Deirdre Purcell was born and brought up in Dublin. She had an eclectic set of careers, including acting at the Abbey Theatre, before she became a journalist and writer, winning awards for her work on the *Sunday Tribune*. She has published fourteen critically acclaimed novels, most recently *The Husband* and *The Winter Gathering*, all of which have been bestsellers in Ireland. She adapted *Falling for a Dancer* into a popular four-part television mini-series, while *Love Like Hate Adore* was shortlisted for the Orange Prize. Deirdre Purcell lives in County Meath with her husband. She has two adult sons.

Also by Deirdre Purcell

FICTION
A Place of Stones
That Childhood Country
Falling for a Dancer
Francey
Sky
Love Like Hate Adore
Entertaining Ambrose
Marble Gardens
Last Summer in Arcadia
Children of Eve
Tell Me Your Secret
Pearl
The Winter Gathering
The Husband

NON-FICTION
The Dark Hunger (with photographer Pat Langan)
On Lough Derg (with photographer Liam Blake)
The Time of My Life (ghostwriter for Gay Byrne)
Be Delighted (tribute to Maureen Potter)
Diamonds and Holes in My Shoes (memoir)
Follow Me Down to Dublin
Days We Remember
Aengus Finucane: In the Heart of Concern

SCREENPLAY
Falling for a Dancer (four episodes for BBC/RTÉ)
Shine On (TV play - Vision Independent and RTÉ)

OPEN DOOR ADULT LITERACY SERIES
Jesus and Billy Are off to Barcelona
Has Anyone Here Seen Larry?

SHORT STORY CONTRIBUTIONS
Ladies' Night at Finbar's Hotel
Moments
Irish Girls are Back in Town

THE
Christmas
Voyage

Deirdre
Purcell

HACHETTE
BOOKS
IRELAND

First published in 2017 by
HACHETTE BOOKS IRELAND
1

A CIP catalogue record for this title is available from the British Library

ISBN 978 1 444 79 949 1

Cover design and typeset by www.redrattledesign.com
Printed and bound in Great Britain by Clays Ltd, St Ives plc.

Hachette Books Ireland policy is to use papers that are natural, renewable and recyclable products and made from wood grown in sustainable forests. The logging and manufacturing processes are expected to conform to the environmental regulations of the country of origin.

Hachette Books Ireland
8 Castlecourt Centre
Castleknock
Dublin 15, Ireland

A division of Hachette UK Ltd.
Carmelite House
50 Victoria Embankment
London EC4Y 0DZ

www.hachettebooksireland.ie

This book is dedicated to Patricia Madigan Byrne,
my dearest friend, pal of my cradle days and
my lighthouse in every stormy sea.
Sleep in peace, Patricia.

The ideal story is that of two people who go into love step for step, with a fluttered consciousness, like a pair of children venturing together into a dark room. From the first moment when they see each other, with a pang of curiosity, through stage after stage of growing pleasure and embarrassment, they can read the expression of their own trouble in each other's eyes. There is no declaration properly so called; the feeling is so plainly shared, that as soon as the man knows what it is in his own heart, he is sure of what is in the woman's.

Robert Louis Stevenson: Virginibus Puerisque

I

Roxy Smith sits in a coach. It is bowling along a motorway, transferring her and a party of fellow travellers from Barcelona airport to the MV *Santa Clara*, moored in the city's port, to begin an eleven-day cruise/hotel-stay holiday, nine nights on the ship and, at the end, two days in Rome in a four-star hotel.

Having represented Portlandis shipping line in the arrivals hall and shepherded her charges on to the bus, their courier, impeccably groomed in her navy and red uniform, has just given her introductory spiel to welcome them all, has turned off her microphone, and is sitting in the front seat to chat with the driver. Throughout the vehicle, like a colony of waking rooks, the voices of Roxy's fellow passengers have erupted, decibels raised so they can be heard above the chug of the diesel engine, the road noise and the blowing of the heating system. Infused with anticipation, the good humour is infectious, especially between members of what seems to be one large family. Roxy believes the woman sitting beside her is one of them, youngish, possibly around the same age as herself. She is craning her neck to address the two men on the seats behind.

The coach has entered a tunnel and, with the window beside her acting as a mirror, she can follow the conversation as the woman complains about the cold: 'I know it's nearly Christmas but, for God's sake, this is Spain! Thank God I brought two jumpers. Just our luck, Jimmy, wha'?'

'You'd have to laugh!' one of the men yells back. 'But at least it's not raining and the sky is blue. Sure what else wouldja want? It'll be grand.'

'Well, cold or not, I don't care,' the man beside Jimmy chimes in. 'I'm feckin' going for a swim the minute we get there. I have to break in me new togs!'

'Hold your horses.' Jimmy gives him a little dig in the ribs. 'It won't be open. There'll be nothing open on the first day, not until dinnertime.'

'An' what makes you such an expert, may I ask?' The second man is affronted. 'Far from cruises you were reared!'

'I know more than you anyway. I read it up. I'm not an illiterate, like some people I might mention.'

'Lads! Lads!' Roxy's seatmate intervenes. 'We're all new to this. Get a grip!' Turning back, she smiles at Roxy, shrugging. 'Men! But they're brothers. What can you expect, eh?'

Roxy smiles back with a conspiratorial nod although, not having a sibling, she wouldn't know.

During check-in at Dublin airport this morning, she had recognised the Dublin accents within this sub-group, having picked them out as fellow travellers because of the Portlandis labels fluttering from their carry-ons. Later, as she and her group had gathered together in the arrivals hall, the inflections could be distinguished from the others. Most, she figured, were from Northern Ireland, although she hadn't lived in the Republic for long enough accurately to tell the difference between Belfast and other counties in, or near, Ulster.

She likes the Dublin accent, had got a handle on it as soon as she learned how to interpret some of its weirder idiosyncrasies, like splitting words to insert an expletive: *That's just desperate. That's abso-fuckin'-lutely appallin', that is...*

After her first novel, *Heartbreak in the Cotswolds*, had been published, she had moved to Ireland from England on the advice of her agent, Tony, because of the Artists' Exemption thingy. It meant that any royalty income due to writers like her (a recent recruit to the profession) and other 'creative artists', such as those working in the visual arts, composing music or choreography, are free of Irish income tax up to fifty thousand euro annually, providing they earn it from that work. 'Don't get too excited, though, Rox,' he had added. 'Publishers are having a hard time, these days, particularly with fiction, and there won't be too many of you getting anywhere near that figure. I wouldn't want to rain on your parade but your contract is in sterling. With that being a movable feast, these days, thanks to Brexit and all that, you can't rely on the exchange rate, so you'll have to factor that in.

'There'll be lots of other little Irish taxes and levies on your income. And don't forget,' he had added, grinning, 'I'll be taking my fifteen per cent before you get any of it! So don't go putting deposits on that Rolex or Jag just yet.'

His advice had included that she find a 'little cottage somewhere in the countryside', if she decided to make the move. 'Renting in Dublin costs a fortune and apparently, from what I hear, there's hardly anything available.' But Roxy was already jumping at the idea because the main phrase she had taken in was *there won't be too many of you*. Tony thought of her as a real writer! He had included her automatically in an exclusive club of which for years she had yearned to be a member. And how exciting it was to be officially recognised as an artist by a whole nation . . .

As for his 'little cottage in the country', no way! Born and bred in London, Roxy is a bright-lights girl. As soon as she'd got home from Tony's shabby little office, she had immediately started an online search for cheap accommodation in Dublin.

Tony Scott had been the first (and only) agent to believe she could make a career out of fiction. Whether sole trader or big firm, every other agency to whom she had sent a proposal and the first chapters of *Heartbreak* hadn't bothered even to acknowledge them, much less send her a formulaic rejection letter. After six months of waiting and hoping, she had almost given up the idea of being a novelist.

So, she had been euphoric to receive Tony's encouraging note – and even more so when, three months later, he had managed to get a two-book publication deal for her with a tiny start-up publisher, whose managing director had decided to specialise in women's fiction. She would never *ever* forget Tony's words on the phone that afternoon: 'Great news, Roxanne. Bellewether has decided to go with you.'

He had had to wait for Roxy's excitement to die down. Then: 'Your advance will be tiny, I'm afraid. I'm working on it with them but they're not likely to budge. The publishers are all, even the big ones, strapped and I wouldn't hold my breath. Don't give up the day job just yet. Anyhow,' he had added, 'you'll have to get down to work immediately. They want this for Christmas – plus they need a proposal and an outline for book two like, yesterday – so it'll be tough going for you, a lot of burning the midnight oil, but it's a start and we're on our way. Congratulations!'

Her advance against royalties had indeed been tiny, tinier still after Tony's cut, but because she had continued to work at the *Weekly Health Advertiser* right up to the move to Ireland, she had managed to keep the money untouched, along with savings she had accrued because she had had no time to shop for anything except food.

That savings account had helped her through the nervy move to Ireland and the hefty deposit she'd had to give to the Dublin estate agent against the flatlet he had found for her in Drumcondra, one of the city's inner suburbs on its north side. But it was now dwindling so she had to get a move on with the second novel, *Heartbreak on the High Seas*. Unfortunately, up to now, the book had remained stalled at the starting gate, her editor rejecting the proposals she was submitting, but she had high hopes of the holiday being the catalyst to get it up and running.

It had not been her idea to set this one on a cruise, with its shipload of possible characters. Her mum had seen a special offer in the *Daily Mail*: 'A thousand people on a ship in a confined space, Rox? And you'll have nothing else to do, will you? No deadlines except for the book, no one like me leeching on you.'

'Don't say that, Mum – please!'

Deep down, though, Roxy had to acknowledge that it would be great to have these days where she had permission to concentrate on work, to make it her sole focus.

It had been a nightmare trying to write *Heartbreak* while

juggling her mother's needs at home with, at work, churning out slimming-aid advertorials or articles on local kids and their hero service dogs for the *Weekly Health Advertiser*. She'd found she preferred the dogs to their owners, had always wanted one, but her mum is allergic to dog hair.

The two of them had lived for most of Roxy's life in Haggerston, one of the now 'coming' London boroughs, near the famous gasometers. Her mum, who had distant relatives somewhere in County Cork, had never married Roxy's dad, of whom Roxy had no memories whatsoever. She didn't even have a photograph because her mother had burned any she'd had. A construction worker, he had moved on before his daughter's second birthday, leaving no trace except, her mum always said, the smell of roll-ups and booze in their garden flat.

Somehow, when the flat had come up for sale, her mum had managed to scrape together a deposit and had found a bank willing to take a chance on a divorced dinner lady with a four-year-old daughter. Her illness was still to develop so she'd passed the bank's insurer's medical examination. They should own the property by 21 August 2021 – her mum had crayoned the date in big red letters on a piece of art paper and had it framed. Now it hangs over the gas fire in their lounge.

Roxy is as proud of her mother's courage as her mother is of her daughter's achievement in getting a novel published at the age of twenty-three. On the day Roxy had come home with the news that she was being offered a contract, her mum had said, 'I can't believe it, Rox! You really amaze me! There's never been any writers in our family – this is just wonderful. And you're so young! You're going to have a fabulous career! Let's ring your nan.'

Like Roxy, her mother was an only child. Her own parents,

Roxy's nan and granddad, live in Glasgow so they don't see them very much, although her nan telephones and there are always presents at Christmas and for birthdays. Although there are a few second cousins scattered about in England – and a good many more distant ones in various parts of County Cork – almost all just names on Christmas cards. So, with just the two of them, they're very close.

Her mum had gone along with the move to Dublin, although it meant she would struggle alone with her emphysema until Roxy decided it was permanent. The plan was then to sell the London flat, hopefully for twice what they'd paid for it, clear the mortgage and, with a little nest egg in the bank, her mum could move to Dublin. And when her money was added to Roxy's income from her tax-free books, they could have a comfortable life together – not that Roxy had given up the notion that her Prince Charming was just around the corner. However, most Irishmen of her age, she'd discovered quickly, while flirty and charming, even up for a bit of offside adventure, seemed to be taken and she wasn't interested in anything except settling down with a bit of security. She and Mum, she would have to emphasise, came as a package.

In the meantime she refuses to contemplate that the second *Heartbreak* may not be successful. That the first had sunk without trace was history. Right now, with this bus chuntering along, all she can think about is her new freedom, the *permission* to spend a day writing and for it to be granted status in others' minds as real work, not an indulgence. Even thinking about what's to come causes excitement to flutter in her tummy.

Mental headlines about the next nine days on the ship vary between 'The Author Sits Inconspicuously to Listen In on

Others' Conversations' (like Maeve Binchy used to do) and 'The Author Tête-à-Tête with Fascinating [name of celebrity, as yet unknown]'. It could be an ex-actress, famous but now divorced and travelling solo, trying to mend a broken heart while drowning in too many martinis. Maybe another Famous Divorced Person will be on board (Roxy finds out by ingenious means) to snag a millionaire or set her sights on the craggy-faced but kindly ship's captain.

Roxy's mum was dead on, she thinks, to have come up with the idea of this trip. She's already thrilled at the tenor of the chat and bonhomie on the bus. Even the brothers behind her are pals again, and she feels a lightening of the load on the back of her neck, resulting from the absence of the cosh that's normally held inches above it.

She takes a quick glance around the vehicle. At a rough count, her seat companion's group appears to number eight, while Roxy and the eight other travellers consist, she reckons, of three couples, mostly middle-aged, and a pair of women friends. No other solos but if the passenger complement on the *Santa Clara* numbers almost a thousand, as her mum had said, there are bound to be some with whom she can have a drink.

But only water, she reminds herself sternly, and only now and then. Should George Clooney himself turn up on board and beg her to come to his suite for a drop of Bolly, she would have to decline. Socialising will play second fiddle to writing.

She turns back to the scene outside the window. Initially, she was disappointed at the industrial landscape fringing the motorway into the city (she'd even seen a pair of Golden Arches, for goodness' sake) but now the coach has slowed to a crawl as it passes through the city centre and they're moving alongside a wide esplanade, with statues, monuments and other sculptures. It's populated with tourists and, to judge by their demeanour, locals. Roxy has been doing her homework and knows not to refer to the latter as Spanish because most are fiercely and nationalistically Catalonian.

And on this showing they're highly confident: even the weightiest old ladies wear their formidable bosoms with aplomb. The girls have bundled themselves into the universal winter uniform of the Western world's young – fur-hooded parkas, huge scarves, and boots over jeggings or jeans. On the streets of London or Dublin, this gear seems merely to be excess wrapping, but here it's über-cool.

It's the gait and the hair, she decides, making notes in the first of four brand-new Moleskine notebooks she's brought with her – an extravagance she justified as confidence-engendering: *Hair, however windblown, remains glossy and dark, casually chic when caught in a comb or a scrunchie, startlingly beautiful when streaming in dark rippling waves from under a woolly hat. And that lovely skin, so darkly golden . . .*

She hesitates, then crosses out *startlingly* – she's not startled: she was expecting this. As for *dark rippling waves*, many women have highlights. She also draws a line through *darkly*. Can you be *darkly golden*? She doesn't think so. The phrases now read: *rippling from under woolly hats* and *that lovely golden skin*.

But she looks again at this. Should she take out *golden*? Isn't that a cliché? Anyhow, some are olive-skinned. And could she refer to the people, mostly men, selling handbags, belts, dream-catchers, carved figurines, scarves and watches on the pavement as 'Nubian'? Would that be more evocative, more literary, than 'black' or would it be racist? Pitfalls, pitfalls – the public has no idea what goes into writing a novel. She decides not to mention skin colour, writing instead: *Street-sellers wearing vividly colour-banded hats are presiding over spreads of their wares.*

Too bare. No atmosphere. She amends it: *As the steely-surfaced Med shushes behind them, street-sellers, wearing hats of vivid colour, preside over their wares, sorted into neat rows on the pavements.* It's essential that this novel be classy. She examines her latest effort as critically as an editor might – actually, she thinks proudly, it's quite good – and turns again to watch the scene on the esplanade. Although she has been to Torremolinos twice and Fuengirola once, this is her first encounter with a sophisticated Spanish city – although the possibility of chatting to anyone, let alone a man, is pretty remote: the cruise isn't a round trip but one way to Italy. She just can't wait to get on board and start work.

*

Many of the men here are so fit, Roxy thinks, you could eat them. Many have wound long scarves several times around their necks and it's like they're inviting you slowly to peel them off. Although she'd had a brief relationship around her twenty-first birthday – he gave her a hairdryer – it had ended in tears and it's been a long time since she's had any romantic encounter, even something as simple as a kiss.

Enviously, with the coach having halted at traffic lights, she watches a couple's progress. The guy is tall, hawk-nosed, like Tom Conti in *Shirley Valentine*, wearing tight jeans and a leather bomber jacket. His scarf is red, his hair gelled and highlighted. The girl is also wearing a bomber, khaki, military-style and belted. It and her jeans fit so well on her slim frame that they could have been custom-made, while her knee-high pale leather boots with discreet brass accents are the most gorgeous Roxy has ever seen.

They're walking slowly, in step, each body curved tightly into the other, heads lowered; his right arm is around her shoulders, her left hand cradles his bottom, and when she taps it lightly, he reacts by breaking stride, but still they don't look at each other . . .

Could they be her models for the lead male and female characters? Could she put them on the cruise, where they provide a story of true love overcoming some awful obstacle, like a vengeful ex? Could one be married to someone else? Endless possibilities. And on present showing, she could certainly give them some heat in the bedroom.

Having been two-timed by someone she'd loved, or so she'd thought at the time, Roxy can write with great authority on betrayal, and Tony had confided that this had won her the publisher's contract.

It had come as a surprise to her that it hadn't been the novel's breadth, the plethora of themes she had introduced – emphysema, marital desertion, alcohol addiction, single-parenting – but the cheating that had got her over the line. 'There are lots of problems with the novel as it stands, Roxanne,' Tony had said, 'and I've emphasised that you're very willing to work on it. Don't worry, dear. This is what editors are paid for . . .'

Now, thinking of it, she is just as excited as she was when submitting *Heartbreak One*, as she now thinks of her first novel, to all those other agents who had been so rude. Here she is, not even on the ship and already seeing opportunities all over the place. It's great to feel so free.

She starts again to scribble but the bus brakes hard,

knocking the pen out of her hand and onto the floor. She and her companion bend simultaneously to retrieve it from under the seat in front, but it's the latter who succeeds. 'Here ye go,' she says, handing it over and then, indicating the note-taking, 'You a reporter?'

'Novelist, actually.' Roxy can't quite believe the little *ping!* of pride she hears in her voice every time she says this.

'That's fascinating,' the girl says. 'I never met a novelist before. Would I know you? Have you been on the *Late Late* or anything? I'm Gemma by the way.' She sticks out her hand. 'Gemma Dunne. My married name is Conroy but everyone in the family still calls me Gemma Dunne.'

They shake. 'Roxy Smith. I'm afraid you wouldn't have heard of me – well, not yet anyway.' She laughs. 'I've only written one book so far, and it was published in England. But I'm living in Dublin now while I'm writing the second, so stand by! My agent is very positive.'

'What's the name of the one you wrote already?'

'*Heartbreak in the Cotswolds.*'

'It's a sad book, then, yeah?'

'I suppose you could say that. But it's not sad all the way through. It's about a girl whose fiancé is cheating on her and she doesn't know until she finds messages on his phone. There's happiness in it too – until she finds out what he's been up to.'

'But she shouldn't be looking at his phone, should she?' Gemma frowns. 'Snooping's a mug's game, yeah?'

'I know. But novels aren't real life. They're . . .' She stops. How to explain the essence of a novel set in the heart of rural England in midsummer as you lurch along a Barcelona motorway in deepest winter? Best generalise: 'I suppose novels give you the highlights and lowlights,' she says slowly, thinking it out. 'Like a long play. You have to hold interest and cut out the boring bits, like having dinner every day, or deciding what you'll order in a restaurant. You can include them but in a novel you see them differently, through the character's eyes, putting in something odd that's never happened before. Hopefully the reader will be interested enough to want to know why it did.'

'Or you can make them get poisoned in the restaurant by a Chinese umbrella,' Gemma joins in.

Roxy laughs. 'Great! You get it! You find the plot, and then you have to, I dunno, use the magic of words to keep things interesting while you're trying to describe what the characters are seeing or hearing.' She's suddenly embarrassed. This has all sounded so trite. 'Something like that anyhow,' she mutters.

But Gemma smiles. '"The magic of words"? I like it. You see, that's the difference between artists and the rest of us. I was no good at English at school, hated writing essays – *"Pride and Prejudice:* is the character of Darcy a misogynist at heart? Discuss –" What's that all about? Who cares? So what's the hardest bit, Roxy? How do you find the plot?'

'Can't answer that,' Roxy confesses. She's delighted all over again at the accolade of being described as an artist, so she's not going to tell this mere acquaintance the whole story, how hard she finds it to nail down what she really wants to write about: she never really knows until she starts, and her first attempts are always a mishmash.

On the starting grid of a novel and looking towards the winding track ahead, with its invisible land mines, her difficulty seems to be that there are always too many roads on offer. This lane or that? The one over there, perhaps? Too many choices lead to a snarl-up as the ideas jostle for pole position so eagerly that they end up in an impenetrable knot and none can go anywhere. She tries to pick them out one by one, but can't discard any in case, with hindsight, they may prove to have been The One. You keep, literally, losing the plot. You stay awake at night selecting, developing, dumping and thinking again. The wretched thing consumes you, churning, keeping you awake at night, and when, exhausted, you wake up in the morning, it's the first item on the agenda.

The plot of *Heartbreak One* had been, in the end, relatively simple. It had been in the title and she had merely followed its prompting. Or so she had thought, until her editor had intervened.

Now as she has to start book two, her brain is again teeming with possibilities. Again too many. She's anxious now. Maybe she won't be able to find a plot. Maybe in the multitude of possibilities she won't be able to identify the single thread that will pull the reader through.

Oh, shut up, Roxy! If you can't find something good in such a great context, with swarms of potential characters, you may as well give up the idea of being an author altogether. To bolster herself, she repeats her self-exhortations:

You won't let this happen, amen.

You've done this before, amen.

You're a confident writer, amen.

You're determined and focused, amen.

'I'm always nervous starting a new novel,' she says to Gemma.

'Is there sex in it?' The other woman seems curious rather than voyeuristic. 'The one you wrote already, I mean.'

'Plenty.'

'From personal experience, of course?'

'Of course!' They both laugh. 'Obviously not enough,' Roxy says ruefully. 'Hardly anyone bought it.'

'Ever read *Fifty Shades of Grey*?'

Roxy shakes her head.

'Well, I did. My husband gave it to me for Christmas. I found it awful, to tell you the truth. I told him he needn't be getting any ideas! But that one who wrote it made a load of money, so you're on the right track, Roxy.' She added, 'You should put a *lot* of sex into this one – not all that hitting stuff, mind. There's enough hitting and slapping going on in real life without putting it into a book. I should know.'

'Why?' Roxy is both alarmed and excited. *Abuse victim?*

'I'm a social worker,' Gemma says, 'not long qualified so don't go asking me for any advice, Roxy. You'd be taking your life in your hands! Listen,' she says then, 'I'm going to buy that first book of yours. I'll get it on my Kindle. What's its name again?'

'*Heartbreak in the Cotswolds.*'

Gemma's quiet for a moment. 'Are you in Ireland a lot?'

'I'm English but I live in Dublin.' And to forestall enquiries about why: 'Thank you, Gemma. Another twopence in the bank.'

'Here, give us a lend of your biro.' Gemma holds out her hand. Roxy gives it to her with a blank page torn from her notebook. 'By the way,' says Gemma, 'don't put me in your book, okay?'

'Of course not.'

'You're writing it already?' She indicates the notebook.

'Only background stuff.'

'So,' Gemma folds her arms comfortably, as though settling in for a long chat, 'you're writing what Barcelona is like and us all here? I saw you looking around the bus.'

'That's the general idea, but I won't be using real people. They'll be made up in my head – I promise I won't write about you and your group. Honestly.'

'But it'll be people *like* us? I get it. I think I could write a book, you know. You wouldn't believe the kind of things I deal with in a day's work. I'd sell a million on the first day and retire to someplace warm and sunny. But it's a Catch-22. I have hardly any free time and, anyway, I'd be sacked if I wrote what I really feel about the Irish system. What are you going to do with your millions, Roxy?'

'I wish!'

'You writers do make a lot of money, though, yeah?'

'Oh, sure! Listen, between stints of consulting my muse, I'm working shifts part-time in a coffee shop in Killester to put bread on the table and pay rent.'

'Put it there!' Abruptly Gemma sticks out her hand, smiling broadly. 'Me too! Not now, obviously, but while I was in college getting my degree. Mine was a café in George's Street. Isn't this gas, though? That the two of us just happened to sit beside each other – and I'm guessing we're around the same age too. I'm twenty-five, next bus stop thirty! Can't believe it, Roxy. It was only yesterday I was in High Babies!'

'I'm twenty-three.' Roxy is liking her. 'We're getting pretty near the port, I think, and I'm sure we'll run into each other on the ship.'

But Gemma is looking up at the ceiling: 'When you think about it, this could be the start of a book. It could be you and me are, like, lesbians and we sit beside each other, at random, like we actually did, and when we're on the ship we start having an affair, and next thing we find out that we're long-lost sisters, like we were both adopted at birth. We're twins and we've been separated to different families, but deep down we've always been pining for each other. Like, there's always been a hole in our souls.'

'But surely we'd have known by looking at each other.' Roxy gets into the game.

'We're not *identical* twins, and it's not until near the end of our cruise that we discover the truth.'

Roxy's stunned. Gemma's given her the plot of an entire novel. More critically, she's added yet another possible strand to her own tangle of ideas. 'Don't tell me if you don't want to, Gemma, but is there some sort of occasion that you and your family are celebrating? I take it that this is your family you're with. Is it something big?'

Her companion visibly hesitates. Then: 'It's big, all right, Roxy, but it's – it's sort of a surprise. I can't really say.'

Roxy has heard, not just in the hesitation but in the inflection, 'Back off!' She does. 'Never mind,' she says. 'The last thing I'd want to do is to intrude.'

The bus has stopped again at traffic lights. 'Oh, look, Gemma – isn't that awfully sad?' She points towards a woman in voluminous layers of tatty clothing, ankles swollen over the sides of flip-flops inadequate for the winter. She is wheeling a shopping trolley containing her belongings in black bin bags – but what is truly affecting is that a piece of string has been attached to the trolley's handle. The other end has been tied around the neck of a greyhound, every rib showing, its head so low its nose almost touches the ground. Roxy's heart almost breaks.

'Poor thing,' Gemma sighs, 'but maybe that's what she wants. We get people like her into the all-night café in Merchant's Quay just opposite the courts there. We find that some of the customers don't want emergency accommodation.'

'You're not saying homelessness is a lifestyle choice? Hello?'

'Of course not. But a small minority will never come in from the cold. It's tragic but unfortunately that's the case.'

'That poor dog hasn't made the choice.' Roxy's heart is still with the greyhound.

'No, he hasn't. But at least he has company.'

'So has she.' She was about to add that if the woman chooses to have a dog she has the obligation to look after it. 'Oh dear, we are getting serious, aren't we?'

'We are.' Gemma shakes her head. 'I've enough seriousness in my job, without bringing it on me holidays. This is going to be a great experience, Roxy – love the name, by the way! What's it short for?'

'Roxanne. My nan is Scottish and her name is Roxanna but my mum preferred Roxanne, so everyone is happy. And, yes, this *is* going to be a great experience. Can't wait!'

'Me too,' says Gemma, for the second time.

'So who's in your group, then?'

'My husband Jimmy – that's him behind us. He's with his brother, Larry, and that's Larry's wife further back. She's one of four aunties of mine on the trip. One of them is my auntie Mary, who's my godmother too.' Using her fingers to count them out, she rattles off all the names, but Roxy can't keep up and reckons it would too obvious to take notes of the roll call. Plenty of time for that, she thinks, as their coach pulls into the port. And there's the ship! The name, *Santa Clara*, is right there, high on the front.

'Omigod, it's huge!' she exclaims, when they're standing on the pier to which the liner is tied. 'Did you know it would be this big?' She turns to Gemma, who is rummaging in her bag for the documents she'll need to board the liner. Roxy has already thought of that: she is carrying hers in a plastic pouch slung around her neck.

'Here they are.' Triumphantly, Gemma produces them. 'And our ship's only about a quarter the size of the one behind it – can you imagine what that one'd be like?'

But Roxy can't wait now to get on board. 'Great to meet you, Gemma,' she says. 'I'll let you go back to your family. We'll have to get together for a drink or something.'

'Yeah. We've all got drinks packages with our tickets so there's going to be some fun, eh? You'll be very welcome to join us.'

'Thanks a million.' But as they part, Roxy's mental klaxon goes off: *Work! Work! WORK!*

She identifies her suitcase to one of the porters, signs some bits of paper and, as the man puts her bag with others, walks quickly towards the ship, following the handy signposts.

As she trots up the entrance ramp, she glances up again. It's one thing to see pictures of your ship, but the size of the thing when you see it in reality is awesome. Above her, near the top of the vessel, she sees some old geezer, wind blowing a white coxcomb of hair upright on his head, hanging out over a rail looking down at her. He's too far above to know for sure, but she thinks he's smiling at her and he even waves. Cheek!

Less than an hour later, she is letting herself into her cabin, having already been on alert for 'colour' – watching how other people behave and interact as they slog down the long, long corridor lined with cabin doors: how some men carry their wives' bags and shopping and some don't; how women travelling together co-operate to spread the burden evenly, even squabble over who has to carry what.

Inside, she finds that her cabin, or stateroom, is tiny, close to the ship's engines – or the fridges or microwaves in the kitchen, maybe – because there's a sort of thrumming noise. No window, and just a few inches to spare on either side of the bed. She sits on it, trying to quash her disappointment because she remains grateful to her mum for splashing the cash to pay for the trip. Anyway, she'll be out and about during the day.

She's lucky to be here at all, she thinks. Her mum had to scrimp to get the money together and had seized on this particular cruise because it had advertised a special offer in huge letters: NO SINGLE SUPPLEMENT.

OK, she's a single traveller: she'll just have to suck this up. Maybe she and Gemma— Well, it's just maybe. By the look of it, she'll be involved with her family. Roxy writes herself a little memo, reiterating the question she mustn't forget to ask: *Occasion for their trip? Big birthday/anniversary?* It may be a good basic setting. Keep things going with them until a big party at the end? On Christmas Day, perhaps?

Roxy intends this novel, whatever plot she comes up with, to end happily. Mysteries and twists along the way, of course, a bit of romance, probably illicit – but it's going to finish with *joy*.

She intends to use herself as a character, maybe as one of those dispassionate narrators who is observing everything, like that man – the name escapes her – Nick something, the guy who's the narrator in *The Great Gatsby*? She hasn't read the book but the movie, the one with Leonardo DiCaprio and Carey Mulligan, is one of her all-time favourites. Depends what she sees in the next few days but, come to think of it, she'd like to feature a man like Gatsby in the romance department, a nice man, a tall man, a bit of an enigma?

Now there's a title: *The Enigma Man.* Doesn't really matter what nationality. In London, she and her mum are surrounded by Asians, Jamaicans and Africans. She'd be perfectly comfortable with any nice, jolly guy who would treat her like any woman would like to be treated. Handsome would be good too, and she'd try not to be greedy, but the occasional unexpected gift would be good – and, of course, he'd have to be pretty good in bed. That's a given.

What about a crew member? Her thoughts are racing. There's bound to be a hot officer or two, and readers love men in uniform. Roxy loves men in uniform.

Then, as she always does when she's writing, she glances at the notes section on her iPhone. During the first lunch she'd had with her agent, to celebrate her book deal, he had said, slowly, so she could tap it in: 'Always ask yourself if what you see is real. Authentic. Always delve, Roxy. Ask yourself, like the movie did, *what lies beneath.*'

Newly excited she unpacks quickly, stowing clothes in the cleverly compact compartments and drawers, putting toiletries and slap in the en-suite shower room, nearly as small as one of those upright sarcophaguses she saw in the Egyptian exhibition at the V & A. But so long as it does the job, she thinks cheerfully, that's all that matters.

Leaving aside Gemma, her family and what possibly lies beneath, her next opportunity for mining gold, she feels, will be at dinner tonight. She's been told she's been allocated a place at a table for eight but that, if she has a problem with it, she can ask to be switched to another. A change is never guaranteed but is possible.

That's a great idea for a novelist, she thinks. Even for a title. Another. *Switching Tables.* It has a good ring.

She sets off down her corridor, stopping when she gets into a big open area with a bank of moving lifts and small queues of people waiting for them or getting out as the doors whoosh open. She consults a *You are here* map on a nearby wall and decides to start her exploration at the very top of the ship, working her way down, while keeping an eye out for Gemma along the way. But that's not a priority: they're bound to run into each other. It's not the *Queen Mary* they're on . . .

She stands with a group of people speaking what she takes to be Spanish (or Catalan?) and can't contain her excitement, strewing smiles around her fellow cruisers and getting answering smiles in return. The adventure begins.

2

Charles Burtonshaw is taking a stroll around the promenade deck of the *Santa Clara*.

Despite his heavy winter coat and tartan wool scarf, he shivers and, pushing his hands into his armpits for warmth, pauses at the seaward rail, gazing beyond the oily waters of the port towards the expanse of the Mediterranean on which, right now, white horses scud like tiny surfers. Not too much sun-bathing in prospect for *Clara*'s passengers, he thinks sadly.

As he always does, he boarded the vessel ahead of paying passengers but this time it feels different, more emotional, and not in a good way. Instead of being optimistic and cheerful, as he normally is on the first day of a cruise, he is mournful. This is the last time he will have boarded the dear old *Clara*. One-way to Rome, one last night moored in port at Civitavecchia and it's all over. All gone. This beautiful ship consigned to history, with one cut of the shipping line's samurai sword or, less fancifully, a stroke of a fountain pen. Probably a Mont Blanc, he thinks, acidly.

The rather distressing news about the *Clara*'s fate had

come from his long-time chum Frank Mitchell, the vessel's cruise director. Being from Liverpool and not a man to mince his words, Frank had offered Charles the usual job and said it would be the last. 'Once more into the breach, Chuck, Barcelona to Rome, the seventeenth of December. It's a Saturday, if that suits you, but then that's it for good, I'm afraid. She's off to Malaysia, and I'm being sent to Miami.'

Charles had thanked him for the job. What else could he do?

His work on board, under the purview of the cruise director's entertainment team, is designed to occupy passengers, particularly during days at sea, when even the most hardened gamblers tire of the ship's casino, and others like to occupy themselves with an improving pursuit. Charles is an actor, his brief to give a short course on acting, a workshop, although he hates the term. *Workshop* – whatever happened to the *magic* of theatre?

So, yes, he's sad but not all that surprised because, for quite a while now, each time he has come on board he has been noticing that the *Clara*'s standards of elegance, the care she gets from her crew, have slipped a little further. Like himself, he thinks wryly, she's showing her age, and while her graceful lines continue to delight, scuff is visible on polished decks, there is a greenish tinge on some of the brass, and this time coming aboard, he had seen a few stains, faint brown stalactites, starting to appear on her hull. The shipping line had obviously decided some time ago to let her go.

Frank had told him that the vessel's owner was intent on squeezing the last few drops of revenue from the *Clara* before sending her to her fate with new owners. 'We're all a bit jittery about what's going to happen or where we'll be assigned. I'll be okay in Miami, probably, until I retire – they've got me a work visa for the States, but you can't depend on that, these days, with Trump. For some of the crew, though, especially in the service area, things are definitely dodgy. They don't know what's going to happen to them yet so don't be surprised if they seem a bit down in the dumps.'

He had also said that one of the company's directors had been designated to represent the board on this last trip. 'Not too happy about it either, I hear. Usually goes to the Caribbean for Christmas. He has a trophy wife half his age and apparently you can't miss her. I've had them put at your table in the Empire room so you can charm the socks off them. So, you play nicely, now, eh, Chuck? Here.' He produced a piece of paper from his breast pocket and handed it over. 'I've written down their names so you can push out the whole polite English thing when you meet them.'

'Of course, dear heart!' Charles detests being called 'Chuck'. He regards even 'Charlie' as an impertinence, but is rarely in a position to demur, certainly not with Frank Mitchell, to whom he has owed so many previous jobs, plus, now, this last one. As usual, therefore, he'd sucked it up.

Now that he has been on board for a couple of hours, the reality of this being the last time has hit. It's the end of an era he has thoroughly enjoyed and, at his level of income, he doubts he will ever be on board a liner again, any liner, certainly not as a passenger. And with Frank based in Florida, it would be far too expensive in a cost-cutting environment to fly him out and back. To get to and from the *Clara* he has always flown Ryanair.

Anyhow, passenger manifests on Portlandis ships based around the Caribbean, he hears, are dominated by senior Floridians, Cubans, Puerto Ricans, New Yorkers and people from New Jersey. Who among that lot, with abundant sunshine and shopping opportunities a-plenty for emeralds and other luxury items, would be interested in an acting course given by a toffee-nosed English nobody?

As for being hired by another shipping company, Charles doubts that very much.

He has reached the *Clara*'s stern, which is at present overshadowed by one of those towering monster vessels, a floating apartment block, sixteen decks above the water, squat, ugly as sin, and no doubt replete with climbing walls, surfing pools, shopping malls, water parks and shooting ranges. This one, he was told by one of the *Clara*'s croupiers, gloomy about her own job prospects, is taller than the Eiffel Tower and longer than Big Ben placed on its side. He won't dignify it with its name, even in his thoughts, as he watches the activity around it. At ground level, it's fringed with supply vehicles and provisioning trucks, ship-to-shore cables and hoses from fresh-water tankers, while on its façade, window cleaners, like busy flies, ply their trade from moving hoists.

The pristine white of the vessel's enormous hull, topped with banks of balcony cabins stacked on top of one another, like giant pallets, nevertheless shames the *Clara*'s. Its sheer bulk is probably eight times hers and brings into stark relief what's about to happen to her: slaughter of the weak, Nature's way. But it doesn't make it easier to stomach.

Charles's relationship with the *Clara* is visceral: for him she lives, breathes and pulses with gentle vitality. At night when the hard-core revellers are finally asleep and she's left in peace, murmuring across glassy waters with engines at half-speed, he, a chronic insomniac, is moving about her open decks above the swish of her wake, hearing her voice. It's in a creak from a place within her, a muffled laugh from the bridge, the clink as a wire strikes the communications mast, even the soft 'Goodnight, sir,' from a crew member taking an illicit smoke near a lifeboat as Charles passes. Where the daytime *Clara* is all hustle and bustle, at night she flexes herself, relaxes and, like a cat, grooms herself for morning. Especially on calm nights, his ship talks to him.

Better make the most of her while you can, old chap! he thinks now, taking a last look at the intruder behind. As he moves on, he mouths at it a derisory *Behemoth!* But it was inevitable, he supposes, that at her age and size, the *Clara* could no longer compete with all that swank and swagger. In her prime, when boarding her, bow cutting an arc into the sky and seagulls wheeling overhead, you felt like a privileged individual, not part of a swarm. That *thing* back there – he glances at it over his shoulder – with her twenty dining rooms and twenty-three pools, is not a thing of nature: you admired the *Clara* for her beauty. When on board, you felt as sleek and silky as she.

At least she's not bound for the breaker's yard. No doubt her refit will be brutal, her comfortable staterooms 'downsized' (that horrible word!), her casino upsized (ugh! Even worse!), and all meals offered as self-service buffets under the pretext of this being what guests want now. Or, perish the thought, her ultimate fate may be as an inter-island ferry – dear God!

He must come up with some way to play his part in commemorating the old dear. In this new, fast-moving and rather frightening world, this is not just his task as one of the faithful: it is his *duty* to ensure that this trip lives on in the minds of the passengers before the *Clara* faces radical surgery.

He sees now that a few passengers, like him swaddled in heavy jackets or coats, are appearing on the promenade deck, peering over the rail into the oily water, taking selfies, waving happily at the tugs and commercial traffic chugging by. From the boat deck far below, he hears a tap-tapping sound accompanied by sporadic, windborne whistling. On peering over the rail to find out where it's coming from, he can see nothing. Perhaps it's one of the crew preparing the lifeboats for the testing of their launching mechanisms prior to the mandatory emergency drill later. Last tests, he thinks, as he examines the sky for a hint of blue. Nothing but grey and, with sailing scheduled for six thirty p.m., by the time the *Clara* gets into open water, it will probably be as dark as the inside of Shylock's pocket. *Oh, stop it, Charles,* he scolds himself. *Life goes on. Chin up!*

Having come on board for the first time nearly three decades ago in Marseille, Charles has lost count of how many times he has plied the waters of the Mediterranean with her, usually west to east, but sometimes skirting Morocco, Tunisia and even Egypt – this, of course, had been before all the terrorist business. He feels he knows her every rivet and stanchion. She has given him a second home, far more elegant than his small townhouse in Shoreditch.

When he is not working, Charles rarely has the chance for conversation, apart from exchanging pleasantries with the proprietor of his local corner shop, a pleasant fellow from Pakistan, when he picks up his *Guardian* or *Telegraph*. In summer, they talk cricket.

He moves off and then, having completed his circuit of the deck, crosses to the portside rail from which he has a gull's-eye view of the gangway.

The familiar rhythm of the boarding ritual soothes him, his mood lifts and he is again simply grateful to be here, not least because of the small but welcome boost to his income. Over the years, his work on the *Clara* has meant he could buy a few decent suits, jackets and the custom-made shirts and shoes he favours, not merely for style and polish and how it feels to wear them but because they're made to last – unlike old ships. 'There, there.' He pats the dowager's rail. 'You've had your day, dear, but we all still love you.'

For his own entertainment, Charles always divides the guests into categories as they arrive shipside. 'Skippers', for instance, are so-called because they seem actually to skip in their enthusiasm to board. 'Celebrators' arrive on the quayside as families or other groups, playfully thumping each other: *Hey! We've actually made it! Now, where's the bar?* 'Lusters' come in pairs: whether same sex or hetero, they touch at every opportunity even while boarding, signalling physically that they can't wait to get into that stateroom. Some couples, such as the one climbing out of a taxi in the set-down area, walk dourly behind one another at a telling distance. He calls this type the 'Reluctants', one of whom doesn't want to be there and has come only to please the other.

Boarding, he thinks now, seems slower than usual although, to be fair, it is still only one o'clock. The chill is getting to him: he won't stay here as long as he usually does. Anyway, his appointment with Frank, to have a little chat about things, is imminent.

Before turning away, he takes one last look at the activity below. He has noticed over the years that, even in her heyday, the *Clara* has never attracted the Louis Vuitton set, and although now the fakes are so convincing that it's hard to tell them from the real thing, at least those who carry them are aiming for class. Charles has long ago accepted that he is a snob, and Vuitton people, he believes, are more likely to attend a theatre now and then, unlike those whose hand luggage is made of canvas, nylon, or carried on their backs.

Snob or not, he did *not* vote for Brexit, and *certainly*, in his own opinion, does not belong to the corps of 'Little Englander' nostalgists. He does, however, secretly long for the days when everyone was sure of the ground under his or her feet.

The two Reluctants now nearing the gangway are pulling cabin-sized wheelie bags in sober charcoal grey, from which flutter American Airlines tags. Could they be the shipping-line director and his wife? But she hardly looks like anyone's trophy, certainly not what the *Sun* newspaper (along with Frank) would term a stunner.

He gives himself a mental slap. *Unkind!* Charles likes to believe his emotional intelligence is superior to that of the average citizen, with EI being a prerequisite for decent acting – but judgement based on a person's appearance? That's a transgression. For instance, that woman could be a trophy in that she's a successful golfer or an award-winning writer.

Anyway, in his case there's pot-and-kettle involved: he knows he is no oil painting. His hooked nose has failed him many film screen-tests, and his agent has urged him more than once to have something done about it. But his mother would have been horrified at the notion of interfering with Nature and now it's too late.

Charles believes defiantly that hooked noses look good on some film actors; any physical quirk, provided it's not too ugly or disabling, can be an advantage when one is classed in agents' and casting sheets as 'character'. It can certainly be advantageous if you're to play a judge on TV. Which he hasn't. Yet.

Charles believes that kindness is the key to everything, to being a good person, to living a good life and, anyhow, he has found that kindness, undertaken for its own sake, tends always to bounce back on the kind. Whether others notice his efforts to behave along these lines is debatable but he continues to try, and little miracles occasionally happen.

So. No harsh judgements on others during this last cruise. What that pair of Reluctants with wheelie bags need is a little TLC. They're probably just tired.

He is about to turn away to go inside when a rush of people, chattering animatedly, emerges from a coach that has pulled up directly beneath him on the pier's plaza. Awestruck, each falls instantly silent for a few seconds as they gaze up at the *Santa Clara*, small and a little battered by contrast with the giant at her tail. Definitely Celebrators, he decides, and they include a Skipper: a woman (girl?), slim, small, blonde, who had been first out of the traps. She is now indicating a modest anonymous black bag to one of the porters and then, moving fast, ponytail bouncing, approaches the gangway. Charles smiles fondly as she glances up to where he stands. He raises his hand to wave at her, but she's already gone. Probably a first-timer, definitely a Skipper.

He loves first-timers, loves their enthusiasm, loves to share with them his own affection for the old *Clara*, to guide them so they discover what cruising is, or should be, all about.

He checks his watch and leaves the rail to meet Frank. They knew one another long before either set foot on the ship, having run into each other during their criss-crossing touring schedules, Charles in repertory as an actor, Frank as a stand-up.

While neither enjoys the capacity to drink at the level of those days, Charles likes the occasional Scotch while Frank, strictly teetotal when on duty, still loves his Guinness. They had met, by chance, for the first time at the counter of an Irish pub in Liverpool during a wrap party for *Antony and Cleopatra* in which Charles had played Demetrius. Frank, enjoying an 'off' night, had attended the show and had afterwards followed the actors to the pub. The two of them had got talking and somehow, despite their completely differing personalities, backgrounds and tastes, they had hit it off.

When he'd got the job as cruise director on the *Santa Clara*, one of Frank's first hires had been his old friend. This lunchtime, they're to have their usual meeting, during which, ostensibly, they will discuss the particulars of the acting course Charles is to give, although Frank now knows the routine so well that their meetings have become merely social catch-ups.

On the way, he passes the main dining room, two leaping dolphins etched into its glass double doors, guarded by two life-sized statues of gilded Roman soldiers.

Charles has always loved the formality of dinners in the MDR, two interconnected rooms, one posher than the other. Both sections offer the same food, but in the Empire, there is added emphasis on presentation, involving silver service, starched linen, tableside flambé and vegetables curled, julienned and arranged like Monet's garden. In the Empire, champagne is free, with a suave sommelier on hand to advise on which reds or whites are most apt for which course.

But unless he responds to a rare invitation to dine at the captain's table, Charles usually sits in the larger, more populous Commonwealth room. And although service is always stepped up a notch, and a small red rosebud placed on each bread plate, you still have to pay extra for beef Wellington, and had you not paid in advance for your 'all-inclusive drinks package' in your fare, wine, never mind bubbly, costs you.

A seat with the Director in the Empire is a step-up. Or

would be. Although he would never admit it, Charles sneakily admires the notion of class-based eating, and for him it's unfortunate that, for this last voyage of the *Clara*, dining is to be single class throughout although, he thinks scornfully, not single price. Staterooms have still been priced on size, facilities, balconies, but on this trip, concierges, valets and the like will be conspicuous by their scarcity on the lower decks. And even among the premier suites their numbers have been stretched because, he's been told, many of them – those with EU passports and visas for the US – have already been switched to the line's more modern 'fun' ships of the Caribbean, with everyone apparently wearing shorts during the day, slacks with open-necked shirts at dinner, and most of the dining buffet-style. It was decided by the powers-that-be that this is what the modern guest prefers.

Oh, really? Charles thinks. *How many people were asked?*

As he passes through one of the two main saloons, he nods graciously at a few of the passengers already ensconced in the seating. He can smell food in the air. Snacks, soft drinks and hot beverages are now available for those who have already boarded, and the kitchens are engaged in gearing up for tonight's dinner.

The door to the bar where he is to meet Frank is closed, but he knows to push it open. Inside, the room is unlit, except for a shaft of daylight filtering through from the deck. Bottles and glasses have been shuttered away: none of the ship's bars is due to open until after the emergency drill for all on board, passengers and crew alike.

He seats himself at the counter, angling his stool so he can watch for his friend's arrival. Ever the theatre man, he always savours these moments alone in semi-darkness, the silence pregnant, reminding him of the hush in an auditorium during the fifteen seconds or so between the dimming of house lights and the revelation of the set for Act One.

Somewhat harassed, the cruise director arrives a few minutes later and they clap each other's shoulders. 'Nice to see you, Frank.' Charles smiles.

'Settled in, Chuck?'

'Taking my time, as usual. I've very little with me because I'm planning to go back to Blighty overland this time after Rome. I don't want to be too burdened.'

His friend looks keenly at him but says nothing, and Charles knows he has deduced that the cost of the flight was a factor in this decision. This being a one-way trip, the company hasn't paid for his flight home. Frank had alerted him to this when booking him for the job. 'Full house again, Frank?'

'Afraid not. Three-quarters, and I didn't see many of the regulars on the manifest. By the way, we've had to change your cabin. Hope it won't be inconvenient, but you're on deck six this time. Six three one. Is that okay? Housekeeping knows.'

Charles is floored. Deck six is all-balcony. He'd never before been given a stateroom with a balcony. His was usually on one of the lower decks, and when the *Clara* was stuffed to her gills, he didn't even get a sea view – a porthole or window. He opens his mouth to say how chuffed he is but his friend continues before he can speak: 'Listen, Chuck, I ask you, who goes on the Med in winter, even for Christmas? *Especially* at Christmas. Last refuge of the lonely, I suppose, although we do have a few groups, including a set of bridge clubs. There's going to be a tournament on Christmas Day.

'Ah, well.' Frank sighs. 'Here we are, last time! I find it hard to believe! I'm going to miss the old girl. You?'

Charles nods. Then: 'Cheer up, old boy.' He forces himself to sound as if he has taken his own advice and, being honest, he has cheered up a little at the news of his new stateroom. 'She's still got nine good days ahead of her, and so have we.' The cruise has been sold as eleven days, but will host passengers for only nine. The package includes two final nights in a four-star Rome hotel. 'And now that applies to me too, along with my posh cabin! Thank you, Frank. I really appreciate it.' His eyes are welling and he's about to reach out to touch Frank's shoulder when the other man slips off his stool, goes behind the counter and ducks under it. 'Don't mention it,' he says, in muffled tones from below. 'Fancy a bevvy? I'm not actually on duty until half past so I stashed a few for us.' He emerges with two bottles of Guinness. 'We may as well drink a toast to the old girl. We mightn't get a chance like this again.' With a flick of his wrist, he tops a bottle by snapping it against the brass finger-rail at the edge of the bar and necks it before the foam can spill over.

'No, thanks, Frank.' Charles is not in the mood for drinking. 'I'm still adjusting to my new status with a balcony, but not yet in a toasting frame of mind. Maybe we'll do it during the Christmas hoo-hah. We'll toast ourselves.'

'I'm sure we will. Mind if I go ahead?'

'Of course not.'

His friend doesn't come back out to his seat, instead leaning on the bar from inside. 'So how goes it, Chuck? At your usual post portside, were you? Picking out prospects for the old thesp training?'

Charles smiles. His friend knows him so well. 'There was one girl I saw, shiny-eyed, definitely her first trip, one of the Skippers. She looked up and seemed surprised to see me. Hope she didn't think I'm the resident voyeur.' He smiles ruefully.

'Come off it, Chuckie.' His companion puts the bottle to his lips and takes another swig. 'You?'

'Well, you never know, do you?' As his friend drinks again, Charles reflects on his single state. After several abortive attempts to build relationships – with either sex – he has concluded he is probably asexual, and has come to terms with that, although he would love to have a life's companion.

'You'd think, wouldn't you, Chuck, that the regulars would come to take this last opportunity, for nostalgia's sake if nothing else? Poor old thing. By the way, remember I told you about one of the directors being on board? Trophy wife and all that? At your table?'

'Sure.'

'Well, they've confirmed. Here's your list. All English speakers. There's a Danish couple on honeymoon, but you know Danes, ten languages nothing to them . . .'

Charles examines the list: he has always asked to be put at a table, no matter what size, with as many English speakers as possible. 'That's great, Frank, thanks. Five men, three women? That's unusual. It's generally the other way round. Solos are usually female.'

'One of them is – some kind of writer. Fellow artist, Chuck?' The gizmo attached to his belt bleeps loudly and he looks at it. 'Gotta take this – sorry. We'll talk again. But quickly, before I go, how're things in the West End, these days? And been in any movies lately?'

In reply, Charles brightly repeats the noncommittal stock phrase he always has ready for these enquiries: 'Treading boards as usual, Frank, grinding it out. Bad penny, that's me.'

'Good lad, good lad, can always rely on you for the good

news. See you in the trenches, eh?' But he's looking again at his watch and Charles knows he has already dropped into cruise-director mode.

'Of course, Frank,' he says. 'I'll look forward to that.' Remaining on his seat, he watches his friend hurry past without looking at him, and the swing doors thump back into place. The encounter may happen, it may not. They may never say goodbye to each other. He looks at the second Guinness bottle. Should he?

'No,' he says aloud. In a funny way, he feels he has already left the *Clara* and taking that bottle would be looting her.

How're things in the West End? How droll. He smiles forlornly as he climbs off the bar stool. In its wisdom, Portlandis has puffed him on its publicity material with a far better CV than reality merited: *Othello with the Royal Shakespeare Company in Stratford-upon-Avon* – yes, he had been *in* that play in Stratford, once, but as the Duke of Venice who appears in scene three of Act One. *A long and distinguished career in London's West End* – indeed, his appearances there have stretched over many years, with highly distinguished and award-laden colleagues, but sporadically and always in minor roles.

In fairness, however, within the profession, he does enjoy one of those halfway reputations as a 'useful' character actor and, if not working, there is usually something in prospect – even the occasional gift of something in a film.

Right now, however, his diary is blank, save for his inscription: 'BBR4?' under its *If Found Please Return To* page at the front of the book, which had happened to be open when he had taken Jeremy's call. His agent was phoning to say that BBC Radio 4 had made an availability check on him in the context of doing a *Book at Bedtime*. 'But,' Jeremy had said, 'if it comes to pass at all, Charles, it'll not happen for at least three months or more. So enjoy your cruise. Get lots of fresh air and sunshine.'

A squall of rain is making its presence felt on the swing doors and the deck outside and he is thinking that, despite the upgrade, the rain matches his mood. Pathetic fallacy. Just wonderful.

But he can't bitch, can he? All things come to an end, and the dear old *Clara* has been a good friend to him, as has Frank. Well, as good a friend as any man can be with another, both now of a certain age with very little in common except their stage experience, their status as single men – Frank had been a widower for many years – and their stated desire to maintain the friendship. Whether it survives the width of the Atlantic, Charles thinks now, remains to be seen.

They see each other only occasionally these days and always in the hothouse atmosphere of a cruise, which is even more artificial than that in the theatre.

Before leaving, he looks around the dim, silent bar. Tonight, after dinner, this bar, one of the favourites on the *Clara* and lit with enough candlepower to illuminate a small football field, will be thronged. Once under way, a cruise liner surrounds one with people, but it can feel like the loneliest place on earth. Even on a balcony.

3

Kitty Golden is in the cavernous passenger hall at the port of Barcelona. Flatbeds in first class notwithstanding, sleep had eluded her during the flight from New York and she can't wait to get to her suite on the *Santa Clara*.

Although this ship is 'a tub', according to Saul, who should know, he has guaranteed they'll have a good voyage. Kitty had nodded dutifully, but had been barely listening at the time. Provided her bed is big, clean and comfortable, closet space is enough for the outfits she has with her, she has access to a decent bathroom and an onboard spa over the next nine days, she'll be fine. Now she just wants to get on with it.

Right now, her legs ache and her ears are ringing. She could sleep for a week and is finding it difficult to resist the urge to take off her jacket, bundle it up and, the hell with what others might think – what Saul might think – use it as a pillow on the floor to take a nap. The hall's roof is high, its surfaces hard, and being surrounded by so many excited, chatting people feels like standing with a thousand-strong flock of parakeets in an aviary, or under a cascading waterfall.

She looks at her watch: the ship had been scheduled to open for boarding at eleven a.m and it's now just after two in the afternoon. She had gone ahead of Saul into the hall, leaving him to talk to the ship's officer who had been there to meet them by the luggage area on the pier when the limo had dropped them off. While she had gone ahead, they had come in together and had been talking near the entrance for more than five minutes now.

Alongside his seats on the boards of myriad construction, oil and gas companies, Kitty's husband, Saul Abelson, is also a non-executive director of Portlandis Shipping Line, here to represent it on the vessel's last cruise before its sale to a firm in Malaysia where, apparently, it is to be stripped down and repurposed before being sent on to serve as a ferry in Bangladesh.

Clearly, it's not the only liner leaving port today. Based on the luminously hued tags on their hand luggage, the vast majority of those in the hall are due to travel on the super-liner she'd seen berthed behind the *Santa Clara*, dwarfing it. And, according to what she has gathered from the loud chat around her, this enormous ship, as big as many US towns and with better facilities, is leaving late this afternoon for the sunshine of Dubai and Oman, prior to the exotic (also sunny) Far East and then Sydney, where, she thinks enviously, it's high summer.

She has zipped her lips, however, not wishing to add to Saul's disappointment at having to spend his sixtieth birthday on Portlandis's old vessel, one of the liners retaining old-fashioned cruising customs. For instance, on the *Santa Clara*, unless one specifies otherwise – if you are part of a group travelling together – table seating is pre-assigned, as are dining companions.

Having had pretty dispiriting experiences with unsuitable

companions on some previous cruises, Saul had recently taken to dictating that the two of them be given one of the 'couples' tables' usually on request by honeymooners or other lovers. It means that the two of you are somewhat isolated from the herd and can dine while gazing into each other's eyes. Not so, this time, to Kitty's (concealed) relief.

This had been her doing, although she hasn't told Saul yet. Her plan is to let things unfold. They'll get to the dining room, find they're at a bigger table, and even Saul won't create a scene in that context. She'll convince him it was just an administrative screw-up on an old ship with tired staff and crew. In fact she had arranged it with his PA, Philippa, with whom she had developed a decent relationship over the years. 'Can I trust you *again*, Pippa?'

'Maybe.' The PA had sounded justifiably cautious. 'Run it by me ...'

As tactfully as she could, Kitty had revealed that she didn't want to be marooned with her husband at a couples' table. 'All kinds of reasons, too boring to go into now. Could you fix that, Pippa, without him finding out that it was my doing? Any other table, four, six, eight, it doesn't matter. Anything but a table for two.' This was not the first time Kitty had asked the woman to divide her loyalties like that but she always rewarded Pippa well, not with cash but with a gift, previously, for instance, a limited-edition flagon, handmade by a glassmaker, of Chanel's Extrait No 5, which cost more than four thousand dollars, an Hermès Birkin 40 bag, which had cost more than thirteen.

Right then, however, Saul's PA was silent.

'Do you think it's too difficult, Pippa?'

'Leave it with me,' the other woman finally answered, rather crisply, Kitty thought. This PA had been with Saul for more than twenty years, knew him probably better than any of his three wives, understood how to handle him and, in Kitty's opinion, was so efficient she could have run the diplomatic service of the UN.

It had taken more than twenty-four hours, but at close of business on the day before they were to fly to Barcelona, the PA had called Kitty to say everything was under control. 'How'd you do it?' Kitty had been half expecting it wouldn't happen.

'I said you couldn't stand your husband.'

'What?'

'Just kidding,' the PA said flatly, then: 'I said it was your idea. The two of you had never been at a big table before, and you'd decided that, with his birthday coming up, it would be a big surprise for him, and everyone at the table could help celebrate. The dining-room manager has arranged it. And he's made sure there are no vacant couples' tables. Have a good time.' She'd hung up, leaving Kitty wondering whether or not she was being ironic. She was usually so friendly. Did she disapprove?

It'd have to be something rather special this time, Saul's wife thought ruefully. A piece of jewellery from the Ponte Vecchio in Florence, maybe. Perhaps she'd pushed her luck just that bit too far. Nothing to be done about it now ...

So, for the birthday itself, will the captain invite them to dine at his table, as Saul – who could sometimes be rather childlike – hopes and is planning to request as subtly as is possible (for him) or, if the response isn't looking good, as unsubtly as possible. For him, birthdays are a very big deal. This one, with its big fat zero, is mega.

She has always privately found it amusing that because of a tiny twist of Fate, her husband, a Jew, great supporter of

Israel and passionate about Jewish culture, should have been born on the same day as Jesus, according to legend. How do astrologers cope with that?

They've discussed the celebration and, at Kitty's suggestion, it should take place (assuming he's granted his wish that the captain will co-operate) on Christmas Eve. 'Christmas Day we're at sea and it's the last night on board before we get off at Rome the next day, Monday morning. People will be packing, Saul. Leaving the dining room early. It's such a big day for you, I've always found that Christmas Eve is nicer than the day itself, which, after you've opened the presents, can be pretty boring. And, anyway, after midnight, you'll be sixty. Christmas Eve is the last day of your sixtieth year. It's sort of more celebratory – honouring six decades before you enter your seventh. Christmas Day is a Sunday. Who likes to party on a Sunday? Saturday night even *sounds* more fun!'

'Oh, God, sixty?' But he had seen the logic and had agreed.

But in general, according to himself, he had drawn the short straw by having to take this trip in the line of duty to Portlandis: during a board meeting, when the company's chairman had asked for a volunteer to represent it on the *Santa Clara*'s last voyage, everyone else had already committed to spending the holiday in the Caribbean, Florida, or the ski resorts of Maine, Whistler or Colorado. 'Or so they said, Kitty,' he'd added glumly to her that evening, 'but I have my suspicions . . .'

The lines of people waiting to go through the formalities of boarding are continuing to lengthen as more passengers come in. Given his status in the company, they could have walked from the pier straight onto their ship, as they usually did on cruises, bypassing crowds and lines, even when the liner belonged to a rival.

So what's going on here? Saul is still gabbing with the ship's officer, no doubt making his wishes clear to the man, who had removed his hat, revealing pepper-and-salt hair. The man's head was bent quite a bit as he listened; her husband's stature is one of the reasons Kitty's shoe collection contains lots of pairs with little or no heels.

Even in sneakers, though, she can't stand for much longer and, looking around, spots a row of seats against the wall. Ignoring the sidelong glances she's attracting as she walks across to it, she folds herself into one and opens her handbag to root.

She is used to attracting undue attention in public. It has persisted even though she gave up working more than ten years previously. As a result, she has developed a personal tunnel vision, head down, gaze fixed on the cover of her book, a boarding pass, the screen of her cell or tablet. If she's carrying nothing, she might be admiring the beauty of the floor; if she's sitting, it's the contents of her bag.

She feels hassled not by people's initial reaction to her, which is flattering and what she had signed up for in her former job, it's because recognition of her in streets and public places has always tended to be fuzzy. Even when, having advertised or endorsed some product, her image has been plastered over the length of a bus, yellow cab or on hoardings all over Manhattan, it has always taken people time to pin down where they had seen her before: 'Don't I know you? Aren'tcha famous or sumpin'?'

Polite by nature, upbringing and early education, by Roman Catholic nuns in Dublin, she has never liked to be rude enough to cut the conversation as they cast around . . . 'What high school did you go to?' or 'Hey! Aren't you one of those girls that got gold medals in the women's basketball at the Olympics?'

'I went to school in Dublin, Ireland,' she would say, but discovered quickly that this frequently led to more questions.

'Dublin, Ireland? Cool! My gran'paw came over from County Clare. You know County Clare?' and all that.

As for the basketball question, 'I'm afraid not,' she'd say, with a smile, as though this was the first time she'd been asked, 'although I sure wish I was. Aren't those women wonderful? But you might have seen me in that new TV commercial for yogurt. Or maybe in a magazine picture.'

She was always uncomfortable when adding this. It sounded so vain. *Of course you should know me!* Throughout home and school life in Dublin, humility and modesty were *the* cardinal virtues, with 'blowing your own trumpet' being narcissistic. Even worse, it meant you were committing the deadly sin of pride, one of the seven that would send you to Hell. But it usually worked: 'Oh, gee! *That*'s where I seen ya! Do ya actually eat that yogurt stuff?'

Her dressing room in the Manhattan apartment, bigger than many designer boutiques on Fifth Avenue, is stuffed with hundreds, if not thousands, of garments, shoes and accessories, but in public she tries to dress inconspicuously. Fair hair stuffed under a light blue baseball cap, today she is wearing denim jeans, like hundreds in the hall but hers have been custom-made to fit; her white sweater and socks are cashmere, her navy jacket is vintage Puffa and her sneakers are ocean leather, so-called because the principal constituent is kelp.

Kitty is vegetarian, but not vegan, as she eats eggs and drinks milk. She still occasionally eats fish but feels increasingly anxious about it. She hates the sight, on TV, of the extraordinary creatures, which have perhaps travelled thousands of miles to the fishing grounds off the coast of the

US, being hauled, suffocating, thrashing about and drowning in the nets closing around the shoals, to be poured like so many tons of silver ingots on to the decks of ships, skidding onwards to the holds and out of sight. What happens down there? She hates to imagine.

As for lobsters – the gourmet world changed for Kitty one day when, in an upmarket French restaurant, the waiter brought the catch of the day to their table so she and Saul could select their lunch from the array of silvery corpses. With them there was a small lobster, claws neatly tied, antennae waving feebly. Jews may not eat shellfish so the lobster had a brief reprieve as Saul plumped for salmon, but to Kitty's horror the lobster made eye contact with her, slowly, very slowly, opening and closing its small, almost black eyes. She nearly fled the table but didn't want to make a scene. It was a famous restaurant, renowned for its glittery clientele. Paparazzi usually lurked in the street outside, and the last thing she needed was to see a social column mention of her behaviour, however defensible in her own eyes. Gulping, almost in tears, she had asked the waiter to bring her a green salad.

That poor doomed creature haunts her still. And every time she enters one of those emporia with a lobster tank on display she cannot bear to eat at all.

Saul, to give him his due, tolerates these foibles, although over the years his puzzlement about this one has emigrated towards exasperation, despite her impassioned efforts to reason with him.

On lobsters, for instance, he dismisses her pleas that they do not take guests to seafood restaurants and to imagine what it must feel like to be a little lobster, marching along with fifty others, nose-to-tail, in a column on the seabed between feeding grounds for forty-eight hours or more. And just when you think you're there, whether you're ten years old or forty-five, the column's leader or safe in the middle of the line, you end up in a basket, then in a small glass tank, still alive but with claws tied, having to fight for space with others, before being plucked out and dropped into boiling water.

But every time she tries to explain her feelings to others, Saul shuts her down with 'Oh, here we go . . .' showily putting his head into his hands, smiling apologetically around fellow guests, then emphatically changing the subject.

She believes the time is imminent when she will become purely vegan. She and Saul rarely dine out with others, except on big occasions, like charity dinners or balls or when one of Saul's companies is entertaining and their presence is required. So her dilemma arises infrequently, and at home she eats mostly alone.

Right now, even though she is busy with the contents of her bag, in her peripheral vision she sees people in her vicinity glancing at her, and because she's seated, it can't be because of her height. Kitty is beautiful. The gene-gods have been good, and at thirty-three, even bare-faced without make-up, as she is today, she could credibly be taken to be in her early twenties.

She had stood out from the herd from the time she went to secondary school, because at around thirteen, her growth had spurted to the extent that, when still fifteen, she had attained her adult height of six feet two inches, eliciting mortifying taunts, such as 'String bean!' or 'What's the weather like up there?' Family members had been mystified since her older sister, Geraldine, at eighteen also taller than average, had finished at a relatively normal five feet eight.

So, in her mid-teens, Kitty had developed a slouch and a

way of moving, sitting and standing with shoulders up and head retracted as far as possible into her neck. But then, one Saturday after she had turned sixteen, with her birthday money zipped into the pocket of ripped jeans, she was lost in futile longing that she could afford one of the bright, optimistic dresses with their promise to overcome the Irish 'summer' displayed in the windows of Brown Thomas on Grafton Street.

For once relaxed and unselfconscious, she was trying to decide whether or not to go into the shop, which was advertising a pre-summer sale, when she felt a tap on her shoulder and turned to a woman who, having seen past the slouching and the grunge, introduced herself as the proprietor of a model agency and asked her to come into a studio for a few test photos. The camera loved her and a career was born.

Her parents had insisted – 'No argument, Catherine' – that she should stay in school to do her Leaving Cert, and for a while she had juggled modelling with exams. But, confidence increasing as she took to the mechanics of how to jut a hip, how to stretch her neck, holding her head at a slight angle so the lights caught cheekbones and lips, she began to enjoy the job. And for a teenager the money, although modest enough at the start, was a terrific bonus.

During those early days, wearing denims, with no make-up, hair trendily crimped but tied up, she could still spend hours in Penneys, Dunnes, or the ILAC shopping centre in Parnell Street, while not attracting too much attention to herself, except from what her sister called 'dirty oul fellas'. The demands on her time began to intrude on study, though, and while she wanted to please her parents, she knew which she preferred.

She was just eighteen when, to her parents' horror, she got

an offer from an agency in New York. Despite entreaties and even threats of dire consequences, she dropped out of school and, with just six weeks to go to the Leaving, flew to the Big Apple, insisting she Go. On. Her. Own. No chaperons.

Saul and the officer are still talking and she is becoming not just impatient but irritated. She truly does not want to be here *at all*, meaning she doesn't want to be here with Saul. She's not sure any more whether she wants to stick with the marriage.

At rock bottom she remains profoundly grateful that Saul had rescued her from penury to the extent that, with difficulty, she overcame Geraldine's warnings that marrying him would end in tears. 'He could be your father, Kit! Have a bit of sense. What have you in common? You're not the same religion, even. Are you going to convert? He'll want you to – his mother will at any rate!'

In the end she had made the difficult call to Ireland to invite her family to her wedding and, of course, her sister had been less than impressed: 'I can't do this, Kit. I just can't watch you throw your life away.' And, as it happened, none of her family attended.

When it became clear that she intended to go ahead with this 'foolishness', as Geraldine termed it, her sister had called her late one night. 'All right, Kit, it's your life. I accept that. But just do one thing, please. I'm begging you. Go to a solicitor and get a decent pre-nup. Promise me that at least. But honest to God, Kitty, you'll get over your current difficulties on your own. You don't need him. Trust me.'

But Kitty's reaction to the shock of her financial ruin, as she had seen it at the time, had been to cave in to Saul's impassioned wooing. She had, though, feeling pretty grubby, fulfilled her sister's urgings to have a pre-nuptial arrangement written and notarised.

To be fair to him, Saul hadn't objected, even though his alimony to his two previous wives and maintenance for his two stepchildren makes for a substantial outgoing. He had even presented her with a list of his associates in his own law firm: 'The choice is yours, honey – don't let me influence you. But we might as well use them. They give discounts!' He had grinned and she had grinned back.

When relaxed and off-duty – a rare occurrence – Saul could be quite funny, even self-deprecating. Along with generosity, it was one of the traits she had used, at the time, in her arguments with her sister to justify her relationship. 'You don't know him, Gerry. You haven't met him.'

'Why not, incidentally? Why is he not here with you to meet your family?' Because their parents were dead now, Geraldine had appointed herself *in loco parentis.*

'He's busy. You know that.' Kitty had become defensive, as she always did, during these arguments. 'You're getting your opinion of him from movies or comedians. He's *not* what you think.'

'Come on! You're to be the third wife, the *new* "younger model".'

'He does love me – he *does*, Ger.'

'Do you love him?'

Kitty hadn't been able to answer that truthfully because she didn't know how. Instead, she had feigned indignation. 'Of course I do! We have a great time together. And he'd do anything for me!'

'I give up.' Her sister had stared at her. They were in the kitchen at Geraldine's house and, pregnant with her first child, she had heaved herself out of her chair to check on a saucepan bubbling on the hob. As she went, she flung over her shoulder, 'On your own head be it.'

It was Kitty's decision not to convert to Judaism. It just didn't feel right. Saul had briefly mentioned that it might be nice if she did, but since he wasn't Orthodox or all that observant, he hadn't pressed the matter.

At the time, Kitty's only real friend in New York was a colleague-model, Ruby Stoneman. She had understood Kitty's dilemma although, when disaster had befallen Kitty, their lifestyles could not have been more different. Ruby's mid-range earnings supported not just herself but her fiancé. He had given up work at the New York stock exchange and, at the time of Kitty's marriage, was in his final year of study to become a professional environmentalist. So, Ruby and her intended were renting cheaply in Ridgewood trying to save for a house upstate to buy after his graduation, although houses there were even then outpacing their little cache. Although Kitty had offered help from time to time, Ruby had always stoutly refused. 'Thanks for the thought, kid, but no thanks.'

Because of their friendship, Kitty, with her husband's rather bemused blessing, is now an ongoing donor to the 11th Hour Theatre Company in Philadelphia, Ruby's hometown. While appearing on stage there in some small part, her friend had been spotted by the model agency to which she still belongs. The theatre's next production will be *Lizzie* – the rock/grunge musical about Lizzie Borden, accused (and acquitted) of axe-murdering her father and stepmother in Massachusetts. Ruby and her friends in grade school had skipped rope to a rhyme about it:

> *Lizzie Borden took an axe*
> *And gave her mother forty whacks;*
> *When she saw what she had done,*
> *She gave her father forty-one.*

Now, thinking about Ruby, in eco-heaven with her two little girls, six cats, numerous dogs, two Shetland ponies and a pet hen, Kitty smiles fondly. Only six weeks to go until the two of them see each other again on a girls' night out at the play. They already have their tickets.

At last! Saul has turned around to give her a thumbs-up. The officer is peering across at her – they must have been talking about her.

She smiles at them and forces her tired body upright. Before going towards them, she struggles to refasten her bag. Of heavy silver brocade, it is vintage, its clasp one of those with a pair of tines, one crossing over the other. They have loosened and won't stay closed if the bag is over-full, as it is today, stuffed not just with toiletries, cosmetics, her bulging wallet and jewellery roll, but her gift-wrapped sixtieth-birthday present to her husband, a Breguet Classique Moonphase watch in 18 carat gold, which had cost her (him) more than forty thousand dollars at Tiffany's and was, with its multiple miniature dials, the kind of timepiece every successful businessman should have, or so the salesman had said. 'He'll love it, madam.'

She eventually manages to get the tines to stay crossed and makes a mental note to have them fixed when she and Saul get home.

It is true, but somewhat morally flabby, she thinks, as she makes her way towards the two men, that while she hadn't married Saul for his money (at least, she thinks not) she sure didn't marry him for love. Instead it was out of a sense of obligation because he had rescued her during that critically upsetting period. She had plumped for security.

Although his divorce from his second wife hadn't yet come through, he had not only represented her as an attorney in a fight against her agency but had pursued her ardently, painting a beguiling picture of leisure and subsequent uncritical support for whatever path she chose for her life. He had been so persuasive and she so badly shaken that she had eventually given in. As soon as his divorce had come through, they had married quietly at City Hall, with only Ruby as a guest, on her twenty-third birthday, 18 April 2006. She'd probably married him from gratitude, but also, she hated to admit, had been grasping at the beguiling possibility of ease from stress and worry, the floor of her career having fallen out from under her.

As she and the two men, officer and husband, weave through the crowds towards each other, she can see that Saul, thank goodness, is in a mellow mood. 'All sorted now, Kit,' he says, as they meet. 'So it's straight through to the suite.' He turns to the officer. 'Captain, this is my wife, Kitty Golden,' then back to her, 'and this is Captain Leifsson, Kitty. We're invited to his table for the big day.'

'That's wonderful, Saul. Thank you, Captain.' Kitty knows that this has been a very important win for Saul because, even though he is a director of the company that employs the captain, an invitation to the captain's table is entirely at Leifsson's discretion. 'How do you do, Captain?' She extends a hand. As they shake, the officer's eyes, of that clichéd Scandinavian ice-blue, are on a level with her own. They widen momentarily but only for an instant, reverting speedily to the wrinkly, avuncular look common, in her experience, to all officers of higher rank on cruise liners. Kitty's accustomed to that kind of look: now and then people actually betray their surprise at the age disparity between herself and Saul, which is all too obvious. She used to get upset but now what people think of her (a gold-digger?) is their own problem, not hers.

'Well,' says Saul, jovially, covering both of them with a broad smile, 'ready to go have fun, honey? Here, give me that.' He takes her wheelie and hands his to the captain, who takes it without comment, and all three, bypassing the check-in counter, head for the doors into the ship.

They are waiting at the elevator bank just beyond the security area when the door of one slides open and a small, excited girl with a blonde ponytail bursts through, trips on one of her shoelaces and cannons into Kitty, dislodging the handbag from her shoulder. It bursts open as it falls to the ground, some of its contents tumbling out, including the jewellery roll and Saul's new watch, swaddled in the distinctive blue gift-wrapping used by Tiffany's. 'I'm so, so sorry.' The girl rushes to pick everything up but is so agitated she drops it again.

'Thank you – thank you. Leave it.' Saul stoops and, without comment, returns everything to the bag – although Kitty sees that, in handling the watch, he had noted the Tiffany wrapping.

'I'm sorry,' the girl says again. 'It's just that I think I might have left my wallet here. I don't have it and the last time I saw it I was putting it through the security tunnel.'

'May I help?' Captain Leifsson steps in. 'If it was left here, it's still here. This is quite common. People forget the most extraordinary things, like their spectacles, their medication. Come with me, madam.'

But the girl is staring at Kitty. 'Don't I know you?'

'I don't think so.' From long practice, Kitty's smile is automatic. 'Are you OK?' she asks. 'You didn't hurt yourself?'

'No. Thank you. But I'm awfully sorry, I hope nothing broke.' The girl, who, in Kitty's ears, sounds English, is still staring.

'Come!' Captain Leifsson takes her arm, and then, to Kitty and Saul: 'We'll leave you here.' With a small inclination of his head, he adds, 'Very nice to meet you, Mr Abelson, and you, Mrs Abelson. You're both very welcome aboard, and we'll see each other again soon, I'm sure. In the meantime, if there's anything you need . . .

'This way, madam.' He takes the girl's arm, indicating a door a little way off.

But as Kitty and her husband pass into the elevator, the girl pulls a little away from his restraining arm. 'Roxy Smith. I'm a novelist. Pleased to meet you, Mrs Abelson.'

She stretches out her hand, leaving Kitty with little option but to hold open the door and, with her free hand, to take the one offered. 'And it's nice to meet you too, Ms Smith.'

'Come.' The captain is smiling but his voice is insistent.

'I'm coming, thanks,' the girl says quickly, but as the elevator doors begin to close, it's her turn to hold them open, blurting, 'You're really beautiful, Mrs Abelson!' She lets the doors go and they slide closed.

'Is she a lesbian or what?' Saul looks at Kitty as the elevator jerks into action.

'I doubt it, Saul,' she says. 'Let's get into that room as quick as we can. I'm out on my feet. I really need a nap.'

But Kitty, whom Saul had introduced to the officer as 'Golden', had noticed the captain's 'Mrs Abelson' response. As she watches the numbers over the door of the elevator count off the decks as it lumbers up to theirs, she's hoping Captain Leifsson hadn't heard Saul's stupid question.

4

Roxy had found it thrilling to respond to the tinny, crackling public-address system by following orders, retrieving her life jacket from the floor of her tiny wardrobe, then following the instructions of crew members standing at intervals on her corridor and at every turn of the staircase leading to the deck with the lifeboats, directing her and her fellow passengers to their emergency stations. There, they had to assemble to learn how to tie on the jackets and how to behave if everyone, including crew, has to abandon ship.

On deck, as the crew practise uncoupling the arms holding the boats to the deck to swing them out over the water, there's a real sense of community (*if it happens for real, we'll all be in it together*) but also of levelling. No distinctions made here between rich, poor, crew or passenger. The only gaps evident are those between the stations assigned, as all gather together to rehearse. An emergency – fire, torpedo attack, whatever – would be a great leveller, Roxy thinks, because the denominator is your life, not your status or what you have in your bank account. And, while they are all smiling at each other, she suspects that many are privately owning up to a small shot of alarm about how real this feels. For her, the whole episode is highly dramatic.

When it's done and they're told they can now disperse, she's still carrying her bulky life jacket as she goes up to the highest deck on the ship to watch their departure from Barcelona, with its ferries to the Balearics and other countries all lit up. Christmas decorations are visible in some of their windows. Lights blaze in buildings all around and reflect on the flat water, creating rainbows near the piers, where the surface is greasy with oil. The plaza in front of the giant hotel nearby sparkles with fairy lights and the giant decorations on its regiment of Christmas trees.

She grips a rail, marvelling at the coordinated, well-practised action on the quay below: nooses on heavy ropes tying them to the quay are slipped off bollards, the ropes whirring into the bowels of the ship, and lozenge-shaped rubber fenders are lifted off the side. And then they're moving, imperceptibly at first. The gap between ship and land widens inch by inch as the *Santa Clara* moves slowly away from the pier and, with her prow set to the harbour entrance, moves into the middle. As they pass ships at other piers, a few passengers on their decks wave at them and Roxy, delighted, waves back.

She jumps with fright as, without warning and right beside her, the ship's funnel emits three loud blasts of what she realises, belatedly, must be its horn.

It's all so exciting.

*

An hour later, with the *Santa Clara* out into the open sea, Roxy is in the main dining room, the first to arrive at her table, number thirty-two, its white cloth laid with plain but heavy cutlery and linens that match. She notices that the drops on all the tablecloths in the room are swaying. Although it's dark outside the windows, she senses that the ship isn't going in a straight line but moving up and down a bit. Staff, however, seem oblivious to this as, unfaltering, they move around, not having to hold on to anything, as she had to when getting here.

It's not 'smooth sailing', as she had expected from the bumf she'd been given prior to the cruise. On the staircase coming up here, she had been close behind a couple, obviously seasoned cruisers, when the man had said to the woman: 'Hang onto that handrail over there, for God's sake, Doris. There's chop and swell and we don't want a repeat of what happened to you the last time! I can't go through that again. *Please!'*

Casting a filthy look at him, Doris had grasped the banister.

Tables are rapidly filling, and at table thirty-three nearby, the family group from Ireland already seems to be having a ball. Roxy had waved to Gemma when the Dunnes had arrived and had received a wave in return, Gemma mouthing: *See you later.* She had been delighted with that.

So far, everyone else seems a little subdued, even tentative. There's a lot of sipping and perusing of menus. This, she thinks, is probably because it's a first night, with tablemates not yet knowing each other.

Her table, like that of the Dunnes, is circular and set for eight. But until others arrive she'll have a few minutes to herself: she needs to absorb her surroundings, to write essential descriptions into the tiny auxiliary notebook she'd brought with her in her evening bag. She has a small digital recorder too but has left it in her stateroom, thinking it would be bad manners to produce it here. Anyway, she enjoys the whole handwriting-into-notebooks thing, the contact between pen and paper. It feels more authorly, somehow, more Jane Austen.

She had loved writing the first *Heartbreak*, had even taken a quick trip to the Cotswolds on a whistle-stop bus tour of its eight hundred square miles for research. Unfortunately, though, she had not been assiduous enough with her notes and had later had difficulty in remembering the names of specific areas. Until she had handed over the manuscript to her publisher, she'd thought she'd managed successfully to gloss over it, thanking God for Google Earth and Google Maps, marvelling at how earlier authors had managed this stuff before the advent of the Internet.

To her chagrin, her tactful but firm editor had recommended she travel back to her various locations, then go through the book to add more vivid atmosphere and context. She had taken the advice and had seen straight away that the novel was the better for it.

At the start, you don't know what detail is going to prove important. Something you've noted in passing and thought trivial may even turn out to be a trigger for a plot development. For instance, if this ship were to go through a bad storm, the ceiling in here, which looks a little cracked, might collapse on top of people. If she decided that were to happen, she'd need to be able to describe why, what the ceiling was made of, what, in its collapsed state, these heaps of materials looked like over mounds of buried human beings. What uninjured passengers and staff had to contend with as, desperately, with their bare hands, they tried to dig people out from under the debris. What was its dominant colour? Was the debris sharp and jagged? Did it cause rescuers' hands to bleed?

Her editor had been right. 'You're not just telling a story, d'you see, Roxy,' she'd said, in the gentle Scottish burr that had belied her steely character. 'Your readers must see pictures. They must feel the wind in your character's hair, smell the rotting rubbish – or corpse – the character recoils from in the gutters of the town. Readers aren't there but you are and it's up to you, as your character's representative, to *show* the readers where she's acting, not just why, and what she's doing. And you don't just say, "It was a beautiful sunny day with the water of the sea glittering." That's too easy. What does the ocean sound like that day? Like crashing thunder? Like a whispering angel? I'm exaggerating, of course, and if you used those similes I'd have a go at you. But you don't merely tell the readers what it's like, you have to give them the best opportunity you can to sense it. You've heard, I'm sure, of the show-don't-tell rule. Well, this is what it means.'

After they had hung up, Roxy had scribbled down as much of this as she could remember, had photocopied it several times and distributed the sheets into her notebook, on her desk and pinned some to the noticeboard above it. The editor's words had turned biblical.

Right now she's scribbling headlines about this room:

> *two huge statues, Ben-Hur types, outside double doors. Glass panels with leaping dolphins ('etched'? NB find out. PR person on board?)*
> *blazing chandeliers inside*
> *delicious smells: beef 'interladen' with fish*
> *nice carpet on the floor, reddish under tables, very worn, pile turned brownish, from feet between the tables*
> *gold paint on decorative plaster on the ceiling, dulled and flaking off in places*

> *curlicues (plaster?) on arches over alcoves for smaller*
> *tables (tables nice, lovely white starched cloths, real*
> *napkins, good cutlery, ordinary glasses)*
>
> *a kind of half-mezzanine eight steps up, tables on it*
> *behind fancy (curly cast-iron?) rails*
>
> *waiters (plus all staff including cleaners, waiters,*
> *captain) wear name badges BUT (use this!) also with*
> *country-of-origin. Capt from Iceland. NB romance*
> *prospect? Saw him when finding lost wallet. Tall, yes.*
> *'Commanding' presence (use but get better word,*
> *sounds punny. Definitely hot tho!). NB find out more.*
> *Age? Looks well preserved mid to late forties? Cd make*
> *him younger?*

She stops. Because here comes the geezer who had ogled her when she was boarding and – oh, God! He seems to be heading straight for this table. Quickly, she slots her little pencil into the spirals across the top of her notebook and slips it into her bag. One of the navy-blazer brigade, the man, who could be in his sixties or even early seventies, is wearing white slacks with black shoes so highly polished they could be patent.

He's smiling when he arrives at the table. 'Well, hello, little lady!' Sitting right beside her and sticking out his hand. 'I'm Charles Burtonshaw,' he adds, and, with a flourish of his hand, 'of the Burtonshaws of Nowhere Muching.' He pauses a little but, then, obviously having noticed her frown of incomprehension, adds more soberly, 'I'm part of the entertainment staff here. And you are?'

'Roxy. Roxy Smith. I'm a novelist.' While initially she'd been inclined to freeze him out, up close he looks like somebody's kindly granddad. A bit like her own, as it happens.

'A novelist?' he asks, responding with what she takes to be admiration. 'Oh, my goodness! You're *much* too young to be a novelist. What's your field?'

'I beg your pardon?'

'You know, crime, adventure, romance – broken hearts sort of thing?' He leans towards her conspiratorially, exuding a whiff of lemony scent. 'I don't like to admit it, but that's what I like. Don't tell anyone, Roxy, this can be our secret, but I have a stack of Mills & Boons at home. My dear mother loved them and I started reading them after she died. Keeps the loneliness at bay and I like it that all the ones I've read so far have happy endings.'

His face softens. 'Mother liked happy endings and maybe that's why I do too. Some novelists these days seem to like blood on the floor. And smut.' He waves away such trash with the back of his hand. 'They don't tie everything up for you either. They leave their stories open-ended, which I find infuriating.'

'Well, not me.' Although Roxy remains a little chary (was this gent for real?), she's warming to him. 'It's women's fiction,' she says, 'and I certainly agree with you, Charles. Every loose end should be tied up. And if an ending can't be happy, at least it should leave a bit of hope. I suppose,' she adds, feeling generously inclusive because he's taking her for real, 'my genre could be called "Romance", but it's deeper than that. My characters do suffer broken hearts, as you say. They're real people . . . to me anyhow.'

'Been published, have you?'

'Yes, actually.'

'Fantastic. Well done, Roxy. That's a lovely name, by the way. Roxanna, I presume?'

'Roxanne. My nan is from Scotland.'

'Ah. How wonderful. I played Cyrano, you know, in rep, the second Anthony Burgess version, which I love, and which, in my opinion, is by far the best translation.' He taps his nose. 'I have the hooter for it.' Then, looking towards the ceiling of the restaurant, he says dreamily, 'Best part I've had the privilege to be cast in. Best audience reception too. That was in Liverpool.' Then, back to her: 'Have you ever seen *Cyrano*, Roxy?'

This is double-Dutch to her. She shakes her head. 'I'm sorry, I really don't know what you're talking about, Charles.'

He sighs. 'I forget far too much about life as it's lived these days. You're too young, m'dear. You're not a theatre-goer, I take it?'

Again she shakes her head.

'What I'm talking about is a wonderful play called *Cyrano de Bergerac*. It's based on the life of a real Frenchman in the seventeenth century. He has a huge nose, like me, and is in love with a gorgeous girl, like you, and because he's fearful of rejection, he has a surrogate woo the woman he loves on his behalf. Also like you, her name is Roxane – with one *n* because they're all French. You should read it for inspiration for your novels, dear. It could be right up your street because, like your stories, it's about a man who is heartbroken, who adores Roxane but thinks that because he has a big proboscis he's too ugly for love— Oh! Here come two of our companions, I'll wager.' He stands, smiling in the direction of two men walking towards their table – at least, one is. The other is trailing several steps behind.

The two men arrive. The first, in an immaculately tailored suit, jacket open over a white T-shirt, probably in his fifties, Roxy judges, is very much older than the second, but it's the second man who captures the eye. Also wearing a tailored suit, this one with a lavender shirt, he is truly gorgeous, around six feet tall, with curly, artfully highlighted hair brushing the collar of his jacket. His eyes are large, almond-shaped, and so dark as to be almost black, each nested in a double fringe of long, thick lashes. After a brief flash of delight (*Might there be some hope for me here? He's utterly stunning! Who could resist?*), Roxy comes back down to earth: they are not father and son, not even uncle and nephew. A couple. Or, if not, definitely a liaison.

And so it proves as Charles presides over the introductions. The new arrivals are 'Barry Lee from London,' the older man says, shaking hands with Roxy and Charles, 'and this,' he extends a hand in the direction of the other, a little wearily, thinks Roxy, whose antennae are raised, 'is Joshua Levitsky, my partner. Josh comes originally from Israel but we live in England now.'

The younger guy's handshake is perfunctory, but despite his orientation, it's impossible not to be bowled over by those eyes, although she recognises that they may as well be beautifully carved lumps of coal for all the interest they show in her or anyone else. Joshua seems supremely bored.

The pair seat themselves two chairs away to the right of Roxy. Each immediately picks up a menu, creating a no-go area around themselves, excluding her and Charles.

Homosexual or not, could she match up this guy with Kitty Golden? Couldn't you just imagine the beauty of their children? Could the younger man discover, on meeting Kitty, that he's bi? Could he desert his long-time and long-suffering partner, who had done nothing but good by him, and ignoring increasingly frantic pleas and promises, spend all his considerable energy and charm in trying to attract her? And could she waver away from her husband?

These thoughts have merely flitted through. Josh, she decides, is acting like a spoiled brat and, no doubt, has got through life on beauty alone. Right now, he has lifted those wonderful eyes and is flicking them over adjacent tables as though prospecting for better companions. Poor Barry.

But she's not yet ready to write about gay relationships, or the struggles of being bi: this novel is on a deadline and to lay the role of protagonist on one or both of these men would require too much research.

She turns back to her immediate companion, searching to find familiarity in his face. Nope. He could be a famous English actor, no reason to doubt that. She's never heard of him, but that's no surprise. Unless he's been in a film with somebody like Hugh Grant or Helen Mirren she's unlikely to have seen him. So she smiles at him and he smiles back, then holds a water carafe up in front of her, with a questioning expression. She accepts and he pours, but halfway through, he puts the carafe down when another couple comes to the table. 'This is table thirty-two?'

'Certainly is,' says Charles, again standing up.

They all introduce one another. The couple are Elise and Aksel Hansen Vestergaard. With a smile he spells his first name: 'If you don't mind, it is not A-X-L like Guns N' Roses!'

'We are from Denmark,' says Elise, 'and we are on honeymoon.'

Barry lifts his eyes from his menu to acknowledge them, then gets up and shakes hands, but when Charles introduces the other man, Josh merely raises his hand a little from his menu so the Danes have to lean down to take it. To make up for such rudeness, Roxy nearly breaks her face with the widest smile she can manage: 'Lovely to meet you both.' And they do seem very sweet, she thinks as, having sat down and without waiting to be asked, they tell her and Charles how they work for a communications company in Copenhagen, how they met there and how each is on a second marriage.

'We married our first spouses when we were young,' says Elise.

'We did not know each other then.' Aksel looks at her, something secret passes between them, and Roxy instantly dismisses them as potential characters. No drama there.

'Are you, perhaps, grandfadder and granddaughter?' Elise asks the other two.

'Dear me, no!' Charles laughs. 'We have just become acquainted. You are in the presence of a published English author,' he adds gallantly, nodding towards Roxy, 'so I do wish we were related. Unfortunately not.'

The Danes seem impressed.

All this at their table already with two spaces yet to fill, and with so many prospects already in view, including Charles (every author probably needs an eccentric), Roxy is getting rattled.

This is what happened with *Heartbreak One*. Too many characters, too many storylines. On her final draft, on her editor's advice to eliminate at least two, she had got rid of four, all of whom, along with their backstories, she had thought, while writing about them, to be essential to the narrative. Once she had dropped them this proved not to be the case and she had found that, after she'd rid the book of them, she didn't miss them in the slightest.

But (*oh, God! Can you believe it?*) here comes the woman she had almost knocked down and whom she had been mentally auditioning as a main character for the new *Heartbreak*. That's her husband and they're both definitely heading for this table. Jack-in-the-box Charles stands up to greet them, but this time his attitude is slightly different, a tad more deferential. Still playing ringmaster, he again presides over the introductions, seeming to know these two: 'Here, ladies and gentlemen, we have Kitty Golden, who is a retired model, and her husband, Saul.'

'We're from Manhattan,' says the husband, then, probably recognising similarity of age, sits beside Barry, leaving his wife with no option but to take the seat next to Roxy, newly mortifying her with 'Thank you, Charles, but Roxy and I have already met! Hello, Roxy!'

Roxy, embarrassed, wonders what had possessed her at the foot of that lift. And now they're sitting together. And, horrible thought, had she led Kitty to think she was gay?

Their waiter, Umar (from Malaysia), who had been hovering as he waited for the table's complement to complete, temporarily saves her as he comes to rattle off the evening's specials. Roxy casts around for ways to make sure there is no misunderstanding. The easiest, she decides, is to talk about a boyfriend – and inventing one might be fun.

She's further saved by the arrival of the wine waiter. Because she can't afford wine, Roxy tells him she'll stick with water. Kitty asks for sparkling San Pellegrino, and as for the other six, it's half a glass of rosé for each of the Danes, 'a decent Château Burgundy but show me the label before you open it,' for Saul, and Josh insists that he and Barry have champagne.

When the waiter brings the bottles, ceremonially opens and pours, they all raise their glasses – even Josh comes out of his torpor – to wish each other a happy and safe voyage.

As for food, Kitty Golden orders beetroot salad followed

by vegetarian pasta while Roxy also goes for the beetroot, and hake for main. Then, with the ex-model now engaged with Charles, she turns to listen to the conversation on her right flank, where Saul, according to Charles's introduction a bigwig in the company that owns the ship, is in full flight, holding forth in long, convoluted sentences and Barry, who's an architect, listens, or pretends to, as Saul rushes on: 'Yeah, be the best available when we've finished with 'em, our sound consultants are the best in class. You go to the movies it has to be a beautiful experience and ours gives you a beautiful experience, believe me, Barry, wide velvet seating, first class, you're right in there with the action! The Mall itself is terrific too, we did great there, great, great stores, really beautiful tenants. I'd love you come see it, Barry, you'd love it . . .'

Roxy tunes out. The starters arrive and she concentrates on her beetroot because, right now, like Joshua, Kitty is emitting a sort of invisible no-go vibe. Yes, beautiful, but quite intimidating, even for Roxy, who prides herself on being able to talk to anyone.

In response to Charles's questioning, Kitty had told the table she'd been a model until she left the business. The only surprise for Roxy is that it seems she had left it more than ten years ago. Unless she's had so much work done that she's the modern equivalent of the protagonist in Fay Weldon's *The Life and Loves of a She-Devil*, that means she's retired – gosh! It's hard to tell, but maybe she stopped modelling in her very late teens or early twenties. So what had happened? It's not as if she isn't still gorgeous, willowy as a whip in her white linen shift with a white faux-fur shrug. Roxy can't believe she could have left such a glamorous job at that age without a damn good reason. So far, she hasn't smiled, at least not showing teeth, and what's more, her husband hasn't even glanced at her since he sat down. Not once. All may not be well there.

Anyway, the actor-geezer, still host of the table in his own opinion, has just turned away from Roxy's neighbour to launch a conversation with the Danes. And with Umar now clearing starter plates, Roxy gets back to Kitty. 'So if I'm not being too nosy, can I ask why you retired from being a model when you were so young? That sounds really bizarre.'

'It's the truth. So what can I do? It's out there, it's never been a secret but, Roxy, it's a long story, too long and boring to talk about now but, yes, it is unusual, I accept that. In my own defence, I do other things. I work with a few charities and things like that.'

'He said,' Roxy indicates the woman's husband, 'that you live in Manhattan? Are you near Fifth Avenue?'

'The park. But, yes, we're not far from Fifth.'

'Central Park?'

'Very near it. We can see it from our roof terrace.'

'I've always wanted to go to New York.' Roxy is wistful. 'It looks amazing on TV. Mum and I just loved *Sex and the City* and *Friends*. Mum was brought up on *Kojak* too. She adored Telly Savalas, always referred to him as "my Telly". The two of us are still watching reruns, especially *Friends*, but I guess *Kojak* has gone to the great lollipop farm in the sky.'

Kitty laughs. 'Life in Manhattan isn't always fast-talking detectives, skinny lattes and great clothes, I'm afraid, although I do agree with you about how good those two sitcoms were. Maybe when you're on a tour for your next book you could get your publisher to send you to the States, and if you're anywhere near New York, you must look us up. You could even stay with us. We've tons of room. Remind me to give you our number before the end of the trip.'

'I will,' Roxy responds fervently, not believing her luck – then, remembering Bellewether's budgets: 'I'll certainly mention it to my editor.'

'Where are you from, Roxy?' Kitty asks then. 'You sound English.'

'London originally, but I'm living in Dublin these days.'

'You're kidding! I'm from Dublin, would you believe? I still have family there!'

'What?' Roxy is taken aback. The woman sounds totally like an American, although not, if TV is anything to go by, like a New Yorker. 'I can't believe it,' she says. 'You don't sound it!'

'I've been in New York for years.'

'They're all from Dublin, by the way.' Roxy gestures towards table thirty-three.

'I've already gathered that.' Kitty laughs, for the first time since she came into the room, and at last showing teeth (perfect, of course). 'They're hard to miss, aren't they?' She seems to have relaxed a little.

'Yeah, they sure are.' Roxy keeps the lightness going: 'Getting back to New York, here's a fun fact from Dublin. Baldies still get insulted in the streets by having "Kojak" shouted at them. Do you remember that, Kitty? It's a popular nickname for them too.'

'I clearly don't get back to Dublin often enough!'

'Sorry again for this afternoon,' Roxy says. 'I don't know what came over me.'

'Did you find your wallet?'

Roxy notices that she hasn't done the normal thing of saying,

'Forget it', or 'No harm done'. 'It was in that room where the captain said it would be. I felt like a right fool.'

'Don't beat yourself up. It happens.'

'Thanks. Thanks for that.' She perks up again. 'The good captain is from Iceland, did you notice? Speaking of TV stuff, he'd be up there with that Dr McDreamy in *Grey's Anatomy* only taller, don't you think?'

'I hadn't noticed. Tell me what it's like to be a novelist.' Again the other woman changes the subject. 'It sounds very exciting – hard work, though?'

'You'd better believe it.'

'How did it happen? Did you always want to write, from the time you were very young – younger than you are now, I mean?' Again Kitty smiles, and Roxy sees, fully, how and why she had been a model. No woman should be this gorgeous. It's hardly fair, she thinks, as she starts on the story of her life so far while continuing to marvel not just at Kitty Golden's beauty but at the smallness of the world. 'So, as I told you at the beginning,' she finishes, 'that's why I'm on this cruise. I'm planning to set the next novel on a ship like this and I want the setting to feel authentic, as though I know what I'm talking about.'

'Of course. But can you do that in just nine days on board?'

'The *Santa Clara* is only two hundred and fifty metres long,' Roxy, priding herself on her research, points out, 'so I'm sure I can. It's not as though I'm researching Greenland or Australia or somewhere like that. Hey, Kitty!' Emboldened, she pretends this has just occurred to her. 'Would you like to meet for a drink or something during the trip? I'm on my own. Know nobody so far.'

'Sure,' she says, without hesitation. Then: 'Provided I'm not part of your research?'

'As if!' Roxy manages to keep her expression neutral.

'What's your stateroom number so I can get in touch?'

'Two hundred and fifteen.'

'That's on deck two?' Kitty pauses. 'How do you find it?'

'It's fine.' Roxy doesn't want to moan. 'It's a little smaller than I'd expected, but there's only myself after all. And my mum had said the wall would have this virtual-reality thing – she saw it on TV – where you can *think* you're looking out at the sea through a porthole but in fact it's a picture from a film camera pointing outwards continuously. I'd been looking forward to that, but I guess she was misinformed.

'But I won't be spending much time there, will I? The only thing is,' she drops her voice, 'I do hope I'll be able to sleep nights. It is a bit noisy because there's machinery or something near me, chugging away all the time. But it's great, really it is.'

'Are you sure you're happy there, Roxy?'

She hadn't noticed Charles had been listening. 'Of course I am, Charles. I'm very happy. Very happy to be here with you all. Honestly. So far it's very exciting.'

'Tell you what, we're planning to go into Nice tomorrow,' Kitty says, 'what shore excursions are you taking? Pompeii is supposed to be well worth it when we dock at Naples next week.'

'I don't need to.' Roxy is chary of confessing that there is the little matter of lack of cash, with very little available for expensive guided trips ashore. 'My characters will probably be on a transatlantic trip,' she's making this up as she goes along, 'so there'll be no shore-going opportunities for them. I'll want them confined to the ship, you see?', then, adding hastily: 'Or maybe not, because of course this is where I'm researching.' She's making an idiot of herself here, she thinks: why would she be taking notes on the Mediterranean ambience if she was sending her characters to America? 'Anyway, you asked about going ashore? I'm certainly planning to take them to Ischia, I know it's really, really romantic out there!'

'But one cruise liner is more or less the same as another? Kitty is getting into the spirit: 'You could do a *Murder on the Transatlantic Express* sort of thing? An Agatha Christie type of story? And if you like, I can fill you in, in detail, about what it's like to go under the Verrazano Bridge on a ship. What your characters would see when they pass the Statue of Liberty and all that?

'Sorry if I'm being an interfering busybody here.' She smiles again. 'You're probably thinking that if you're sending them to America you'll have to take the transatlantic trip yourself? Nothing like the real experience, right? And,' she continues thoughtfully, 'if you're going to confine your characters on board, you're right, there's usually nowhere for them to go ashore until they get to New York. Hey!' Kitty is enjoying this, 'you could make the ship sink?'

'Naah. *Titanic* got there first. I'm on a deadline, so I don't think there'll be time or, being honest with you, Kitty, the money for me to set my novel on a voyage to America. That was just a fleeting thought. Bane of my existence. Anyway, I'm not a thriller writer, I'm afraid!'

'I guess I'm just being ignorant. You see, apart from you, the only other author I've ever met is Tom Wolfe.'

Now Roxy isn't sure whether or not she's being sent up: mentioning her in the same sentence as the author of *Bonfire of the Vanities*? It turns out, however, that the other woman is simply thinking aloud: 'All I knew about him beforehand,' she says reflectively, 'was that he was famous for wearing a white suit. I met him after he gave the Jefferson Lecture for the National Endowment for the Humanities, I think it was in the Kennedy Center, but it was definitely in Washington. Very clever man. We only got to exchange a few words after he spoke – it was Saul who was invited.

'You know, Roxy,' she smiles, 'a writer's mind is a wonderful thing to behold. Fascinating for ordinary mortals. Tell you what, let's meet for a drink before dinner tomorrow. Say six thirty in front of the doors here? We can find a nice bar or a nook somewhere.'

'I'd love that.' Roxy's heart thumps with pleasure.

Then the other woman spoils it: 'And you, Charles? Would you like to join us?'

'It would be an honour, madam.' Theatrically, Charles raises his eyes to the ceiling and throws both arms wide, as though taking a curtain call to an upper circle, but one hand knocks against two of Umar's plates, one of pasta, the other of hake. They fall out of his hands and tumble to the carpet.

5

Barry Lee and Joshua Levitsky are in their suite following their first dinner on board the *Santa Clara*. Josh had been all set to go to the casino but after the last time, in Cannes, Barry had mentally called a halt. Knowing all too well that Josh doesn't have the money even for five or six minutes at the roulette wheel, he has said, rather cruelly, he thought, in retrospect, 'I'm for bed – I'm bushed – but you go ahead, if you like.'

As expected, Josh had sulked for an hour or so, but then bounced back and had gone into the bathroom for evening ablutions. He has been there for at least forty minutes when he pokes his head out. 'We need to switch tables, Bar. That lot is so *dreary* – there's the *One Foot in the Grave* character, the sickly sweet honeymooners, that Saul – ugh! And if that girl with the horrible earrings is a famous English author, I'm telling you, Barry, you can call me Elvis!'

'I'll see what we can do tomorrow.' Barry hadn't lied when he said he was tired. 'Are you nearly finished? I want to go to sleep and I need a few minutes in there myself.'

'Not long now, my prince . . .'

Josh, as he does every evening, is moisturising every inch of his beautiful face and magnificent body. He will approach their bed in a cloud of vetiver, redolent of Barry's childhood afternoons spent in church as, one by one, his mum's friends and a lot of her patients were dispatched from this earth, coffins shining, priests waving all the perfumes of Arabia over them in fragrant clouds, censers clinking rhythmically – up, two, three, *down* . . . up, two, three, *down* . . .

Even as a boy, he had mentally rued the efforts expended on varnishing that wood, whether pine or mahogany, sometimes with intricate carved images, polished brass handles. All for what? A quick flash up the aisle, then down again, a journey to the bone yard to be sunk in filthy wet clay, all that polishing and carving never to be seen again. What's that all about? Certainly, the person for whom all this is being done can't appreciate it, although Barry's mum believes that during his or her funeral the coffin's inhabitant is out-of-body, watching from a heavenly perch, delighted and honoured by all the fuss. Each time he hears the monotonous funeral refrain 'She [or he] would have loved this!' he feels like vomiting.

She or he wouldn't have loved it. They would have wanted to be alive, saying that to someone else about a corpse that wasn't her or him.

Ah, shit, he thinks now. He doesn't really think it's all nonsense. He's just being a pill this evening.

He's been thinking of death a lot, tonight more than ever when all around him in bars, nightclubs, the casino and at a midnight chocolate buffet, people are celebrating their luck to be on board a cruise liner now well under way on the Mediterranean. In his present mood, however, Barry, is ultra-aware that this pretty sea is now a mass grave. The *Santa Clara* could be motoring merrily along, screws turning, while in the depths of the disturbed water, the remains of dreams roll over and drift with the drowned.

What's got into him tonight? *You can't take on the woes of the world. You're not Atlas.*

He mustn't let it get to him. He mustn't. He must keep up with everyone else's pleasure. Santa Claus will come, ringing bells down the ship's passageways, warning off the wraiths from the deep, soon to be joined by himself, possibly in less than five months. He hasn't told anyone of his diagnosis, not family, not Josh.

That boy will never be lonely. At least, not until his spectacular looks fade, and they will, he thinks sadly. No matter how assiduous the moisturising regime, cheeks always puff and sag, jowls and dewlaps form, ugly pads of crêpy flesh emerge from hiding places under the eyes. As he lies in the large bed, he is pierced with a shaft of premonitory loneliness at the thought of what is to come and of an interim period without Josh.

Because Josh will be off as soon as he finds out about the diagnosis and its pal, the prognosis. And who could blame him?

Will the boy even attend the funeral?

For now Barry has been able to conceal his increasing physical weakness with steroids prescribed by his consultant, good makeup, deft tailoring and a deliberate slowing of his gait, under the pretence he is having trouble with an ankle. He hadn't wanted to come on this trip but Josh had nagged and threatened, said he would go insane if he had to spend another Christmas Day eating overcooked veg and soggy turkey slices cooked by Barry's mum, or be subject, again, to descriptions of the exploits of famous Manchester United footballers of the fifties and sixties revered by Barry's dad.

A cruise at Christmas had been his idea to get away from suburbia. 'Your parents will accept it, Bar. It's just for this year. We can tell them we'll do Christmas with them again next year. Come on, Bar – please? Pretty please?' He had actually flounced.

Barry is neither camp nor dramatic – at least, he doesn't think he is – and it was probably Josh's prodigious energy and extroversion that had first intrigued him. It hadn't been his beauty, not then, because Barry had been late to the club, and had had to stand at the back until there was a pause on stage. As he'd arrived, Josh's drag act was just ending. He was heavily made-up, and so, because of his distance from the stage, Barry hadn't perceived how physically perfect he was.

But after the show some of the performers had mingled with the audience in the club's small bar and it was there, *sans* greasepaint, lipstick and eyeliner, his hair damp from the shower, that Josh had cast his spell. Barry had never seen such a creature. Almost twice the boy's age, he had fallen instantly, completely and irrevocably in love.

He couldn't believe his luck when this wonderful child of nature (an oxymoron but that was how he saw him) had agreed to a date the following week, not, Barry saw, before taking into account the older man's shoes, his Armani jacket and his gold Rolex watch. But he didn't care about venality, that night or any other. He'd won the prize. He was besotted but, even before that first date, he knew he would never hold on to him, that he would forever be running after him and that, if the relationship developed, it would be like housing a flame in his heart. He didn't care.

What he did care about was his own decrepitude by comparison with the boy's beauty: the thickening skin, the hint of brown patches on the hands, the receding hairline. When Joshua was away in Israel on a visit to his parents, Barry had taken advantage of his absence to have Botox and an eyelift, knowing that, on his return, the child wouldn't even notice. He did it to distract himself from the certainty that, while in Tel Aviv, Josh would play away, and the painful images the knowledge engendered.

He's Catholic by birth and education and had boarded with the Benedictines at Ampleforth, but had escaped the sex abuse because he wasn't pretty enough. He had seen enough of it, though, to drop Catholicism from the day he went to Cambridge and had the freedom to do so.

But that time when Josh went to Israel, Barry, eyes still black and blue after his treatment, had slunk into the London Oratory one Saturday evening in May, with sunlight slanting on the gilding. He didn't really know why he'd come. With his lifestyle, and the official attitude of the Church to homosexuality, he had no business being there asking for peace and help in his agony of suspicion and jealousy.

There was no official service in progress but the Schola, the young boys' choir, was rehearsing a descant above the sonorous voice of a lay reader intoning the incantations of the Litany of the Blessed Virgin Mary, with which Barry was familiar from his schooldays. He had come in just as the choir director cut the practice session to consult the reader, the echo of the singing continuing for a second or two, then dying gently into silence.

He slipped into one of the pews near the entrance. Apart from the performers, there were only three other people in the gorgeous building, Italianate, neo-Baroque, deeply satisfying to his architect's soul; an old woman, whose scoliosis was pronounced, fed her rosary through her fingers, lips moving, and nearer where he sat, a couple, Oriental, probably tourists, maps of London and the Underground protruding from the man's backpack, were as still as two of the statues presiding in the chapels.

'From the same place, okay?' The director lifted both hands and, on his signal, reader and choir, trebles piercing in unison, resumed the haunting call of praise and petition.

Mirror of justice, intoned the reader.

Pray for us, the boys sang.

Seat of wisdom, he called.

Pray for us, they responded.

> *Cause of our joy, pray for us.*
> *Spiritual vessel, pray for us.*
> *Vessel of honour, pray for us.*
> *Vessel of devotion, pray for us.*
> *Mystical rose, pray for us.*
> *Tower of David, pray for us.*
> *Tower of ivory, pray for us.*
> *House of gold, pray for us.*
> *Ark of the Covenant, pray for us.*
> *Gate of Heaven, pray for us.*
> *Morning star, pray for us . . .*

Barry had closed his eyes with the aim of immersing himself, trying to draw comfort from these words of his childhood and youth.

Health of the sick, pray for us.
Refuge of sinners, pray for us.
Comforter of the afflicted, pray for us.
Help of Christians, pray for us.

But it wasn't working. There was a lot more to come and he could take no more. It was too raw – these choristers were so innocent and pure, as he had been once. He had no place here.

Guts twisting, he had left the church and gone back out into the evening sunshine.

This Christmas cruise on the *Santa Clara* had been a last-minute decision. Barry could deny Josh nothing now, especially with those little aliens worming their way through his blood and bones. He was due to start chemo in the new year in an effort to get a few extra weeks, maybe even months, but he had become newly conscious of what he was leaving by departing this world: he had eased back on work commitments, citing temporary burnout and the need for rebooting, and in his now-expanded leisure time he was belatedly consuming box sets of *Planet Earth* and *Blue Planet*, having bought and stored them with a view to watching them 'when I have more time'.

Abruptly, of course, there was no more time.

Craving sunshine and blue skies, he had offered a cruise in the Caribbean but Josh had been adamant that it had to be Europe and had found this one – 'Two nights in Roma! Those wonderful restaurants, Bar.'

Those limpid-eyed boys on their Vespas, Barry thought ruefully, but he had telephoned the cruise company, despite being stricken with guilt at the knowledge that his parents would find out he had elected not to spend his final Christmas with them.

The last eighteen months had been hard for them, accepting Josh as family, but they had done their best during the two years and three months he and Josh had been together. Barry's mum had even taken to ironing Josh's shirts since, she maintained, he made a dreadful job of it himself.

Barry had remonstrated, 'No need, Mum, we can send them to the laundry,' but she would have none of it, and it had taken him a few days to realise it was her way, not only of showing her son that she would accept any choice he made, but of having some tangible contact with him. Because, of course, it was he who always called at his parents' house to drop off and pick up the shirts. Josh hadn't passed his driving test yet.

Having agreed to the cruise, Barry wasn't going to ruin it for Josh by breaking bad news. He would enjoy his boy as much as he could with his compromised store of energy, put up with the tantrums and wheedling, would go with him to the casino, but not every night.

And not tonight. Although he is only fifty-six, he feels what he is, an ageing, very sick man who has been placed on a conveyor belt rushing towards the crematorium.

After Josh has left him he can call on various supports, medical and family, but not until then.

Again, he feels the stab of loneliness. He's had other liaisons, lots of sex, even relationships where the sex was loving, but this is the first time he has totally fallen under the spell of another human being, when he can lavish love, and lovemaking is like exposing everything about himself, not just mutual pleasuring. He would have given his life for Josh. Now he has to give up his life.

Josh wouldn't last a week with that news infecting the air between them. He would weep and would genuinely feel the emotion of the moment but, like the child he is, he would recover. They would embrace, even make love, and then, some days later, having probably left a note awash with tears and heartbreak, he would vanish.

'Ta-dah!' Like a genie out of a bottle, he appears now in the doorway of their en-suite and performs a pirouette. He's naked, his torso, back and front, his thighs, shins, calves and shoulders gleaming in the dim light of the stateroom's wall sconces; his wet, curly hair lies in crisp layers, as though rendered in black marble by a sculptor. 'All ready!' he sings, leaping under the covers, pulling them up to his chin and peering over them at Barry, eyes merry with anticipation. 'Who's been a good boy, then, Daddy?'

Barry takes him in his arms, burying his head in the boy's fragrant neck.

*

Later that evening, with Josh asleep and snoring slightly, Barry, moving as quietly as he can, slides out of the bed, pulls on his winter dressing gown and goes out onto their balcony. Having given up smoking nearly fifteen years ago, he has started again, arguing with his doctor about what difference it can make now.

The sea was rough earlier but the wind has died down and the sky has largely cleared. With the ship's engines at what he judges to be less than half speed, her prow cuts gently through the water, creating twin white waves luminous under a gibbous, waning moon, hanging halfway up its orbit and still bright enough to create a narrow path of beaten silver.

It's not quite midnight and this moon will not be at its full height until three a.m. With his mathematical mind – much good it's going to do him now – Barry likes to know these things and the shipping company obliges, including moon phases in the chirpy but informative events bulletin slipped under every stateroom door in the early evenings. It lists the weather to be expected next day, facts about the hinterland and attractions around the next port of call, all the 'fun' activities to be had on board from after breakfast until late at night.

He lights his cigarette and, inhaling deeply, leans on the rail, flicking ash, although this entire deck has a non-smoking designation. So what are they going to do to him? Drown him? At least it would be quick, unlike what he faces.

Unlike Barry, whose nicotine addiction has flared into full bloom since his diagnosis, Josh smokes only as a style statement. Barry has seen him pose in front of a full-length mirror, trying out various angles at which to hold the little tube. He is a dabbler, puffing the smoke out again almost on the instant he has taken it in.

The older man pulls his fleece tighter around his neck and sits in one of the balcony's deck chairs, again pulling in the warm smoke. How many more nights like this?

He weeps.

*

Next morning, day two of the nine days on board, at about half past nine, with Joshua still asleep, mouth half open and an arm thrown casually across Barry's pillow, there is a discreet knock on their door. Answering it, Barry finds Charles, the actor, standing outside. 'A few of us are thinking of going into Nice, Barry. Would you care to come?' With the door to the balcony closed and the curtains pulled, it isn't cold, the ship's heating system perhaps too efficient, but Barry shivers: there's something about the timbre of the man's voice, something in his penetrating eyes, that spooks him. 'Thank you, you're so kind, Charles,' he says quietly, 'but I'm just out of bed – as you can see I'm not even dressed yet – and Josh is still asleep. So we'll pass, if you don't mind.'

'Of course not. Just thought you might enjoy it. Nice is a lovely, calming city.'

'Thanks for thinking of us, Charles. We'll see you around.'

The other man smiles and turns away, but as Barry closes the stateroom door, he pauses before clicking home the lock. What had Charles meant by Nice being 'calming'? Had he, Barry, given something away about himself last night during the dinner? He had mentioned that he was an architect but . . .

He shakes his head clear of such thoughts. You're being paranoid, he says to himself, opening the door again and hanging the *Do Not Disturb* sign on the outside handle, then gently closing it and slotting in the little brass security chain.

Of course he hadn't given anything away last night. He had behaved as he always does.

Anyway, Saul is the one who needs calming. Barry had had clients like him. Talk about A-type personalities, they're always a nightmare to deal with. No way would he work for him in California or anywhere. Even if he could.

He crosses back into the suite and sits on the sofa at the wall, facing the bed, staying very still to watch Joshua sleep.

6

The previous evening, still Day One, Charles Burtonshaw had been standing on the balcony of his suite. He had come outside to hear the music of the night: the clink of glasses from another balcony, followed by a woman's giggle, the faint thump of a disco beat far below, and the steady hum of the vessel's big diesels. Although he couldn't see it from the midship positioning of his new stateroom, the overall sound in his ears was the soft rush of water passing the *Santa Clara*'s hull.

He had spent the first couple of hours immediately after dinner savouring his new room. He'd watched TV from its big bed, rearranged his meagre store of toiletries in his bathroom (unaccustomed as he was to having the space to do so) and carefully laid out his clothes for the following day on his sofa before coming out here for a last breath of fresh night air and to watch the sea.

Not entirely due to the chilly temperature, he had shivered. For the three-quarters moon was fading, as he was, and although the water sliding by the *Clara*'s hull was lit by feeble yellow necklaces of reflections from the ship's internal lighting, the sea looked dark and forbidding, foretelling, he thought, the nature of his future.

Since receiving the *Clara*'s final gift of a stateroom with a balcony, he has tried hard to retain the sense of gratitude and even euphoria he'd experienced then, but having been alone since dinner, with no one to jolly along, he let his guard down, and with dropping the mask came fear and loneliness.

Being the performer in public keeps his demons at bay. His mother, bless her, used to call him the Angel of Granby Street, not necessarily with approval. 'You've a kind heart, Charles. But you let people take advantage of you.'

'No, I don't, Mother. And look at it this way. All I'm doing when I'm nice to people is depositing in Heaven's piggy bank. When I was little you always told me that kindness is like a boomerang: it always comes back to you if you throw it right. So I'm trying to throw it right. Tell you what, let me put the kettle on. How's the stock of ginger nuts?' Early in life he had learned how to deflect, had become an expert at it – he'd had to.

At prep school, he had regularly suffered bullying because he was 'other' – not a nerd, which could be cool, but excelling in school shows, many times playing female roles. All through, he'd pretended he didn't care that his performance of Ophelia or Rosalind was a source of jibes and mockery for some, attracting attention from others with homosexual tendencies, even when he and his companions were of such a tender age. Somehow, though, he had managed to divert the worst of the unwanted attention from doing him too much harm with the use of charm and self-deprecating humour, traits that have lasted.

Eventually, after a similarly rocky ride in grammar school, he got into RADA, which, given the intensity and self-absorption of everyone there, had been a cakewalk by comparison, even great fun, despite the backbiting and sniggering about his having got his place only by dint of having famous parents.

Charles himself suspected as much. But he thrived on the discipline and, unlike some of his more rackety contemporaries, worked diligently, took all advice, and did so well at the graduate show that he secured an agent, Jeremy Barber from the mid-ranking AWTF agency.

The acronym for Actors Working in Theatre and Film is a source of mirth for many, even some of AWTF's clients, since in medical notes for some patients, it denotes Away With The Fairies. Wits commonly abbreviate it by removing the A to make it WTF: What The F−k?

But the excitement of securing an agent has been, it turns out, the highlight of Charles's acting career. About six years later, after yet another failed audition for the National, Jeremy, who had many clients far busier and more lucrative for his agency than Charles, had said, 'I don't know what it is, Charlie boy, but whatever it is, looks, charisma, who knows, we haven't been able to get you into the front line. Not yet anyway. We'll keep trying, of course, and don't worry, we'll ensure you'll always make a living.'

Jeremy, Charles has suspected for years, keeps him on AWTF's books because he is loyal, doesn't cause trouble either for the agency or for the producers and directors who hire him, and is willing to take anything on offer, trusting his mentor that he wouldn't be landed with a booby. And, thankfully, that trait had stood him in good stead when many of those with soaring talents had crashed and burned out quickly while he plodded steadily along.

So Jeremy's promise to keep him in work has been fulfilled

and he has knocked a living out of the profession. Sure, like all actors, except the crème de la crème, he has no pension, no savings, and now with what have been the relatively reliable quasi-acting gigs on the *Clara* bowing out, he'll have to mind his pennies even more than usual.

And that money has been good, a cruise of this length paying more than twice the total he'd get from a whole month of touring, one and a half times what he'd be offered for supporting a lead in a telly.

Film, of course, is a different matter.

At least he has no mortgage. Shoreditch is now a fancy place to live and much in demand. His mother and father were both actors, but in a far less crowded arena where it had been easier to attract attention and fame. Buying their house as a doer-upper when the area was not fashionable had proved prescient for them and himself; if not, he would never have been able to live the life of an actor. For instance, periods of 'resting' are always alarming when they stretch out a bit, but for him are made bearable because he knows that, come what may, he has two major assets: Jeremy's loyalty and, far more importantly as he gets older, that roof over his head.

Although he hasn't considered selling his little house, and has managed quite well to keep up with the council tax and so on, with the *Clara* gone, he may have to.

When he worries at Jeremy that there's nothing in the diary, his agent always comes back with the retort that he should start seeing his home as an asset. 'I don't know what your parents paid for Granby Street, Charles, but I'm willing to bet that it was less than a tenth of what it's worth now. Last time I was up there I saw Audis in those little driveways, the occasional Beemer, and lots of fairly new Golfs. You have three bedrooms? They're paying up to a million for 'em – strike while it's hot, Charles. None of us really knows what's going to happen after Brexit.'

'But where would I live?'

'Like all the rest of us, you're not going to live for ever, old chum, but if you sell, you'll have money in the bank, enough and more to see you through if you rent in somewhere like Lewisham or Haringey or Ealing. Ealing, I hear, is Central Line heaven. You'd be made up. Don't forget if you're a tenant and the roof falls in, it's your landlord's problem, not yours . . . Or you could take a lodger if you want to stay where you are. A fellow actor? Come, come now, old chap, cheer up. We'll get you a few more jobs before you go to the great theatre in the sky. I promise.'

Dear Lord, just one featured character, even a decent cameo – I'm good at eccentrics. Just one, please, and I'll be happy and I won't have to petition a committee or whatever to allow me to move into an actors' retirement home.

Yes, morose as he can become sometimes, as he looked out at the black sea, he acknowledged that, taking everything in the round, he's had a good life, with only his mother's death and the break-up of his marriage contributing deep and lasting sorrow.

His father had died of a brain haemorrhage when Charles was just eleven years old, but although such a crucial bereavement at that age, for boys in particular, is said to be damaging, that hasn't been his experience. His memory of it is sad but not unduly so: Father was here, then suddenly, quite dramatically, not. Even at eleven, Charles was taking in the details, the bee-baw outside, siren silent but lights rotating on the roof, the strange objects strapped to the ambulance men's uniforms, their quiet, kind air of authority. Father was taken away on a stretcher with what he now knew was an oxygen mask over his face and didn't come back. There was a great deal of fuss for a day or two, then everyone had accepted that he had gone to Heaven, which was a much nicer place than Earth, with plenty of pale ale to drink with your dinner or at any time you wanted, and God offering the best show in town, with all the actors and actresses who had been Father and Mother's friends and were up there already, rehearsing their lines, while other friends were making costumes and changing scenery and operating the main curtain, which was made of peacock feathers and pure gold. They made it sound so terrific he'd wanted to hurry up and go there himself. But there was Mother to consider. He and Mother had become closer after he had taken on the role of little man of the household.

He had moved out of Granby Street after graduating from RADA, renting a bedsit only a tube ride away from Kensington on the Piccadilly Line. But when his mother's osteoarthritis had deteriorated so that she could no longer properly look after herself or Roger, her little Jack Russell, she had asked him to move back because her fear of having to go into a home was more crippling than her disease.

Charles had been happy to oblige. With a contribution from her savings, he could afford to hire professional carers to live-in when he was away for periods, which, Jeremy understood, could, for now, last no longer than a couple of weeks. In that context, the gigs on the *Santa Clara* had proved to be a godsend. They all managed, and he had even become quite fond of Roger, almost as old as his mistress in dog years.

For the next five years, the three had co-existed happily, and on the day before she died, in hospital, crippled and on heavy morphine, his mother had, during a period of lucidity, grabbed his hand. 'I'm so, so grateful, darling. Thank you. And don't forget to be kind. That'll see you through no matter what. It always does.' Her last words. Charles had regarded them as her Dying Declaration, a sacred command.

Having died so often on stage, he'd always been interested in the drama inherent in death. Shakespeare, of course, had majored in it, littering his plays with murder, battlefield killings and so on.

Because Jeremy had recommended it, Charles had even accepted a role in a TV play where he'd played a corpse: 'You'll be in an open coffin but popping up all the time on screen, even close-ups according to the script, with a voice-over expressing your thoughts.'

'Do I get to do the VO?'

'Not sure about that, but lots of screen time, Charlie. It's good to keep your face up there.'

He didn't get the VO, but Jeremy had been bang on: there had indeed been a large number of close-ups as, all around him, his family tore themselves apart in a dispute over his will. The writer had based it on a notorious court case of 1906 where two women, this corpse's mother and his wife, each believed that his three-line will *All to Mother* referred to her: he'd always called his wife 'Mother' because she was the mother of his children. The wife won in court on the grounds that, on balance, he must have meant to safeguard his children who were now in her care.

After the death of his mother, combining work commitments with Roger's needs had proved difficult enough, Charles had found. The little fellow had lost the sight of an eye and was almost as crippled with arthritis as his mistress had been, but with the help of a good vet and accommodating neighbours, Charles had somehow managed to look after him for two years until one morning he came down into the kitchen and found the dog's small body half in and half out of the basket in front of the Aga.

It was peculiar, he has thought many times since, that although he was sad, of course, he had never wept for his mother, even throughout her memorial service, perhaps because he believed she was ready to go because she was in such pain.

Her funeral had been full of his former colleagues, some of whom he recognised only from TV as they hugged and air-kissed him, calling him 'darling' and 'dear heart' even though they hadn't been near Shoreditch for decades. He'd worried about getting back to Roger, who, after his mother had been removed to hospital, had cried and whined and couldn't settle anywhere. The little dog had crawled under her bed and had stayed there until, days later, Charles had enticed him back to his basket with a trail of chopped-up sausages down the stairs and into the kitchen.

He can't remember crying for his father, but seeing that tiny brown and white body, which used to turn itself almost inside out with joy each time Roger heard Charles's footsteps on the Victorian tiles leading to the front door, hit hard. Rather than stoop to touch it, he had stood for a long time remembering how he used to resent those little paws, now so still, for having ruined the hall door as they scrabbled for quicker reunification.

And the open eyes, opaque in death, had been in old age so expressive. As he stood there, they breached Charles's defences and brought the floods, so painful his body doubled. He'd wept until every muscle in his body hurt and his voice hoarsened. The tears eventually dried because the reservoir had emptied.

Eventually, he'd called the vet to take Roger away for cremation, but as soon as she'd picked up the body to take it away, he'd wept again, not caring what she thought of his lack of restraint or manliness.

Despite advice from well-meaning people, he didn't go to a rescue centre to get another dog. He knew that to experience such depth of emotion again could break his heart. It was better not to become attached to any living creature, including, perhaps, humans.

Over the Med, a stiff breeze was coming up and the water was beginning to chop. Despite his greatcoat and gloves, he felt cold out here. What had brought on that maudlin nonsense? 'You're a foolish, mawkish old man,' he muttered into the breeze.

He left his rail and was about to go inside when he thought he heard a sound from one of the balconies on a deck above him. It could have been a cough, but he stopped, listening hard. Almost unbelievably, given what he'd been thinking, it may have been a sob. Wondering if he was suffering from delusions now, again he listened hard. There it was again, definitely a sob, a male sob, chiming with his own mood.

Feeling like an intruder on someone else's grief, he went inside to the brightness and warmth of his suite, closed the balcony door, pulled his curtain to end the show, and quickly turned on CNN to see what was happening in the real world.

7

At the time of Charles's retreat to his stateroom, Roxy, dressed only in her underwear, laptop open on her thighs, is on the bed in her hot, noisy little room.

Transcribing from both big and small notebooks, she wants to tie down as much as possible right from the start so she'll get home with settings vividly described, potential lead characters lined up, plot and plot devices noted and narrowed to manageable proportions, useful quotes nailed down.

Fingers flying over the keyboard, she's pleased with today's output. It had certainly been fruitful, she thinks, so much so that she's wondering if, by some divine or fateful intervention, she was placed at the best dining table on the ship. Except for the ultra-polite and happy Danes, all the others offer possibilities.

On the other hand, the very fruitfulness may make difficulties for her. The potential she has seen already seems so big that she knows she will have problems about whom to choose as main characters. She's getting confused.

When people ask about what they think is 'the terror of the blank page' as an author faces into a novel, what they don't know is that this isn't the problem at all. It's that the writer's poor old brain is swarming with far too many ideas, dementedly hopping from one to another and back again in a frenzy as to which to choose. Right now, she's less than twenty-four hours into this venture and this is what's happening. Should she start eliminating? Is it too soon to strike out the brash American lawyer, Saul?

He does go on a bit although, like herself, he and his wife have an understandable reason for being here. This in itself may prove useful: *the heart-breaking fate of a once-glorious and great little ship*? At dessert stage, Saul had revealed what a bigwig he was, on board representing the ship's owners because this was her last trip as a cruise liner, which had been news to the rest of them. Is it too early to get rid of him as a main character?

Anyhow, haven't some of the male writers majored in that kind of character – overbearing, full of himself, verbose, always right but always slated for a downfall? Roxy types a note to herself, colouring it red, indicating that, where Saul is concerned, this is for further consideration, positive or negative, when she comes to write her first draft . . .

'Always ask yourself if what you see is real, authentic. Always delve, Roxy. Ask yourself, like the movie did, *what lies beneath*?' That had been good advice from Tony, her agent, but she's already under pressure. This has to be a sure-fire bestseller or she'll have to call time on her (very) short career.

What's more, she can't bear to think of her mum's disappointment if *Heartbreak on the High Seas* suffers the same fate as *Heartbreak in the Cotswolds.* This time there can be no excuses, after her mum's gift: a shipload of fascination. And now that she's discovered it, even the ship itself being on its last legs offers background potential at the very least.

Possibly more. Could she sink the ship in this novel? Have her entire group at table thrown together into the last available lifeboat? Could Captain Fantastic, last to abandon ship, join them? Could there be a big storm with waves so high they can't be reached except by helicopter? She types another NB in red: *check out frequency of bad storms (i.e. how bad?) in the Med @ Christmas & WHO has to die? Maybe fall back in water? The last thing to be seen just a hand before it's sucked under a huge wave?*

She types faster. She can't bear to think that she might have to go back to journalism, which she had initially thought would be very exciting, with (eventually) her world exclusives attracting attention. Very quickly, however, she had found herself dismayed by the grind and triviality of the daily grunt work, the repetitive, intrusive interviews: 'What was your reaction? How does it make you feel now?'

What are people supposed to say? That their tragedy, the death of a loved one, their homes going up in flames, their discovery that a hospital has made a fatal mistake in a diagnosis, makes them feel great? That they reacted with delight?

She had not expected either that, being last in and thereby lowest on the totem pole, she was expected to do most of the advertorials, even to make tea for others occupying loftier perches. 'So this is your last chance, Rox,' she murmurs aloud. 'Get a grip! No whingeing that this is too hard, no slacking. Use the gift. Don't waste this time. Get everything, no matter how insignificant it seems right now, into that computer. And back it up!'

She doubts if she'll ever get such an opportunity again and, okay, she's not all that thrilled about being categorised as women's fiction instead of just fiction, but she has to suck it up, leave the new *War and Peace* to others and stop being such an up-her-own-arse ninny. This book has been handed to her on a plate – like, what woman (and, in the main, women are the people who buy fiction) doesn't want to read about luxury and great food, gorgeous, fit officers and goings-on in cabins?

Then, for the second time in five minutes, perhaps as a result of her renewed onslaught on its keyboard, the laptop slides off her thighs, slick with perspiration. It thumps into the tiny space between the bed and the wall. Muttering, 'Shit,' under her breath, trying not to disturb the arrangement of pillows, one behind her head, one under her knees, she fishes awkwardly in the gap and while she manages to snag it, her hand proves just as sweaty as her legs and the bloody thing slips back again to the floor.

The heat is really getting to her.

The control for the air conditioning unit is on the wall and, heaving herself onto her knees, she reaches for the little knob but twists too hard and it comes off in her hand: 'Shit, shit, *shit*!' loudly this time.

Throwing the thing away, not caring where it lands, she manoeuvres herself off the bed and into the shower. She is, sourly, not now a bit surprised that this is the last voyage of the *Santa Clara*. Should she ring somebody about the useless air conditioner control?

At least this works, she thinks, calming down as cool water flows through her hair, over her shoulders, down her back and between her breasts.

'The Med in winter,' Saul had said, during one of his many monologues at the dining table, 'who'da thought it, eh? But, hey, you guys, it's surprisingly peaceful here, yeah? No Russkies, no Germans – they're in search of the sun, of course. Most of all, no kids. We nearly went crazy last time we spent Christmas in the Caribbean – couldn't find anyone like ourselves to talk to. Those lines for the breakfast and buffet lunches – you guys over here in Europe call 'em "queues", right? So, those queues were terrible. We couldn't hear a thing with all the kids, couldn't get into a Jacuzzi – right, Kitty?' She had just smiled at him.

Kitty smiles a lot, Roxy thinks, but very quietly. Quite a lot to work on there, if Roxy's any judge. Still waters and all that. *What lies beneath?*

She turns the shower's thermostat up a little because the water has become a bit too cool. What about Charles, then? Nice. But probably too nice? So it's a no there, for the moment anyway, although he could definitely become a minor character. She could certainly use him as a bit of colour. More of that from the two gays, of course.

Then there's Gemma and her family... What to do with them?

Just as she'd left the table in the dining room, Gemma had come over. 'If you're not too tired, we're going upstairs for a couple of drinks. Want to join us?'

And that, too, had proven fruitful in the story stakes. Dear God, Roxy thought, who'd blame her for being bamboozled by the choices on offer?

Soothed, she turns off the water and, perfunctorily flicking a towel over herself, goes back to the bed. This time, she manages to retrieve the laptop and, pulling a sheet over her legs to absorb the damp, resumes typing.

Kitty, Saul and Charles had mentioned their plan to take a taxi into Nice after breakfast next morning and have lunch there. She envied them and, to be fair, they had invited her but she can't afford it, even to watch Kitty at close quarters. She has to be very careful with money and if she's to keep her subjects on board – ha-ha! – she certainly doesn't want them to think she's a sponger. She'll pay her way, like a proper journalist – or the professional novelist she is now.

She's not quite finished her transcriptions when she hears

a soft knock on the door. 'Just a minute,' she calls, checking her watch. It's just after ten o'clock. Hastily she pulls on her new Primark dressing gown and opens the door a crack, to find, out in the corridor, two men wearing name-badged uniforms and wide smiles. 'Good evening, madam,' says one. 'We are from Housekeeping and we are here for your room.'

'I beg your pardon?' Roxy frowns. 'I don't understand.' But she is not familiar with the routines on ships. Do they clean rooms in the middle of the night? She peers at the first man's name tag, which shows him to be from the Philippines. 'Thank you very much, Dilip,' she says, and then, speaking very slowly, 'but I arrived only today and I have not even used the sheets yet.' She gestures at the bed, on which a dent shows where she has been lying. 'I have used the shower.' She points in its direction. 'You could perhaps clean that? And the towels have been used.'

She opens the door wider to let them in but the two look confused and stay where they are. Dilip says something to the second man, who is from Colombia and whose name is Angelo, in a language she doesn't recognise. Then: 'Is very nice room.' He makes a circular motion and widens his arms.

'Yes, nice room.' This from Angelo.

'Yes, it is a nice room. I am happy with this room. Thank you.'

'Big.' Dilip's smile widens further, which she would have thought to be a physical impossibility. She smiles back, but a little sceptically. Are they having her on? She looks up and down the corridor but can see no sign of a cleaning trolley.

'You have bag?' asks Angelo.

'Yes, I have bags. But I can take care of bags myself.' She is speaking slowly and, she hopes, very authoritatively.

'We take?' offers Dilip.

'No, thank you.' He has just confirmed that this is some kind of scam. Young woman on her own? Idiot English girl? 'You are very kind but thank you, not tonight.' She closes the door. It's so blatant it's laughable. She has just picked up the laptop to continue her task when they knock again.

For God's sake! Angry now, she jumps to the door. 'What? I said no. Now please go away.'

'Madam, I think you do not understand.' Dilip puts out a hand to hold the door. 'We are here to take you to other room.'

She isn't falling for this. 'Listen—'

'Please, madam, nice room.'

'Nicer room, madam.' Angelo, too, looks anxious and, for the first time, Roxy hesitates.

Then: 'But this is a nice room. I like this room. I am happy here.'

'Happy room on six floor.' Dilip looks a little nonplussed.

'You mean you're here to show me a better room?'

'Yes, madam.'

'But I can't afford—'

'You not pay, madam.' Earnestly, Dilip cuts across her. 'You,' he points at her, 'no money. Company,' he places a hand on his chest, 'company, yes, pay. We take you there. Upstair.' He points to the ceiling of the corridor. Then: 'Upgrad.'

'You mean an upgrade?'

'Yes, madam,' they chorus, obviously with relief. The smiles are back. 'You have much bags?'

Dilip indicates the room behind her and the penny finally drops for Roxy. Wordlessly, still only half believing what's happening, she stands aside to let them in. 'I have to pack.'

'No problem, madam,' Angelo says, as both men ease past her and, with experienced eyes, survey the contents of the room, then immediately begin to open doors and drawers.

Too late, Roxy realises that she has left her underwear, both top and bottom, on the bathroom floor, but before she can get to it, Dilip has gathered it up. 'For ship laundry, madam?'

'No, thank you.' She reddens. 'I'll take care of it.' She snatches both garments from him and, since Angelo is already opening her bag, she stuffs them into her handbag. Finished in the bathroom, having slotted her toiletries into her (luckily new) washbag, Dilip joins the other man and the two work in tandem, with Angelo extracting her clothes, Dilip folding and packing. The entire operation takes less than five minutes before, still beaming at her, they stand back to allow her to go before them into the corridor.

'You will like room,' says Dilip. 'Follow me, please, madam.'

'Who ordered this? Who sent you?' Roxy asks, when they're waiting outside the lift at the end of her corridor. Still bemused, she hasn't yet come to terms with what's happening and is holding tightly to her laptop and handbag. She's finding it difficult to be fully convinced that this isn't an elaborate scam. Could they ambush her, stab her to death in the lift?

But as the lift arrives they seem to be consulting in that other language. Then inside, Dilip pushes the button for deck six. 'Frank,' he says. 'He is cruise director.'

'What's his other name?'

'Frank.' Angelo takes this one, speaking to her as though she's a child. 'He is cruise director. Big boss.'

They ascend to their floor in silence and, to Roxy's amazement, the corridor is silent too, no thrumming, no banging of machinery, and it also seems beautifully cool. It's empty as well . . . She allows herself one last twinge of suspicion. If she's to be attacked, it'll probably be here, with no one around.

But they walk ahead of her to her new room, 625, without incident. Dilip opens the door with a keycard, inserts it in the slot inside the door and both stand back to allow her to precede them.

As she enters her new room, Roxy feels she is being assaulted with pleasure. She is stunned. The bed alone, with lockers on both sides, seems as big as the entirety of her last room. There's a desk. A sofa. A coffee table. Oodles of carpeted space, a dressing table with six drawers, table lamps and a big mirror. Having given her a moment, Dilip gently deposits her bag on a stand and, with some ceremony, gives a little bow. 'New room, madam.' He hands her the spare keycard. 'You are welcome. And this, madam,' he opens a door, 'is your new bathroom.'

Roxy looks. It's at least three times the size of the last, with space to take a few steps. There is shelving, a far bigger cabinet over the washbasin and a more than adequate shower cubicle. Rooted to the carpet, she wants to pinch herself. Instead, she rummages hurriedly in her handbag and, retrieving her wallet, extracts a five-euro note. 'Thank you so much.' She hands the money to Dilip, who receives it with another small bow and another wide, delighted smile.

But he hasn't finished. He crosses the floor towards a set of thick wall-to-wall curtains and, with a flourish, pulls one aside, along with a voile panel, which hangs against French windows. Quickly, he slides open one of the doors, allowing a rush of cold sea breeze into the room, stirring her hair, still damp from the shower. Then he stands aside to allow her sight of the sea and its narrow, moonlit pathway all the way from the horizon. Roxy has a balcony.

8

Kitty Golden, lying beside her sleeping husband, has been awake for more than thirty minutes and is now watching a sliver of pale light seep under the heavy drapes across the balcony doors of her suite while her thoughts range back and forth across events of the past twenty-four hours. It's the second day of the *Santa Clara*'s voyage, the morning of 18 December 2016.

Contrary to Saul's fears, their suite, dead centre astern (and named, absurdly in her opinion, the Duchess), has turned out to be fine, a little worn but, at 1100 square feet, would have housed an entire family from the projects in New York or Chicago. If the Duchess's guests are musically talented, they can entertain themselves on her baby grand.

Lying there, she can imagine her late mother's tart response if she'd seen a video of all this, the Manhattan apartment, the condo in Miami: 'Far from this you were reared, Catherine Golden!' with its implied slap-down.

Too true, Kitty thinks now. But in many ways she has become so accustomed to luxury that she no longer notices it.

Up here on deck eight, insulated from engine noise and the ruckus of the entertainment, shopping, dining and atrium circulation areas, it's quiet. The suite's huge terrace is sheltered by two side walls of glass when the ship is under way, except on the rare occasion when there is a strong tailwind. Even at peak periods when they're sailing and there's lots of activity on board, the overall sound remains that of the sea, wake creaming off into the distance. 'You should watch out,' the English actor, Charles, had said at dinner the previous evening, 'because you'll see dolphins playing in and out of that wake. It happens all the time and they're easy to spot from up there.'

Right now she's concerned less with her surroundings than with the small verbal bombshell Saul had launched as they were making their way to their first dinner the previous evening. He had entered a twist to her plot.

Before leaving the States, she had checked the Portlandis company website for a name she could employ as having authorised the switch of tables. Having found a Jason Halyard and a Jerold Habowski listed among the executives in administration, she had melded them into the mythical John Heldowsman. So if things went pear-shaped to the extent that Saul checked up on Mr Heldowsman – although she doubted even he would go that far – he would get nowhere. She hated behaving like a trickster but . . .

At the last possible moment, when they were emerging from the elevator and were even within sight of the dining-room doors, she had taken a deep breath to plunge into her spiel about her call to this obliging manager but he'd grabbed her arm. 'Hold it, Kitty, there's something I have to tell you.' Then, fast: 'I hope you don't mind, but seeing it's my birthday and all, I have a surprise for you, honey.'

She had frowned. 'Saul, it's your birthday, not mine.'

'I know, I know, sweetie, but it's not . . .' he'd hesitated '. . . it's not a thing or a gift, it's a bit of, I dunno, it's nothin' bad. Honestly . . .'

'I don't understand – spit it out, Saul.'

'Kit, I know you like those li'l couples' tables on these cruises, so the two of us can just be private, yeah? But just this once, if it's okay with you, I've organised it so we're at a bigger table. Pippa thought that because it was my birthday . . . Just this once, okay? I guess it's like I'm getting old and I just felt like a bit of outside company. It's nothing to do with you, honest. I love you, honey, I love your company, you know that . . .'

She had managed to convert a laugh into an explosive coughing fit.

'You okay, honey?' He had clapped her on the back: 'You want I get you some water?'

Red-faced, avoiding his gaze: 'I'm fine, Saul, it'll pass.' Then, gasping, 'Just give me a minute.' But as they'd resumed walking, she couldn't credit her own idiocy. All that thought! All that dragging of Saul's poor PA into a conspiracy.

She was also amused. At what point had Philippa known about the double request? Before or after Kitty's? She sure hoped that, in this instance, the woman would remain as discreet as she normally was. Just to be sure she didn't drop Pippa in it (whatever about his own reasons for making the request, Saul would *not* like to know that his wife hadn't wanted to sit with him alone, even if his PA thought it was a hoot that they had both asked) Kitty had better get on to New York as soon as possible, before Saul made his usual check-in call, and with the ship now anchored in a bay opposite the town of Villefranche, there would be network coverage.

Given the time difference, the PA won't be in her office for a few hours yet, but a message could be left; best-case scenario, she would have a good laugh at the story's farcical nature but would keep the joke to herself.

There is a serious side to this, Kitty thinks now. It's telling that neither partner had relished the idea of being with each other at a dining-room table without others present. It was even more telling that neither had felt it possible to come right out and say as much.

It's unfair but true that, for her, an additional light was shone on herself and Saul by the glow, almost tangible, that had emanated from the charming Danish couple. For with the exception of Joshua, who had remained visibly bored, everyone else had been captivated as, throughout the meal, they had taken every opportunity to touch, a deliberate brush of hands as one poured wine or water for the other, a shared reaction, eye to eye, about what one of their neighbours had said.

By contrast, for the past ten years – in fact, right from the beginning – the words 'glow' and 'passion' could never have been used about Kitty and Saul by observers.

They had jogged along, amicably enough. Serious rows had been infrequent but one-sided. Saul under pressure could be tempestuous, irritation could blow up very quickly into irrational fury and, except in very rare cases when he apologised, they were resolved with pacification by her because she had fully accepted responsibility for her own action in marrying a man she liked but didn't love.

In the interests of fairness, materially at least, Kitty reminds herself now, she should have little to complain about. So Saul can be choleric and impatient? He is fundamentally kind and certainly generous, as exhibited by the appurtenances of her life: wealth, fine clothes, living arrangements beyond what would have been her parents' wildest imaginings.

However, her sister's admonitions, sounding intermittently in the distance, like the braying of a lone donkey, were louder, closer and more persistent.

And, on top of them, she is increasingly having to recognise the beating of an internal drum, monthly, weekly and now daily. More than a decade, no children. So far, her husband has refused to undergo investigations that could lead to IVF or other procedures. She, covertly, had had her gynaecologist check out her own fertility, which, the woman had confirmed, is normal for someone of her age: 'That's as far as the tests show and I can judge, but you're in your thirties now, Kitty, and I wouldn't wait too much longer. You must take into account, however, that sometimes we have no idea why a woman can't conceive. You have to act as a couple here. Your husband should get checked out.'

'What if he won't?'

The woman had shrugged. 'Come back to me,' she'd said, expectantly in Kitty's opinion. 'We'll talk then.' But, while thanking her, Kitty hadn't been ready to confide the details of her relationship with Saul to a person who, although aware of her most intimate physical secrets, was a virtual stranger.

A month afterwards, she and Saul did talk. Or she did.

They were on one of their Caribbean vacations, this time in Grenada, and she had brought up the subject of IVF, having researched Jewish law, in case scientific interference with 'nature' was forbidden.

On the contrary, she discovered that, in the case of infertility, this procedure and other aids are actively encouraged by most rabbis, even within those communities who follow the Orthodox way of life. Because one of the main and overriding commandments God handed down was that Jews must be fruitful. They must multiply.

So, on their third day abroad, judging he had relaxed sufficiently at least to hear her out, she was ready to argue her case.

And he did hear her out. Mirrored sunglasses staying firmly in place, he continued, unmoving, to lie prone on his sunlounger while she spoke as clearly and confidently as she could. 'So, honey,' she'd concluded, 'will you at least consider going to your doctor? I sure will.' She'd felt it prudent not to reveal she had been to hers already.

'Let's see what happens, sweetie.' He still didn't move. 'We've plenty of time. Plenty. I'm still a youngster, after all – anyway, I can't bear the thought of anyone fooling around with the family jewels!' Said jocosely, touching himself, but she knew he meant it. Then, at last, sitting up, he removed the shades. 'Want I should get you some ice cream?'

'I don't want ice cream, Saul. Please, will you take this seriously?'

'I am, sweetie. Honest. Look, let's give it another year, huh? Speaking of which, I'm feeling horny right now. Wanna go back to the room and try again? Right now? The way I feel with all this sunshine and oil and the way you look in that white bikini – wow! Did I buy you that? Whatever I paid it was worth every dime. Come on.' He swung his feet onto the poolside patio. 'Let's do it! I'd bet this time I'm feelin' so good, we could even hit the jackpot!'

Instead of answering, Kitty had got up from her own lounger and dived into the pool, swimming length after length as though in training for a race. When she had climbed back out, Saul had gone.

The reaction of her sister, when Kitty called her to fill her in, had been: 'Of course he's the problem. You've checked out. He's just being selfish and ridiculous. If he loves you, Kit, he'll at least have himself looked at – but listen . . .' She stopped for a couple of seconds. 'Didn't you tell me before that he's being done by one of his other wives for maintenance for two kids?'

'They're hers from a previous marriage.'

'Sorry, I forgot, baby brain again.' Geraldine, who had just given birth to her second, still less than six weeks old, had laughed. 'So that's QED, isn't it? He's definitely the one in trouble. And he has to do something about it. You have to make him. Look, I know I'm a stuck record about this but I'm sick of telling you that money isn't everything, Kitty. Why do you stay with him? It's not just about having children, it's the whole damn relationship. You're not happy and I know it. And you could be. You've only one life and you're still young enough to live it like you deserve.'

Recently, Kitty's regular responses – *It'll come good, you'll see!* – have sounded hollow even to her, although she continues to cling to the hope that, somehow, things will change – for instance, if Saul eases up a little on his work commitments so for some sustained period they could spend time together, particularly at home because most evenings, once Kitty closes her front door, she is alone until bedtime. 'All right, all right,' she'd said to Geraldine, having to grip her phone tightly because her hands were slippery from applying sunscreen. Having come home from Grenada, she'd been topping up her tan on the roof terrace of her 'posh pad', as her sister always referred to their triplex. 'I'll do it, she'd said. 'Somehow I'll make him go to a specialist in this field.'

On past experience, however, she wasn't all that hopeful she could 'make' Saul do anything.

But, she decides now, glancing at his comatose form, this cruise is the ideal time to bring all this up again. After all, he can't flee to the office, can he? He could vanish into the ship's business centre, but she can follow him there: it's open to all passengers. And, dander raised now, she doesn't care who hears what she's saying. She'll offer him the option of privacy in their suite, and if he doesn't accept, that's his own business.

Last night, when they were in their suite after dinner, he had glanced over his shoulder, while he was pulling off his tie, to where she was sitting on the side of the bed, massaging body oil into her shins. 'Were you genuinely surprised about the table, sweetie?'

'I sure was.' By focusing on her legs, she had been able to be forensically truthful.

'That's good.' He was now unbuttoning his shirt. 'I was a bit worried about it, but just for this once, I thought— Pippa's terrific, isn't she?'

'It was a great idea, as it turned out,' she said, before he could go too far with it. 'We might keep it in mind for the future, Saul. These are very interesting people, don't you think? You certainly seemed to be getting on with that English architect beside you.'

'Barry is terrific,' he'd said. 'Great ideas. Seems to be on top of his game – I might bring him over to have a look at the Northern California project. It's not too late, we haven't broken ground.'

'Why don't you do that? Fresh eyes and all that?'

She had tried to show interest in her husband's work but had found it very difficult because it was so diverse and he always became irritated when she mixed up the three strands, legal, property development and construction. Although he did let her know where he'd be on any given day, she found it difficult to keep track. But as their lives have gone on, and he's been relating some work tale, she has developed a lexicon of interchangeable phrases to show she's been paying attention.

The four-eyes principle, I understand?

Fresh eyes for sure?

That's great (on news about some exchange or other 'rocketing'). *You selling now?*

And for the legal side: *It's the law, though, isn't it? First, last and always?*

The devil is in the detail?

We're in funds, are we?

All she had to ask, for instance, in the case of a class action involving the introduction of more severe regulations to do with, for instance, smoking (or using mobile phones while driving, or carrying concealed weapons): *We're in luck, are we, this time? We get the judge who hates Big Government?*

Construction matters are simple. All she has to ask is: *Have we broken ground? Is it first* (or second or final) *fix at this stage? Roofers in yet? Building watertight? Scaffolders still on board?*

One of his current projects with a construction company of which he is a partner involves building a condominium complex in Boise, Idaho. The contracted scaffolding outfit on the build is unionised, threatening strike action for reasons that are exercising her husband greatly but, because they're so technical, Kitty hasn't bothered to keep up.

'I will bring Barry on board,' Saul is musing now. 'He's the type of guy who'd do well in the US, I think, even under Trump. I know a guy who'd fast-track a visa for us ... And, by the way, speaking of doing well, I'll bet you were wondering what I was talking to the captain about in that entrance hall earlier. I was telling him about the table, how we wanted a nice one with people who are interesting and speak English.' He took off the shirt and put it on the armrest of the couch on which he was sitting. 'He's a good guy, that captain. That's what held me up. Did I tell you he's from Iceland?'

'I think so,' she'd murmured. 'If it wasn't you, somebody did mention it.'

'Well, he is. They're great seafarers, those Icelanders, it's kinda in their blood. I think we're gonna have a beautiful cruise, honey.'

'Yeah, I think so too.' She had meant it when she'd said that their table companions were interesting and, for herself, thought that maybe she could make friends with Roxy who, if not exactly her own age, is at least a contemporary.

From experience, though, she knows that such temporary friendships, forged in the hothouse of living so close to others at sea, evaporate very quickly. Despite promises to write to your new friend, even to visit his or her city, when people disembark to take up lives and work worries where they left off, they fizzle out. These acquaintanceships are fun while they last. They even engender confidences, possibly because all parties know how transient they are.

She checks again to make sure that Saul is breathing. This isn't paranoia. They've been told by medics that he's on the cusp of developing sleep apnoea but for now he's still borderline and the CPAP machine, the ugly but lifesaving contraption designed to keep airways open during sleep, is in their future. He's been warned he needs to plan for it and has been given the loan of one for the duration of this cruise to see how it and he get along. He has postponed its use for a couple of nights to see if the sea air will help on its own.

He's lying in the foetal position, left arm dangling over the side of the bed, right hand holding his forehead as though soothing a headache. His mouth is slightly open, and although he's not snoring, there is a soft, intermittent gurgling at the back of his throat.

Like this, expression relaxed, cowlick raised and tousled, he could be a small boy, except for the stubble and hair colour. Along with incorruptible gratitude, whatever her reservations about their relationship, she sometimes finds him endearing. Despite her sister's campaign, she can't claim to be unhappy with Saul all of the time. She's just bloody mixed up.

Last night, watching this master of the universe sitting on the couch in their stateroom to struggle with his shoelaces, which as always he had double-knotted too tightly, she'd had to smile.

She's looking forward to how he will react to his new watch, safely concealed in the handbag with the defective clasp and stored in her closet with the rest of her luggage. For all his riches, hard-nosed careerism and luxury living, sometimes, when he opens a gift, he shows small-boy delight, as though it were his very first bicycle or train set. She's confident that the Breguet watch, with its multiple tiny hands, delicate as the legs of spiders and all pointing in different directions, will hit the spot. The salesman was right: he'll love it.

With it she will give him her customary Christmas gift, a voucher, alternating it year on year, one from the travel company they use, the other for the bespoke tailor he patronises.

He will thank her for the vacation, store away the voucher, and some day, Amilia, their Salvadoran housekeeper, will come to her with it to say she had been cleaning out Mister's dressing room and had found it stuffed into the tie section or perhaps on the floor onto which it has fallen from a suit pocket. 'It might be important, missus,' she will say, and because of the travel shop's logo, she will know only too well what's in the envelope. But it will be almost certainly out of date and no use to her, her family, or on eBay. Kitty will toss it. But that week she'll give extra money to Amilia so she can treat her family to a meal out, or a movie.

The following Christmas, she will buy Saul the tailoring coupon. He's fussy about fabrics and likes his clothes to fit properly. 'This is terrific, sweetie,' he'll say. 'With a belly like mine you can't buy suits from Sears!'

'Those laces are a bitch,' he had panted the previous night, when at last he had succeeded in untying them, part of the problem being he'd had to stretch over his protruding belly to reach them. Then, pulling off his socks, placing them on top of the shirt: 'I hafta hand it to that captain, Kitty. Never batted an eyelid about me asking him to do me the favour about the table. There are some of 'em who'd brush off little details like that, thinking it was not in their job spec.

'Confidentially,' he'd said then, 'when we were briefed at the board about selling this tub, it appears that this guy's not interested in staying on with Portlandis because he doesn't like Miami and there are no other openings right now at his level. He'd have to re-document or retrain, whatever it is they do to take on one of the really big vessels. So he can retire, if he wants. He has the years and he'll have a decent pension. I know he doesn't look it but he's coming up on fifty. Been with our company for twenty-two years, youngest captain ever for Portlandis when he got to take on the *Clara* at thirty-six, and apparently he doesn't want to go any further. He's a widower, no kids. Maybe that has something to do with it – maybe he just wants to take advantage of freedom and see the world on his terms now – but, hey, all that's for your ears only.'

'Of course, Saul.' Kitty, sitting on her side of the bed, continued to concentrate, hard, on her moisturising.

'Because, you see, honey,' he'd gone on, 'our CEO's trying to get him to change his mind. Good guys like him, we were told, are hard to find, and who am I to say otherwise? It's not my area of expertise. So, anyway, there's plenty of hotshots dying to get a captaincy, whatever. I'm glad you were surprised about the table. In a good way?'

'Mm. You certainly caught me on the hop!' But mention of the captain meant Kitty had been right. She remembered his arrival at their table in the course of their meal. He'd gone straight for her husband, touching him on the shoulder. 'Everything satisfactory, Mr Abelson?' Until he actually retired he was a company man. Knew whose side he was on.

'Perfect, Captain, thank you so much.' Saul had been effusive. 'We really appreciate what you've done for us! Great people here – couldn't be better.' He'd beamed at Barry, then turned to her. 'Right, honey?'

'Thank you, Captain,' she'd murmured. 'My husband's right, we couldn't be better served.'

Leifsson had responded with that courteous little half-bow of his, inclining his head with a smile, then moved on to Roxy and Charles, greeting both. In his whites, with his back to her, she could see he was broad-shouldered. And then, as he made his way around the table, she had also registered his amused delight as he'd reacted, just like all her tablemates had, at the Danes' beaming joy while informing him they were on honeymoon.

Before going any further with this particular reminiscence, she'd slipped off her side of the bed, jar of moisturiser still in her hand. 'Can I use the bathroom before you, Saul?'

He was now reading the leaflet that had come with the loaned CPAP machine. 'Sure thing, sweetie,' he'd said absently. 'Enjoy!'

It's now eight hours after that dinner, and on this early morning, careful not to wake her husband, she slides out from under the bedclothes and, moving stealthily, picks up her cashmere robe and a wool throw from the bottom of the bed. Then, inch by inch, she opens the sliding glass doors and goes out onto the balcony where she sits at the little dining table and, breath showing on the calm air, snuggles herself into the warmth of the wraps. At this level, on deck eight, the sounds of a waking ship are muted. At peace for now, the gulls, becalmed, bide their time on the glassy waters between the *Santa Clara* and France, while the growing light in the eastern sky sparks ice crystals on the vessel's rails.

The town of Villefranche, she judges, is about a quarter of a mile away and it, too, is waking, with people moving about on the quayside to open up a small number of what look like stalls, sited to catch loose-walleted guests from the *Clara* and from another, smaller, cruise ship anchored nearby. Both vessels, she figures, will be conducting their passengers ashore in tenders, since from this perspective at least, the quay has to be too small to berth either. Meanwhile, decks are being swabbed on both ships, and from far below inside her own, Kitty can hear a high-toned, muffled singing. Someone, whether male or female she can't judge, has woken up happy. It's a new day and her heart lifts.

Happiness, she knows only too well, is like a bird on the wing, hard to catch. It flies in almost always unexpectedly. You can't buy it, you can't manufacture it, but you can learn to recognise it as it passes. And here it is, in this peaceful interlude before the racket of activity and mask-donning of the day intrudes to put it again on standby.

Although the layers of cashmere and wool are warm around her body, her face is seriously chilly so she goes back inside. She is able to have her shower and slip into her clothes without waking her husband.

At the buffet breakfast bar, she finds herself at the same cereal station as her neighbour of the previous night, the actor, Charles, whose attire stands out from that of others already in the room. Male and female, they are mostly clad in tracksuits with the addition of scarves, jerkins and fleeces. He, though, is dressed as though for winter cricket, if there is such a thing, caramel-coloured slacks with knife-edged creases, a Pringle sweater in baby pink, and tasselled brown loafers. Around his shoulders is slung an unbuttoned and obviously expensive camel-hair overcoat.

On seeing Kitty, he escorts her, stagily gallant, to their table, which, as it's so early, they have to themselves. Once there, however, he drops his public persona and they have a real conversation, cautious at first, about their lives. He reveals he has lived alone since his mother's death. 'Even her little dog died last year.'

'I'm so sorry, Charles. What was his name?'

'Roger,' he responds, looking off into the distance. 'He was a little Jack Russell. More than twelve years old.'

'Oh, Charles,' Kitty touches his arm. 'It must be very lonely for you now.'

'Oh dear! How awful of me to do this to you. I'm sorry, Kitty.' He has reassumed his public voice. 'That was really selfish. Your first morning and here I am, an old man bleeding all over you!' Then, briskly: 'Is Saul joining us for breakfast?'

'I believe so,' she says, and then, remembering her mission: 'If you'll excuse me, please, for a moment. Before I start eating, I need to make a phone call home.'

Out on deck, she makes the call, and when the machine kicks in, she leaves Saul's PA a message, making it as impersonal as she can, highlighting the absurdity of the situation, and finishing with: 'So anyhow, Pippa, I apologise from the bottom of my heart for putting you to all that unnecessary bother. But in the end you'd have to laugh, wouldn't you? Talk again soon.'

When she gets back inside, her husband, somewhat bleary-eyed, is coming in through the door at the other end of the room. 'Hi,' he says, when they meet in the middle. 'You're up early.'

'So are you! I didn't want to disturb you.'

'Housekeeping knocked and I couldn't get back to sleep.'

'Ah, well.'

'Making a call?' He indicates the phone in her hand.

'Yeah,' she says, glancing at it. 'I was checking in with Geraldine. They're only an hour behind and I knew she'd have been up for hours with the kids.' It's very upsetting, she thinks, how easy she finds it these days to lie.

'And how is she?' But he's looking towards the buffet tables. 'What's good over there?'

'Everything. There's lots of fruit, Saul. Fresh juice?'

He makes a moue. 'Yeah, yeah. Bagels?'

'I'm sure there are. Why don't you go and see? Or you can ask – I think I'll have melon. I'll go with you.'

When they get back to the table, Saul's plate heaped with scrambled egg, gravlax, cream cheese and, in the absence of bagels, a second plate bearing warm white rolls, Roxy, the English girl, wearing jeans and a sweater, a vivid cerise to Charles's pale pink, has arrived and is sitting chatting with him. 'Hello.' She dimples up at Kitty. 'Isn't it a lovely morning out there? I think it's going to be sunny.'

'Let's hope so.' Kitty, who has yielded to the delights of the cereal dispensers, slides melon onto her Rice Krispies and sits down. 'You're in good form, if I may say so, Roxy! Listen, if you remember from last night, we're taking a cab into Nice today for lunch and Charles is joining us. We could double-date!' She smiles. 'Are you sure you don't want to hitch a ride with us? Nice, I hear, is a lovely city. Very relaxed.'

'Thank you, but unfortunately,' Roxy taps the notebook beside her plate, 'I have to do a bit of work.'

'You could make notes. If they're on a cruise, your characters would probably be taking these excursions?'

'I really appreciate the offer, but maybe some other time?'

'Of course. You did mention Ischia? Is it really that romantic?'

'So I've heard anyway – right now, though,' Roxy looks towards the breakfast buffet, 'I suppose I'd better have a look at that fantastic spread over there. Makes you hungry just to look at it, eh?' She hops up and makes a beeline for the covered hotplates.

'And you're sure you don't mind if I tag along?' Charles asks Kitty.

'Of course not. That'd be great for sure, Charles.'

'And that's all right with you, Saul?' The actor looks across her towards her husband.

'It's fine,' Saul says, through a mouthful of food, then taps his lips to show it would be rude to continue.

Within minutes, Roxy is back and there follows an oddly tuned breakfast, with the other three trying not to see Roxy's notetaking, or at least not to comment on it – until, turning to Kitty, she says, 'Don't answer this if you don't want to, Kitty, but why *did* you retire so young?'

'Actually . . .' Kitty reddens but Charles, a model of genial urbanity, comes in with a jovial 'My goodness, child! You're a bit eager, aren't you? Not even half past nine and you're up and at 'em. Time enough for such a serious issue. At least let the woman have her breakfast!' Then he embarks on a story about first having met John Gielgud in the Lyons Corner House on the Strand, 'long before he became a "sir". Poor old Johnny, we all had to lobby for that knighthood for him, all that stupid homophobic nonsense of the time. Good old Sybil Thorndike led the brigade. He had an amazing voice, of course, but legs like they were broken off an old thorn bush.

'Speaking of legs, darling,' he addresses Roxy now, 'I've a couple of twinges in mine. It's the cold, d'you see. I'm wondering if there's a chance in the world I could ask you, fit as a fawn as you are, to go over there and fetch me a fresh cup of tea, please?'

'Of course, Charles, no bother!' Roxy jumps immediately to her feet and goes off as Kitty flashes him a grateful smile.

9

After breakfast on the morning of the first full day, the second officially of her cruise, Roxy is standing on the portside rail of the ship on one of the lower decks, watching tenders come and go. Inside she's alternately bubbling with joy at her good fortune in living the rich life on deck six but, as a counter to that, she can't get out of her mind the poor greyhound she saw in Barcelona with the homeless woman. Since coming to Dublin she's noticed many homeless people, far more than she'd expected. Some of them have dogs. One had a kitten, another a rabbit. Her personal jury is out as to whether or not she approves of this. On the one hand, she can only assume that their owners care for them sufficiently to keep them alive and may even value the animals as company on the cold pavements. On the other, she worries about welfare. What kind of a life is it for an animal, especially a young one, to be tied up, immobile all day? And in comes the treacherous thought: *What if they're being used purely as pull factors for donations?* She has to accept that at least some of them are.

But there'd been something about that poor greyhound, created for speed and agility, plodding morosely along on that piece of string. In her experience, dogs being walked, even on leads, frequently check in with their owners, raising their heads to seek approval before trotting on. Even those running free return to them every so often. This one's head had drooped so low its nose was only inches from the ground and she'd had the feeling it was never raised.

Although she's chuffed about her new digs and couldn't keep it to herself (the news was sort of knocking at her chest to get out), she'd tried to keep it as low key as she could, and while telling the others at breakfast about her good fortune, she hadn't gone on about it too much, beyond saying she couldn't wait to tell her mum. She believes she was quite discreet, keeping a lid on her excitement. You'd never know, one or other of her tablemates may resent her being given a free upgrade. Although they'd all seemed happy enough with their own accommodation, in Roxy's experience human nature is such that people don't like to see others getting above themselves. Supposing her new gaff is better than, say, Charles's? She wouldn't like to upset him.

Right now she's freezing her tail off. Who would've thought that the South of France would be this cold? Her mum had said it'd be sunny, and for Roxy sunny meant hot. At least she'd brought her anorak with the furry hood, thinking she'd need it for rainy old Dublin when she got off the plane from Rome.

She's watching the comings and goings while making 'ambience' scene-setting notes, descriptions of busy sea traffic, cataloguing low-slung buildings on the shore, the slight bumping against the ship's hull as one of the tenders rides the wake of another, departing *on the restless surface of the sea*. Searching for precise words to convey these images, she describes the tenders as *large, squashed, hollowed-out oranges*. Then, remembering the advice of her editor to be careful with descriptions ('Think about them a little, Roxy. Ask yourself, "Can I do better than this?" Revise. They're important, of course, but, frequently, less is more'), she crosses this out, substituting: *Orange-coloured boats, little Chinese lanterns adding gaiety to the busy surface of the sea.* 'That's pretty good,' she murmurs, pleased with herself at getting the hang of this imagery thing. It's all to do with experience, isn't it?

Having kept an eye, between scribbles, on the activities on the decks below, she now spots her three tablemates, Kitty, Saul and Charles, as, one by one holding a rope rail, they step along the gangplank and bend their heads to climb down inside the tender's opening, Kitty glowing in a blush-coloured windcheater, her fair hair *wafting in the breeze. Natural or very expensive?* Roxy asks her notebook.

She sighs. There's no point in being envious of someone who wins the birth lottery. The woman did nothing to cause it unless you go with the dippy theory that we choose our parents! And, anyway, Roxy is inclined to like her.

As for the actor, she can't get a handle on him. Nobody's that nice, and the scuttlebutt in places like the *Daily Mirror* and *Daily Mail* is that all these old geezers are total prima donnas. *Prima dons?* She'll have to google . . .

She is kind of sad now that she's not going ashore with them to have a bit of an adventure.

She closes her notebook, thinking it's a good omen that none of 'her' three had looked up to see her taking notes as they disembarked. She checks her watch. Eleven o'clock and, so far, she hasn't spotted any other immediate targets, such as the Dunnes, three older and two younger women, the older slightly overweight but all with dark hair, and three men – all husbands?

But are family sagas passé, these days? And aren't they hard to write – all those characters with different problems?

The gay couple might prove simpler. Despite all the research involved, she'd have to have another look at them: she hasn't seen them disembark so they could still be somewhere on board. 'To work, Rox,' she tells herself, in case they are. But, first, she has to run an errand.

She goes first to the reception desk on one of the main decks. It might be before noon, but already the bars and cafés on the ship are busy, with people scoffing snacks and fast food with their beers and Cokes, and even some of the harder stuff. It seems to be non-stop food on board. She and her mum had heard about this, but it's different seeing it for real. She'll have to be careful. She suffered enough through her Weight Watchers years to know how hard it is to get the pounds off – and how easy to put them on. But the general mood of cheer and fun is rather attractive – although most of those socialising are in couples or groups. So far, apart from Charles, she hasn't spotted another single. She had again encountered the pair of friends from the coach, waiting for one of the lifts, and they had exchanged smiles and a few words about the weather outside, but a quick glance had confirmed that they were both wearing wedding rings.

There are fairly long queues at the desk. People are exchanging currency, buying stamps, paying deposits as they book excursions – about which they ask, in great detail, exactly what they'll get for their money.

When it's her turn, she's lucky enough to be served by a

charming young man, Wolfgang (from, where else, Germany). 'If you don't mind,' she smiles, radiantly she hopes, 'I need to get in contact with one of your officials called Frank. I gather he's the cruise director?'

'Of course, madam. You'll probably find him right now in the theatre, rehearsing. If he is not there, please come back and I shall find him for you.'

Roxy wants to engage him further, but can't think of anything to say other than the shockingly bland, 'May I have a few of your excursion lists and brochures, please?'

'One moment.' He searches under his desk. 'Anything in particular of interest to you?'

'Pompeii,' she responds, as this seems to be the most popular excursion for everyone, as far as she can see.

'Here you are.' He hands her a printed sheet. 'Every excursion we offer is on there, but with regard to Pompeii,' he hands her the particular leaflet, 'this is the one that always fills up first. So, if you're interested, madam, I could put your name down right away.' His English is formal, faultless and, as far as accents go, unplaceable.

'I don't have my wallet with me, I'm afraid.'

'I could hold a place for you until this afternoon?'

'That's fine, Wolfgang. How much is it?'

'With lunch or without?'

'Without! I'll eat a big breakfast!'

'You'll find many people do.' He leans forward confidentially. 'And we don't like to broadcast this, but if you ask the waiting staff at breakfast to provide you with a box lunch, they will be happy to oblige.'

'That's great, Wolfgang, but how much?'

'A hundred and thirty dollars. You are alone or is it for two persons?'

'I'm alone.' Roxy is finding it difficult to conceal her shock at the price but then he smiles at her. It's hard to guess at his height – there may be a raised floor behind the desk.

'I am sure you will not be long so, madam. On this ship, you will find friends and perhaps even more . . .' He continues to smile, showing perfect, even teeth. Is he flirting with her? Sorry for her? What? She can't tell as, the consummate desk clerk, he does his job, handing her a sheaf of literature: 'Schedules and excursion details, madam!'

'Thank you. I'll see you again this afternoon. You're on duty until when?'

'Six o'clock.' Almost imperceptibly, keeping a straight face otherwise, he winks.

He is. He's flirting. As Roxy turns away from the desk, she's wondering if this trip can get any better.

She finds the theatre, which, to her untutored eyes, is as big as the one to which she took her mum as a birthday treat to see *Jersey Boys*. And it looks far more comfortable, with plush red velvet seats, armrests with drinks holders and a little table for every two, wide aisles and plenty of leg room between the rows. She judged the stage not to be quite as wide as the one at the Piccadilly, the theatre she and Mum had attended, but would give it stiff competition.

She stands for a while at the back, watching eight female dancers, wearing leotards, tiny little skirts and tap shoes, going through a routine. There's no music, and the only light is a big one dangling from the roof over the stage. One of them is calling the steps, 'One-two-three-TURN, two-two-three-TURN, three-two three-TURN,' and so on. The sound is as precise and loud as that of a drum corps, she's thinking, regretting that, for once, she hasn't her notebook with her. Then she spots a man who could be Frank, standing not far away from her, watching the stage. She goes over but sees that he doesn't have a name badge. 'Sorry to interrupt, but I'm wondering if you're Frank.'

'That's me,' he says, without taking his eyes off the stage.

'You're the cruise director, right?'

'Guilty as charged. What have I done now?' The voice is cheerful, but when he glances sideways at her, his expression is wary.

'I'm so grateful to you. My name is Roxy Smith, I'm a passenger, and last night—'

'Hang on a sec. Stay there, Roxy.' He walks away from her and down the centre aisle. 'That's good, Patti. Well done. Really works. Take a break, okay?'

As he walks back towards Roxy, the girls disband, three of them clattering down the steps leading to the auditorium, one taking out a packet of cigarettes from a pocket in her skirt while rushing for the exit. 'Right-oh,' says Frank, as he reaches Roxy and, holding out his hand, adds, 'Nice to meet you.'

'To meet you nice.' Roxy can't resist it. She and her mum were Brucie fans.

'The old ones are the best, eh?' Frank smiles. 'I think I know why you're here, Roxy. Hope everything went smoothly.'

'So smoothly I couldn't believe my luck. It was an amazing surprise. I can't thank you enough, Frank!'

'Well, we can't have our bestselling novelist cooped up in a little room on deck two, now, can we? We couldn't expect a five-star review in that case, eh?'

'How did you know?'

He taps his nose. 'Part of the job, Rox. My job is to know everything about everything!'

'Still . . .'

'Look, I'd say it's Charles who did the needful. Apart from yourself, Roxy, we have another VIP on board this time. Charles somehow found out that you weren't getting the recognition you deserve, and I suspect he informed someone influential – like the wife of one of our directors?'

'Kitty? Saul? Are their names Saul and Kitty?'

'My lips are sealed but you wouldn't be far away from that road – so no thanks needed. We're light this trip, and there are several staterooms we could have given you. Hope you like the one you did get? Deck six?'

'It's amazing.' Roxy is fervent.

'Give us a good mention in your next book!'

'I sure will. Thank you so much.'

'My thanks will be if you enjoy your cruise. And if you're nice to Charles. He's a good 'un and there aren't that many around these days.'

'I'll love him to death!'

'No need to go that far. Sorry, but I need to have a word here.' He indicates one of the dancers standing a little way off in one of the aisles, clearly waiting for him. 'Enjoy, Roxy,' he pats her shoulder, 'and don't forget to come to a few of our shows.'

'I won't. Thanks again.'

But he has already turned away. 'Yes, Patti? What can I do you for today?'

Roxy walks out of the theatre, conscious of the plushness under her feet. This day is just getting better and better. But she looks back over her shoulder from the doorway. What's going to happen to this lovely theatre in Malaysia? And not least to Charles, who seems, according to himself, to love this ship to bits and to depend on it for work?

More importantly right now, though, she's wondering if it's wise, for a person with her limited budget, to spend a hundred and thirty dollars on a trip she had opted for only because she was staring at Wolfgang.

He is fit, though . . .

*

Just after three o'clock, she is in the large ballroom, where four members of the Dunne family, Gemma among them, are taking a line-dancing class with about fourteen others. There is an audience, many of whom have drinks in their hands, sitting on the sidelines to watch, jogging in their seats to Garth Brooks on the sound system at top volume.

Wouldn't you know it? It'd have to be sodding Garth Brooks with his friends in low places. Roxy can tolerate some country music but, for some reason, that of Garth Brooks is not included. Anyway, she remains loyal to poor Amy Winehouse. She joins the audience. Even for her art, she's not going to descend to line dancing with Garth Brooks.

She's about to leave when the lesson ends – and then Gemma approaches with one of what must be her aunties. 'Hi, Roxy, on your own? Come and join us for a drink. We have the drinks package – nothing too good for this family.' She turns to the other woman. 'This is Roxy, the girl I was telling you about. It's her first cruise too.' She turns back. 'This is my fairy godmother, Roxy, my lovely auntie Mary, the woman none of us in our family can do without. That right, Mary?'

'Right.' The woman is wearing a blue M&S dress Roxy

recognises from her mum's wardrobe. She is well-upholstered around the middle but with slim arms and legs. 'How do you do, Roxy?' She holds out her hand. 'Yeah, fairy godmother is right. If only!'

'But it did work, Mary!' Gemma says. 'You waved your wand and we're all here!'

'Thanks to you, pet.'

When the three of them are seated at the bar, Gemma reveals that she won a quarter of a million euro in the Irish lottery on Lotto Plus One. 'It was a last-minute Quick Pick,' she explains to Roxy. 'Mary was with me in EuroSpar, we were buying sandwiches and it was her idea I should add the price of a ticket to the cost of them because the jackpot that night was eight point six million. So I did – and here we all are.'

'There was no need.' This is Mary.

'I keep telling you,' Gemma says, 'youse are all to shut up about that! I wouldn't have bought that ticket if you hadn't told me to, and if you hadn't been there. We all only live once, Roxy,' she says now to her. 'Isn't that the God's truth? And even after all this, I'll still have enough left over to enjoy life for years, maybe the rest of my life. What's the point of being young like us if you don't enjoy yourself? Isn't that right, Roxy? In anyway, I got us a great deal,' she adds. 'Four cabins, thirteen grand for us all – they're not all together, mind, I'd have liked that, we all would, but thirteen grand for eight people? All food and drink included? Including Christmas dinner? Sure where would you get it? Let's have another drink, yeah?'

*

That night, Roxy is in for a surprise. With everyone at her own table having another early night, she's invited to join

Gemma's family and, sitting next to Mary, whose tongue has been loosened by gin and orange, discovers the other reason why the Dunnes are on this cruise en masse. 'Not everyone, of course, Roxy, some are a bit iffy, and that's understandable, although Gemma offered to bring the whole caboodle, in-laws an' all. We're having a great time, as I'm sure you can see but . . .' Mary hesitates. Then: 'Don't tell Gemma I told you, she worries about me, about strangers knowing our business, but I can take care of myself.'

Then she tells Roxy about getting pregnant at the age of sixteen in the midlands town where she was brought up. Her horrified and deeply ashamed family had confided in a priest friend who had organised for her to stay in a convent in Wales, where she had her daughter who was given up for a prearranged adoption with an Italian-American couple in Chicago. She had consented to the adoption at the time but has regretted it bitterly ever since, especially because, having suffered infection during childbirth, she had been left infertile.

'But I have a daughter and I'm going to meet her. She's divorced from her Italian fella, Roberto, and she and my granddaughters live in Rome now so as the kids can see him regularly. It's working out for them. I'm not complaining, Roxy,' she adds. 'I've had a good life and I've had plenty of kids to look after. My three sisters are all working, couldn't afford childcare when their kids were younger, so I stepped in. Sort of like an unofficial crèche! But the kids didn't come all together and were all different ages so it wasn't too hard.

'Anyways,' she adds cheerfully, 'I've found my daughter. She's done good and works in the Irish embassy in Rome. We're all going to meet the three of them, her and the two kids, there. I can't believe it. I keep thinkin' I'm going to wake up and it's all a dream . . .'

'All of you are meeting them?' Roxy's imagination goes into overdrive.

'Me first, of course, but then, we hope, all of us.'

'Would it not be simpler just to have taken a flight?'

'Course it would – but Gemma wanted to spread her good fortune around. She was my first to mind. Well, after Alessandra . . .'

'That's her name? Alessandra?'

'Apparently. I called her Maria. From the day I discovered I was pregnant I asked Our Lady to look after both of us, me and my little baby – and she did.'

'Have you spoken to her? To Alessandra?' Roxy, not believing her luck, novel-wise, but already trying to figure out to what use she can put this story, leans forward.

'Yes. She has an American accent.' But Mary's expression has closed in. Abruptly she stops talking, holding up her glass to the bartender, signalling for another drink, and Roxy is experienced enough by now not to push any further. There is more, she's sure of it, and she's equally sure she'll get it. She marvels at the existence of some smiling little god somewhere, the one who had arranged to place her between a pair of goldmines, her table and the one beside it. She couldn't have made this stuff up if she'd tried. She can't wait to get back to her wonderful posh room to get it all down.

IO

Kitty Golden is on the balcony of her suite. She holds her face to the sun, while the gulls, somnolence overcome, ride watchfully overhead to get on with the business of their day. They remind her of Roxy, questing for her story.

Under normal circumstances Kitty doesn't hide what for her is old news, but this morning she had been caught off guard by the abruptness of the questioning on her former life in front of Charles and, more significantly, with Saul present: if she had started on that narrative, some of what she's been feeling about their relationship might unwittingly have filtered through. Roxy might be young but she's bright.

Thank God for Charles, she thinks now. He may present himself as a doddery old has-been, but where people are concerned, he is alert to feelings and undertows, and is kind with it. She believes she can trust him.

On the other hand, in the matter of trusting people, she has to be cautious: her instincts in that regard have let her down in the past.

In many ways, the personality of the young novelist reminds

her of the breezy, sunny side of her pal Ruby – certainly Ruby as she was during the time when both she and Kitty were at the age Roxy is now.

She smiles as she thinks of Ruby. Only six weeks to go until the two of them see each other again on a girls' night out at the theatre to see *Lizzie*. She can't wait. Although she and Ruby Skype each other, it's a pale reflection of the real thing.

Roxy's digging had brought all that palaver of more than ten years ago to the fore again, the trauma, the fear, the agitation, the uncontrollable physical manifestations of shock, certified as such by her doctor. Suddenly she'd found she couldn't make a decision about what to have for lunch, much less what to do with her life.

Her abandonment of modelling had had nothing to do with her popularity within the industry. She was liked by most booking agents for her work ethic and lack of diva-esque behaviour. They'd even worked around her well-known refusal to wear animal skins.

But, given what had happened, she could no longer face the relentless posing and grooming, and pretending not to care that, while doing a summer shoot in an Alberta forest during January, she was so cold it was difficult to keep her teeth from chattering and spoiling her smile. In light of what had happened, her profession seemed abruptly so trivial. So shallow. And so dangerous.

Just as her career was burgeoning – she had been seen for a *Marie Claire* cover shoot and her agent had said the omens were good – the floor had fallen from under her feet at just after nine p.m. on Thursday, 1 December 2005 when she was twenty-two years old.

Having showered, she was at home in her apartment

wearing only a pyjama top. Long legs curled under her on the sofa, she was eating cornflakes for dinner in front of the TV.

Uncomplaining, she had suffered through a particularly long and gruelling fashion shoot that day while clad in a scratchy faux-fur loincloth, with platelets of fake porcupine quills concealing her nipples and stuck individually at weird angles into her wildly backcombed hair.

She had finished the cereal and was trying to decide whether or not to turn off the TV and go to bed, when, beside her, her mobile had piped. On consulting the little screen, she saw it was her agency.

At this time? She'd hesitated, but because the timing was so unusual, she put the cornflakes bowl aside and answered it. 'Hi, Sherman, have you no home to go to? What's up?'

The caller, however, wasn't her agent in the firm, Sherman Read, but the head of the agency who told her, with little preamble, that Sherman had absconded with the money in her account. What was left was negligible.

'Absconded?' Her initial reaction was confusion. The word had sounded silly, even preposterous. Sherman was always in her corner, always wheedling more and better jobs for her from casting executives. What did this woman mean? *Absconded?* Only jailbirds did that.

She was not one of those girls who lived the high life with aspirations to nab high-rollers but, with an eye to the future, had been prudent with her money. At that point, over the four years she had been with the agency, she had accrued almost three and a quarter million dollars in her primary account, with a second account for Sherman's commission, to pay taxes, and the modest 'salary' she took every month to cover rent, food, gifts and the few bob (she still frequently thought in

Dublinese) for her sister and nieces to help with communions, confirmations, back-to-school expenses and so on. Her needs were few: she ate frugally, while shoes and many of her 'good' garments came largely free, as designers gave them to her with the proviso she wear them on gala occasions.

She had a legal agreement with the agency that it would invest her money safely until retirement, which, Sherman had assured her, would be comfortable. 'You bet, Pussycat!' Sherman called all his models 'Pussycat' and referred to them, en masse, as 'The Kitten Crèche', although some of the women were now in their forties and working in catalogues. 'Sorry,' she said now, into her mobile. 'I don't quite understand, Carmel.'

She didn't. Not Sherman, surely. He who had told her he was *in loco parentis* and was prone to scolding her when he felt she was starving herself too much. 'Getting to healthy middle age and out of this rat run is more important than catwalks, commercials and cover shoots, darlin'.'

She agreed with him. He had provided her with meticulous quarterly statements and up to that moment, as per the last one she'd seen, in her own estimation, with a little bit of luck and a lot of hard work, she was well on her way to being able to retire at thirty. Her dream was then to go to college and, knowing she could never qualify as a vet, at least study for a qualification in one of the peripheral professions, veterinary nursing, perhaps, even business administration, so she could get work in some area associated with knowledge of and caring for animals.

It was just the previous week she had discussed with Sherman why they should, as Geraldine had urged, reposition her money. 'Somewhere it'll earn better interest than you're getting in that deposit account they set up for you,' her sister had advised. 'Some kind of a bond maybe. Or ask them to invest it in a pension fund, one where you can get at the money if you find you really need it, if there's an emergency medical situation or something. You're not going to be earning that kind of money for ever, Kitty, are you? You're gorgeous and in demand right now but you have to think of your future. College is expensive in the States, remember.' Then, laughing: 'Or at the very least you could marry a rich man like most of your colleagues seem to do!'

Kitty had laughed with her but the conversation had set her thinking.

Sherman had agreed it was a good idea when, almost verbatim, she'd put these suggestions to him shortly afterwards. 'You leave it with me, Pussycat,' he'd said. 'I'll do some research and get back to you. Gimme a week,' he'd added, 'and I'll be back with a proposal.'

Her intervention had obviously spurred this disaster.

Absconded. As the agency woman continued to talk, Kitty noticed that the hand holding her mobile was shaking as panic, yellow and toxic as vomit, moved from her stomach into her throat and threatened to cut off the air. Somehow, she managed to tune back in: '. . . five thousand,' the woman was saying. 'I guess he must have left that so you could fly home to Ireland if that was your reaction. And there will be money coming in from today's shoot, and the one you're booked for next week. As a gesture, we won't be taking any commission for either of those, but unfortunately your taxes will have to be put aside as normal.' Although she was speaking more rapidly than she usually did, the tone of the woman's voice sounded the same as always, as though this were just a normal call on a normal day. 'So, all in all, I reckon you'll have about eighteen thousand dollars left in the shake-out.'

'But I was getting statements.' Kitty didn't recognise her intonation.

'I know, hon. That's really the worst thing of all. We have them all here. We've been on to the cops and sent them copies.'

'He said he'd take care of everything, that all I had to do was to concentrate on work.'

'Well, all I can say is, on behalf of the agency, we're real, real sorry, Kitty. But right now there's very little more we can do. We've handed over the shyster's address, every phone number, right back to when we hired him, his mother's address in New Jersey in the event he died, everything we have. So, you never know, he mightn't have gotten away with it all. Don't panic just yet.

'But for such a thing to happen, we're not the first and probably won't be the last – it's human fucking nature. Sorry for the cussin'. I know it's no consolation, but you're not the only one he scammed. Bertha and Abegunde are in the same situation, although neither of them had nearly as much in the bank as you had.' She'd added quickly, as though conscious she'd said too much, 'Of course you know that's confidential, Kitty. You've been our rising star. You still are, of course.' She'd paused as though waiting for a response.

But Kitty could no longer speak.

'Are you still there, hon?'

The mock fireplace in Kitty's apartment was pulsing, rhythmically enlarging and fading; her TV was still blathering. 'Look . . .' the woman hesitated '. . . would – eh – would you like me to come around? I can hop in a cab right now.'

But her client still couldn't answer as she gazed around

her tiny but comfortable bolthole, furnished from the better offerings at the Goodwill and Salvation Army stores when she'd first arrived in New York at the age of eighteen. What was she going to do with everything? Where would she live now? Whom should she call?

What about the ten grand she'd planned to give Geraldine and her bus-driver husband so they could have a nice Christmas with their little family and book a decent summer vacation? She'd been due to fly home for the holiday and had planned to take the money with her in cash, parcelling it up in a fancy box tied with ribbon so they'd all think it was just candy or something. She simply hadn't gotten around yet to making the withdrawal and now she couldn't . . .

'Is anyone with you, hon?' For the first time, the woman at the other end of the phone sounded anxious.

Something came out of Kitty's mouth but to this day she cannot remember what it was. She broke the connection, and when the woman called back, didn't pick up, her brain scrabbling as she gazed at the little machine, as though she were trying to decipher its pinging.

Eighteen thousand would pay rent on her one-bed apartment and her living expenses for less than four months . . .

She had bookings the following week and the *Marie Claire* decision was imminent too, but the way she felt now . . .

Her brain tried to engage with figures: *subtract eighteen thousand from three and a half million?* Or was it the other way round? Should she put a plus in front of the eighteen?

One thing was certain: Christmas largesse had to be cancelled – even her trip to Dublin? But Aer Lingus didn't do refunds except in the case of death. Could this disaster be categorised with the same seriousness as a death in the family? For a moment she tried to construct an argument along those lines but her brain wouldn't work: it felt like a lump of soggy porridge. She saw it, grey and sagging – and, in an effort to douse sudden nausea, opened the refrigerator, poured herself a glass of Sancerre and, mindlessly, drank it as though it were soda.

Then, while the TV, without a care in the world, chattered to itself, she'd crossed to her bureau to check if passport, bank books, Green Card and that kind of stuff were all there. They were. She picked up the printout of her airline confirmation. From JFK to DUB on 12 December 2005. From DUB to JFK 29 December 2005.

She was being silly. Of course these things were still there: she hadn't been mugged. She'd closed the drawer, her brain continuing to whirl uselessly through figures – ten thousand for Geraldine, eighteen thousand, three and a quarter million. Back to eighteen thousand.

She called Ruby. Although her friend frequently worked abroad, Kitty knew she was currently in the city. 'It's gone, Rube, it's all gone!' she blurted, when her friend answered. Somehow saying it out loud in her own voice made it more horrifyingly real.

'What's gone?' Ruby didn't understand.

'My . . .' But Kitty couldn't say the word.

'Kitty honey, what's gone? What are you talking about?'

'Money. Fees. Bank account. All gone.'

'You're not making sense, sugar. Gone where?'

But again Kitty couldn't speak.

'Kitty, please, what's happened? Hey – you been fired?'

'The money. It's gone.'

'You been burgled? You *kept your money in your apartment*? In *New York*?' Ruby was screeching.

'N-no. Swindled. I've been swindled out of it. It's – it's all gone. My agent's gone. He stole all my money.'

'*What?* That Sherman?'

'I got a call . . .' Kitty, faltering, then, all in a rush, explained, starting with the call from the agency head.

From a farming background in Tennessee, Ruby was as practical about money as Kitty, to her cost, had been vague. 'Tell you what, honey . . .' she'd said, after they'd talked for half an hour and Kitty, although still disbelieving, had calmed down a little.

Now, on the eighth deck of the *Santa Clara* more than a decade later, Kitty watches from her balcony as two gulls spiral and whoosh over the water just yards from where she's standing, one chasing the other in an effort to snatch what it has in its beak. In retrospect she finds it odd that during the emergency call with Ruby, every detail still sharp, she hadn't wept, she hadn't complained, she had set out the situation as though reading a play script or a set of words for some dumb TV commercial. From down the line, she'd heard guttural sounds, as if her friend's throat was being constricted, but throughout, Ruby hadn't interrupted and at the end of the recital had simply said: 'I'm coming over. But first I'm making a call to a guy I know. Well, I don't actually know him – he's an attorney and I know his PA. We met at Pilates and liked each other, and ever since we've had a few skinny lattes together after class. She says he's real tough. The kind who kicks butt. I'll have an appointment set up for you in the next few days. Okay, sugar?

'You're a strong lady. So you go do your stuff and let the cops do theirs in the next few weeks. Then you go be with your family over the holiday. No matter what they say, darlin', that agency is liable – you'll see. That's my opinion anyway, and I'm always right, yeah? Are you at home?'

'Yes.'

'You got wine, honey?'

'Yes.'

'Is it drinkable?'

'Yes.'

'Well, you just break it out there, but don't start without me. I'll take a cab and be right over.'

'Okay.' But, having laid it all out, seemingly with such calm, Kitty was hit by the enormity of what had happened and this time it wasn't just her hand that shook: her entire body contorted and she fell backwards into the sofa, dropping the phone.

'You there? Kitty! Kit! You there?' From the floor, she could hear Ruby's shouts. 'Kitty? Where'd you go? What happened?'

'I'm all right.' Still trembling, Kitty managed to retrieve the phone.

'Thank God,' Ruby gasped with relief, 'but you sure don't sound it. Stand by.'

Less than half an hour later, Ruby had burst through the door of the apartment bearing an overnight bag, an enormous pizza, chocolate bars, a bottle of wine and, in her purse, a small packet of sleeping pills. 'I got him.' She was breathless: the elevator in Kitty's block didn't work all that often. 'His name is Abelson. Saul Abelson. He'll see you tomorrow, ten forty-five, thanks to Pippa. She got a hold of him – he was at a club or something like that. Anyway, he's expectin' you. Here's his address and Pippa's direct line.' She thrust a piece of notepaper into Kitty's hand. 'You won't like him, probably, but aggression is a *good* thing for his clients, yeah? Remember that, Kitty. Wine in the icebox?' She whirled across the room into the alcove kitchen and wrenched open the door of the refrigerator.

Kitty already felt a little bit better.

With the aid of the alcohol and Ruby's little pills, she slept that night. And the following morning, just after seven thirty, her phone piped and a warm-voiced woman named Philippa said she was calling to confirm that morning's appointment with Mr Abelson.

Ruby's forecast that Kitty would not like Saul proved accurate, but the attorney's new client appreciated his evident commitment and his assurances that while he mightn't be able to get all her money back for her. 'I've thought overnight about this, Kitty,' he said, 'and I recommend we go for the immediate option to scare 'em into submission. You okay with that, Kitty? Or would you prefer if we take the slow route, when it could go either way, and your costs would mount up with every postage stamp, shoutin' match and email?'

When he put it like that Kitty thought she had to take his advice and so had gone for the shorter option. At least she had upcoming work to distract her while she let the lawyer do his.

But as it turned out her personal plan proved not to be all that simple. Modelling is a competitive but close-knit business, and as soon as word got around about the suits launched by the three models who'd been scammed, all three had found that, suddenly, they were no longer being put forward for castings and not just by their own agency, which, Kitty supposed, would have been understandable. Bertha and Abegunde had each told her separately that they had found most other agencies were closed to them as well; this was confirmed by the latter during a tearful phone call following a consultation with her own attorney. 'You won't believe it, Kit, but he said there's very little to be done about this, unless we all get together and take a class action against all those goddamned agencies that have blackballed us. He – he said I should move to another state, Kitty! Can you believe it? I was horrified. He said I should move to LA or Seattle!' Abegunde, who'd always been a drama queen, had then wept bitterly. Born and bred in the Bronx, she'd said, between sobs, that she'd rather eat rats. 'I'm a New Yorker, goddammit!'

On learning about this fatwa against the three models, Saul Abelson was all for making efforts to avenge the outrage with a separate suit about discrimination, cartels and so on, but Kitty, worn out by tension and stress, had had enough and he had accepted her view. 'Fine, sweetie. Better to lie low for a while, but you're still okay with the action against your own agency?'

Within days, he had issued proceedings citing negligence on the agency's part as Sherman Read was its employee, it had oversight of the man's activities, and could therefore be charged, with Sherman's whereabouts, still unknown, as a co-defendant.

He had worked quickly and efficiently, bargaining hard, face to face with the agency that, despite all the sympathising initially expressed by its management, was insisting ('Bluffing,' he said to Kitty) that it would fight this suit, to the Supreme Court if necessary.

Over that weekend, she had consulted with Ruby. She spoke again to Bertha and Abegunde, both of whom remained as flabbergasted and angry as she was and, despite Abegunde's reservations about hers, were in daily contact with their own legal people.

Then on the morning of Friday, 9 December, the agency's lawyers came back with a take-it-or-leave-it settlement offer of one million dollars. 'Final offer, or so they say,' Saul said down the phone. 'Otherwise they insist it's a see-you-in-court situation. I still think we could win, but I hafta warn you it could take years. The offer is net, by the way. They'll pay all costs – hang on a minute.' Kitty heard him yell at his PA: 'Those Golden papers arrive yet?' Philippa had shouted something back, then Saul was again on the line. 'Offer's in. It's your call, Kitty. Wanna think about it until Monday?'

'Thank you, Mr Abelson, I will.'

'Oh, God, what's with the "Mr Abelson" crap-doodle? How many times I have to tell ya, Kitty, it's *Saul*! Ya want me to call you Miss Golden? Maybe Ms?'

'I guess not.'

'You guess not, what?'

Kitty hesitated, then: 'I guess not, Saul.'

She hadn't yet told her sister, still expecting her to make an appearance later in the month for Christmas, about any of this. But when things settled down a little, she could think more clearly. She'd had a series of conversations with a horrified Geraldine who was urging Kitty to accept the offer: 'A bird in the hand, Kit? And, lookit, let's get real here. To ordinary mortals, a million dollars is a lot of cash.'

Kitty agreed to the offer. Saul, to his credit, had refrained from applying pressure either way.

She had accepted for all kinds of reasons. While of course she agreed that a million bucks was a lot in anybody's terms, it was still less than a third of what she'd lost, but her sister had hit a nerve with her reference to 'ordinary mortals'.

Over the next few days, though, she discovered she'd lost

more than money: she'd lost confidence. Those ten days following her acceptance of the offer had passed in a whirl of interviews with police, appointments with her doctor and shrink, work commitments already in her calendar – and, yes, consultations with Saul Abelson, who had dictated that she should not, under any circumstance, make contact with her former agency. He would, on her behalf, personally conduct all necessary dialogue concerning her work.

Then, with all contractual commitments fulfilled, she had flown home for Christmas where, in her sister's northside Dublin semi-d, she had been loved to death by her two little nieces, who had been as delighted with their gifts of dressing-up clothes from Kitty's own stock of glitter as they would have been with the most expensive stuff from the Lego Store or Dinosaur Hill.

Back in the States, the legal proceedings were coming to a conclusion more swiftly than she could have imagined (far faster than Geraldine had envisaged would happen in Ireland) but that million dollars was not enough to house her in Manhattan for more than a few years, certainly not enough to secure her future. With her strength of purpose on the floor, the notion of starting again from the very bottom – even moving states, as Abegunde's guy had suggested – was, she felt, akin to putting on a blindfold and stepping off the rim of the Grand Canyon, believing in the existence of a magic mattress. She castigated herself for her lack of courage. Ruby's constant refrain about her strength of character was becoming a little irritating: 'I might look and sound it, Rube, but I don't *feel* it. I feel like a blob on the floor.'

Her shrink had advised she take a rest from modelling – that she should do something completely different. 'Temping, for instance? You can type? You familiar with computers? Ever think of working in a flower shop? Nice ambience, happy clients – except for funeral wreaths, of course.'

But Kitty's feelings of guilt, inadequacy and even humiliation at allowing herself to be scammed, to have been so stupidly trusting, were overwhelming. She couldn't see herself in a flower shop anyhow, with people stopping dead in the doorway when they recognised her and she had to explain . . .

There was something else. Saul was smitten with her. He had made that absolutely clear almost from the beginning.

He continued to woo her with daily calls, an avalanche of bouquets, fruit baskets and, in his efforts to get her to agree to a date, even the offer of a puppy: 'He's already house-trained, honest, Kitty. You'll *love* him!' She had made the mistake of mentioning her love of dogs during one of his less ardent calls when the conversation had, surprisingly to her, opened out a little and away from subjects other than her, her beauty, and his frustration that she wouldn't go out with him.

She had at first tried to keep him at bay, saying her shrink had warned her she was in a state perilously close to PTSD and in no fit state to date anyone. But he had waived his fee and had been so persistent she had felt, eventually, she owed it to him to go on one date.

He had called her at three o'clock, Irish time, on Christmas Day, just as she was about to sit down with everyone for the turkey dinner. 'Wish me a happy birthday, Kitty!'

'Hang on!' She went out into Geraldine's hall to take the call. 'Happy birthday!'

'"Happy birthday, Saul!" I'm all alone over here. I'm an orphan, you know.'

'But your step-kids?' He had two, both adults, from his first marriage.

'They're with their mother for the holiday.'

'All right, all right.' Conscious that, in Geraldine's kitchen, everyone was waiting for her before they started eating, she said, 'I'll go out with you. One dinner. I'll bring you a birthday present from Ireland. New Year's Eve, okay? My calendar is a little bare just now. And it's just to get you off my back. So we agree? Just once?'

'Great. And you'll give me my present then?'

'Yes. Goodbye, Saul, happy Christmas, happy birthday.'

'Thanks! This is great.' He sounded like a kid. 'So go eat bagels or brunch or whatever. I'm trying to!'

Her misgivings were not trivial, she thought, as she went back in to join the others around her sister's Christmas table. Technically Saul Abelson was still married. She had never dated a married man but, she reasoned, this one date might settle matters once and for all between them.

Six days later, at five in the afternoon of 31 December, having returned from Ireland two days previously, she was wearing an off-the shoulder Donatella Versace dress in blush pink, full model make-up and heels as she waited for him to collect her. She would tower over him, but that was part of the plan to put him off.

It had been his suggestion that they eat early, avoiding the scramble in every restaurant in town, but when she opened her door to him she found him wearing a white linen suit with an open-necked Hawaiian-style shirt in vivid colours, a black fedora with a white band, tilted rakishly to the left à la Al Capone, and tan and white leather Spectator shoes. On seeing her, he stuck a huge, unlit cigar into his mouth. 'Happy

New Year, Dollface! Love the Jimmy Choos.' He seemed not in the least put out by the disparity in their height. 'You look even more spectacular than usual. Let's go. Limo's waitin' and dinner's gettin' cold.'

She had to laugh. At least he had a sense of humour.

Their dinner proved to be on board a private plane he'd hired, which was already turning over when they got to LaGuardia. They were going to Miami for New Year.

During that first date and then a second the next day – because, of course, they had to stay over (in separate rooms), she tried not to be snowed by his repeated promises to take care of her: 'You'll never have to lift a finger again, Kitty. I'll take care of everything. I'll give you the life you deserve, I promise. You want to go to college? I'll find the best one. You love animals? A menagerie is not out of the question. You want a taller guy? I'll get lifts put in my shoes.'

In this mood, he was funny, self-deprecating. 'My mom always told me not to be bragging about my good looks. Not to look in the mirror. So I didn't. Couldn't reach any of 'em, even on tippytoes, and she'd hid all the stools and ladders.'

And to give him his due when, exhausted in every way, emotionally, physically and psychologically, she caved in and married him, materially he had kept his multiple pledges.

Throughout their marriage, she had frequently been embarrassed by Saul's thrusting, sometimes discourteous and uncouth behaviour in public, and his abrupt carnal activities in private, but had managed to come to terms with both. He hadn't trussed her up in chains and rolled her into City Hall to marry him, and in the Irish phrase, she had made her bed and must lie in it.

In any event it was hard not to admire her husband's

confidence, character, achievements, innate sense of fair play, even his generosity: he frequently, and quietly, worked *pro bono* for clients who, like her when he'd taken her on, required legal expertise but were largely without the means to pay for it. 'Work for a shelter,' he'd said, 'or in the office of another attorney, go to college – whatever, Kit. All fine by me. Whatever you want, sweetie.'

All fine, except, it seems, her becoming a mother.

11

Kitty and Saul arrive at the captain's cocktail party about fifteen minutes after the appointed time but the captain himself, as far as she can see, is not yet at his own event.

His absence is the first thing she notices when they walk into the venue, one of the many bars on the *Santa Clara*. Furnished with extra-deep rugs and plush, comfortable seating, it's at the bow on deck nine, glassed at the front and on each side with floor-to-ceiling windows, and runs the width of the ship's superstructure. The circular bar is raised a little and approached via three steps. Neither the brass rail and fittings surrounding its counter nor the handrails on the four sets of steps approaching it show any sign of verdigris or wear. Of money spent on the *Santa Clara*'s upkeep recently, a lot of it seems to have been used here.

As it is on many cruise liners, although lately not on all, she knows that this party is a tradition, with guests coming from the ranks of 'top people' on board, VIPs and senior management, like Saul (and his adjunct, herself), and those who'd paid through the nose for suites.

'I was expecting this.' On arriving back from Nice, Saul had grabbed the gold-shouldered envelope placed exactly in the middle of their bed beside a towel – someone in Housekeeping had laboured to morph it into the shape of a swan. 'Our company includes repeats at this party,' he'd told her, 'people who've been loyal over the years, even if they can afford only a balcony cabin. I kind of like that, fraternity, equality, blah-di-blah, all that good stuff, eh, sweetie?' Having shrugged off his coat and jacket, he put the invitation on his night table.

'That all came from the French Revolution, except they added "or death". They dropped that sharpish. And I'd bet you don't know that this whole premise is the basis of what we call now natural law, as in the First Article of the Universal Declaration of Human Rights.' Without waiting for her reaction, he said, 'I'm going to take a shower. We won't stay long. By the way, I meant to tell you, I saw our Danish friends down on my walk by the sea. I waved but they didn't see me. I was going to cross the road to say hello but, hell, I thought, why bother? I'll see 'em at dinner.'

'Wrapped around each other?' Kitty, who had kicked off her shoes and was resting on the bed, had smiled affectionately. 'Do they ever talk to anyone else?' She was slightly envious. She and Saul— *Ah! Don't go there . . .*

'Schlock!'

It had always been one of Saul's all-encompassing words, not just for cheap goods, but for anything soft and fuzzy, movies such as *Sleepless in Seattle* or *Love Actually* (both of which Kitty loves), TV ads involving laughing, hugging families, kittens, puppies . . . 'Funny enough,' he was unlacing his shoes, 'they weren't gazing into each other's eyes, they were talking to someone, another passenger, I guess. He was wearing one of those yellow baseball caps with *Santa Clara* written on it – the ones they sell on board?'

'Anyone we'd know already?'

'We haven't been here long enough, eh? I'm hoping we'll meet a few interesting folks this evening. But only half an hour or so at that party, forty-five minutes, tops! Promise!'

'Thanks, Saul, I'm tired.' She's tempted to close her eyes but is afraid she'll fall asleep. Sometimes, she thinks idly, she can be inclined to forget how highly educated her husband is, or at what level he operates in some of the complex legal work. He can still surprise her with his knowledge of world history and so forth.

'But it should be fun.' He's unbuttoning his slacks – Saul doesn't do zipper flies. 'All the ship's top brass should be there, including the captain, first officer and probably a few of the engineers too – I sure hope so, they're always enjoyable. So it'll be cool, honey, and after my speech, we can just slip away – I'll have to say a few words on behalf of the company but Pippa's emailed me an outline of what's expected. Okay?'

'Sure. That's great, Saul, thanks. Oh, listen, I was talking to Geraldine earlier today when we were in Nice, she phoned, and on the way back I had an idea. Their fifteenth wedding anniversary is coming up, but with the kids and everything, it's challenging financially and I was thinking how's about we give them a few days in Venice? Thursday evening to Sunday. We're there on Friday, right? We could meet them for lunch in some nice restaurant. They've never been to Venice – and neither have I. Wouldn't it be a nice thing to do?'

'Would we get them a trip in time? This is Sunday, sweetie.'

'I'm sure it's possible. There are all these last-minute offers online I hear about and she told me she was actually looking at places like Croatia, one of the cheaper Christmas-market trips, but they couldn't afford even that. Wouldn't it be good to give them a decent anniversary gift? The fifteenth is crystal, so what I was thinking, a piece of Murano glass? I could go in early that morning to find something appropriate and we'd all meet in the restaurant. Wouldn't that be nice?'

'Okay, whatever you think. Tomorrow's Monday. I'll see what we can do – I'll get Philippa on the job tomorrow.'

'Thanks, Saul.'

'You're welcome. I'd better get into that shower or we'll be late.'

Now Kitty finds herself half glad the captain isn't there. She's simply not in the mood to make trivial conversation with him. And not just with him, with anybody. Still suffering from jet lag, all she wants for this evening is to get out of here as quickly as possible, to have her dinner, then, hoping the food will act as a soporific, to take a long hot bath and slide under the bedcovers.

They accept drinks – sparkling water for her, Scotch for Saul. 'There's food, honey,' he says then. 'You want I should get you a plate?'

'No, thanks.' Kitty, a veteran of such parties, whether intimate like this one or gargantuan like the Met Gala to which, even as a retiree from the fashion business, she continues to be invited, has always struggled to manage drinks and food while still trying to shake hands with people or, increasingly common these days, to give them a hug. She finds it irritating how comedians and even some social diarists nonchalantly deride the custom of air-kissing. What else can you do when someone is holding out a cheek and both pairs of hands are full? 'I'll wait for dinner, if you don't mind, Saul.'

'Sure – oh! There's Barry – gotta have a word.' He zooms off, face set with purpose, bypassing the waiters circulating with silver trays offering minute crustless sandwiches and miniature canapés.

Poor Barry, thinks Kitty, watching her husband launch into one of his monologues.

Saul, for her, is a strange mixture of shyness and bravado: when there's no one present except themselves, his speech patterns, complete with pauses, are almost normal (for a New Yorker), but with strangers, especially those he esteems, he speeds up, eliminating breaks, words slaloming across sentences and clauses as though engaged in a downhill ski race. She used to intervene sometimes to rescue the recipients but, in recent years, has given that up. He's an adult and can take care of himself and so, she tells herself, can they.

Standing well to the side of one of the bar's entrance doors, she sips her water, content with her own company although she is aware, as usual, of being subject to stares and covert glances, presumably as Americans (of a certain age) try to remember where they've seen her, while others react to her height. In social situations such as this, she usually tries to dress discreetly, her taste running to monochrome shift and slip dresses: patterns and ornamental frills, bustles, panniers (intermittently fashionable Vivienne Westwood-style) and other decorative folderols make her feel she's dressed like an Eastern European folk dancer and serve only to draw attention to her.

The irony, of course, is that with some designers, the plainer the dress, the more expensive it is, largely because of the trickier body-form tailoring and more precise cutting of fabric, revealing the skill of the expert and leaving no room for sloppiness, such as a seam with a lumpy stitch or two or an ill-concealed zipper.

Is she guilty about being rich? About being able to splash cash on this kind of stuff? About being, in truth, a kept woman? Looking around the bar, knowing a lot about couture and fashion, she can't pick out all that many women from Saul's liberty-equality-fraternity group. There is at least one Dior outfit, she reckons, quite a few Donna Karans, two Burberrys, as far as she can judge, and lots of Louboutin shoes.

So, yes, guilt, like a little black asp, can strike and sink its venom into her without warning. For instance, having picked up some rock chick's designer perfume in Bloomingdale's, and having checked only its animal-testing credentials, she can hand over one of her credit cards and, without looking at the price either on the flagon or the receipt, sling both into her handbag.

Millions of women all over the world struggle to live for a year on what she, bedizened by Tiffany's and dressed by Balmain, spends in a second. The bellies of countless women in hundreds of nations are swollen from eating grass or the leaves of trees while she, a picky princess with a coat-rack frame, is fed, by choice, with vegetarian morsels by world-class chefs who have sourced them from some faraway, exotic half-acre, accessible only by mule.

She even has a limo at her disposal, should she be too lazy that day to walk four blocks to get an ice cream from a teeny-weeny shop so fashionable and famous it doesn't deliver.

Because of her upbringing in a not-so-fashionable part of Dublin, one of her mam's acerbic admonitions, *It's far from this you were reared*, all too frequently buzzes like a bluebottle trapped in her brain, getting louder during the cheeping around her at the charity lunches and gala benefits she and Saul ride on the social carousel of elite Manhattan.

You want a diamond not just bigger than the one slung around your neck, but bigger than the one slung around hers? No problem.

Maserati has brought out a new saloon model, one that practically drives itself but still sounds like Formula One. And you can have it in any colour of the rainbow? And you need one, like, *yesterday* because the car you *thought* you liked eleven months ago no longer matches the colour of your front door? So you go to the showroom and talk nice to that new hot young guy from Costa Rica on the floor. *No problem, madam. I can have it for you – in violet, you say? – in six days.*

And at a girls-only lunch when they were swapping news, one of the women had announced that she had tired of the colour of the Louis XVI *bureau plat*, brown burr walnut with inset marquetry and brass mountings. She'd fallen in love with it at a Sotheby's auction and just *had* to have it. Now: 'It's lovely of course, in the showroom, but to live with? That colour? So depressing, like drying mud or *you know what* in a baby's diaper – ugh!' A careful moue designed not to tamper with the surface of 'flawless' foundation. Then, first taking a sip from her glass of organic, mountain-sourced water from the Himalayas: 'I found the most darling little upcycling place in the Bronx . . .'

So, right at that very moment, her table was in the shop being redone in an overall hue of pale but cheery yellow, 'Like, distressed? With the woodgrain showing through? These people know what they're doing, ladies. They have a guy from Florence working there and I just can't wait to see it. You all have to come visit. And of course I'd be happy to share the shop's number . . .'

So, yes. She does feel guilty. But, like all those in the circles she inhabits with Saul, she gets over it.

Kitty has housed self-criticism since childhood but its tone becomes increasingly caustic the longer she remains married to Saul and his wealth. Now, it seems, she can't entertain the slightest negativity about him (or about her sense of loneliness) without triggering an instant mental response: *Poor little rich girl!*

As she continually reminds herself, Saul hasn't chained her to the apartment and she is free to walk away, should she choose to do so. But if she is brutally honest with herself, although she hates to admit it, the money has helped her stay, and she doesn't need any voice in her head to point out that it has been all too easy to go with the flow.

And, fretful with the repetitive gossip – shopping, fashion, interior designers, calibre of Filipina maids and South American childminders – she's also bored.

It isn't hard to recognise that many of the wives of Saul's business associates are equally bored and restless. Many had married for money and stay for it – so did and does she, which is something she hates to admit, no matter what the reasons or excuses.

What she hasn't done, as many have, not yet anyway, is to take the next step, which is to divorce for money. The women who get satisfactory settlements instantly fall away from their circle, changing country clubs and tennis coaches. They have a bit of work done to their bodies and faces, and find a truly amazing personal trainer. They begin to spend a lot more time in places such as Palm Springs, Malibu or, for boasting cachet, Èze-sur-Mer in the South of France where the members of U2 have holiday homes and can be seen occasionally out and about, looking and behaving like ordinary men – thereby bestowing cachet and boasting rights on those who catch sight of them.

So just because she entertains thoughts like this, can she claim to be all that morally superior? No, says Guilt. No, says the woman she'd seen just yesterday, shuffling along a Barcelona pavement with all she possessed stacked in a shopping trolley, to which she had attached, on a string, a depressed and underweight greyhound.

Retirement and life as a woman of leisure had had its benefits – she no longer had to compete or even keep up with the stellar cast and style at the Met Gala. They always include almost every A-list film and pop star, every supermodel not just in New York but on the planet (and all the aspirants), dressed by the starriest and most famous couturiers. She'd been delighted to see Ireland's Saoirse Ronan there last time, wearing a lovely white feathered gown by Christopher Kane.

Thinking of young people, there's no sign of Roxy at this party. Perhaps even her improved stateroom status on deck six hasn't been sufficiently good enough to rate an appearance here, although, in fairness, the invitations had probably been printed before the ship sailed.

Kitty smiles to herself as she sips her water. The girl had been bubbling with excitement about the move at breakfast this morning: 'Oh, it's so wonderful, Kitty. When I'm out on that balcony I feel I have wings – that I'm actually flying over the sea. And the bed, and the bathroom – and the quietness. Honestly, I can't believe my luck! I sure could learn to like this, I can tell you! Actually, I can't wait until I can get a proper signal and to hell with the cost! I'm ringing Mum to give her the news. She'll be delighted but she probably won't believe it. She's always saying that because I'm a writer I exaggerate everything. I still can't believe it myself. It's like – like . . .' She'd stopped to search for a suitable metaphor. 'Oh, I dunno! I can't put it into proper words, but I feel this ship is like a fairy palace and I'm the princess! Oh, God, that sounded so childish . . .'

'Not at all.' Kitty had smiled. 'It's a lovely image. All you need now is your prince to knock on the door!'

'Exactly.' The girl had beamed in return. 'But he's not going to *knock* on my door, that'd be too ordinary, he's going to swim up through the sea and I'll let down a rope made with sheets – they're huge sheets on that bed – and he'll climb up them, up the side of the ship and over the rail, and he'll grab me and kiss the breath out of me right there on my balcony!'

Sipping her water, smiling again at the recollection of all this, Kitty rests her back on the glass wall beside her, wishing not that she was twenty-three again but that she could still access the twenty-three-year-old spirit she had enjoyed before her personal crash, the kind of belief that everything was possible and that the possible could be made concrete with just a sprinkling of Roxy's fairy dust. The English girl is only ten years younger but, with her enthusiasm, she makes Kitty feel a lot older than that.

She likes Roxy: her energy is impossible to resist. Surrounded as Kitty is, mostly, with sophisticates (and pseudo-sophisticates), it's refreshing to see the girl's delight at being on board her first cruise. As yet, however, she doesn't altogether trust this. She could become a nuisance. She's upfront about scoping background material for her new novel, not quite so open about fingering people like Kitty as characters – too many 'naïve', seemingly innocent questions . . .

Maybe she's going overboard, Kitty tells herself. Maybe the girl is merely wearing her curiosity on her sleeve, and maybe that's common to all novelists and journalists – she had said she'd originally come from that side of writing. Kitty is no admirer of Donald Trump, or the ditzy crew now preparing to 'transition' into the White House, and certainly wouldn't pan the media for its biases, which are at least transparent in most democracies. The president-elect's constant trumpeting about 'fake' news has been such overkill that it's perfectly clear the description applies simply to adverse reactions to his own tweets, statements or behaviour or to any reports with which he doesn't agree.

She has to admit, though, that there is a tiny grain of truth, perhaps point zero zero one of one per cent, at the core of his complaints about press monoculture and group-think.

On the other hand, with some honourable exceptions, because of the relentless competition from social media, 'citizen journalists', for instance, some practitioners and their editors have become ruthless, prurient and, in some cases, outright nasty. As yet she doesn't categorise Roxy as such – how could she on such short acquaintance? But she's on her guard.

Apart from all of this, she is secretly relieved that, other than she and Roxy having connections with Dublin, another coincidence had arisen at their table during that getting-acquainted phase the previous evening. Quite quickly, she had discovered that no one there, with all the varying ages and relationships, has any children so she won't have to endure the torture of cooing over photographs of cute kids and hearing tales of their little doings. It's not because of boredom she dislikes this: it's because of her needle-like longing to join the club.

On the cruise she and Saul had taken the previous year through eastern and southern Asia, it had seemed that all those at adjacent tables to theirs had children and were only waiting for an excuse to whip out the pictures. Many of the kids were actually on board because it was half-term, so there was no escaping their joyful, rampaging presence. While simultaneously castigating herself for being so ungenerous, she'd found them, and the natural affinity between them and their parents, upsetting.

Charles isn't here tonight either – perhaps his status as a casual employee is too lowly.

She'd been delighted he had come with her and Saul to Nice: having a third person at table is always good. At first, he had tried to divert them from the main drag to eat at a small local fish restaurant he knew on the seafront, but Saul had already had Philippa (who, thank God, thought Kitty, was keeping schtum about other matters) book them into a small but palatial and very expensive place because it had a Michelin star and was, according to reviews, possibly up for a second. Grandly, he'd invited Charles to join them, brooking no argument, calling the maître d' on his mobile when they were on their way there to announce that a famous English actor would be joining them.

On arrival, she could see that the poor Englishman had been embarrassed because, while greeting them and leading them to their table, the maître d' had, unsubtly but understandably, enquired about the movies in which he might have seen his eminent guest. (Kitty suspects he may not be as eminent as Portlandis has portrayed him in its literature: if he's that good, why is he on board a clapped-out ship bound for semi-destruction?)

But throughout lunch, Charles had been charming (professionally, she suspects), beautifully mannered and, with his store of gentle anecdotes and gossip, just outrageous enough to be amusing, without being scurrilous, about people who *were* famous. At heart he is, she thinks fondly, what in Ireland would be termed 'a dote', meaning you'd like to tuck him under your arm and run away with him. In enjoying his company, she was reminded of another saying of her mother's: *Wouldn't you just like to put him in a glass case and throw sugar at him?*

It had been one of those still, bright but chilly winter days, and after lunch, in place of taking a walk along the promenade to admire the yachts, sheathed in coverings, Saul had wanted to go to Galeries Lafayette to buy her a dress, despite her protestations: 'I don't need any more dresses, Saul. My closets at home are full to bursting.'

'Come on, sweetie!' He had winked at Charles. 'What woman can't do with another nice dress, especially from France?'

But Kitty didn't want to tramp around a department store. If the one in Paris was anything to go by, this branch of Galeries Lafayette would probably be on a similar scale. In other words, imposing but big and tiring. 'I haven't the shoes for it, Saul.'

'We'll buy you a pair.'

'Could we not just find a nice café to sit and watch the world go by for a little while?'

'If I may intervene?' Charles had said quietly. 'I know exactly the street you need. Lots of craft shops and boutiques – just around the corner. I can take you.'

'That's what I want, Saul. You can wait here, okay? Have another coffee?'

Saul gave in. 'I know when I'm outnumbered. I've had

enough coffee but, tell you what, sweetie, I'll meet you back here. I'd like to go down to that promenade, see where that awful thing happened last July, with all those people mown down by a truck. I'm assuming it's marked in some way.'

'Great.' Decisively, Kitty had stood up and set off with Charles, following him into the little side streets, lined with small houses and cafés, ateliers and craft shops, stopping at the window of the first fashion boutique they'd come across, its window displaying only a single dress, beautifully cut in black linen with cap sleeves. Her experienced eye told her it would fit. 'I love this, Charles. Can we go in?'

Inside, a middle-aged woman, who was probably the shop's owner, turned herself inside out with delight on seeing them, so effusively, Kitty thought, she must have been having a slow day. The stock was monochrome, from white, through cream, sludgy khaki and into charcoal and black. She indicated the dress in the window – '*Celui-là, s'il vous plaît, Madame?*' Although she hadn't actually sat her Leaving Cert, French had been her favourite subject at school, and you can't be around the fashion industry without absorbing a bit of pidgin French and Italian.

'*Oui, oui, bien sûr! Tout de suite!*' The woman scurried into the window to take the dress off its form.

When Kitty, wearing it, came out from the curtained cubicle at the back of the shop, which was doubling as both sewing and fitting room, the woman clapped her hands: '*Ravissante, Madame. Parfait! Parfait pour vous!*' And turning to Charles: '*N'est-ce pas vrai, m'sieur?*'

Charles had merely nodded. 'I've no French,' he'd said to Kitty, as the woman, clearly eager to seal the deal, took one of her stiff, branded bags from a small stack on a table nearby, then pulled a length of brown satin ribbon from a roll, expertly snipping it. '*Voilà, Madame! Votre père est d'accord!*'

'What's she saying?'

'That my father is in agreement. Anyway, the gist is that we all love this dress on me so we should buy it – hope you're not insulted?'

'Not at all. Of course not.' Charles's gallantry surfaced. 'It's an honour to serve as the dad of someone so beautiful. She's obviously clever, and sees you have inherited my incomparable bone structure.'

As they left the shop, Kitty's mobile rang. It was her sister, calling simply for a chat. 'I'll ring you back,' she said immediately. 'This'll cost you a fortune, Geraldine – it's just a chat? Everything okay?'

'Sure, everything's fine.'

'Hope you don't mind, Charles?' She'd apologised as she'd tapped out the number. 'I won't stay on long.'

'Not at all – please. Talk as long as you like.' Discreetly, Charles had moved ahead of her.

'*Oui, merci* – thank you,' she'd said to the woman. '*J'aime ça, je lui accepte.*'

The grammar wasn't great but the woman, standing there with her bag and her length of ribbon, had had no problem in understanding. '*Merveilleux!*' She'd beamed. '*Merci, Madame, M'sieur . . .*'

'Even I understand that.' Charles had smiled back at her, as Kitty went back into the cubicle to take the dress off.

Saul had liked the dress too, when she'd shown it to him. 'Pretty chic, I'd say – why don't you wear it this evening at the cocktail party?'

'If you like. You bought it after all!'

She is wearing it now – the shopkeeper had been right about it: with the hem just above the knee to emphasise the length of her legs, it fitted and suited her perfectly. What's more, it's so comfortable she can forget about it.

She's watching Saul, across the room, as he continues to talk with (at) Barry, gesticulating as though in persuasion mode, while the general chatter swirls around them. Barry, she notices, although inclining his head politely towards Saul, is never losing sight of Joshua, his partner.

For his part, Josh, a little way off, is openly surveying the room over the head of a woman who, seemingly unaware of his rude inattention, is chatting away. She is squeezed too tightly into her shiny violet bodycon dress, Kitty thinks – then gives herself a mental slap. This woman, any woman, is entitled to wear anything and everything she likes without having people diss her for her taste or shape. But she continues to watch as the woman chatters on, even batting her eyes upwards as though flirting. Could it be that she normally wears spectacles? Too myopic to recognise the guy's lack of interest?

Given what she'd seen of the relationship between him and Barry, and Barry's watchfulness, Kitty doesn't believe it will survive even the length of this cruise.

In the course of her previous career, she had come in contact with many of the Joshuas of this world, spanning both sexes, who have one overarching trait in common: while physically stunning (she would include the Israeli in her roster of those who would stand out in a world entirely populated by the beautiful), they have their focus entirely on the main chance and would throw their firstborn down the stairs if it would get them on the front cover of *Vogue* or *Elle.* That sounds harsh, she knows, but truth does hurt.

Poor Barry, she thinks now. It's definitely a relationship of unequals.

On impulse, she makes her way across the room to where Barry's partner is still standing with the woman, who is now gesturing, describing something. Could he be wearing kohl? When she gets nearer the pair, she sees the kohl effect around his eyes is natural, created by those gorgeous lashes.

Just as she reaches him, she is suddenly aware that something is happening behind her. The room doesn't exactly hush, but some conversations have paused and people around her are glancing towards the door.

Given her height advantage over most of those near her, she turns to see what has caused the stir, and her eyes meet those of Captain Leifsson, who, bareheaded, wearing whites, gold stripes gleaming on the cuffs of his jacket, is finally making his appearance. The floor of Kitty's stomach plunges.

Dear God she thinks. *What the hell is going on here?*

As if you don't know! admonishes a little voice, gleefully, at the back of her brain. Without acknowledging her, Leifsson turns away immediately, holding out his hand to shake those of the two women sitting nearest the door, then progresses towards others, sitting on sofas or lounging by the rails surrounding the bar, greeting them with professional cordiality.

She turns back to Barry's partner. 'Hello there, Joshua,' she says brightly, and then, wearing her most brilliant smile, to the woman with him, 'Hi. I'm Kitty Golden. Very nice to meet you. And you are?' But, while grasping the woman's hand, she doesn't catch the name. 'Sorry? It's a little noisy in here.' She leans down to listen, focusing, overriding other thoughts, putting them as far from reach as she can, concentrating while the woman repeats it.

She becomes aware of a familiar smell wafting from Joshua, just a whiff but unmistakable, the sweetish pong of weed, utterly familiar since the time of her early career when many of the girls smoked as a matter of routine, especially at parties.

While the woman chunters on about how wonderful everything is, she glances at Barry's boyfriend: the eyes, those wonderful eyes, darting from right to left as he continues to survey the bar, give the game away. They are too bright and, at such close quarters, she can see the pupils have enlarged.

In addition, she detects that by contrast to the previous night, when at the dinner table he'd seemed half asleep, limp and oh-so-bored, right now he seems a little agitated so he may also be on something heavier than marijuana.

12

While the *Santa Clara*'s elite guests enjoy the captain's company, along with the canapés on deck nine, Roxy Smith is ensconced at a window table in one of the large open areas midship, where the temperature is comfortably warm but rather humid because the entire area, sporting a heated swimming pool, Jacuzzis and a number of food and beverage stands, is covered with a retractable glass roof, now snugly closed.

She's waiting for Gemma Dunne to come back from the Ladies, while other members of the Irish family splash around happily in the water. She's continuing to marvel at finding herself here – and at the variety of locations available for socialising, eating, entertainment, and shopping, for clothes, jewellery, electronics, souvenirs and what her mum would categorise as 'gewgaws'. She's come across organised events, such as bridge tournaments, card games, people making small bets with each other while playing crazy golf. There are sports available – archery, snooker, volleyball. And although the casino is closed while they are in port, there's the cinema, the ballroom where she'd run into the Dunnes, the theatre where she saw the dancers rehearse, and where this evening there's an after-dinner show with a comedian on offer, and more. The list of what's available would make you dizzy. She is taking advantage currently of being alone to jot down a few descriptive notes.

Seating and tables have been placed around the periphery of the central pool area, which has been configured along the lines of pictures she's seen of Roman baths. It features intricate mosaic tiling, tall pillars, columns and more-than-life-sized statuary of men and women with curled hair bearing jars, bowls or bunches of grapes, lush tree ferns and other tall tropical plants in bronze urns. *Feels a bit like Palm House in Dublin's Botanic Gardens,* she scribbles, *not as sweaty . . .*

She pauses to watch people help themselves to little glassfuls of melted chocolate from the chocolate fountain just at the entrance. Nearer to where she's sitting, she hears a little girl give her order, in *very* firm tones, to the amused chef behind the counter at the pizza stand: 'Just pepperoni, please. Nothing else. Only pepperoni.'

It's hard to get used to the idea that, for free, you can help yourselves to glassfuls of melted chocolate, take away a pizza, with or without fries, select what you like from the patisserie counter, even order coffee or various teas. And if your fare has included a drinks package, beverages, whether alcoholic or not, are also free.

Roxy's diet hasn't been the healthiest of late, especially while she's writing when time shrinks alarmingly and it's far easier to eat biscuits or Mars bars when you're hungry but in a hurry to get back to the keyboard, and the fastest dinner available is cheese on toast or a Bovril sandwich.

At least she always has bananas close at hand. Cheap and cheerful, bananas can save your life. She hasn't tried it herself but someone once told her that a person can actually live for a long time on a diet consisting solely of bananas and milk. At one stage she'd sketched out the first page of a screenplay outline where someone was stranded on a desert island, like Tom Hanks in *Castaway*, but although there were banana trees there was no water and no coconuts from which the protagonist could drink. But then, one calm night, she heard what she thought was a faint mooing coming from another tiny, rocky island nearby, really only an outcrop. She managed to swim over and found the wreckage of a little open boat, the dead body of a man, and a very thin cow with a suckling calf... *but there was grass too.*

She'd never got around to developing this any further than that opening sequence because life had intervened, as B-list stars frequently say when being interviewed about disappointments and failure to progress their careers.

With a large percentage of the ship's passengers having gone ashore that morning, it had been peaceful on board for most of the day, but the pace is now picking up, the atmosphere increasingly buzzy as the tenders, again operating in rotation, bring them back.

Although she has enjoyed her day, she believes she made a mistake in not taking up the opportunity offered by Kitty Golden to go ashore with her small group of three. All right, she doesn't have much money to spare but still . . .

When they dock at Naples, her plan had been to blow her budget, if necessary, to get to the island of Ischia because her mum and she have always longed to see for themselves the location where one of their favourite movies of all time

(*Avanti* with Jack Lemmon and Juliet Mills) was filmed. She has promised her mum she'll take loads of photos and make copious notes. For her novel, she might send one or more of her characters to the island where, as a result of the romantic atmosphere, he or she could be enticed into a deep dalliance, leading to heartbreak, of course, when they have to go their separate ways.

As soon as the cruise confirmation came through with a visit to Ischia presenting as possibility, she'd discussed it as a storyline with her pal, Ruth. And in a way that means she's half committed to it – although as yet her mind is open. In a way, all this descriptive stuff she's cataloguing, as well as being for the novel, is part of a daily journal of the trip she's writing for Ruth because she's promised to keep her fully up to date.

They've been friends since schooldays, and with Ruth at present halfway through her year on a kibbutz in Israel, Roxy worries that because of all the matiness Ruth is experiencing while picking oranges or washing dishes alongside guys of her own age from all over the world – there's one in particular from Chicago – this 'great fun' is turning into romance. Although she hasn't hinted at such in her emails, not yet, Ruth mightn't go back to rainy old London at all. Roxy's heard that this happens a lot on kibbutzim, as she now knows to call them. Maybe she could tempt her to Dublin. Get a trip on Ryanair for half nothing. She could even get Ruth the ticket as a belated Christmas present.

All day today she's had her laptop with her to cut out the tiresome transcribing, and right now, having gone into detail about the luxury and exclusiveness of her new accommodation, she is describing for Ruth the people on board, Kitty, Charles, Gemma and her tribe, Frank, the beautiful Wolfgang in

Reception (*charm the socks – or the pants – off you, wouldn't kick him out of bed, Ruth!*) and, right now, the two she'd met at lunch that day.

Middle-aged, gay as Christmas and lovely. Buffet lunch in a huge café-style self-service restaurant. All the window tables were taken but Lara from Latvia comes over, would I share? And took me over to them. Guess what? They're from Ireland! (This whole boat is riddled with Irish people, apparently, according to these two. Cruising is the new sex in Ireland!) Anyway, they've been together for eighteen years, married last month. Very proud that Ireland let them do it legally, and they're on board to celebrate. Their names are Finian (pronounced Fineen) and Tom, and they're hilarious. Sample:

Finian: 'Luckily I'm from Cork, he's from Leitrim. Have you heard of Leitrim? It's in the middle of Nowheresville, God love him, God love 'em all up there!'

Tom: 'Shut up, you! We're hiding from Christmas.'

Finian: 'From our families.'

Tom: 'From your family you mean!'

Well, sorry, Ruth, it sounded better than it reads! I'll have to make a scene out of it if I'm putting it into Heartbreak Two, as I'm calling it for short.

So I really enjoyed them but you'd want to hear the viciousness when they were talking about people they didn't like. I felt so-ooo guilty for laughing along but I couldn't help it!

Glancing up from the laptop now, she sees Gemma and her

auntie Mary at the pool's coffee counter just a few yards away. Quickly, she saves, then closes the machine. She can finish later.

'God, it's all go around here, isn't it, Roxy?' Gemma's aunt turns to address her. 'Have you any plans for this evening, pet? Going to one of the shows or anything? I see they're doing *Grease* one night. I just loved John Travolta in that picture. What age was he when he did that?'

'Same age as me, Mary! Twenty-three,' says Roxy. 'Can you imagine having a film like that under your belt at that age?'

'Look what's talking here!' Mary unwinds the towel from her shoulders, revealing a one-piece swimsuit illustrated with a multi-coloured, rather villainous-looking parrot. 'And you already an accomplished author?'

Throughout this exchange Roxy has been getting anxious about her timetable. She's due to meet Kitty Golden at half past six and before that has to change her clothes and apply a bit of slap because they'd be going straight into dinner afterwards. 'Lovely talking to you, Gemma, Mary.' She acknowledges them with a smile and a nod, just as the PA system crackles into life, announcing that in the Orchid Room the next event would be: 'Stand by, ladies and gentlemen! Don't go anywhere because . . . it's . . . the . . . Grandparents' Bragging Session! Get on down there right now or you'll miss it. Don't forget your photos!'

Roxy hauls herself to her feet.

'If you're doing nothing after dinner, pet, don't be a stranger.' Mary points upwards. 'We'll be having a few drinks if you'd care to join us – but we'll be doing a bit of shopping first.'

'Thanks, Mary, that'd be lovely. I'll do that.' Roxy leaves them, hurrying off to the atrium and the lifts, where, among the waiting crowd, she bumps into Charles.

'Good evening, young lady.' Although he's not wearing a hat, she can almost see him doff it. 'How was your day?'

'Very interesting, thank you, Charles. By the way, does anyone ever call you "Charlie"? "Charles" is a bit, I dunno, Prince-of-Walesy?'

'Not really, my dear.' His tone is firm. 'If you don't mind, of course?'

'Sure. No problem. It's a nice name whichever way you have it. You know, Charles, I think I could be here for a week and not get around everything on this boat. It's amazing.'

'Agreed!' The lift arrives and he stands back to let her go before him. They ascend in the usual silence that descends on a group of strangers sharing a lift, and as they get out at their deck, he touches her arm. 'Don't want to detain you, Roxy, but could I tempt you, d'you think, to partake in my little acting class? We're starting tomorrow. Three o'clock in the ballroom.'

'Sure. Well, actually . . .' she pauses '. . . now that I think about it I'll have to get back to you. I may have to work, but perhaps.' She doesn't want to be too hasty in making commitments in case something better comes along.

'Shall I, as they say, pencil you in?'

'Do that, Charles, yes. See you at dinner.' And they go their separate ways.

The arrangement with Kitty Golden is to meet at the doors of the dining room, and when Roxy gets there Kitty, in a stunning but very simple black dress and bronze gladiator sandals with wedge heels, is already waiting. 'Sorry, Kitty, I'm not late, am I? How was the cocktail party? Was it fun?'

'The usual. These things follow a formula, this one was just from five to six and the kind of people who show up are a bit jaded and don't stay long, put in an appearance, a bit of jaw-

jaw, haw-haw, and they're on to the next. That's why they're scheduled for just an hour or an hour and a half. It's a courtesy thing, really. Anyway, I've just got here. Where shall we go? I'm a bit tired, jet-lagged still. I didn't sleep all that well and we were traipsing around Nice today so I think I'm due a well-stirred Manhattan. Something alcoholic anyway.'

'I'm sticking with the water for now. Looking at you, Kitty, I feel ashamed of myself and my blubber.'

'Oh, for goodness' sake, Roxy. You're not fat! Anything but.'

'I'm looking at you, Kitty.'

'It's the greyhound blood.'

'It's lovely by that indoor pool. I was there this afternoon, comfortable chairs as well as the loungers, and with everyone getting ready for dinner now, we'll probably have it to ourselves.'

'Lead the way.'

When they get there, Roxy's forecast proves accurate: the pool area is empty. 'There's a bar right through those end doors.' She leaves her wrap on a table to reserve it and a couple of minutes afterwards they're at the bar.

'Are you sure you wouldn't like a drink, Roxy?' Kitty says. 'Do you not drink alcohol at all?'

They're standing in front of Steve (from Wales) who is using instinct and experience rather than measures, with bourbon, sweet Cinzano and Fernet Branca.

Roxy knows all about Fernet Branca. Her nan, in Glasgow, always uses it to counter the effects of her granddad's overindulgences of the night before – or for his penance. She's fascinated to see it being used in a real cocktail. 'You know what, Kitty?' Roxy says. 'Thank you. I'll try one of those. I've never had one and it looks terrific!'

'You won't be sorry. But if you are, we can change it.' Kitty nods at Steve, who repeats the process with the bottles and a fresh glass and then, with a flourish, pops a maraschino cherry into both drinks.

A couple of minutes later they're sitting in the covered pool area, sipping. The doors onto the deck outside are open, probably to disperse the humidity, Roxy thinks, and although the temperature is still comfortable enough, it's far cooler than previously and she puts her wrap back on over the thin cotton of her dress.

'That's a wonderful engagement ring.' It's the first time she's had a chance to look closely at Kitty's ring, displayed as it is now against the stem of the cocktail glass. 'Is it an antique?'

'No.' Kitty glances at it. 'One of Saul's jeweller buddies made it for our wedding – I suppose you could say it's a combined wedding and engagement ring. We had a very short engagement, just less than two months, actually. Anyhow, a wedding ring wouldn't fit under it.'

Roxy can't place her tone. Reflective? Serious? She settles on peculiar, making a mental note to put words to it later. The other woman seems, however, to recover from whatever it was that had flashed through her mind as quickly as it had occurred to her. She takes off the ring, holding it out. 'Would you like to try it on? Do the Irish thing of twisting it three times while making a wish?'

'Sure – if you'd trust me not to drop it into the sea. It looks very valuable.'

'Aren't all engagement rings valuable in their own way?'

Roxy parks her half-drunk cocktail beside her to put on the ring but, to her dismay, warm from its owner's finger, it fits only the little finger of her left hand. 'God, you have very thin hands, Kitty!'

'Comes with the territory!' The response is dry. 'One of my first jobs when I went to the States was as a hand model. I hated it but I think the agency was testing my temperament so I was as sweet as pie for the six hours – *six hours*, Roxy – it took them to get their angles and lighting right. I had cramps in my hands and arms all night.'

'Was the shoot for a ring display?'

'No. Fairy Liquid, would you believe? For the close-up at the end of the commercial.'

'Gosh. Isn't it a small world? Those were your hands? My mum used to go round humming that jingle: '. . . *with mild green Fairy Liquid*,' they finish it in unison and then laugh.

'What are we like? But you're far too young to remember that?' Kitty is surprised.

'Me and Mum watch a lot of telly – or we used to until I got so busy. She has emphysema so she doesn't move around a lot. There's always something to watch and we saw it on one of those nostalgia things where they rerun famous ads. We laugh at the hair-dos and the frilly aprons and so on. It's amazing what you do remember, isn't it, Kitty?' Having taken off the ring, Roxy is holding it up, angling it this way and that. 'This is gorgeous. Do you love it?'

'It's a lovely ring. Yes. A Daisy.'

'I can see why it's called that.' She looks again. One very large diamond at the centre is surrounded by a dozen or more others, slightly smaller, but in its own right, she thinks, each would have made a very decent solitaire. To admire it properly she stretches her arm to view it. 'Do you have lots of lovely jewellery?'

'I have some, yes. It's a bit of a waste – most of the good pieces spend almost all of their sad lives in a bank deposit box.

Saul is convinced that sooner or later we're going to be burgled. You know,' Kitty laughs, 'I think he buys jewellery for me so he can look at it himself!' She has now relaxed. 'Listen, Roxy,' she opens her beaded bag and withdraws a small, beautifully wrapped package, about six inches by four, 'knowing we were meeting tonight, when I saw this I thought of you.' She puts the package on the table between them. 'Now don't get excited, it isn't jewellery or anything like that, but I think it's beautiful. Have it as a souvenir of Nice, since you couldn't get there today – or as a welcome gift from Saul and me to celebrate your new suite on the *Santa Clara*. I hope you like it.'

'Can I open it?' Roxy, somewhat overwhelmed, puts the Daisy ring on the table and picks up the package.

'Of course!' Kitty smiles. 'It's yours. That's what it's for!'

Inside the wrappings she finds a notebook with a delicate silver filigree clasp, bound in shimmering white silk, verging also on silver. 'It's moiré, watered silk,' Kitty explains, 'and when you open it, the writing paper inside is also handmade. It's for your really special, *special* notes, and to wish you luck with your new novel. They had a leather one, which might have been a bit more practical, certainly easier to keep clean, but I don't do leather, I'm afraid.'

'It's wonderful,' Roxy says, feeling this is inadequate. 'I mean it, Kitty. I've never seen anything as lovely.' *Can it get any better?* she's thinking for the umpteenth time, landing herself a suite, and now this?

'Thank you so much.' She gets up from her seat to give the woman a hug, but is stopped in her tracks. 'Jesus! Look who's coming – it's the Captain – you giving me that notebook, it's a complete omen, Kitty.' Without thinking, she goes to step out into the aisle, but the corner of her wrap catches the ring on the table and sweeps both it and her half-full Manhattan glass onto the terrazza, still damp from condensation and wet feet. The glass smashes while the ring hops then skids a little towards the pool, dangerously so.

Captain Leifsson, seeing what's happening, speeds up and gets to it before Roxy, frozen with horror, can move. Gingerly, feet crunching on the glass, he retrieves the ring from the edge of the pool, then presses a pager on his belt. 'This is yours, I believe, Mrs Abelson?' he asks, handing the ring to her. 'And please,' he says then to Roxy, 'be seated again and don't touch the table. There may be tiny splinters you can't see easily with the naked eye. What was in the glass?'

'A Manhattan,' Roxy says feebly, 'but please don't . . .'

'A Manhattan it is. You have good taste. I've called for help, which will be here immediately. Your drink will be refreshed and the staff will tell you when it's safe to move again. Apart from accidents, I hope you are having a good time? Were you reunited with your wallet, by the way?'

He thinks I'm the biggest klutz in the world. Roxy is newly mortified. 'Thank you,' she says. 'I did. Your staff are wonderful down there.'

'We aim to please.' He glances out towards the deck, where two members of the housekeeping staff are rushing towards the open doors with brooms, dustpans and other cleaning stuff. 'Ah. The cavalry has arrived.' He smiles.

Roxy feels sick. She had planned to buttonhole him for an interview but, given present circumstances, this would now be inappropriate. 'Thank you so much, Captain.' In her own ears, her voice still sounds faint.

'Well, good evening, ladies. I'm due on the bridge. We're about to depart.'

'Can I watch? Not now, of course, Captain,' Roxy adds hurriedly. 'Just sometime?'

'We'll see what we can do.' He smiles again, then: 'How about you, Mrs Abelson? But I'm sure you and your husband have been before?'

'I'd love to,' Kitty says quietly, and Roxy notices she's having some difficulty, it seems, getting her ring back on the correct finger.

Heightening Roxy's embarrassment, the two men who arrive to clean up are the two, Dilip and Angelo, to whom she initially gave such a frosty reception when they'd come to move her from room to room. Both, she sees, recognise her but don't betray anything as the captain, speaking quietly, asks them to get a replacement drink for Roxy, adding, 'When you're done here, of course.'

Then: 'I must leave you, ladies. As I've said, I have to be on the bridge to prepare for departure. Theoretically we can go when we like since we're not docked, but we have a time slot to leave port and the French are a little particular that we keep to it.' He smiles at them, but as he takes a step away from where he's been standing, his foot crunches on a shard, invisible against the mosaic. 'I'm making things worse, it seems, so I must wait a little. Allow me to sit for a minute or so, please?' And, as the two cleaners bustle about, treading slowly and cautiously, he goes to the empty chair beside Roxy's and seats himself.

For a few moments, all that can be heard is the gurgling of the two poolside Jacuzzis and the sound of glass being swept. 'Isn't it amazing how widely the pieces from one little cocktail glass can spread?' The captain is speaking apparently to no one in particular, his gaze glued to the work ongoing around them.

And nobody answers, Roxy because she's so embarrassed. She glances sideways at the other woman, who seems to find the work of the two young men absolutely fascinating. Maybe she's embarrassed on Roxy's behalf.

For whatever reason, an odd haze of tension seems to have descended on the group. The two staffers are working in silence, Kitty has barely opened her mouth since the captain's arrival, and as for Roxy, what an idiot she must seem to this man. First the wallet and now this. Her tongue has tied itself to the floor of her mouth.

But after enduring this weird atmosphere for what seems like minutes, but may have been mere seconds, she manages to untie it sufficiently to murmur an even worse idiocy: 'Yes, it sure is.' Then she manages to retrieve a little of her mojo. 'Now that you're here, Captain, I wonder if I could ask you a favour, please.'

His head snaps towards her: 'Yes?' It's a holding response, not an invitation to treat.

'I'm actually writing an article about the ship for a newspaper and I'm wondering if sometime, not now because you're so busy, you could give me five or ten minutes, at your convenience, for an interview?'

'I wasn't made aware there was a journalist on board. I was told you were researching a book.'

'Yes, I am, and that's absolutely my priority,' Roxy stumbles on, 'but I'm also a freelance journalist. I'm on the level, Captain, and I'm not the kind who picks holes in everything. This is for a travel supplement.'

'About the *Santa Clara*?' The officer raises his eyebrows. 'What newspaper is this?'

'I've been in touch with the travel editor of the London *Times* in London – it's about to start publishing an Irish edition and I'm based in Dublin.' Roxy is already feeling braver. This guy is the captain of a big ship but he puts his trousers on one leg at a time like every other man. 'They're definitely interested,' she adds, defying her mother's admonition at the back of her brain: You're making things up again, you're exaggerating, Rox!'

'Even though this vessel will be scrapped by the time your article is published?' Leifsson's tone is civil but disbelieving.

'The piece is about cruising in general.' Roxy hopes she'd sounded earnest and that he hasn't noticed her miss a beat. 'I can give you my card – although I don't have one with me now.' She had taken the precaution of having a hundred Bizquip cards printed before she left. 'Do you have yours on you, Kitty?' By staring hard at Kitty, she's signalling her to play along, and Kitty, thankfully, while keeping a straight face, gets it.

'Unfortunately not, Roxy. Sorry.'

'Frank will vouch for me – the cruise director, I mean,' the other woman rushes on.

'Well, if Frank thinks you're okay.' Leifsson's mouth twitches, then: 'Five minutes it will be, maximum ten, but, as you say, not now.' He indicates the two workers, one of whom, holding the dustpan, is now carefully pacing a wide half-circle around the table while the other, bent double, is eyeballing the edge of the pool, walking slowly along it, dropping to his knees every so often to peer into the water.

'All clear, fellows?' Leifsson stands up.

'Can I have a selfie before you go?' Roxy stands too.

'Certainly, but please be quick.'

'Here we go.' Roxy picks up her mobile. 'How about you, Kitty? Do you want to stand in too?'

'You go ahead, Roxy. We don't want to delay the captain.'

'Okay.' Roxy cuddles in as much as the man will allow – he's standing stiffly, she thinks, but as she holds up the little screen, he does smile. She clicks. 'Thanks a million. I'll treasure that.'

'I'll be in touch about your interview.' He detaches himself. 'We'll see what we can do.' This time, Leifsson's smile is resigned, rather wry, and Roxy exults. She's home and dry. He turns then to Kitty and, rather casually, Roxy thinks, considering the woman is a Portlandis board director's wife: 'How about you, Mrs Abelson? Would you two ladies like to visit the bridge together?'

'That would be lovely, if it's OK with Roxy? She's the one doing the feature.'

'Fine. Of course, Kitty, that'd be great.' But Roxy is a teeny bit disappointed. She had seen herself as the sole object of the dreamboat's attention up on the bridge.

Is it a real bridge over the whole boat? She must check to see if you can tell from the deck. Even google it to know what to expect before she gets up there so she won't make a complete muppet of herself.

'I look forward to it.' Then, again with that practised inclination of the head, the captain goes off, leaving Roxy, looking after him, to breathe again. He's old enough to be her father, she knows, but, God, he's scrumptious. Still gazing after him, she asks Kitty if she knows anything about his personal circumstances. 'Like, he has to be married? Would Saul know? Could you ask him?'

'If I get the right opportunity. He mightn't know, of course.'

'We'll do this again, Roxy.' Kitty stands, just as Dilip returns and, with a smile, hands Roxy the fresh glass. 'Enjoy, madam,' he says, with a wink, as though she and he are co-conspirators in some happy but under-the-radar scheme.

'I'm actually hungry now.' Kitty sounds preoccupied. 'I need to freshen up a little before dinner. I'm sure you do too.

'I'm hungry too,' Roxy says. 'Is it awful, on the food side, having to watch what you're eating, especially here? I had a huge lunch. The food is irresistible when it's all laid out in front of you, like in the Sail Away café or whatever it's called.'

'You get used to it.' Kitty is moving away, leaving Roxy with little option but to follow, unless she wants to sit down alone by the deserted pool.

But as they leave the pool area to go to the atrium, base camp for the lifts, she is chalking one up to her mum. She sure was right to warn her about all the food. It is non-stop. *And guess what, Mum, a hot Scandi captain to boot.* This is major. She'll hold off saying it, though, because her mum would run away with it. Better wait at least until they know whether the man is married or not. But she can tell Ruth! Hopefully she'll get another selfie on the bridge. And there's Wolfgang as well. God, any woman would be spoiled for choice on this ship, or at least for fantasy. It's not as though she hasn't a chance. A few pounds to lose, for sure, but at her age that's a doddle.

She reckons that the captain is about forty-five. A twenty-two-year age gap isn't all that big a deal as age gaps go, is it? Look at Rupert Murdoch and Jerry Hall!

*

Meanwhile, on their way to the lifts, as Kitty paces quietly beside the younger woman, who is clutching her fresh Manhattan, she is thinking that Roxy must never know that her response to the question about the captain's marital status had been ambiguous if not downright misleading. Kitty already knows from her husband that Einar Leifsson is a widower.

13

Charles is sitting with his friend, Frank, the cruise director, on the pool deck. They are at a drinks table just in front of the hi-fi and speakers (thankfully, now silent and unblinking).

It's late morning on day three, and the meeting is not by appointment: the two had bumped into one another as Frank was on a tour of quasi-inspection and Charles was taking the air before going down to the ballroom to set out his stall for the first class of his acting course.

The *Santa Clara*, now docked in Livorno, is quiet, largely deserted by most of the passengers, who have gone ashore to take advantage of another calm, sunny day. On board, it's warm in her more sheltered nooks, bringing out a few swimmers and sunbathers. In front of the two men, on a single line of sun loungers a few dozen guests, faces held to the sun, have tucked themselves in against the windward side of the glass wall surrounding the fringes of the pool and the water slide. Some are swaddled, only heads and hands showing. Others, the more intrepid, are wearing T-shirts and shorts.

Livorno is billed in the bumf as a jumping-off point for excursions to Florence and its hinterland, Siena, the shopping outlets in Pisa and the ancient town of Lucca, its fully intact city walls, dating from the Renaissance, being a sight to behold. Charles has visited them more than once.

According to his friend, by far the most popular excursion booked by the *Clara*'s guests today has been to the UNESCO Heritage Site of Cinque Terre. Charles is not surprised: he had taken that jaunt two years ago and the cliff walk linking the five villages had been extraordinary, with, above it, village houses, row on top of row, clinging to the slopes over the blue, blue Ligurian Sea far below.

Cars from the outside aren't allowed to enter the territory, the villages are linked only by trains, boats and that precipitous pathway, billed as one of the most scenic in the world. Walkers are, however, warned of rock falls (although it is safe, with rock nets much in evidence) and where you seem sometimes to be walking in the sky. By deliberately tuning out the chatter, snapping and device-pinging of your fellow tourists traversing the route at various speeds, you can use your imagination to time-travel back to medieval times. Charles had done so, inserting the earbuds of his iPod, tuned to Sir Neville Marriner's *The Art of Fugue* with the Academy of St Martin in the Fields, and let Shakespeare's medieval scene-setting direct his steps.

'It'd be lovely today,' Frank goes on, 'but you watch, some of 'em will come back with hair-raising stories of almost tumbling off the cliff, or having to dodge a falling boulder. There was that horrible landslide back in 2011, but unless something extraordinary happens with the weather today, that walk is a jog in the park. But you'll see. The human brain is very good at exaggeration, but who am I telling, eh?'

Charles, gloomy, is barely listening. 'Doubt I'll get much business today, Frank. The ship is empty. There's only one signed on, maybe two,' he's thinking of his invitation to Roxy Smith, 'but only one definite. I'm betting she's an octogenarian with no English! Mind you,' he makes an effort to sound perkier, 'could be Maggie Smith or Angela Lansbury, in which case I'd have to pull my socks up. Either of 'em on board to your knowledge, Frank?'

'Even if they were, my lips are sealed.' The other man grins. 'Anyway, why would they want to take a class?'

'That was a joke.' But Charles is still fretting. 'This one has signed in as J. Merriweather. Ring any bells?'

'Don't think so. Not marked as anyone special anyway. I think I'd have been notified,' his friend says drily. 'You know, Chuck, sometimes I don't get you. Cheer up, eh? There's a few about – they'll get bored sitting around doing nothing, and you can tell anyone who does turn up that it's a lucky day. Individual attention and all that. But what do you care anyway? You'll get your fee, it's your last trip, you'll never see any of these people again.'

'That's the point. I'd like this final outing to be one to remember. I'd hate to be written off by Portlandis as a dud hire, a failure.'

'Sorry to give you the bad news, old chap, but Portlandis won't remember a single one of us on this ship. Maybe the captain, but I don't know what the plans are for him, or indeed what he wants. Trust me. We're toast, as the Americans say, forgotten but not gone. We're little blips on an enormous radar, and when poor old *Clara* steams off to face her fate, our particular set of little blips will be extinguished with the press of a computer key.'

'Yours won't. You're going to Miami.'

'Yes, I am. But the day's not far away when I'm surplus to requirements or there's some shiny new thirty-year-old on the radar and his blip will override mine. The world turns, Chuck. We can't stop it.'

'You're right, of course you are. You always are, Frank. Sorry if I'm a bit glum today.' Charles shakes his shoulders as though shrugging off a heavy coat, then straightens them. 'All right, it's heigh-ho, just carry on as normal and pretend I'm playing to a full house. And, yes, whoever does turn up will get my full attention.'

'I'll rev the desk. Get them to sell you when people come up for exchange rates, or to book something, anything. I saw Wolfgang Becker's on today and he can sell anything.'

'Even me?'

'Oh, for God's sake, Charlie. Get a grip! You turn up, that's the main thing. It's not your fault if they don't get what a privilege they're being offered.'

Charles looks keenly at his friend. Sometimes he doesn't know whether or not Frank is sending him up – but the other man's expression is bland. 'Sorry, Frank,' he says. 'I know I shouldn't get so het up. To Hell with reputations.'

'Good lad.' Frank glances at his watch. 'Duty calls, I'm afraid. For the poor cruise director it's not all schmoozing with passengers, cocktails and cronies like you. There's an awful lot of administration – paperwork, travel logs, scheduling. It makes my head spin. Right now there's a woman down in the medical area. She's sprained her ankle and says it's our fault. And, by the way, you and your nerves are in good company today. It must be something in the water because there's a very jumpy ventriloquist down there on the stage. Like you, he's worried that nobody will show up for his peerless performance this evening and he's taking it out on the sparks, giving the poor guy a hard time, feels our sound system isn't up to scratch. You think you're nervous? I am too. All this going on, and this is only the little *Clara*. I hope I haven't bitten off more than I can chew by moving to Miami and working on something four times the size of this. Have to run. We'll talk again.'

'Thanks, Frank. I feel better. Sorry for unloading.'

'Think nothing of it. What are friends for, eh? Why don't you go to the spa for an hour? I can talk to Marnie – she can't be busy with everyone gone ashore. You've plenty of time to have a massage or a face mask or whatever.'

Although he knows his friend means well, Charles, feeling a little patronised now, demurs: 'Thanks, and I know it's still early, but I'll just get straight to prep in the ballroom. I do have a good bit to do for this afternoon. Even if it will be for only one person.'

'Good lad. Chin up!' Frank pats him on the shoulder. Charles watches him go, but looking at the line of sunbathers, all of whom seem perfectly contented, his gloom again descends. In his present mood, he feels more than ever that, in success terms, his achievements during his allotted lifespan on this planet have been found miserably wanting. Why haven't some of these people signed up? All he needs is eight of them, for God's sake – he sees them as a long row of silent jurists, who have found him not worth the price of anything above what they've paid for their cruise.

Perhaps it's his impending forced retirement, *Book at Bedtime* notwithstanding, or maybe it's having had interesting company at dinner for the past two nights. It's left him ultra-aware of how shorn of companionship his life will be when he's back in London.

Most likely, though, he feels empty and sad because his insignificance in the grand scheme of things has at last fully dawned. While in public he goes about pretending he's a happy chappy, the uncaring world continues relentlessly to turn, regardless of his moods or fears, shrugging him off as though he's a fly. A 'blip'.

Yes, he has the roof over his head, and thank God for it, but what else? Who else? His loneliness, the loneliness of an old man, is particularly sharp today, and as he walks away from the pool in the direction of the ballroom to set up his class, he's wondering where Maggie is, what she's doing, whom she's with now.

The way he found out his wife was leaving him after decades of marriage had been bizarre by any measure. On coming home from tour a day early, while she was still at work, he'd gone upstairs to unpack his suitcase and found the bed pristine, pillows plumped, coverlet pulled tight, hotel-style, and when, at first merely piqued with curiosity, he had pulled it back, he'd found the bed dressed with fresh linens, sheets tucked under with hospital corners.

Hospital corners?

He and his wife were perfunctory bedmakers. Sometimes whoever got out of bed last pulled up the covers without straightening them, not even bothering to puff the pillows. 'What's the point?' Maggie had always said. 'They're just going to be all messed up again in a few hours.'

Their charlady was not due until the following day and making beds was not her forte either.

Charles hated conflict and confrontation in any sphere of

life, to the extent that many times, rather than disagree, he had given way to what other actors would have regarded as bullying by a tyrant director. Privately and sadly, he acknowledged that this trait had probably impeded his career: the temperamental, explosive types got more attention. Of course they were entitled to it because they were obviously more talented than he— *Oh, shut up, Charles!* He gives himself a virtual kick as he leaves the pool deck and goes inside. Like Frank had said, *Get a grip!*

That day, he'd had time to think out a strategy before Maggie was due home from work at tea-time, but he couldn't get his brain to work properly. Afflicted with actors' imagination, his brain wouldn't operate in straight lines but, like an ancient zoetrope, spun successions of still images, flicking one after the other in quick rotation to produce the illusion of moving pictures, including some that were very disturbing: Maggie's mouth open as she screamed in orgasm, a sound he had never heard even when they had initially got together. The two of them laughing at Charles's sexual ineptitude, and quipping merrily while he shows her the finer points of bedmaking.

Charles had dashed to the washing machine, but it was empty, and upstairs on the landing, the airing cupboard was as neat as it always was, sheets and pillowcases innocently folded and stacked in tidy white piles. They'd been careful not to make any silly mistakes.

Except for those hospital corners.

When he heard her key turn in the lock he had tackled her immediately, springing up from 'his' chair in the sitting room and going into the hall to intercept her, breaking into her surprised 'Hello, darling, didn't expect you until tomorrow?' with his 'You didn't make that bed upstairs. You're having an affair.'

After a fraction of a beat, so fast that, if he hadn't been so alert and watchful he'd have missed it, she'd laughed and with a sturdy 'What are you on about now, Charles? I'm worried about you these days,' she'd turned her back to shake rain off her umbrella into the porch. Every time he thought over this scene, which he did frequently because there was a chance that if he hadn't been so hasty in challenging her the affair might have run its course, he always had to admire her aplomb.

At the time, however, he had persisted, but so had she, scoffing at him over her shoulder while closing the door and shrugging off her mackintosh to hang it on the mirrored hallstand. 'You've lost it, Charles.' Looking at her reflection and patting her hair into place. 'You know what? I'm going to make a doctor's appointment for you tomorrow morning, if there's one available. You're muddled. Fantasising. You clearly need a brain test so at least we can know where we stand.'

But Charles had found reserves of anger and passion he hadn't known were in him, those of a man much younger and more impetuous than he. His marriage had been sexless for years, he had believed by mutual consent (although they had never discussed it, sex had merely faded away), but over the next couple of days he'd been stunned by the depth of his agitation at the thought of Maggie with another man.

Up to then he had thought his only concern about his marriage was which of them would die first, leaving the other to cope. For his part, he'd been working as hard as he could, accepting cameos, one-liners and even humiliating himself with walk-ons on TV soaps so as to salt away at least a little money to tide her over before her pension kicked in, should he go before her. He had no pension, of course, so if she went first, he'd have to move in with his mother, if she was still alive, because the house he and Maggie shared was rented.

Although he felt slightly guilty about it, he continued to use a tailor and shoemaker because to him they provided his work attire. These days actors came scruffy to rehearsals. Charles didn't care how antediluvian he seemed, with his well-pressed slacks and tweed jackets: he had standards to maintain. But he denied himself luxuries, such as a decent watch, insisting that all he needed was something that told the time and that the old Timex on his wrist, which he hated, was perfectly good and never lost a second. He didn't smoke, drank very little (the *Clara* gigs, where the wine flowed, were much appreciated on that score, as were the perks of trips ashore), took no trips abroad, other than in conjunction with the *Clara*, and didn't squander on eating out.

The list of what he had denied himself – and Maggie, in some cases – was long. How stupid did that seem now? His brain, rapidly turning over and over, like a highly tuned engine, tortured him during those nights when he lay awake in their spare room.

He'd pestered her as those first fraught days had played themselves out: 'Who is he? How long has this been going on? Stop denying it, just tell me the truth, that's all I ask!' She, at first puzzled by a side of him she'd never seen before, but then increasingly irritated, denied, denied, denied, calling him a blithering old man, accusing him again and again of being a fantasist, swearing his behaviour was so bad she couldn't stand it. 'You're driving me out of the door, Charles. Do you know that?'

By day four of this, exhausted, they ran out of vitriol. It had been the first and only fight of this depth and bitterness during their long time together.

That observational third eye, with which Charles always

watched his own behaviour as well as that of others, had been operational throughout and he'd been astonished at some of the words he had used. She had excelled too. He had always thought of her as settled and contented, a sort of mother hen who looked after their home and him, whose companionship was as dependable as her fidelity. He had never questioned the latter.

By the afternoon of day four they were both limp, bereft of anything further to say, but now the silence between them was poisoned as each sat in the chairs they had always jokingly referred to as his 'n' hers. He had been so heedless, so *smug*, he'd thought forlornly. It had never occurred to him that she might stray. He realised now that the break-up of a marriage takes two people: his fault was that he had never seen her as separate from theirs.

In a very weird way, despite his hurt and despair, now that she was about to leave him, his respect for her strength, for a fighting spirit he had been too blind to see, had grown. When one thought of it in football parlance, neither had left anything on the field after this fight, which, instinctively, he knew was terminal. If he had surprised himself, she had matched him insult for insult and there was no going back.

It was a Sunday, and at about a quarter to five, hating what had become of them, of him, Charles turned on *Songs of Praise*, which, when he was at home, they had always watched together. That afternoon's broadcast, apparently, had been a special one. He had cut into it just as the congregation, so harmonious and perfectly in tune they must consist of pre-selected choirs, was singing 'Nearer, My God, to Thee' accompanied by a single sweet-toned violin played by an old man while a picture of a lighthouse, assailed by a storm, slowly faded from its superimposition on the faces of some of the participants. The programme, he thought, had evidently been recorded in some seaside place.

Or had it something to do with the *Titanic*? 'Nearer, My God' was popularly believed to have been played on her deck by the ship's band of valiant, even heroic musicians until, right at the end, still playing, they had gone down with her.

The emotional trigger of music is potent in any case and he'd always found the old hymn particularly so, causing his eyes to prick, especially when it was sung at funerals. But on that afternoon, to his horror, weakened by the four-day storm of his own, whatever equanimity he had left finally caved in and he had erupted in tears, sobbing, bent double, nose streaming, foam collecting at the corners of his mouth.

Oblivious, the choir sang on:

> *Though like the wanderer, the sun gone down,*
> *Darkness be over me, my rest a stone;*
> *Yet in my dreams I'd be nearer, my God, to Thee.*

Quickly, she was over to him, climbing onto his lap, throwing her arms around his neck, pulling him into her while he spoke incoherent words into her shoulder, words, words, words. He didn't know what he was saying.

'Sssh, sssh.' She'd rocked him. 'Oh, my dear Charles, sssh, my darling, sssh, don't cry . . . I can't stand it, don't break my heart . . .' But there was no consoling him while the choir sang their hearts out and the violinist drew sorrow from his instrument:

> *Then, with my waking thoughts bright with Thy praise,*
> *Out of my stony griefs Bethel I'll raise;*
> *So by my woes to be nearer, my God, to Thee.*

He broke away, roughly thrusting her off his lap, groping for the remote. 'I'm sorry. I'm sorry, Maggie, I don't know what came over me. Please forgive me.' He'd found the control and turned off the TV, not knowing for what he was apologising. For weeping? For being semi-violent with her in getting her off his knees?

She was standing in front of him, tears in her own eyes and clearly perplexed as to what to do next. Had he hurt her? 'Of course I forgive you,' she'd said quietly. 'But forgive you for what, Charles? For being human? There's nothing to forgive.'

She made as though to approach him again but, hiccuping painfully, he put out a hand to impede her. 'Excuse me for a moment, please.' Still hiccuping, he bolted for the cloakroom off the hall. In there he snatched length after length of toilet roll from its holder so the cardboard core spun, unleashing swathes, paper pooling on the tiled floor. He tore it off, took a fistful and swabbed his face, eyes, mouth, nose, even the lapels of his jacket, which, he saw in the mirror over the washbasin, bore snail-trails of mucus.

Tears subsiding, he stood for a while gazing at the wreckage of his face, until, having recovered sufficiently to tidy up the mess of paper on the floor, blow his nose in it, throw it into the toilet bowl and, not caring if he blocked the system, flush, then watch as the water rose right to the rim, slowly sank and vanished, taking the paper mess with it.

Unsteadily, he went back into the sitting room. She was standing at the window nets, staring through them into the street. Hearing him come in, she turned around, eyes wide, shoulders straight. 'All right. Sit down, Charles. Let me tell you. Let's talk like civilised people ...'

And by the end of the ten minutes following, whatever

smidgen of hope he'd had left that this was a nightmare from which they could recover had been dashed and Charles's domestic world had burned to ashes.

Right now, in the *Santa Clara*'s atrium, bound for her theatre with the unwinking glare of the winter sun over Italy generating little rainbows in the bevelled glass of the lifts, why, he wonders, had all that come into his head?

Not unusual. Dormant for most of the time, the scenes around the break-up of his marriage flared into vivid life now and then and this was just one of the nows. Probably because he's feeling so defeated.

Maggie's lover, it turned out, had been a lieutenant colonel in the British Army's Nursing Corps and had recently retired at the age of fifty. The pair had met randomly when, having visited the HMS *Belfast* on the Thames, each had separately taken the recommendation of their guide to go for a coffee in the café-bar, the Upper Deck, because it offers a panoramic view of Tower Bridge, the Tower of London and the bulbous glass bulk of City Hall.

'May I sit here, please?' Without waiting for a response, the lover who would displace Charles had taken a vacant seat on one of the picnic-style benches at Maggie's table. She had introduced herself.

'And from then on,' Maggie had said quietly to her husband on that awful day, 'we both just knew.'

Her name, his wife told him, was Leonie. 'If you want to know what she looks like – you seem to want details, Charles – this is her.' She'd gone to her handbag, taken out her wallet and pulled a small colour snapshot from one of the compartments. Because he was insane at that point, he thought later, Charles took it. Smiling up at him was a woman, undoubtedly in her fifties, with curly dark hair in corn rows, large brown eyes, and lips outlined with bright red lipstick. 'Yes,' said Maggie. 'Before you ask, she's Jamaican. And I love her. I'm sorry, Charles, I really am. I didn't ask for this – I never thought it would happen to us, you and me. I can't say how sorry I am that it did. But it did, I love her and I have to be with her.'

Just before he reaches the doors of the *Clara's* theatre, he goes out onto the deck to take a last breath of fresh air. And as though to highlight his sense of nothingness, a truck draws up alongside the ship, disgorging a group of very young musicians onto the pier. Tousled, bleary-eyed from God knows what, they're chatting and joshing each other in high good humour. The two boys first out are carrying cheap canvas guitar cases, the girl bears a sax, while two older men wrest a drum kit from the bowels of the vehicle. Clearly the band hired to add background or to play support to tonight's ventriloquist, probably thinking it's just a step towards world domination in music. The girl with the sax case is petite, long hair piled messily, beehive high, on top of her head, as though to give her height.

In his current mood he can't bear the sights and sounds of their communal good cheer and obvious optimism so he steps quickly away from the rail, away from the brightness, to go back inside.

Once in the sanctuary and quiet of the ballroom, at present lit only by working lights, the overhead glitter ball hanging motionless and looking a little tawdry, the old black magic of theatre casts its soothing spell, all-enveloping after the brightness of the sun and reflective water outside.

When working in the old days, it had always been Charles's habit to get to the theatre in late afternoon, to sit in the stalls in a row halfway down from the back wall, when the sets were ready to receive the play and no one was there except himself. In those seats you could sense the ghost voices of actors, directors, lighting, sound, rigging and technical crews across the generations. You could feel jiggery anticipation flowing throughout the audience avid for mystery, enjoyment and suspense of disbelief, knowing that anything might happen.

On his side of the curtain later, with the stage manager's 'Five-minute call, please,' on the backstage Tannoy, there came a sharpening of tension in the dressing rooms with 'Beginners, please,' shortly afterwards, bringing those in the first scene to their marks onstage.

Most stomach-churning of all, in a good way, was the SM's 'Houselights, please,' the auditorium darkening, a tide of hush spreading across it and the curtain swishing away as the stage lights clunked on.

Nowadays, of course, there is rarely a curtain.

Charles misses it all dreadfully, while readily admitting he's a relic, an old fart, a duffer, a throwback, a dinosaur, one of those annoying old thespians who chunters on about footlights and the day Ellen Terry showed him how to own his space on stage.

All around him now, everyone is a 'theatre worker' in the 'performance space'; everyone, front or backstage is 'making theatre' and plays are 'made' instead of written by a playwright. Even the *Clara*'s ballroom would probably, in certain quarters, be referred to as a 'found space'. He's sick of this.

But he's had to accept that one showing of a *Harry Potter* or *Pirates of the Caribbean* franchise (ugh! He hates that word) will be seen by countless millions all over the world in one week, whereas a Shakespeare play in Stratford, however brilliantly acted or staged, could not match these figures over ten generations of a typical audience. The same holds true even for a musical in the West End or on Broadway.

He has learned to keep his mouth shut about all of this: nothing more boring to people than an old fogey pontificating about 'the old days' so he tries, when in company with non-theatre 'workers' (ugh!), such as those he gets to know here on the *Clara*, to confine his personal anecdotes to disasters he's experienced, like sets falling down, or the shenanigans of a drunken director. He also limits his name-dropping, mentioning only the very famous colleagues with whom he has worked or socialised, however briefly or humbly: Sir John Gielgud, Judi Dench, Maggie Smith, Helen Mirren, Sinéad Cusack, even Richard Harris, with all of whom he can legitimately say he is or was acquainted. He had run into Harris during the period the Irish actor had lived in a suite at the Savoy in London while, having just completed *The Field* for which he was Oscar-nominated, he was starring onstage at Wyndham's in Pirandello's *Henry IV*.

For two glorious hours in the early afternoon Charles, who had dropped into the hotel lobby merely to get out of the rain and have a cup of tea, had found himself gathered into a Harris entourage that seemed to gravitate towards the star wherever he was. He had found the man to be doggedly opinionated and argumentative, yes, but supremely intelligent and entertaining, the antithesis of the public image in which he seemed to take such delight.

One of the traits Charles had most admired in him that afternoon had been his egalitarianism: he treated everyone, waiter, barman, fan and Charles, who had seen the Pirandello – Harris had given a towering performance – with the same courtesy and interest.

He sighs as he sets out nine of the ballroom's spindly gilded chairs, eight in a semi-circle, the ninth, for himself, facing them. Despite his forebodings that only the mysterious J. Merriweather would show up, he had to be professional about this and carry on as normal.

He has always limited his student numbers to eight because each deserves equal airtime and, in any case, Frank had insisted that Portlandis's marketing department puff up his classes as 'exclusive and individual attention from a master-actor'.

He checks the Timex. Still twenty minutes to go, before the Mysterious J. Merriweather, as he now thinks of him or her, arrives, if he or she is punctual and turns up at all.

With no one to tell him to bloody cheer up, he sighs again as he sits in his chair, facing his empty semi-circle, to wait.

Wouldn't it be great if Kitty Golden, or even Roxy, were to appear? That might be a bit of fun.

Except for being enclosed in a taxi with the odious Saul, the trip to Nice the day before had been quite a good outing, with crisp, bright weather and a chance to partake in the actors' pastime, pavement observation, particularly enjoyable in France: the self-possession, the careless glamour, self-confident gait, the glances (supercilious, curious, flirtatious, 'get-out-of-my-way, Tourist!'), the distance between people ostensibly walking together; the women bearing 'handbag dogs' with ball-bearing eyes yapping self-importantly at indifferent Rottweilers and Alsatians under café tables.

And, in the outside air, the smell of Gitanes, which you don't get any more in Britain.

He's intrigued by the relationship between Saul and his lovely wife. He had liked her instantly: his actor's radar detected at the dinner table and again during the Nice lunch that underneath her quiet, even demure mien there exists a very different woman.

He's seen this phenomenon many times before: an extraordinarily beautiful, intelligent, but inexplicably submissive wife or girlfriend in a relationship with a domineering male. He has watched as many bright, attractive, witty actresses (oops! theatre workers!), full of fun at break time during rehearsals, the life and soul of an after-party, become quiet and reticent when their husbands or boyfriends join the company.

Women are psychologically impenetrable, he's decided, and he should know, having lived with one for decades and never for a second having detected her true nature and sexuality.

The Taming of the Shrew represents only half of the story because even Katherine eventually submits. The behaviour of women . . . You take your life in your hands when you marry one. He has often wondered if it has to do with biology. An ancient stone-age throwback to do with provider and provided-for, both comfortable in their respective roles?

As for Barry Lee and his partner, what about them? A mismatch if ever Charles saw one and a very interesting one, in many ways a reversal of usual roles, with youth dominating age for reasons glaringly apparent. He has been long enough around the gay community to recognise the Barry/Joshua thing for what it is, an older man blown away by the physical beauty of the younger and desperate to hold on to him, while the younger, more powerful entity in the relationship, by virtue of the elder's passion, sees himself as merely passing through.

Charles isn't sufficiently catty to see Joshua's treatment of Barry as venal and exploitative – he's probably too young to be that calculating and is merely, in his own eyes, living each day as it comes: today it's Barry, but who'll drop into his life tonight?

The table sittings on the *Clara* are a lottery. Even if his have always been benignly mediated by Frank, his chum can't divine, simply by perusal of a factual passenger manifest, an individual's or couple's emotional provenance. This gathering, while not exceptional by any means, does rate as one of the more interesting.

Roxy is great company. If he'd ever had a daughter, he'd have loved her to be like this girl, who plays younger than she is, he thinks. But, then, he's so far away from dealing directly with modern young women he could be as wrong about that as he was about Maggie. At twenty-three, however, he had already graduated from drama school, and his contemporaries, while full of life and enjoyment, were also singularly hell-bent on their careers.

Roxy talks that way but he feels she may need a few more years on the clock before she settles seriously into the sweatiness and discipline of creative work: Goethe's *Sturm und Drang*, the storm one has to go through to create something worthwhile, the angst that goes with it, and the prodding of the critical will that forces one to delve for the truth in any artistic work.

As for the two Danes, they seem like decent sorts, although they don't participate all that much in the general conversation at table. At present, understandably, they are enclosed in that haze of adoration, when nothing matters except to be in the presence of the beloved.

The *Clara* is quiet enough now for Charles to hear footsteps approaching from outside. J. Merriweather, he thinks, standing to receive his pupil, without, however, his hopes being high. A class needs spurs, of ambition, jealousy and envy, of competition, if it is to be what he considers successful. These people, who are amateurs, should enjoy themselves, but they should also experience the joys and sorrows of acting and get to know and appreciate the effort that goes into the lifelong learning, training, stress and striving to 'fail better' so as to provide a few hours' entertainment for people who sit in the comfortable seats with the wherewithal to pay for them.

He expects nature to overcome reticence in his classes and usually, however much people protest they're there only for fun, by the last session there is always competition.

The feet stop outside the door, as though their owner is checking something, probably the sign advertising the class, Charles thinks. Then, as though pushed forcefully, the ballroom's double doors crash open and: 'Jay Merriweather reporting for duty, *sah!*' Charles's recruit (in his own mind) clicks his heels and gives an approximation of a salute.

To the older man's surprise, this is not the old woman he had half expected. He's Barry's partner and, even at a distance of twenty feet or so, he can see that the young man's upper lip shows traces of blood.

Instantly, having seen this many times, Charles knows that Josh has taken cocaine.

14

Roxy Smith has, sort of, come down to earth. She's at a loose end until six o'clock when she's to meet Gemma and Auntie Mary again to get the full story about the latter. It's still just after half past two, however; the Dunnes, who travel in packs, are evidently all ashore in Livorno or further afield since she could find no trace of them anywhere on board so she could suggest meeting earlier.

She's sitting on the top deck of the *Santa Clara*, starboard side – the lingo is now coming easily – where it's currently sunny enough to open the zipper of her anorak. As far as she can see, theirs is the only liner here.

The view is towards the business side of the harbour, in which small boats chug to and fro across the water, with, on the dock opposite, passenger and ro-ro ferries, along with huge container ships, going about their business on this last Monday before Christmas Day, the following Sunday.

Her notebook, pen and pencil lie idle beside her on her bench seat because she feels she's up to date with her scene-setting notes and transcriptions and, right now, can see nothing of any value to add. At this rate, she thinks sourly, she's so familiar with the layout and facilities of the ship she'd be able to design one herself.

Against all well-meaning advice, including that of Kitty and that gorgeous bloke, Wolfgang whatever behind the reception desk, she had decided to stick to her guns and to go to Ischia from Naples the following day, rather than Pompeii; so, early this morning, soon after the reception desk opened and having organised her queuing so she could deal with Wolfgang rather than his female colleague, she'd been about to make a very large dent in her budget to hand over ninety-eight pounds for the 120-dollar cost of the excursion to Ischia, due back on board at six o'clock for a six thirty departure from Naples. While waiting for her turn in Wolfgang's queue, she'd noticed he has one of those Kirk Douglas cleft chins, which she's always found attractive.

She couldn't help noticing lots of other things about him too: he had a straight nose, his eyes, hazel, were widely spaced, with dark, angular brows, of a type for which women pay fortunes in trendy eyebrow bars. Her first impression having been that he is seriously fit, she had modified that: this guy is very, *very* seriously fit. She can't take her eyes off him.

'Pompeii, isn't it, Ms Smith?' He'd smiled, showing those perfect, even white teeth and Roxy's inner self had cheered. *He remembers me!* 'So what can I do for you this morning?'

Take me to bed!!! the inner self screamed. But she had thanked him politely and then: 'I've decided on Ischia. I'm really looking forward to it. I've been planning it for ages. I don't suppose you'd be willing to give me a short interview?'

'I beg your pardon?'

'Background for my novel. I'm a writer and I'm on board

researching because my story is to be set on a cruise. I'd imagine you and your colleagues have a very interesting and varied job.'

For the first time, he'd seemed put off his game: 'I'd – I'd have to check that with my superior.'

'Of course. You can tell him or her that you wouldn't be identified. I'm just interested in the mechanics of the way things work, from cleaners to captain. I do want to know how a ship like the *Clara* runs so smoothly,' she had said, hoping she was keeping it light but professional; she was also conscious, however, that a little queue was building up behind her, so speeded it up a bit: 'I'll be speaking to as many staff and crew as I can. Including, of course, the captain.'

'I shall check, and if it's accepted, I'll be happy to talk to you, Ms Smith. Your ticket for Ischia, as I'm sure you know, would include a visit to the natural hot springs. We hope to see you again and, don't forget, we're always here.'

It was the 'we' and 'we're' that got to her. It was a bazz-off. 'Bet you say that to all the girls,' she ventured, and was rewarded with a smile, but this time, the teeth were a no-show.

'How much for Ischia?'

'A hundred and twenty dollars. That would be ninety-eight pounds in sterling, Ms Smith – or I can quote in euro if you like?' Only ten dollars less than Pompeii. She'd quailed. 'Look, Wolfgang, could you please call me Roxy? "Ms Smith" makes me sound like a schoolteacher!'

'Of course – Roxy!' He had smiled again. 'Shall I book you for Ischia?'

She had hesitated and he saw it. 'There is another option, Ms Sm— Roxy! The hydrofoil from the port takes one hour each way and costs just under forty euro for the round trip.

That would be approximately thirty-five pounds sterling. You will be without a guide on the island of course – but people do enjoy exploring – and it means you can go as early as you like and come back at any time up to half an hour before departure.'

The man behind Roxy had coughed loudly. 'Thank you, Wolfgang.' Roxy, although reacting to the man's impatience, had not turned around. 'I'll do that. Do you have the hydrofoil tickets?'

'Unfortunately not. You can get them easily at Napoli Port. There is a ticket office.'

She had thanked him and left the desk. *He had remembered her name. And now he's calling her 'Roxy' . . .*

She hates to admit it but other than chatting to this Adonis and gazing at him, she's bored. She could go ashore to Livorno, of course, take a bus somewhere, but she's fed up with her own company, something she'd never imagined could happen when she'd envisaged this cruise.

But once you've walked down a central shopping mall, on which most of the shops are closed until the boat sails again, there's nothing to do except walk back past the same closed premises, the same window displays promising discounts on stuff you still can't afford.

Roxy loves jewellery but today she can't even browse the window of the jeweller's, let alone go inside to drool, because the display shelves are empty, presumably for security reasons. Are they expecting a raid? Difficult to achieve, she'd think, even James Bond-style.

After dinner the previous night she had lingered at that window, its directional lighting activating prisms of colour within diamonds, emeralds, rubies and sapphires while less valuable pearls, citrines, peridots and aquamarines played support in their own exquisite way.

Taking pride of place in the centre of the display, however, had been a large pendant, prominently labelled 'precious opal'. Its surface mixed tropical green and indigo but it offered flashes of red when you moved to see it from different angles, and it had been enhanced by its setter with an oval of diamonds. In vain, she covets it. No prices visible anywhere, of course.

Maybe she'll write about it some day. It could be a wedding gift to a bride from her rich-beyond-Croesus groom on their wedding day. A source of jealousy and division between a pair of sisters, each believing she is entitled to it because of a will in which a mother had specified that her two daughters could choose one piece of her jewellery with the rest to be sold in aid of a dog shelter.

She'd gone inside, just to get an idea of what kind of person might have the money to buy such beauty and found just one customer, whose Slavic cheekbones spoke of her origins, trying on a diamond tennis bracelet. She herself had been approached instantly by a man wearing a spotless blazer: 'May I show you anything, madam? Are you looking for something in particular?' Intimidated, she'd muttered an excuse and retreated.

She watches the rectangular frame of a huge crane move along a track on the quayside opposite, lower its arm to the top of a container and somehow lock on to it before lifting it into the air. How? Maybe with powerful magnets. She picks up the notebook: she'll use Google to find out how this works.

This is the kind of unusual detail that can fascinate readers like herself and her mum, who reads and rereads her stack of Arthur Hailey novels, *Wheels, Hotel, Airport* and the others, all based on meticulous research. 'You feel you're right there with him, Roxy. He tells you how all the systems work in hotels and cars and everything. Reading his books is like taking a university course in whatever subject he's writing about.'

In many ways, Roxy thinks, it's her mum who should have been the writer: she's so interested in stories and storytelling and discovering new facts, even if only from reality TV, like *Judge Judy* or *Grand Designs*.

She sighs. How to fill in the time? Her stomach is still full from lunch, uncomfortably so, and she makes a vow that she has to watch what she's eating if she's not to waddle home.

She could go back to her suite, begin the actual writing, but although it will only be part of a first draft, she's still afraid of starting it.

It's to do with reluctance to commit, fear of that first sentence: as soon as that's down on paper or on screen, choices have been made and options narrow.

Even if you know that a first draft rarely survives in its initial form, with editors advising that your entire first chapter, the one over which you've agonised most and re-written most often, be ditched, it will have a psychological hold over you, like that crane over there has a physical hold on the container it's depositing on the dock opposite . . .

'Oh, God.' She groans. She's losing the plot. Her editor would strike that out as ridiculous, an analogy too far . . .

She'd been late to breakfast this morning and neither the Dunnes nor her own tablemates had been in evidence. That's probably why she's feeling so lethargic. There's been no one with whom to chat. So, what now? She could have more bloody coffee, go to the spa – but that place, like all but the most souvenir-y of shops, was far too expensive for her resources. She could use one of the pools or the Jacuzzis or, like the hard-core sun-worshippers she'd seen on the pool deck, could occupy a lounger.

Although she has her bikini with her she doesn't swim; her mum has warned her not to use Jacuzzis because they're full of horrible viruses; and she gets even more bored lying with her eyes closed on a sunbed. She's been to the small library where she'd found nothing that interested her, except a couple of copies of *Hello!* magazine she'd already read. That visit had been somewhat productive, though, as by pretending she was bringing back a copy of *Heartbreak in the Cotswolds* and openly placing it in the returns bin, she'd managed to get it, she hopes, into circulation. For certain authors, her agent has told her more than once, word of mouth is crucial.

None of the events scheduled for the ship's much diminished crowd on board – bingo, a singalong with Marty in the piano bar, a cocktail-making demonstration, a table-tennis tournament, an archery lesson, a 'Getting Fit with Antonia' session, and certainly not circuits of the jogging track on the upper deck – attracts her today. As for the cinema, it's showing a *Minions* movie.

She could learn 'how to make the perfect cheese soufflé with Chef Andy', but she'd already consumed more food and snacks during the first three days than she normally does in a Dublin or, indeed, a London week.

'Think, Rox!' She's speaking aloud: with no one else in earshot she can talk to herself without feeling stupid. She does so regularly to settle her brain when it's whirring about like a hummingbird, alighting only now and then. Sometimes when you hear words spoken aloud, rather than having them passing for mere nano-seconds through a brain continually offering alternatives, you can clarify things.

'Will you stop faffing around, Roxy Smith!' She's vehement. 'You're seeing too many possibilities and not enough *probabilities*.' She thumps the bench. 'You have to decide. Rule out a few people!'

She could start by telling her brain to draw a line through Wolfgang's name on the roster. That had been an overexcited, too personal distraction. Anyway, as staff, he's probably bound by rules and regulations about not fraternising with guests? He is gorgeous, though . . .

The crane opposite has now deposited its load, raised its arm and is tracking back again to the stack on the patiently waiting container ship.

Enough. No more watching paint dry. She will go back to her suite to seize the moment and write that dreaded first line, *any* first line. By the time she has to meet the Dunnes after dinner this evening, she will have written not just a first line but the whole first page of *Heartbreak on the High Seas*. Only 299 to go then . . .

She stands up and gives herself a little shake. 'Get to work, Roxy Smith. You're a disgrace! Call yourself an author?' Again she has spoken aloud, not realising she has company on the deck. A man and a woman, she in a wheelchair, he pushing it, have emerged onto the deck and, bemused, are staring at her. Roxy picks up her equipment, including her phone, and ostentatiously pushes a few buttons as though turning it off.

'Good afternoon,' she says airily to the couple, as she passes them to go inside. 'Beautiful day, isn't it? Aren't we so lucky with the weather? I can't believe it's only two days to midwinter and the shortest day of the year.'

*

Back in her stateroom, Roxy opens the envelope she'd been given by the Cruise Director whom she'd encountered by chance in the atrium. At least she has this to look forward to tomorrow. 'The very woman!' Frank Mitchell had smiled at her, giving her one of two envelopes he was carrying. 'I was going to Reception to leave this for you, with instructions to deliver it to your stateroom.'

'What's in it?' Roxy hadn't wanted to open it in front of him.

'Apparently you've asked for a visit to the bridge?'

'Yes?' She'd cheered up immediately. 'That's brilliant! When?'

'Tomorrow evening, before dinner. Mrs Abelson has apparently expressed an interest too,' he had indicated the second envelope, 'so obviously I've included her husband. We've arranged for the three of you to be taken up together. I've asked one of the senior receptionists, Wolfgang is his name, to meet you in the atrium in front of Starbucks at about ten past six. He's off duty at six but happy to take you. Barring alarms elsewhere, Captain Leifsson will be on the bridge at the time so you'll be able to ask him questions. Some captains are stuffy and rigid, standing on protocol, but he's not like that so you're in luck, Roxy. He'll explain everything, and you'll see how the local pilot and the officer-of-the-watch negotiate the ship out of port and so on. You'll see computers and it will be explained to you how the ship is steered – it should all be fascinating for someone like you. And Portlandis, one of the premier cruise lines on the Med, is delighted to facilitate you. Happy?'

'Very happy. That's terrific, thank you very much.' But despite her enthusiastic response to his spiel, she couldn't help but think it sounded practised, by rote. The man was a speaking leaflet.

But that was mean, she had decided instantly, taking it back. After all, she does owe him. 'I very much appreciate it, Frank.'

'Having a good time on the *Santa Clara*?' He hadn't detected any negativity. 'Oh, God, yes. And thanks again for the room change. Right now, though, I'm at a bit of a loose end. Would you have time to sit down with me for a general chat about the *Santa Clara*? Don't worry, I won't quote you directly, nothing attributable. This will be fiction, and anything you tell me or describe would be only for my novel's authenticity. I won't even be calling my ship by this name. I have in mind the *Roxanna*. It's my nan's name. I've looked it up and there doesn't seem to be any real liner of that name.'

'Don't think so, offhand.'

'I just need to know what's what and who plays what role in the running of the ship.'

'Some other time I'd be honoured, but there's a lot of paperwork on my desk. I'll rope in the staff captain too. He's second in command and would take over if the captain got beriberi. He's a mine of information and not only about the *Clara* but a lot of other ships too – he's been around the block. But in the meantime, if you've nothing better to do, Roxy, why don't you pop along to the ballroom? Charles will be just starting his first acting class in about a quarter of an hour and I can personally guarantee it won't be boring. It's only ninety minutes.'

'But if he's already started?'

'It was due to start at three, it's just after ten past and he's on for ninety minutes.'

'I would need to go to my stateroom first, Frank?'

'He won't mind if you're a bit late. I know he'd love to see you and, in a way, you'd be doing me a personal favour – he's an old pal of mine and he's a bit glum, these days. This is his last job with us, you see. He's part of the *Clara*'s furniture and her demise is hitting him hard. I hate to see it.'

'Okay.' Roxy had tried to sound eager. 'Maybe I will.' She had completely forgotten Charles's personal invitation to her.

'Good girl. Got to run.' He had walked away, and, over his shoulder, 'Don't forget now, ten past six tomorrow, Starbucks.'

'I won't!'

Roxy, staring at the invitation in her cabin, sod's law, will have to be sure to go exceptionally early to Ischia to get back in time to have enough time on the island to get the most out of her trip there. She had noticed that the hydrofoils were pretty frequent. Shit! She thinks now: You wait for a bus and you wait and then . . . Her head is mashed.

She puts the invitation safely away in the drawer of her bedside locker and, wondering what one wears to an acting class, decides that what she's wearing, jeans and a sweatshirt, will do fine. She lets her ponytail down, drags a brush through it and then puts it up again because they might be doing strenuous things during that class; she'd read something somewhere about actors having to pretend they're a tree. Or a bumblebee. Or a crab. To know what they felt like. She sighs, takes another look at her reflection. 'You'll do,' she says, again aloud, consoling herself that it might be fun. Anyhow, she does want to stay in the cruise director's good books.

She'll be out from the class by half past four and can have a leisurely shower before dinner and the appointment with the Dunnes, this time with tape recorder rather than notebook because she has a feeling that she'll acquire Plot Material. Upper case. She'll need the nuances of the dialogue, how they express things.

Her interview list is lengthening substantially, at least that's one good thing; along with the captain, Kitty Golden, Wolfgang and Frank Mitchell, after today it will include Charles, Gemma and Mary.

These two will be part of her narrative. Not quite main characters, not yet – but no matter how horrific – or uplifting – Mary's full story is, Roxy will have to keep in mind that this is the woman's real life she's dealing with. Mary won't see herself as fodder: what would she have to gain from it?

She lets herself out of the stateroom again and hurries back down towards the ballroom, slowing down only when she gets to within a few yards of it, and in case it's already in session, and although she's thinking, *What the hell am I doing here?*, tiptoes up to the double doors and pulls one open very slowly and carefully. She's unfamiliar with how actors work and doesn't want to wreck the atmosphere, or whatever—

She's expecting to find one of two scenarios: a reverent silence, with Charles standing at a lectern while his respectful class sits agog at the pearls of wisdom dropping from his mouth or, alternatively, since the class will already have started, one hapless guinea pig, script in hand, reading lines of a play, while the rest stifle giggles behind their hands.

She finds neither. Instead Charles, in the middle of the ballroom, surrounded by scattered, upturned chairs, is leaning over Barry Lee's partner, Joshua, who, sprawled face down on the wooden dance floor, legs spread-eagled, one arm beneath him, is not moving. She knows it's Josh because of his wonderful thick hair, now unruly. Neither man seems to be playacting.

Having sensed her standing, transfixed, inside the door, Charles looks in her direction and says, desperation in his voice: 'Thank God! Help me turn him over, Roxy.' Despite his distress, there'd been an underlying tone of command, and while her strong instinct is to wheel around and run, she obeys, dashing across to the centre of the floor and together, Charles at Josh's nearest shoulder, she at a hip, they roll the young man over on to his back whereupon she's horrified to see a stream of fresh blood pouring from his nose and flowing gently over his mouth on to his neck. It's already spreading, roughly fan-shaped, over his shirtfront. 'Go and find someone in a uniform or even not,' Charles barks. 'Get anyone. Say we need a doctor urgently in here – but, first, help me clear his mouth. Have you tissues or a hanky?'

Unable to move, Roxy shakes her head.

Quickly, Charles pulls off his jacket, yanks the tail of his white shirt out of his trousers and, with some difficulty because the fabric is substantial, manages to tear off a tea-towel-sized section to use as a swab. 'Go! Go!' he shouts at Roxy. 'Tell whoever you meet that I'm doing CPR but I won't be able to keep it up. We need a defibrillator. Will you remember that?'

But Roxy, appalled, finds she still can't move her feet as she watches him clean up Josh's face, which to her seems lifeless. She can't tell, either, if he's breathing. She has never seen a dead body before. 'Will he be all right, Charles?'

From somewhere deep in his diaphragm, Charles summons a huge roar: 'For Christ's sake, are you still here? Will you bloody well go and get someone and stop dithering?' It's so loud and unexpected she jumps and, for a second or two, remains frozen while he turns his attention back to Josh, feeling around on the chest, finding a spot under the breastbone and then, linking both his hands, begins to pump: 'One, two, three, four, five, six . . .'

Roxy, galvanised at last, flies for the doors.

15

itty Golden is tired. After an early breakfast this morning, she and Saul had set off on the Cinque Terre excursion, which had initially involved being bussed to the first of five medieval Ligurian villages, then walking along one of two trails that link them.

When they'd boarded their tour bus on the pier, there was no one on it she had recognised from the ship, but that hadn't surprised her since, apart from chatting to their immediate companions at table during mealtimes, and with Roxy a couple of times, she hadn't fraternised. She hadn't gone to any of the shows and, apart from a few room-service snack meals at lunchtime in their suite, had eaten only in the formal dining room. As for Saul, he might as well not have left Manhattan: since they'd boarded the ship, she reckons he's spent at least 70 per cent of his time in the second bedroom of the suite, which he'd fixed up as a temporary office.

This is a pattern for their vacations. They'd go somewhere, probably at huge expense. They'd check in, then after the first dinner, and maybe an orientation walk next morning, he'd appear mainly for food or, if the location involved the sun, by the pool or on the beach for an hour or so. But his phone, if not in his hand, was always within earshot.

She tolerated it because she had to, and had developed a modus operandi: sunbathing, wandering around local museums, shopping, sipping coffee outside cafés, reading books on their balcony or terrace, and having beauty treatments.

But this time she's finding his workaholic lifestyle more irksome than usual and had persisted in her efforts to get him to come on this shore excursion. 'We're supposed to be a married *couple*, Saul. We do hardly *anything* together.'

'What about yesterday? We went to Nice, didn't we?'

'Yeah, and we brought along a referee.'

'That's not fair.'

'No,' she'd conceded, 'it's probably not. But we do go to lovely places and it would be nice to have a companion to come with me to *share*, Saul, the scenery, local opera, cute little cafés and shops. I get fed up discussing it with myself or with total strangers on tour buses.'

'Okay, okay. I get it! Go put our names down.'

Reputed to be one of the most spectacularly scenic areas in Europe, Cinque Terre, named for the hinterland around its five villages, lies within one of Italy's national parks. The two designated walking trails are labelled Red and Blue, Red being higher, longer and more strenuous than Blue, which is easier on the feet and fairly level. Most tourists, especially the cosseted clientele of cruise liners, who are not given enough time ashore to traverse the Red, go Blue, set into the lower reaches of the cliff along which the villages are strung.

Before they left the *Clara*, they'd been warned that it takes five hours to walk the length of this trail, but Kitty had been up for it and Saul had surprised her by agreeing to walk it with her. 'Are you sure, Saul? No business to attend to? On the other hand, some of these villages might have Wi-Fi – after all, it is 2016.'

She'd meant it sardonically but, as usual, he didn't get it. 'It's okay, honey. I have satellite.'

Saul is irony-free. For one of his birthdays, along with the usual travel voucher, she'd given him, via Amazon, *The Three Stooges Collection 1934–1959.* It was one of his all-time favourite gifts and he had registered such delight she might as well not have bothered with the voucher. And late into the night, long after she'd gone to bed, she'd hear, streaming from under the door of his study, his giggle which, when he was really amused, hit the higher reaches of a soprano. 'The time difference works in our favour, honey,' he'd added then, settling into his seat on the coach. 'We'll be back on board long before the closing bell. Anyway, I have my smartphone powered up, so don't worry.'

I'm not worried, I'm pissed off – but she'd put on her glad face. 'Great!'

Determined to make the most of the day, she had relaxed once they'd got off the bus at the limits of where it was permitted to go, the village of Monterosso, the first of the chain. The weather had been benign. Although they had dressed warmly, it was a crisp, sunny morning and, within minutes of setting off, both had removed their jackets, tying them around their waists by the sleeves. 'We look like proper hikers now, eh, Saul?'

'Mm.' He was repeatedly making figures-of-eight in the air with his smartphone, trying to attract a signal.

She'd tried again: 'We got real lucky with the weather too, eh?'

'So far.' He was squinting at the little screen.

After that, she'd kept her mouth shut.

But then he'd become frustrated. 'Can't see anything, it's too bright. Here.' He'd thrust the phone at her. 'You have better eyesight than me. Will you see if it's showing any service?'

She turned her body so that it cast her shadow over the screen. The top left-hand corner showed two little white dots, indicating a weak signal. 'No dice.' She turned back, holding the phone out to him. 'Sorry. It says "no service". Why don't you put it away?'

'Thanks.' He'd taken it back but kept it in his hand.

'You regretting coming, Saul?'

'Of course not. It's lovely.' Again he'd raised the phone to make a figure-of-eight.

She speeded up slightly and got a few feet ahead of him, calling on all her mental resources to refrain from snapping at him. What's got into her this trip? She normally manages to deal with him quite well.

To her surprise, within the time frame given as guidance in their brochure, they soon found themselves below Vernazza, the second of these magical little villages. From this perspective, the closely packed gaggle of little houses, painted in bright colours, seemed to live on top of each other on the face of the cliff. 'Next stop Corniglia and lunch,' she'd called over her shoulder, but then, when he hadn't replied, turned to see that Saul's energy was fading. While he was wearing state-of-the-art trainers, with custom-fitted support insoles, his step had become heavy, more a trudge. While she felt a little sorry for him, she said nothing. There was no point. He lived his life in the glare of digital screens, kept a Town Car on standby for journeys of a few blocks, and was on his feet only in courtrooms or on building sites.

She tried not to anticipate that they might have to truncate this experience. It was not only scenic, its tranquillity had so far been interrupted only twice by the putt-putting engine of a small boat close to shore below the path and once by the passing of a train.

They were less than ten minutes beyond Vernazza, when, behind her, she heard Saul call out, 'Kitty? Kitty, please!'

Turning, she'd seen him, face contorted with pain, leaning against the boulder net that, like massive chicken wire, secured cliff falls from landing on the pathway. An old injury, sustained several years ago to one of his knees, had suddenly flared up.

They had no choice but to peel off and, with her supporting him, made their way back to Vernazza where, it was advised in the brochure – it was a stroke of luck she'd brought it – they could pick up a train to get back to where they'd started.

The problem was, the coach was not scheduled to take them to the ship for at least three hours, so they decided, Saul decided, to have lunch in Vernazza.

Their day out was over. She was disappointed, but she had to deal with it. No point in eking it out with lunch. In any case, it was not even noon yet. 'We could forget the train? Take a cab back to the ship?'

'We could, but it hurts only when I move it. I need to sit, give it a rest. Anyhow, I'm hungry. Let's eat.'

The nearest restaurant, which was just opening, proved to be one of those with a laminated menu showing pictures of what was on offer. During their lunch, a (very good) pasta dish with tomatoes and flaked fish, he was irritable but, thankfully, quietly so, annoyed with himself for agreeing to come. 'I should never have done this. I shouldn't have let you talk me into it. It's my own goddamned fault . . .'

They finished with a selection of ice creams, including

pistachio, which was Saul's favourite and which even he had to admit was to die for. 'Love it, love it, don't care if it's a heart attack on a plate!'

'When was the last time you walked more than fifty yards, Saul? This walk was madness, but I didn't think you'd do it. I thought you'd stay in that first village, you and your smartphone having a ball together!'

'I know, I know, sweetie. I'll join that gym in the basement in the New Year, I promise. Top of the New Year resolutions, eh? Will we have seconds?' He held up his empty sundae dish to the waitress, hovering nearby.

During previous trips, to Rome, for instance, Kitty had found that Italians, by and large, speak or understand English poorly but had to admit that the score was level. How much Italian does she know? *Spaghetti, linguini, fettuccine, ciabatta . . . Pavarotti, Schillaci . . .* But with shrugs, a few words of French, a lot of gesturing and body language – including miming a steering wheel – she and Saul managed to get the waitress to call a local cab to take them back to Monterosso. And, it being open to the outside world, as it were, she felt it would be relatively easy to get back to the ship.

And so it had worked out. It had been one of those occasions when Kitty, although not guilt-free about it, had been glad that money talks.

Back in Livorno, by the time they're in the elevator on the ship taking them upwards from the security area, Kitty's knees feel like jelly from the strain of supporting Saul, and her head is thumping from fatigue. She pushes the button for the atrium and reception level, brooking no argument: 'You go on up, Saul. Here's the key.' She shoves it into the pocket of his jacket. 'I have to tell them we came back independently, or there'll be search parties organised. But I'm also getting help for you. Medical help. You have to see a doctor, at least to have that knee strapped up and get a few painkillers.'

'We could call from the suite.'

'Yes, we could. You do that if you like, but I'm going to Reception to organise things.'

'All right.' To her surprise, he gives in. 'But I'll come with you.'

'Fine!' She sighs as the doors open. 'Suit yourself. Find a chair. I won't be long.'

But when they're emerging from the elevator it's he who spots Roxy, running fast along the corridor towards the desk in the atrium, which they're approaching from the opposite side. 'She looks like she's being chased,' Saul says. 'What's happening here?'

'Sit over there. I'll find out.' This trip, Kitty is surprising herself with the way she's handling Saul. It's as if, since they put to sea, she's been freed from a restrictive corset and can breathe properly.

She's also surprised at Saul's new mellowness, his acquiescence – it's even a little disconcerting – but, she warns herself, it's early days yet. Nevertheless, she's promised herself that she, for one, will step off the circular tracks they customarily tread in Manhattan – business, money, company stuff, the changing roster of wives concerned mostly with kids, self-beautification and spending, or saving, money. 'She's definitely scared,' she says now thinking the worst, as she watches Roxy nearing them. 'Something dreadful has happened to her.'

'Give me your arm again,' Saul demands. She does so but he's slow, and by the time they get to the desk, there is all kinds of organised chaos in progress. Roxy, panting hard and in a state of semi-collapse, is leaning against it and the two clerks are on separate phones. The second, as well as cradling her receiver between her shoulder and neck, is tapping the pager strapped to her belt over and over again.

'Are you okay?' Kitty touches Roxy's arm, but the girl bursts into tears and can't speak. Kitty puts an arm around her shoulders and hugs her. It's the only appropriate action she can think of.

The first receptionist, although keeping his voice low, is speaking with some urgency, and now a few guests are standing around, trying to divine the situation.

'Excuse me?' Saul limps to the desk as the male receptionist, whose name is Wolfgang and who seems calm enough, raises his voice to whoever is on the other end of the call: 'Yes, yes, immediately! . . . Ballroom . . . Yes . . . CPR is being administered.'

'Can someone tell me what's going on, please?' Saul taps the counter and, then, loudly, looking from one to the other of the receptionists: '"CPR is being administered"? Where? What's happened?' But when neither responds, he turns to Roxy. 'You obviously know something.'

Roxy, still trying to get her breath, gulps to Wolfgang: 'He – Charles, I mean – he said to tell you they need a defibrillator, I think that's right.'

Wolfgang covers his mouthpiece: 'I've asked for it. Everything's under control. The doctor's on his way and so are the paramedics.'

'A defibrillator? Paramedics?' Saul persists. 'Someone's had a heart attack?'

The receptionist puts down the phone. 'One of our guests has fallen ill in the ballroom. We are taking care of it. You are yourself limping, I see. May I help you in any way?'

'Yes, you can.' In his best lawyer's voice: 'You can give me some information. I'm one of the directors of this company so will you please inform me what's happening?'

'Of course, Mr Abelson. We are aware of your position and, yes, it may be that someone has had or is having a heart attack, but we are waiting for information from our medical staff. We are doing all we can, sir.'

'You heard him, Saul,' Kitty intervenes. 'There's nothing for us to do so let the professionals do their jobs. We can call the medics for ourselves up in our room when they're clear of this.'

'Listen, er – Wolfgang,' Saul is peering at the young man's badge, 'I want to be kept informed. If our company is at hazard . . .'

'Of course, sir. One of our nurses on duty has gone to the ballroom with the paramedics but may I send the other up to your suite?' Still cool, he picks up the phone.

'Yes, that would be great.' Kitty loosens her grip on Roxy and then, to her: 'Are you all right? You're very pale.'

'It's Josh,' Roxy quavers. 'He's the one. There was blood. Charles was great, but I was useless, I'm afraid, but I think I helped . . .'

'Our Josh?' This is Saul. 'Barry's friend, from our table? What happened to him? He's the one with the heart attack? But he's just a kid!'

Roxy seems to realise she is now the centre of attention as those who have been merely spectators up to now crowd around the desk to listen in. 'I actually don't know,' she falters, then steadies herself. 'When I got there, he was lying on the floor and the chairs were all over the place. His nose was bleeding badly, really badly, all over his face, and he was unconscious. Charles and I turned him over . . . I'll never forget what he looked like.' She puts her head into her hands.

Kitty again gives her that one-armed hug. 'You've done everything you can, Roxy,' she says, 'and from what you say, it sounds as though you did really, really well. Come on up with us to our suite, and when the nurse comes, we'll have her take a look at you too. We all need a bit of quiet now. Let's leave things to the experts. Does Barry know what's happened?'

Roxy shakes her head. 'I don't know. It was all so fast.'

Kitty turns to the desk. 'Has anyone told the man's partner?'

'And she is? Do you know their room number?' Wolfgang pulls over a pad.

'They dine with us at table thirty-two,' Kitty says. 'Their names are Barry Lee and Joshua Levitsky. Josh is the one injured.'

'Thank you, Mrs Abelson. I'll take it from here.' He taps on his keyboard. 'I see their room number – and I can see that both have mobile phones.'

'Barry is a he, in case there's any confusion.'

'Thank you. I shall make sure that Mr Lee is alerted. I shall try in person first. I shall need a master key . . .' He murmurs a few words to his colleague, who leaves her post and goes through a service door behind them. 'As soon as possible, I'll go up to their suite. I've already passed this matter upwards and all officers on the *Clara* who need to know about it have been informed.'

'Let's go, Saul. Roxy? We're done here.' Kitty tugs at the girl, then offers her arm to her husband. 'And please don't forget to organise that nurse for us,' she adds, speaking to the clerk. 'We understand, of course, that other things will take priority. But do stay in touch, please.'

They move off, Saul again surprisingly compliant. But in

Kitty's experience, he's never been stoic. Pain, even toothache, fells him. He'll need painkillers and a bit of TLC too.

When they get into the suite Roxy, who'd also been silent and uncharacteristically sorrowful as they'd travelled up in the elevator, stops dead in the open doorway as wonderment overcomes other emotions. 'Jesus!' She takes in the breadth of the huge windows, the terrace beyond them, the port buildings and seascape beyond that. 'I don't believe this.' She takes a few steps into the suite. 'You have a *piano*?'

'Do you play?' Kitty is steering Saul towards one of the two big sofas in the living area.

'No.' Roxy is still taking it all in: the bar counter – at one end of which is a massive arrangement of white lilies and roses and behind it, the large fridge and brass-railed shelf holding a full array of drinks, the archway, leading into a small but fully equipped kitchen, the other three doors, now closed. 'This is incredible.'

'Sit down, Roxy.' Kitty deposits Saul, moves an ottoman in front of him to prop up his bad leg, then crosses to the bar, going behind the counter: 'I'll tell you what else we have.' She reaches up and takes down two bottles, Scotch and cognac. 'You could do with some of this.' She holds up the brandy bottle. 'Both of you could.'

She takes three glasses, adds ice from the icemaker in the door of the fridge and splashes liberal measures of the alcohol, two brandies, one whiskey, on top. Then she comes back with a little silver tray. 'Here, drink this, no excuses.' She hands one of the brandy glasses to Roxy, now sitting in a winged armchair, then gives Saul the whiskey before seating herself on the second sofa. 'I, for one, certainly need this. Down the hatch, as my dad used to say.' She upends her glass.

'So tell me what happened, Roxy?' Isn't he too young to have had a heart attack?'

'I don't know. Honestly. You read about these things, don't you?'

'You say there was a lot of blood? Did you get a chance to look at his eyes? Were they open?'

'I – I don't know,' the girl says miserably. 'It was all very confused and it took, maybe, less than a minute in total, but I do remember his eyes were kind of invisible. Rolled up? And ...' she looks into space as though recreating '... all red. Like he had hay fever.' She drinks. 'But that's just an instant impression. Charles and I turned him over a few seconds after I got there. I didn't have a hanky to stop the blood so he ...' She seems to be losing it again but takes another swig of the brandy. 'Charles tore off the tail of his shirt to mop up the poor guy – and then he ordered me, he *roared* at me, Kitty, you wouldn't *believe* how *loud* he was, scared the shit out of me.' Again she drinks.

'Why was he angry with you?'

'I don't think he was angry. He wanted me to get help and I was, like, paralysed. Before I'd even got to the doors, he'd started to count out loud, and he was thumping with his two hands together on Josh's chest. I know about CPR and all that but I didn't know you had to press so *hard* . . . It was, like, kind of violent. Like he was trying to kill something inside Josh's chest. And with the blood wiped off, well, most of it anyway, Josh's poor face was as white as a sheet – oh, God!' She shudders and empties her glass.

'Let me get you a refill.' Kitty gets up and takes the cognac bottle from the bar counter where she'd left it.

'Well, he's in good hands now,' Saul says, as his wife pours another hefty measure into their visitor's glass. 'As you said yourself, sweetie, nothing more we can do.'

'We can make sure Barry's okay. This is going to hit him hard.' Kitty is remembering the cocktail party, the expression on the architect's face as he continually monitored the younger man's whereabouts and behaviour over her husband's head while Saul continued with his monologue. Her prediction about the relationship may be coming to pass, but – poor Barry – she hadn't envisaged it might end like this. She stands up. 'I won't be long. I'll just make sure the young man at Reception has found him. Barry has to know that somebody cares for him, nothing to do with compensation suits.'

'That's not fair.' Saul tries to jump up from his sofa but his gammy knee complains and he falls back.

'Isn't it? You're a company man, Saul, first, last and always!'

Saul looks at Roxy, then back at his wife. 'It's not the time or the place, Kitty.'

'You're right. Sorry. It's the brandy talking.' Kitty was not a big drinker, rarely indulging in spirits. 'Sorry,' she repeats, and then, to Roxy, 'You too, Roxy, it was very rude of me to talk like that in front of you. Help yourself.' She waves in the direction of the bar. 'I won't be long. I just want to make sure that poor Barry's all right.' She adds hastily, 'Josh too, of course. I'll try to find out what's happening with him. Keep that foot up, Saul. I'll leave the door on the latch for the nurse but I'm sure she'll have a key. See you later.'

'I'll come with you.' For the second time, Roxy empties her glass. 'I want to get back to my own room.'

A few minutes after they left the suite, and parted company, on going down to the atrium, Kitty found that the male clerk, Wolfgang, was now missing from the desk and his colleague was busy dealing with a complaint from an elderly customer in a wheelchair and her very angry husband. She thinks hard. Anyone searching for Barry, if anyone had, would have investigated the outside decks, the restaurants, pools, all the public spaces, so she consults one of the wall maps to locate the more unusual venues.

She goes first to the ship's oratory, which proves to be a little sanctuary of secular tranquillity, tealights burning in red glass holders, the scent of lilies sweet on the air, a solitary painting of a seascape on its back wall. It's empty.

Then she hurries to the small ship's library, where the ambience is cosy and insulated. A youngish man, presumably the librarian, is sitting behind his desk, with Saturday's two-day-old *Guardian* newspaper spread out before him. He looks up and smiles as she enters but then goes back immediately to his reading.

Barry is sitting at a table, a large pictorial volume open in front of him. Hearing her come in, he too has looked up and, as she approaches him, says, 'Oh! Hello, Kitty! Nice to see you. How was Cinque Terre?'

'Hi, it was great.' But she's now full of dread as she recognises that the poor man has no idea what she must tell him. Her instinct is immediately to hedge, to call someone official, but that would be cowardly and just plain wrong. However, she does stall a little, in order to adopt the right tone, and sits in the chair opposite. 'You've been here a while?'

'It's not huge, for sure, with limited options for someone like me, but it's a bolthole, isn't it? And, in fairness, there are a few interesting books, off-piste, as it were. Like this one.' He smiles. 'I doubt it'll ever be top of anyone's bestseller list, but I find it fascinating.'

'What is it?' *Why is she still treating this like a normal conversation?*

He flips over a few of the pages. 'It's actually a catalogue, would you believe, but beautifully produced and illustrated, even has a slipcover.' He indicates this on the floor beside him. 'It was published with an exhibition in New York about the architect Gaudí and his Sagrada Família. Have you and Saul ever been there, Kitty?'

She shakes her head.

'Well, it's the extraordinary basilica he designed in Barcelona.' His voice, fuelled by passion for his subject, has risen – and it occurs to her that, on day three of this cruise, despite their being tablemates, this is the first time she has had a one-on-one conversation with the man. Up to now she's merely observed him in the roles of listener (to Saul) and as half-panicked monitor of his lover. But this is another Barry, engaged, highly articulate, attractive in his enthusiasms. As she watches him speak, experienced as she is, she notices that his forehead is slightly frozen and the area around his eyes is a little too smooth and stretched when compared to the impending wattles on his neck. He's had work done, she thinks compassionately, no doubt due to the disparity of his and Josh's ages.

What a context in which to meet him. How, she asks herself, is she going to cut in, to destroy him? No matter what happens with Josh, whether he lives or dies, the boy's lover will never forget being in the library when he got this news – and who imparted it. He'll even link this book, that church in Barcelona, to the words she will say to him now.

'It won't be finished until 2021.' Happily oblivious to all of this, he's stroking the glossy pages. 'And that will be the centenary of the turning of the first sod. Imagine! A hundred years! Four generations of artists in stone and other materials completing one church! Put it on your bucket list, Kitty. Everyone should see it, even if it's only once. I think of it as the world's biggest and finest piece of art, a massively intriguing and fascinating sculpture, which is the apogee of that art. You could look at it every day for a year and continue to find new little things. The last time I was there I spotted a poor little carved tortoise with his mouth open, probably calling for help,' his smile is sympathetic, 'because he's supporting a huge pillar on the back of his shell! I hope I'm alive to see it finished. Amazing!

'Oh, and guess what?' He rises from his chair and goes to one of the fiction shelves, fingering the S section and pulls out a paperback. 'Sorry,' he grins, 'got a little bit carried away there. Look what I found when I was browsing?' He hands her the small volume, its cover depicting an artist's rather hazy impression of rolling hills, a little cottage, a church steeple: '*Heartbreak in the Cotswolds* – by guess who! You know, I only half believed the poor girl. Turns out she's for real!'

Without comment, she gives it back to him; and as he returns it to the shelves, he asks, over his shoulder, 'You looking for anything special, Kitty? Or just a bit of a read?'

Kitty can bear this no longer. 'No. No, thank you.' She steels herself, and when he sits down again: 'Barry, I've actually been searching the ship for you. I think others were too – probably still are, nobody came in here looking for you?'

'No.' Instantly Barry's expression closes in. Slowly, he shuts the Gaudí book, tucking in the ear of the dustcover so it's tidy. 'Why would anyone be looking for me?'

'It's Josh.'

'He's in our suite.' He speaks in a monotone, such a contrast with the vivid, excited way he'd been talking only seconds previously. 'He was exhausted after lunch, said he needed a nap. I was with him in the room up to about an hour ago.' He stares at her, an unmistakable appeal in his eyes: *Please don't tell me . . .*

'He—' She stumbles. 'Barry, he's had an accident. Apparently he went into the ballroom to join Charles's acting course and collapsed there. Charles gave him CPR, and he's in the infirmary now . . .' She trails off.

Barry opens the book again and, concentrating very hard, runs a finger down the ear of the dustjacket as though he hadn't neatened it enough the last time. Carefully, he once more closes the cover, squaring it so each of the book's rectangular lines runs precisely parallel with its equivalent table edge. Then, with his head to one side: 'This is rosewood, I'd say. It's rare enough these days.' Hand on the table now, as still as one of the photographs in his book, he looks across at Kitty. 'Is he dead?'

She can't lie, even to save him a few minutes' grief. 'I honestly don't know, Barry. It happened, I believe, less than half an hour ago. The medics went in very quickly. I'll come with you to the desk, if you like. You shouldn't be alone.'

But he sits back in his chair, shoulders very straight, settling his gaze on the ceiling.

Use of facial expressions is part of a model's toolkit, with photographers constantly yelling instructions: 'More of that, no, a little moodier, get *angry*, Kitty, you're in *love*, dammit, Kitty, but you're scared too – hey, that's it! Hold that one!' And to her Barry, having been so animated, instantly looks spent, depleted, and yet there is an element of something else. Relief? A sort of psychic lifting? So far there's no sign of what she'd been expecting: grief, panic, some kind of outburst.

She scolds herself. Facial analysis is not what's called for right now. The poor man's thoughts and reactions are private and his alone. Should she get up to hug him? Somehow she knows that this, too, would be inappropriate so she waits silently as he continues to stare at the ceiling, a perfectly ordinary expanse of plaster, flat and white as most ceilings are. Lighting in the library comes from green- and gold-shaded floor and desk lamps. For atmosphere, she supposes.

'Barry,' she says gently, when he doesn't move. 'We don't know yet if it's bad news. Why don't we go and find out? And don't worry, you won't have to do this by yourself.'

'Thank you.' He stands up. 'That's very kind of you,' he says, with such dignity she feels humbled.

When they get near it, she sees that the reception desk in the atrium is quiet. There's no sign of Roxy and everything seems to have got back to normal – at least, for those who weren't there to observe the crisis.

The young man named Wolfgang, who is dealing with a guest, spots them before they get to him. He says something to his female colleague and she replaces him while he comes out from behind his desk. 'Madam – and good afternoon, Mr Lee.' He shakes Barry's listless hand. 'You'll find Mr Levitsky in our infirmary. The medical staff are working on him now and it is possible he is to be transferred to a hospital in the city shortly. Captain Leifsson has asked to be informed as soon as you were located. He wishes to go down to the infirmary with you. May I call him now? He is not far away and can be here presently.'

'Is he dead? Is Joshua dead?' Barry's monotone continues to hold.

'The last information I received, Mr Lee, which was about ten minutes ago, is that the doctors were working on him, as I said. Just a moment, please.' He goes behind the desk and picks up his phone, which is answered immediately. He murmurs something into the mouthpiece and replaces it. 'The captain is on his way. May I get you anything? Some water?'

'No, thank you. You're very kind.'

The silence that descends next is so profound that a guest, only feet away, there to exchange currency, is affected by it: instead of speaking normally as he had been until then, he lowers his voice to a whisper.

Kitty now sees this entire situation as surreal, maybe in line with the basilica Barry had been admiring? It's hard to take in the formal speech patterns of the clerk and, indeed, of Barry himself while his lover possibly lies on a slab and he himself, in this glitzy atrium, is surrounded by huge floral arrangements, Rococo folderols and people on chairs with beers in front of them. To Kitty, the scene and the way it feels resembles something you might dream about, or see in a foreign movie.

Right now she feels extraordinarily detached, as though it has nothing to do with her while at the same time being right in the middle of it. Her headache is now bothering her badly.

Adding to the strangeness, she sees the captain, in his immaculate whites and cap, striding purposefully towards them. It's odd to see him so grim-faced when at the cocktail party he had been so gregarious.

Before he gets to them, Barry grabs her arm. 'If he dies, I killed him.'

'What?' she gasps.

'It's my fault. I gave him the money. He had none of his own—'

The captain is upon them. Kitty, reeling, manages to don her bland model-mask as he greets her courteously, almost as formally as though they've never met before. He shakes

Barry's hand. 'I'm sure you won't want to delay any longer, Mr Lee. Shall we go?'

'Just one moment, please, Captain.' Kitty, trying to process everything, speaks to the clerk, employing the syntax everyone now seems to favour. 'My husband has asked to be informed should I find Mr Lee. Could you call him for me, please? The Duchess Suite. And please tell him I'll call him myself on his mobile phone when we know what the situation is.'

'Certainly, madam.' Wolfgang picks up the phone.

As she and the captain accompany Barry in the elevator down to the security floor where the infirmary is housed, silence, weighty as rocks and just as dense, fills the multi-mirrored space, reflecting all three faces, her eyes wide with stress and the pain in her head, the captain's, in the shade of his peaked cap, expressionless, ice-blue.

As for Barry, given the circumstances, his eyes, too, are weirdly blank but she can feel the stiffness of his body, its rigid self-control as he continues, successfully, to contain his emotions.

She regrets what has happened to the younger man, of course she does, as would anyone with an ounce of humanity, but it's difficult to feel sympathy for him, now she suspects that his collapse had been due to coke. Maybe a bad batch. Again, she glances at Barry's reflection: what has he been thinking? You can't live intimately with someone on drugs without at least suspecting and yet his blurted confession, if that's what it had been, proclaimed that he knew only too well of his lover's predilections. Appalled that she can entertain such a thought, she is nevertheless conflicted as to whether poor Barry would be better off in the long run if Joshua were to die. But what of Captain Leifsson? What are his thoughts and can anyone ever tell with him? Is he a cold fish or, like Barry (she assumes), monumentally self-controlled, not letting his anger show? He has to be annoyed that such an episode, cocaine on his vessel – if it is cocaine, she needs to be cautious about this – should be visited on him during his last watch on the *Santa Clara*, when, if Saul had it right, he was anticipating a peaceful retirement.

She has noticed that, when dealing with passengers, the *Santa Clara*'s captain usually takes off his cap. In keeping it on his head right now is he, like a cop on duty, indicating that he's already conducting a formal investigation? Will Barry, poor guy, to add to his grief, have to go through an interrogation?

With Barry behind, the captain is physically so close to her she can see, peripherally, that his jaw is set and his gaze is fixed, not on the descending numerals as would be normal, but on the elevator doors, his eyeline as straight as his back and shoulders. She can smell the starch used to stiffen the creases on his uniform trousers.

*

Meanwhile, back in the ship's small library, the attendant comes out from behind his desk and, glancing towards his door to make sure his customer is not coming back, bends over the Gaudí catalogue and opens it to admire the quality of the reproduction, but also the clarity and font of the captions and text. He runs his hand appreciatively over one of the two smooth, glossy pages in front of him, closes the book again, picks up the discarded slipcover from the floor beside the chair to put it where it belongs. Then, almost reverently, he carries the volume to the short section of one of the shelves, over which is the legend *Art and Architecture*, and slots it back into its position between *The Future of Music* and *Gauguin: 16 Art Stickers*.

16

Charles, seated on a plastic stacking chair, is outside the door of the infirmary while inside, medics do their thing with Joshua.

He is so physically drained from his efforts to revive the boy that one of his knees is jigging uncontrollably as though it has a life of its own. On top of everything else he is embarrassed because never in his life until now, except when wearing bloodstained tatters as Old Mahon in Synge's *Playboy of the Western World*, has he appeared in public in such a state of dishevelment. He hasn't been able to summon the energy to ask if he may go up to his room to change into something more respectable.

He's in the business heart of the ship, a utilitarian corridor punctuated by a series of doors that, as they open and close, reveal office interiors, a pharmacy, mysterious staircases and large pieces of equipment, with people, some in uniform, others in civilian dress, passing up and down carrying files, cleaning materials, tools and medical equipment. Directly under the ceiling, on each facing wall, there are runs of large ugly ducts, their contents, he imagines, equally hideous.

Relative to the rest of the vessel, it's dark down here, with no windows to the outside; one of the strip-lights over his head is buzzing and flickering, disturbing no one, it seems, except him. He hopes it's more comfortable inside the infirmary for Josh, although that boy will have bigger worries if he survives.

When Charles had arrived here with the stretcher and the first responders, a nurse walking alongside holding a drip bottle high in the air had asked him, politely, if he wouldn't mind sitting outside the door instead of in the treatment area. 'You're not family, are you, Mr Burtonshaw?'

'No.'

As the stretcher was being manoeuvred through the doors of the infirmary, she had yielded the drip to a colleague, then brought out the chair so Charles could sit. 'I'm sorry you can't be in there with him, but it's a bit hectic right now. I'm sure you understand.'

'It's fine.' Charles had had no wish to be in there. He'd come simply because they'd asked him to in case they needed to talk to him again about what had happened. If he's honest, while he's trying to remain empathic, he's too busy recovering his own energy and equilibrium to care not a whit if he never sees the boy again. He's sorry for Barry, though. He's a decent sort and to say that the poor man had done nothing to deserve this is less than understatement.

While they had made him go through his recital of events more than once, he acknowledges that the first responders had been kind, with one telling him over and over that he'd done the right thing throughout: 'Nobody on earth could have done better, sir. Your reaction was exactly right. First rate.' That young man, like the nurse, had looked like a teenager.

To Charles, everyone looks like a teenager, or even younger.

So why, after all that praise and validation, does he feel so frazzled and unworthy? By the time help had arrived, he had been about to give up: he was out of puff and his wrists felt like flaccid pieces of raw meat.

All over, as far as he's concerned. *Nothing to see here now. Please, someone, let me go to my room . . .*

How long had it been since Josh had scared the lights out of him by bursting into the ballroom the way he did? An hour? Two hours? Forty-five minutes? Less? How long had he, Charles, worked on him?

He has no clue. What time is it now?

Probably because he had used so much pressure on Josh's chest, Charles's watchstrap had snapped. He hadn't felt it at the time, discovered it only when the medical staff had come to take over from him. As he'd heaved himself upright and away from Josh, he'd seen it face down on the floor and felt almost too exhausted to pick it up. But he did – and saw that it wasn't only the strap that had suffered, the watch was damaged as well. It had stopped at just after a quarter past three.

Maybe it's recovered. Mindlessly, he takes it out of his pocket to examine it, but no. He's disappointed. His mother had bought it for his thirtieth birthday.

Unwilling to give up, he shakes it a little, puts it against his ear, can't hear any tick, shakes it again, then checks to see if the second hand is moving. It isn't. As far as this watch is concerned, it's just a quarter past three. To mangle that famous phrase of John Cleese, this is a Dead Watch . . .

Definition of madness, of course, repeating actions to get the same result. It's a cliché but he's always liked it.

His brain, he thinks now, is not working in straight lines.

His thirtieth. How many years have passed since then? He puts the watch back into the pocket of his jacket.

The urge to lie down, even on the cement floor, painted a shiny grey, is becoming acute. He's been told to sip water and had promised he would. At least, he thinks he did. He can't remember properly. He checks the level of the water in the plastic cup he's holding. Still quite a bit there. He means to sip, but the next time he checks, the level hasn't gone down.

He remembers it was the staff captain, whom he knows of old and who is inside with Joshua, who had brought him the water. 'Sorry we can't let you in but, as I'm sure they've told you, they need to have him to themselves for a while, Charles. They'll probably also want you to answer a few questions for them. You're a hero, you know.'

The SC, who'd been at sea for decades, is Scottish and his burr has never weakened. He rolls his *rs*. Charles, sensitive to the nuances of an accent, likes to hear it.

'It could prove to be necessary but we'll let you go as quickly as possible.'

'Could I have a drink of water, please?' He had sounded childish, but at that point Charles had felt like a child. A good boy.

'Water? Certainly, and I think we can do better than that.' The other man had gone back into the infirmary and had come out with two disposable plastic glasses, one filled with a pale yellow liquid. 'Drink this first.' He'd proffered it.

'Is it wee?' The words were out before Charles could stop them. Mother would have been so upset – she had no time for crude language.

'Oh, dearie me, no.' The *Clara*'s second-in-command had found this amusing. 'Think of it as Lucozade. It's a pale American substitute, I can never remember the name of the bleddy stuff. You've had a shock, Charles, a bad one, so you need a sugary top-up. Go ahead, drink it.'

Charles had gulped the sweetish liquid in one go.

'There's a good lad. Now the water – you're probably dehydrated too. Don't you go faintin' on me. If you do feel weak, just knock or send the nearest person over to knock on your behalf. Okay? I'll be right out. I promise that this,' he'd jerked his head in the direction of the infirmary behind him, 'won't take much longer.'

But the wait seemed interminable as people hurried past, smiling curiously at him because, he believed, of his bloody get-up.

He's still gripping the plastic beaker when, shortly afterwards, he sees the captain come towards him from the lift. Kitty Golden is there too, and so is Barry. An odd little group, he thinks, one that doesn't make sense. The need to lie down is more urgent than ever, but the captain is coming. He needs to stand up for the captain: it's the correct thing to do.

He tries to get to his feet but his knee won't co-operate. It gives way and he stumbles backwards into the hard plastic chair, almost overturning it but managing to catch it just in time and flopping back into it.

He's become so clumsy, he thinks. His trousers are wet all down the front. He's spilled his water . . .

All he wants to do is to lie down.

*

Next thing Charles knows, he's lying on the bed in his suite, and through the gap where the curtains across his windows don't quite meet, he can see that it's dark on his balcony and the ship is rocking slightly. He can also hear wind. But he's so comfortable and snug and warm . . . He closes his eyes again. He feels a little woozy too, as though someone had slipped him a Mickey . . .

Slipping a Mickey – now there's a phrase he hasn't heard for a long time. Smiling a little, he drifts off, not quite to sleep but into that delicious, misty anteroom of sleep, back to a time when he was young and just starting out in the profession, facing the world with his agent, Jeremy, having his back, Mother proud of him . . .

Almost immediately after graduation, he'd had a bit of luck: a jobbing actor, about ten years older than Charles, had broken his leg. He'd been one of a young troupe bringing Shakespeare to festivals and fairs and the accident had happened in the first week. Jeremy had put him up as a replacement and Charles had got it because, Jeremy'd said, 'You were born with a face older than your years, kid.'

'Say what you mean, Jeremy.'

'And that nose of yours could, after all, become your fortune.'

How wrong *that* had proved to be.

But the tour had sealed his love of stage acting, and although he was poverty stricken, with barely enough cash to pay for fish and chips every night, the group, about ten actors in all, became a tight little family, gambling that there was still a market in the rural towns and villages for the late lamented fit-ups of the recent past: traditional theatre. Rather obscurely, he'd thought, for the demographic of the audiences they hoped to attract, they'd named themselves On with the Motley and moved in tracks all over the British Isles laid by theatre companies of the recent past. They performed in sunshine and rain, and once even in a blizzard, with only the man who owned the field in which they'd pitched their tent, his wife, two daughters and their collie as the audience. The dog had got bored and left.

The canvas of their tent was tatty and smelt faintly of

manure, but while Charles continues to acknowledge that Jeremy's taking him on for the AWTF agency was the highlight of his career, that first tour, where he had had no option but to become a fast study, to learn how to work as part of an ensemble, how to pitch a tent no matter how uneven the ground, to erect the sets and wire in stage-lights, take tickets, conduct raffles – and, as a result, overcome his fear of making an idiot of himself.

Part of the deal was that, having arrived at a new place, when the tent was safely up, one member of the company had to go out in public, in costume, with a small drum belted around his or her waist and an ancient trumpet strung around the neck, to walk the streets, entering pubs, factories, barbers, hairdressing salons and other premises to publicise the show. Like a town crier, you had to make your noisy presence felt wherever you were playing. The group couldn't afford flyers.

He learned to improvise on stage if someone else fluffed, forgot or skipped a crucial line, how to perform quick changes without help, how, if someone was genuinely unable to perform, to take on his – or on one occasion her – role as well as his own. It meant you had to have a good memory and, since the programme changed depending on the venue, to retain the lines of every play and (almost) every character in the repertoire.

There were disasters. In the north of England, they were run out of two separate towns when the punters thought they weren't worth the money. Sometimes, when they didn't have enough cash for digs, they had to sleep in their tent, if the farmer or factory owner agreed to let them keep it up that night.

Often they weren't paid by their 'actor-manager' and had to settle for the price of a pint and a sandwich in the pub. That guy had left the profession near the end of the tour to become a welder because his girlfriend had announced she was pregnant and her dad had become involved. It meant two things for the players: he had to be replaced and stage roles had to be recast and distributed. Probably because Charles had *looked* older than the rest of them, the company, by secret ballot, had voted and the result was that, by a narrow margin, he had become the new manager.

He had no desire to be a manager of anything or anyone except himself; his desire was to be *on stage* with the spotlight shining directly into his eyes so the audience retreated into darkness. The notion of dealing with box-office takings, rosters and casting, banks, farmers and county councils would have come between him and sleep, so he'd declined, not before thanking everyone in the company for the honour they'd bestowed on him.

By the end of the twenty-seven-venue tour he'd found the experience had been a wonderful boost, not just enhancing skills he could draw on for the rest of his career but also his confidence. That tour still reigns in his mind as the most enjoyable period of his professional life, physical hardships notwithstanding.

He was in Newcastle, of all places, and it was winter, stormy and wet. It had been his turn again to drum up business, so he banged away on his drum, tooted his trumpet and yelled, 'Tonight! Tonight! Eight o'clock! Come in! Come in! All welcome, only one shilling and sixpence,' as he moved in and out of the pubs. But the people were turning their backs. He wasn't fazed, he'd done it before, they'd done it before, so he banged ever harder, shouted louder . . .

Suddenly he becomes aware that he isn't in Newcastle but in his *Santa Clara* suite and someone's knocking hard on his door and calling his name: 'Mr Burtonshaw? Mr Burtonshaw?

Charlie?' Then he hears whoever it is insert a key and, still dozy, forces himself up on one elbow. 'Yes? Who is it?'

The door opens and it's his old pal the staff captain. 'Are you okay, Charlie? You gave us a fright.'

'What happened?'

'I might ask you the same thing. Cap'n Birdseye had to pull you off the floor. Have you eaten today, lad?'

Come to think of it, he hadn't had any lunch. 'Not since breakfast, no.'

'Leifsson wants to see you as soon as you feel up to it.'

'Okay. Where do I go? How's the boy?' The mist is rapidly lifting and, while there's still a blank in his memory about how he got to his suite, Charles now remembers, only too well, what happened this afternoon. He sees his slacks, neatly folded, across the back of an armchair. They'd been wet, he remembers now, embarrassment spreading like a rash. Had he spilled his water – or had a terribly embarrassing accident? That didn't bear thinking about. 'Was it you brought me up here, Jock?'

The SC's name is Stuart but no one, not even the captain, calls him that. 'Guilty as charged. Don't worry, we didn't fuss. Your timing was good, ship was half empty . . .' He notices Charles is still glancing askance towards the armchair. 'And, yes, Charlie, your virginity is intact! It was me undressed you – you're wiry but, Lord, don't you have heavy legs!'

'How's the boy?'

'He'll be taken off. Hospital ashore. No good way to say this, Charlie, the police are involved.'

'But he's alive?'

'Last I heard, yes. Thanks to you, they're all saying. In his favour he's young. Against him is the amount of coke he snorted. Ambulance is coming, but you know the Italians. There's no great hurry. There's very little anyone can do now, anyway, they say, except wait and keep him hydrated. Maybe pray – but a fat lot of good that'll do him.'

'And his partner, Barry? Where's he?'

'He's with the captain now. You up for it, Charlie? His office. I'll take you there.'

'I know where it is.'

'Of course you do. But I'll take you there anyway.'

Charles, who is rapidly coming back to himself, sits up and swings his bare legs over the side of the bed.

'Take it handy, lad.'

'I need to get this over with. And obviously I need to put on some clothes. By the way, what was in that yellow drink you gave me?'

'Nothing except about sixteen spoons of sugar. It's dynamite, isn't it?'

'Had the opposite effect, clearly. What time is it?'

'Twenty to six. Departure at seven.'

'Okay, just give me a minute to get respectable.'

Less than ten minutes later, the two men are on their way down to Captain Leifsson's office. The weather had changed dramatically during the afternoon: rain, torrential by Mediterranean standards, driven by a gusting, whipping wind, is sweeping the decks outside the public areas and, unless they're wearing hats or caps, the hair of guests returning from outside excursions is slick, their clothing dripping.

While Charles knows that the captain's personal quarters are spacious by comparison with those of other crew members, they are not as fancy as even a balcony cabin. There is a porthole. His office is small, less than thirty square feet to the actor's trained eye, and, although tidy, rendered even smaller by filing cabinets and office furniture, with just three chairs, one for the captain behind his desk, two for visitors in front of it. With Barry Lee, Roxy Smith and Kitty Golden already there, the two women occupying the chairs, it's a squeeze for the new arrivals. On seeing them, Barry, who is standing and as pale as Banquo's ghost, Charles thinks, steps aside to make space for them. Instinctively, Charles sticks out his hand. 'I'm dreadfully sorry for what happened to Josh.'

The other man grips, tears standing in his eyes. 'Thank you for what you did.'

The captain clears his throat. 'It's very uncomfortable in here with so many people, I know, but I shall try to make this as quick and painless as possible. Thank you for coming. As we speak, Mr Levitsky should be on his way to hospital in Livorno and we have arranged to keep in touch with his progress. I'm assuming, Mr Lee, that you will want to disembark to be in the hospital with him. We'll arrange a taxi. Will you organise that, Jock?'

'Sure thing,' the SC says quietly.

'And since we don't want to delay our departure, would you like to go to your suite to collect your luggage? I have already arranged for the housekeeping staff to pack it for you – you've spoken to the police already, I know, but they've indicated they will want to speak to you again. Mr Lee, I hesitate to intrude on your upset, but I must ask you this before you go. What do you think was the cause of your partner's collapse?'

'A heart attack?' Barry whispers.

'Did he have a history of heart problems – that you know of?'

Barry shakes his head.

'As I say, this is difficult, Mr Lee, but I must ask you. Could illegal drugs have been involved?'

Barry shakes his head again, the rest of his body remaining stiff. The effect, thinks Charles, is rather like the dummy used by the ventriloquist, where the head can turn but the rest of the body remains soft and inert. With difficulty, it seems, he himself tunes in again to the captain, who is speaking in a level voice, his expression set: 'You do understand, Mr Lee, we must cooperate with the local police? That it's procedure?'

'Of course.' Poor Barry's voice, even though he is whispering, cracks on an intake of breath. He is visibly starting to shake.

The captain stands up and comes out from behind the desk, but as he does so, his own veneer splinters: 'I'm very sorry that this has happened to you, Mr Lee. I can barely imagine how you must feel. Please accept my sincerest sympathy, and that of Portlandis. I hope, again sincerely, that Mr Levitsky may make a recovery.'

Barry's nod is barely perceptible.

As Charles watches this play out, the word 'frangible' jumps into his head. Barry's body is frangible: anyone wishing him harm has merely to place two hands on it and it will shatter. He can feel his eyes stinging.

Watching as the captain clasps Barry's hand, his free hand touching the other man's shoulder, both women in the room are similarly affected. Roxy's eyes are closed and she is holding a hand over her mouth. Kitty has bowed her head.

Barry holds it together almost to the end. 'Thank you, Captain, I appreciate your kindness and understanding, and I'm desperately sorry that Josh—' he's losing it, gulping, swallowing, but then, although barely audible, manages to continue. 'I'm sorry he has caused such trouble for you,

Captain, personally, and to all your –' he is overcome and his voice, driven by tears, has risen as he loses his control of it '– your s-staff.'

The atmosphere quickens. This small functional room, thinks Charles, who is also trying not to break down, is no place for such high drama.

'Please don't upset yourself, Mr Lee, but as I say, I do know how painful this must be for you. Please accept my commiseration and, of course, may I reiterate the concern of Portlandis Shipping Line.' He nods in the direction of his second-in-command, who comes forward to usher Barry, gently, out of the office. And while the others signal to him with their eyes that they, too, wish to express their sympathy, Leifsson, granite-faced, goes back to sit again behind his desk and begins to write.

No one else speaks or moves. The room is not quiet, however: under the pounding of the storm, the *Clara* is shuddering and jerking a little at her moorings, and although the office has no egress to the outside, the noise of the combined wind and monsoon-like rain seems to be getting louder.

In such a tense situation Charles, acting as class clown, can usually come in with a quip or even an appropriate anecdote to relieve the pressure. He is so upset, however, that he cannot think of anything even vaguely appropriate. Instead, while waiting for someone else to take the initiative, he retreats into the kind of dramatic imagery that can lighten whatever scenario is stressing him, usually something connected with it. This time it's the storm.

He is a veteran of Shakespeare's *The Tempest* – permanently in On with the Motley's repertoire. He had played Stephano, the drunken butler. He had performed it again at least three or four times for different companies and had happily accepted a minor role in the movie of the play, Peter Greenaway's *Prospero's Books* in 1991.

But comedy, even comedy with a serious undertone as in that play, is out of order now and he switches away from it when the ship shakes particularly strongly. Now he's wondering if they'll be able to leave at seven o'clock as scheduled.

It's Roxy, obviously worrying along the same lines, who breaks the tension: 'Will we be able to sail in this kind of weather, Captain?'

He looks up. 'It's a passing squall. The forecast is for it to clear this coast in an hour or so. We may cast off a bit late but not much. The ship may be getting old, like her master,' he smiles, 'but her last refit gave her an up-to-date set of stabilisers and she'll do fine. She's been through far worse than this. It may be a little bumpy for a while, once we're on the open sea, but nothing we can't handle. Just ask your wine waiter not to fill your glass too full!' His attempt at another smile doesn't work this time.

'I won't detain you much longer. But the reason the three of you are here, if you don't mind, is for completeness, since all of you were involved in different ways with this incident, and I need to get a picture of what happened, three-dimensional if you will.

'And,' he reaches into one of the drawers in his desk, 'if you have no objections, I shall record you. I don't have shorthand, I'm afraid. Anyone object to this?'

'No.' All three looked at each other.

Charles, who needs the bathroom and whose legs are telling him they've been standing long enough, asks if he can go first. 'That's if no one minds? I'll be brief.'

Not waiting for a response because the bathroom need is getting more urgent by the minute, he goes ahead, telling of his preparation for his course, his setting out of scripts on his half-circle of chairs. 'But, to be truthful, I was getting upset when, by ten past three or thereabouts, no one had turned up. Then Josh did.' He describes the young man's absurd entrance. 'And for those first few seconds I thought he was doing this to impress me, shock me, if you like, into watching his version of how a military man in a stage role behaves or how he imagines he would behave. He certainly achieved the shock effect. It was bizarre but attention-grabbing, a sort of preliminary audition, if you like, although it was a bit . . .' he hesitates '. . . I don't like to criticise the poor fellow, but it was all a bit Gilbert and Sullivan.

'But then he flipped – that's the only way to describe it. He was demented, racing around like a whirlwind, picking up chairs and throwing them like missiles in different directions, kicking them violently when they were down, and although he wasn't aiming them at me directly, he was behaving so fiercely and so – so *savagely*, I was having to duck out of the way. I got more and more scared. He was making strange noises in his throat, and yelling at a chair he was kicking, "Well, how does that feel, matey?" To a chair! Or "You thought you'd got away with it, didn't you? You have another thing coming!" He'd pick another one up and fling it in the air, shouting, "Have a nice flight, bollocks!"' Charles glanced at the women. 'Apologies, ladies. His behaviour was insane and my instinct was to get out of there as quickly as I could. I wasn't even thinking of seeking help at that point, just safety. I was planning my route as to how to get to the doors, but before I could move, blood started to pump out of his nose and he collapsed, face down, onto the floor.

'Although I've never seen it happen I thought he must be having a brain haemorrhage and maybe that would explain the behaviour. I tried to find a pulse in his neck but couldn't feel any. I'm not an expert in this. All I've had is a demonstration of it, years ago when I was rehearsing for a TV play . . .

'And then, well,' he looks towards Roxy, 'thank God, Roxy came in. She helped me turn him over so I could start CPR. I knew how to do it. And then she left to get help. That's the whole story. I have to go – I need the bathroom. Is it all right if I leave now? Please, Captain?'

'Is this the way you remember it, Ms Smith?'

Roxy nods.

'And I believe you became involved, Mrs Abelson, only when you went in search of Mr Lee, so you didn't observe any of this?'

Her turn to nod.

'Captain, I really must go.' Charles fears he's in trouble.

'Thank you.' Leifsson pauses his recording. 'We're all most grateful to you, whatever the outcome. You certainly did your best, and if he recovers, that young man will owe his life to you. Thank you.'

Both women smile agreement and approbation and Charles makes his escape.

After his departure, Captain Leifsson looks at his watch. 'I think I have the picture, at least for now. Unfortunately, I must leave shortly. Have you anything to add, Ms Smith?'

Roxy shakes her head.

'If you don't mind, may I ask you one or two quick questions, please?' He presses his record button again. 'About those chairs in the ballroom, were any of them broken?'

'I don't know.' Roxy is taken aback. 'Maybe one or two. I

wasn't looking at them in detail, although I did notice they were scattered all over the place. I can't really say.'

'Please don't jump to any conclusions about what I'm going to ask you next, Ms Smith. I'm trying to get a general sense of the incident. Would there be any possibility that the two men, Mr Burtonshaw and Mr Levitsky, were physically fighting? Could Mr Levitsky, for instance, have insulted Mr Burtonshaw in some way, leading him to react?'

'That nice old man? Fighting?' Horrified, Roxy exchanges glances with Kitty, who, beside her, seems equally appalled.

'But *could* it have happened? There was an argument and it spiralled out of control?' the captain persists.

'I definitely don't think so. I don't think it's even a theory – I *absolutely* take the word of Charles, Mr Burtonshaw I mean, that what he's told you is exactly what happened.'

The captain turns his attention to Kitty. 'I shall need to talk to you, Mrs Abelson, because there was no third party involved in your meeting with Mr Lee. We've spoken to the librarian on duty this afternoon, who said that the library was very quiet at the time and that he certainly would have noticed had there been anything unusual in your conversation but, of course, he could not throw any light on its content.

'He did register, apparently, that you were both very quietly spoken and that Mr Lee was showing you pictures from the book he had in front of him. I have Mr Lee's version of that meeting and what you talked about, but I should like to ask you for yours, plus anything further you may have to contribute, such as his state of mind, or his reaction when you told him what had happened to his partner, that kind of thing. May we make arrangements to meet later?'

'Of course.'

Kitty's response is so low that Roxy turns to her. 'Are you okay, Kitty?'

'I'm fine.'

'And, of course,' Leifsson goes on, 'your husband, as representative of the company, will have my report on the incident as quickly as possible. He will need to apprise himself of the full story for his own report to the board.' He glances at his watch. 'Right now, however, I regret to say that I must be elsewhere.' He stands up. 'Let me open the door.'

Quickly, while the two women are getting out of their chairs, he walks the short distance past them and pulls the heavy door open just as the staff captain, right hand raised as though he had been about to knock, is revealed. He's breathless. 'Einar?'

'Yes?'

'Joshua Levitsky died in the ambulance on the way to the hospital.'

17

The *Santa Clara* cast off from the quayside in Livorno port just after twenty-five past seven, almost half an hour after her scheduled departure time. The delay had not been due to the storm, which had eased twenty minutes earlier, leaving only showers and a grumpy sea. It was mainly because the ship's master, Captain Einar Leifsson, had had to go ashore to deal with the Italian authorities in the matter of a passenger's death.

The storm, or 'squall', as he'd termed it, had moved away and, although still suffering the occasional jolt, the *Clara* was motoring quietly towards her next port, Naples. Although Kitty has booked herself and Saul into the next day's excursion to Pompeii, at heart she doesn't expect her husband to come with her and now doubts she'll use even her own ticket. She feels flattened in every way, physically, psychologically and emotionally, and can't see how, even after a night's sleep, if she does sleep, she'll be up to viewing bodies, including those of little children (and 'writhing pet dogs', according to the information leaflets), who had been petrified at the moment of their agonising deaths. Again according to the bumf, she would be able to see even the terror on their faces, 'frozen for all time'. *Not right now, thank you.*

She and Saul have been invited on a private tour of the bridge. They haven't discussed it, but when Saul had opened the invitation, he'd seemed a little lukewarm, somewhat along the lines of *You've seen one bridge* . . . 'Nothing to see here, nothing new, for obvious reasons. It's a tiddler anyhow. We'll see how we feel at the time, okay?'

Kitty had made no comment.

Somewhat to her surprise, when she and Saul had arrived, last to the table, for dinner that evening, the Danish woman, Elise, whom she'd never seen interacting with Joshua, had looked as though she had taken the news of his death particularly hard: she was pale, seemed shocked and, as they sat down, had looked at them almost fearfully. 'You've heard what's happened? Roxy has just told us. What a dreadful thing. He was so young.' She had turned to her husband. 'So young, Aksel!' In response, he had just stared at her. He seemed tongue-tied, it's still new news to both of them and he's probably only beginning to absorb the horror of what had happened, Kitty thought. Everyone deals with bad – or good – news in his or her own way.

With its complement reduced by two, it was a sober gathering at table thirty-two that evening. The management had re-spaced the table settings, leaving wider gaps between each in a well-meant effort to cover the absence of Barry Lee and Josh Levitsky. In Kitty's mind the move had had the opposite effect. After what had happened, the couple's non-attendance had moved them to the forefront of everyone's mind.

As a pair, their absence was tangible, if ghostly. It was hard, she thought, to express it in words but if she were an artist she could draw it, with Josh being the bigger figure on the paper because he, even when sulking, had sucked all the oxygen from around the two of them, leaving Barry's quiet and cultured presence (as she now knows it to be) deceptively dull by comparison. She'd had almost no conversation with the man until that last one and, too late now, believes they could have been friends.

The waiter had arrived immediately after she and Saul had taken their seats and, unlike the two previous nights when they had bantered with him and with each other while selecting their meals, tonight's interaction among themselves and with Umar had been brief, terse all round.

But although not as bubbly as usual, there were pockets of chat from other tables in the room – not everyone was as affected, clearly, but overall, when compared with the atmosphere of the previous two evenings, tonight's was serious and even at table thirty-three, where customarily the Dunne family could be depended on to be in loud, high good humour, there was chat, for sure, but in a far more subdued manner than heretofore. The news must have spread, as it does in any closed community. Oddly, there was little discussion about it at Kitty's table and people ate their first and main courses quietly; there was little or no wine consumed.

Tonight's show is to begin in the theatre in half an hour, and in some parts of the room, people are becoming restive. The reason for the hiatus becomes apparent when Captain Leifsson arrives and, using a microphone, introduces himself, apologises for the delay in leaving port, then explains, in outline, what had happened, referring to it as a 'tragic accident'. 'I have decided to speak about the episode, without going into detail, rather than have rumours circulate and swell into unhelpful speculation and untruths. The sad fact is that one of our guests fell ill. We did all we could for him but eventually he had to be taken off the ship by ambulance to go to a hospital ashore. His partner went with him but, very unfortunately, the young man died in the ambulance before he could get there.'

There is an audible reaction in some parts of the room. For some, a very few, this was the first they'd heard of it.

Leifsson waits, mike in hand, until the minor hubbub dies down. 'We have been in touch with the young man's family and I know you will join me and the Portlandis Shipping Line in extending our deepest sympathy to his mother and father, sibling and friends. I am available if any of you care to talk to me immediately after dinner but, as you can imagine, I can't give you any personal details. These events do happen on ships but I'd like to reassure you they are rare. Our medical facilities are modern and fully equipped to deal with all emergencies up to and including the most extreme, but this one proved to be one of those uncommon occasions when disembarkation to an onshore hospital becomes necessary.

'I know this comes as a shock, ladies and gentlemen. Because of shared experience on board, our cruise communities, especially our repeat visitors, do evolve, become families.' He smiles in the direction of a particular table where four people, delighted to be acknowledged, react with discreet little waves. 'We have arranged for our chaplain to be available. She is an ecumenical pastor and serves those of all faiths and none, and our oratory on deck four will be open all night, should you like to spend some time there. There will be a book of condolences open there too, should you wish to express your personal sympathies, and we shall make sure that the family of this unfortunate young man will receive it in due course. It will be available all through the voyage for signing until we dock at Civitavecchia, for Rome, next Monday morning.

'As I say, I shall be happy to answer some of the questions you may have and, as you know, I am available from time to time in various parts of the ship, usually passing through, when I will have time for a short chat. Again, I'm sure you will understand that there are many things I cannot discuss. The investigation about what happened this afternoon is only beginning and, I believe, will be ongoing for some time.

'Ladies and gentlemen, I apologise again for being the bearer of such bad news and hope it will not spoil your evening too much. Thank you.' He switches off the microphone, hands it to the maître d' and, for the next twenty minutes or so, circulates through the room, pausing at each table.

No one at table thirty-two is talking. The desserts had been brought out by waves of waiters within seconds of the captain having completed his speech and Kitty, who has refused any, casts her eye around her five companions: Roxy, predictably, is excavating her ice cream with one hand but surreptitiously, thumbing the phone balanced on her lap with the other. More notes, Kitty thinks. Does the girl ever relax?

Charles, his craggy face sagging even more than usual, is methodically spooning crème caramel into his mouth and, beside her, Saul is lashing into his chocolate mousse. Both Danes had ordered fresh fruit salad on all three evenings so far, and while Aksel digs into his, Elise is pushing pieces of melon and apple around her plate.

Kitty has been following the progress of the captain on his odyssey around the tables in the huge room, feeling once again that she is living through something surreal, a reality TV show, maybe, that is anything but real: she is half expecting some grinning host, teeth like the White Cliffs of Dover, to spring out from behind a door. She has watched brides and grooms performing these visits with their guests at weddings, and this parallel ritual feels out of place, inverting the norm given the reason for the captain's presence tonight, but then what is the norm?

The other five have now finished their dessert and are, with herself, waiting politely for the captain to reach them.

'It's like waiting for the Queen to shake your hand at a garden party!' Roxy mutters, under her breath.

'Have you been?' Kitty, too, keeps her voice low.

'Nah,' Roxy whispers, 'but my mum's a royal-watcher and anything, I mean *anything* – cutting the grass, feeding the corgis – if it's happening at a palace and it's on TV? Mum's glued to it. Even if it's a visit from horsy Princess Anne to an old folks' home, Mum's there.'

The captain, now with the Dunnes, is nearing their table.

'No need to curtsy but sit up straight,' Roxy hisses, and Kitty envies her irreverence. Levity is probably her way of dealing with tragedy. Oh, to be like her!

There had been a time when she was, Kitty thinks ruefully. She and Ruby had had wonderful times together in her early days as a model, while Bertha, Abegunde and herself had operated as a little team, specialising in dressing up to the nines to gate-crash, together, dozens of ritzy A-list-infested parties, sweeping haughtily past security men at the doors, exuding a sense of entitlement with a toss of their hair extensions. They were so impressively beautiful, triply so when together (Kitty blonde, Bertha, red-haired with eyes the colour of the Caribbean and Abegunde, Jamaican/Sudanese, tallest of the three, whose abundant hair, most of it real, cascaded to her waist) that they were rarely challenged.

'May I join you, please?'

To the astonishment of everyone at table thirty-two, including Kitty, the captain of the *Santa Clara* takes a vacant chair from a nearby table, waits until she and Roxy shuffle apart to leave a gap, pushes in and sits, beginning his spiel with a reiteration of his gratitude for the parts that Charles, Roxy and Kitty had played in the drama that afternoon. 'I owe it to you to give you at least some detail, on the understanding that you will not gossip. And I must include you all, even you, Mr Abelson.' In their various ways, they all reassured him of their discretion.

During his visit to the police station ashore, he tells them, the formalities had been difficult and complex. The results of toxicology tests on Josh's body would not be available until after the *Santa Clara* was due to sail.

In his steady, almost flawless English (with, to Kitty's ear, just the faintest Scandinavian intonation), he tells them that, with the help of international agencies, such as Interpol, they had managed to intercept Josh's parents on their arrival at Doha airport to start a vacation, and that the authorities there had also been helpful in facilitating the couple's immediate turnaround to board the first flight available to Italy. 'As for the authorities here, the Italian legal and police systems are bureaucratic but I was banking on that because in general, officials of all agencies drown in paperwork and they have bigger worries here, including the fragility of local and national government and the dreadful refugee crisis. But in truth, I believe that if I hadn't lost my temper, or intimated that I was about to, I might yet be in the police station.

'Is there anything, outside what I've said, that I can help you with?'

'Was it cocaine? That's what some people are saying.' This is Roxy.

'As I've said,' he responds smoothly, 'the results of toxicology screening won't be available for a while, so we shall have to wait and see.' He scans again, waiting for someone else to contribute.

'How's Barry?' This from Kitty.

'I'm afraid I can't answer that. Nothing to do with secrecy or privacy, I simply don't know. No information whatsoever. I haven't seen him, and neither, say the police officers I've met, have they – which doesn't imply that Barry isn't in the hospital with his partner's body. I did not have time to go to the hospital, but when I telephoned from the ship before we left, I found those in charge there less than helpful since Mr Lee is not a patient. I do find communications difficult in Italy – so few people speak any of my languages, but then, I guess, they don't have to and it's churlish of me to say such a thing since Italian is not one of mine. I did leave my personal number with the police, with instructions that, when Mr Lee appears, he should call me at any time, day or night.'

'Ah! But will you have a signal?' asks Saul.

Leifsson smiles. 'I get the joke, Mr Abelson, but, as you probably know, we have ways and means on the bridge.' Again, he scans for questions. 'Nothing more?' Then, to Saul: 'May I steal your wife for a few minutes, Mr Abelson?'

'What for?' Saul frowns.

'Unfortunately, our interview in the immediate aftermath of the incident this afternoon was cut short and I need to ask her a few questions. It's merely procedure but it's necessary for the paperwork and I promise I shall allow her back to you presently.'

'What questions?' Saul glances at Kitty, then back at the captain. 'About what? And what interview?'

'About her encounter with Mr Lee.'

'What encounter?' Now he stares at Kitty.

'You were working when I got back to the suite after meeting Barry, which was at around half past three, before four anyway, I think,' Kitty says swiftly. 'Remember I said I was going to look for him after we got back from the excursion? Roxy was there with us in the suite. But then you were asleep when I got back again after talking, with Charles and Roxy, in the captain's office. I can't be sure now about the time – everything was so muddled and so quick. I did tell you the three of us were being formally interviewed.' This is over-explaining. She stops.

'Without representation?' Saul is still frowning. 'I'd have remembered that.'

'The presence of a lawyer is not necessary in the slightest, Mr Abelson. As you must know, I have legal jurisdiction here in any case. But legalities don't come into it for your wife. There has been no suspicion of anything untoward on her part, none at all.'

On the surface, Leifsson remains unruffled although, if anything, thinks Kitty, he is becoming a little impatient. 'Saul,' she says, 'I was going to tell you about Barry as well but then time ran out. We both had to get a move on and dress for dinner. Remember all that kerfuffle because of your knee injury?' Again she stops. When she gets flustered, the residue of her Dublin accent becomes stronger and she's conscious that that's happening, also that she's inadvertently illuminating her domestic relationship for the others at the table, including the captain. She reddens, thinking she might even have made herself sound guilty about meeting Barry – it wouldn't be the first time Saul has become suspicious about what he, quaintly she's always thought, terms a 'tryst'.

The captain breaks in again, ignoring Saul and addressing her directly: 'Would now be convenient for you, Mrs Abelson?'

'Okay, okay, I'll come with you.' Saul, hampered by his strapped knee, struggles to get up.

But the captain, his tone silky, also stands. 'That won't be necessary, Mr Abelson.'

'But—'

'Were you in the library with Mr Lee and your wife?'

'No, but—'

'Then I'm afraid you're not material to this investigation. Unless, perhaps, you might know something about Mr Lee – or Mr Levitsky – that we don't?'

'I never met either of them before. But I was very impressed with Barry. I was planning to offer him a job.'

'That may be possible, of course, but we believe he is still in Livorno. Or he may not be. Would you like his phone number? I'm afraid I don't have it to hand, and we shall have to secure his permission first, of course. As a director, I'm sure you know how important it is, these days, to comply with data protection legislation.'

'Fine, fine!' Saul bundles up his napkin and throws it onto the table. 'Do what you have to and, yes, get me that number.'

He addresses Kitty, still sitting and growing more embarrassed by the minute: 'My knee is killing me so I'm going back to the suite. Okay, sweetie?' The tone is low and level but Kitty can tell he's furious at being challenged. She believes that the captain's position is defensible in the circumstances, but has the feeling that the spat, small as it was, had been a rout for Saul.

'Cancel that trip to Pompeii tomorrow, Kitty. Thank you – '

Saul takes his crutch that Charles has retrieved for him from under the table. 'By the way, sweetie, there's no way in hell I can manage a trip to Pompeii, or any trip at all, in this condition.'

'I might go by myself, then.' Although she had decided she wouldn't, Kitty certainly doesn't want to convey the impression that part of her job description as Saul's wife is to be his supine assistant. Not in front of this tableful of people. Not in front of Roxy making notes. Not in front of Captain Einar Leifsson.

'Fine. Do whatever you like.' Saul, not yet accustomed to his crutch, takes an awkward step and grimaces. 'I'm going up.'

'Shall we go, Mrs Abelson?' Leifsson gets to his feet and steps aside to allow her to pass him.

Stuck for words, Kitty stands and heads for the door, Leifsson falling into step beside her. As they walk, she is conscious of hundreds of eyes, from their table and others, boring into their backs, a flashback to her days on the catwalk when she sashayed and twirled for rich fashionistas and big noises in the business. She's also ultra-conscious of Saul's gaze too, as on his crutch, he hobbles after them to take the elevator.

When they are outside the room and are safely past the elevator bank, Leifsson turns to her. 'I'm afraid it will have to be my office again, Mrs Abelson. I know it is not the most comfortable place on the ship, but I will be recording you as I did the others. I hope you don't mind?'

'It'll be my first time ever to be taped. I did a radio interview once, but it was live. I think I'd be very embarrassed to hear my own voice.'

'Everyone is.'

Conversation peters out.

She already knows that the little office is a couple of decks below the level of the atrium but, not wishing to have to share an elevator with him again, she's about to say something facile about needing to walk off her dinner when he supersedes her: 'Shall we take the stairs, Mrs Abelson, or do you prefer the elevator?'

'The stairs will be fine.'

'This way.' Lightly, for an instant, he touches her back, guiding her towards a brass, semi-circular rail, from which a red-carpeted flight of stairs curves downwards, but before they reach it, he's stopped by a middle-aged couple who wish to condole with him on the loss of a passenger. 'Such a tragedy, Captain, and him so young,' the woman says. 'He was from the Middle East, was he?'

'Israel.' Leifsson's tone is polite but not warm. He is not inviting expansion of the conversation, thinks Kitty, but they don't pick this up.

'It was a heart attack, I believe?' This is the man.

'The jury is out on that one until we have the results of the post-mortem examination. Everything will be covered.'

'Well, I heard that the ballroom floor was too slippy and he fell down and cracked his head wide open and there was lots and lots of blood.' The woman's eyes are avid. She's probably the type, Kitty believes, who glories in misery, the deeper the better.

'As I told everyone in the dining room—'

'- we don't eat dinner,' the man says, patting his ample belly, as though making a virtue of it. 'We like to eat before four o'clock, but we heard you made a lovely speech. We'll definitely sign your memory book,' he adds kindly. 'You mustn't blame yourself, Captain. These things happen. In the chapel, is it?'

'You mean the book of condolence? That's right. We're happy to facilitate it. Many people wish to express their feelings.

Well,' Leifsson makes a small move towards the stairs, 'it was nice to meet you.'

But the woman hasn't finished. 'Is this your wife, Captain?' She's smiling at Kitty, stepping back a little to accord her that swift up-and-down assessment, common among women the world over.

'Oh, no!' Kitty and the captain say simultaneously.

He gets them away and they descend the staircase in silence, he two steps ahead of her, she holding the rail all the way down, but taking the opportunity furtively to touch the spot he had touched, checking that all is smooth, that there's no little bulge to be felt under the clasp of her bra.

The silence between them persists as they walk along one of the ship's internal corridors until they reach the door of his office. It continues as they go inside, he opening the door, holding it for her so she can precede him.

'Will I sit here again?' Kitty indicates one of the two chairs in front of the desk.

'Would you be more comfortable in the other one? The light won't be in your eyes.' He has just switched on his desk lamp.

'This will be good, thank you.'

He retrieves his digital voice recorder and opens what looks like a ledger or logbook, uncaps a fountain pen and turns on the machine, fumbling a little with the switches. 'These are so tiny. You'd think that the manufacturers would take into account that some of us— there! Cool!' Given his normal mode of speech, that word doesn't fit.

For a few seconds they both gaze at the little red light at the top of the matchbox-sized appliance. Then he checks his watch. 'Twenty-one zero six, Monday, the nineteenth of December two thousand and sixteen, captain's office. Present, Captain

Einar Leifsson and witness, Mrs Kitty Golden Abelson.' Then, covering the top of the machine, presumably to muffle it, 'This has to be formal, Mrs Abelson. It's a legal requirement for me.'

As he uncovers the machine again, he smiles at her, and it strikes Kitty that the extra formality is for her husband's benefit, should Saul ever demand to hear it. But she's worried she won't be able to remember how she and Charles dealt with the story, that their versions will be different. Her brain, protecting her, has already smoothed out some details. 'Captain, I hope I can help you here and that I won't be contradicting what the others have said. My mind feels very muddled right now.'

'Just tell me what you remember, Mrs Abelson. Are we ready?'

She nods and he launches straight into it. 'May I take you back some hours to this afternoon, please,' he begins, 'and the conversation you had with Mr Barry Lee in the library of the *Santa Clara*? What time was it, do you remember, and for how long did the two of you speak?'

'I can't be definite about either timing, Captain.' If he was going to be by-the-book, she had to be too. 'I was upset at the time.'

'Your best estimate?'

'I found him, I think, around three thirty.'

'And the length of your conversation?'

'Maybe fifteen minutes, I'd say, or a few more. No more than twenty.'

'You were the first person to tell him what had happened to his partner. Did you tell him immediately?'

'No.'

'Why not?'

She thinks. In this situation with the little machine winking between them, she's not going to quantify the psychological mishmash she'd undergone on seeing Barry, so peaceful and happy in the library when she'd walked in. 'It wouldn't have been the right thing to do.'

'Why not? Was a delay going to help in any way?'

'I just couldn't do it. He seemed so – so absorbed in the book he was reading. In a restful way. I'm sorry I can't put it better than that.'

'And were you well positioned to assess his mood at that point? You're sure he didn't know already?'

'I'm sure.' But this line of questioning is bothering her. She pauses to think.

'Mrs Abelson?'

'He *seemed* relaxed.'

'Do you happen to remember the name of that book?'

'Yes. No. Not quite – sorry. Is this relevant, Captain?'

'I apologise if I seem pedantic but, as policemen say when they're appealing for information, "the smallest detail" can prove to be important.'

She thinks hard. 'It was a coffee table book, a catalogue of some exhibition about a man who designed a church in Barcelona. Barry said it was the greatest sculpture in the world and it should be on everyone's bucket list . . .' Try as she might she couldn't remember the name of the architect. 'The more he talked about this man,' she was racking her brains, 'the more excited Barry got. You could see he really loved this church.' Abruptly, she remembers the little tortoise holding up the giant pillar. Barry had seemed so affectionate, so – so *tender* about it. Tears pool in her eyes.

He sees them and softens considerably: 'Gaudí's Sagrada Familia?'

'That's it!' She's superficially relieved, but Barry's revelation earlier was tugging at her tongue. 'I'm sorry you had to prompt me,' she says.

'So at that stage, Mrs Abelson,' he gets back to officialese, 'before you told him about Joshua, he seemed relaxed. But you also said he was "excited" – could he have been a little agitated?'

She frowns. 'No. If it was agitation, it was because he was talking about his hero. Agitation in a good way.'

'Sorry to press you, Mrs Abelson, but you're absolutely certain that at the time you met him Mr Lee was thinking of nothing but the book about Gaudí you saw him reading?'

'Yes. I'm certain.' She's becoming irked. Rather than react, she pauses again. Then: 'But how does anyone know what people are thinking? To me, though, he was loving this book. Like Gaudí was, he is an architect so I believe I did understand his excitement about that. It was catching.'

'You mean you yourself became excited?'

'Happy that he was happy. But knowing how short-lived that was going to be, that what I had to tell him would probably destroy not only his happiness but his whole life, I got a little bit upset. I think I did anyway. Anybody would.' She feels defensive now.

'So then did you tell him about Joshua?'

'I postponed it. I was having to pluck up the courage.'

'And during the postponement what did you do? What did he do? Or say?'

'We talked some more about Gaudí and he described the church. Oh – I've just remembered. He had found a novel by

Roxy Smith on the bookshelves. He fetched it to show it to me. He told me he was surprised to find it because he hadn't altogether believed her when she'd told us all at the table she was a published author. He seemed amused about finding it, but not harshly so. My impression was that he liked Roxy and that he was relieved she'd been telling the truth. And then he put the book back.' Kitty wipes her eyes with a fist.

'And then what?' His tone has softened again. He turns off the recorder. 'Are you happy enough to continue, Kitty? We can take a short break if you wish.'

'When he came back to where we were sitting, I told him.' But she has registered his name-slip, and as they lapse into renewed silence over the currently dead recorder, so, she thinks, has he.

'Sorry, Mrs Abelson,' he says, then. 'For the record, it will have to be Mrs Abelson.'

He's embarrassed, she thinks, and refuses his offer of water. 'No thank you.' She's off balance.

He switches on the machine again. 'So how did Mr Lee behave when you told him his partner was taken seriously ill?'

He ordered an ice cream – how do you think he reacted? Kitty has recovered somewhat. 'He froze.'

'Froze?'

'Froze, went still. Like his limbs wouldn't move.'

'Did he perform any actions? Cover his face, for instance? Weep?'

'He closed the Gaudí book. Fiddled with the cover of it, kind of lined it up so it sat right in the centre of the table.'

'Did he say anything at that point?'

'I actually can't remember, Captain. He may have but I just can't remember. He was kind of locked onto the book. But then

I do remember he looked at the ceiling. Staring. I told him I'd go with him to find out where Joshua was. And he sort of behaved like a school pupil with a teacher. Obedient when I said, "So let's go," or something like that. Anyhow he left with me to go to the desk but I could tell he was distraught. The contrast between his stiffness and silence and the way he'd been when he was talking about the book couldn't have been bigger.'

Leifsson again switches off the recorder. 'Thank you, Mrs Abelson, you've been very helpful.'

She hesitates, then: 'I don't know whether I should say this or not and, for Barry's sake, I don't want to put it on the record, but at your party last evening, I definitely smelt marijuana on Josh.'

'So did I, Kitty.' He sounds sad. 'Such a waste of a beautiful young man.'

He looks up and his eyes are different, less blue or something, she thinks fancifully, but this could be because the lighting in here is currently so low. 'Some of those questions you asked me,' she says quietly, 'you think Barry was involved?'

He studies the surface of his desk. 'Joshua was unemployed. As far as we've been able to ascertain, he had no money of his own.'

That was quick, she thinks. 'His parents?'

'In a way I hope that's what happened because parents are usually the last to know.'

'You've no doubt it was cocaine, then?'

'Are we in lodge, Kitty?'

There's that flip of the stomach again. He's trusting her, his gaze steady. And he called her 'Kitty'. 'Yes, if you mean are we speaking in confidence.'

'Over the years,' he goes on, 'we've had it with crew. You get to know.'

'How do they bring it on board?'

'They find professionals to tell them how – or, more likely, the professionals find them, particularly when they go ashore for a few hours in certain cities, Nice being one of them, I'm afraid. Some of the younger ones are kids from poverty-stricken countries. Most of them send all of their salaries home, keeping enough only to buy a few soda cans at the crew bar although our ship, in fairness to Portlandis, is not the worst of these liners in employment terms, but it's not the best either.

'Of course they're tempted when they're offered cash and reassured that the risks are covered. Once or twice we've been convinced that our security guards have been bribed to look the other way when the drugs come on board, but we haven't been able to prove it – yet.

'Who'd blame them when you think about it? And then you do think about it because Joshua Levitsky paid for his high with his life.'

'Crew members sell it on to passengers? Is that how Josh got the stuff?'

'Regular users always find what they need, or believe they need. It's a sort of talent they have.' He sighs, adding sadly, 'And it's not always crew either. During my time on the *Clara*, we've had to deal with a few passengers too.'

'What happens to them?'

'They leave the ship at the next port of call and are usually met by the authorities.' His voice has hardened. 'If they've paid for a fun holiday on a cruise liner, they're certainly not poor. My sympathy is not extended in their direction. But in life, these days, nothing is ever black and white, is it? For me anyway, it's a matter of balancing things out. Oh dear,' he shakes his head, 'that sounds so – so *lame*. I'm what they call in Iceland a "*Hvað er gangandi klisja*".'

'What? I didn't catch that.'

'I'm a walking cliché, or I can be one, I think you would say in America. In this instance, the crew is under investigation – but you won't see it. None of the passengers will. If we find the right guy or guys, he or they will be taken off at the next port, and handed over to the police. They'll never work again at sea, probably, certainly never on a cruise liner from any country.

'The reality is that at the lower levels – although in my experience they're cared for by Portlandis with health benefits and such – on all ships, not just this one, they're badly paid, have an awful, very restrictive life and are scheduled on duty for appalling, almost inhuman hours. I'm top dog here, with truly extraordinary powers but, basically, I'm as much of an employee as they are and there's little I can do about the corporate side of things except, when on board and in charge of literally every aspect of the running of this ship, to treat them well when their problems reach my desk, humanely when they're up before me on charges.

'I'm from Iceland, Kitty, where we've had our financial problems recently but where we are exceedingly rich by the standards of the regions from which many of our crew members have come. Sometimes, when I see these tiny, puny Filipinos and Mexicans working these shifts, the physical toll it takes on them, I find it hard to be harsh if they transgress.

'The drugs rules are different, though. The bottom line on the *Clara*, on all cruise liners, is that there is an absolute no-drugs policy, no three-strikes-you're-out. It's first-strike-you're-out. No matter what your motivation, you, who went off to El Dorado as the bright hope of your family, will be in prison for years, perhaps in certain countries for the rest of your life, or even receive the death penalty. And every day in your prison cell you will know that, as a result of what you've done, your family will maybe starve, your sisters could be trafficked and you'll probably never get another job. Certainly never on any cruise liner. Some, a tiny minority, continue to find it worth the risk.

'During this voyage, I would love to have a conversation with your husband about all of this, if he's open to it. Portlandis has other ships besides this one.'

She gazes at him. There's something indefinable in the air. Not so, she thinks. It's perfectly definable. 'I can ask Saul to come down now.' Her look, although she's trying to control it, is brazen.

He's staring back at her, his expression now inscrutable. 'No,' he says simply. 'That won't be necessary.' He averts his eyes. 'It's been a long and terrible day for all of us. I'll call him in a couple of days. What more can I say? I've said far too much as it is.

'There is one thing, however.' He is playing with his recorder. 'In case you think I'm using you as a conduit to your husband, I'm not. I give you my word on that. It's just that . . .'

'Yes?' Her breath seems stuck somewhere in her throat.

'Your empathy shows,' he says quietly, turning the little digital machine over and over in one hand, watching it as though it's a new and intriguing toy. 'I've taken advantage. I apologise. It won't happen again.'

'I'd like it to . . .'

Kitty-Kat Golden and her big fat gob. She can hear the jeers of her classmates when, once again, hauled up before the Sister Principal, she hadn't been able to prevent herself from confessing the truth following some misdemeanour of which they'd all been accused . . .

The captain puts the recorder down as delicately as though it's a rare, fragile bird's egg, then stares at her across the desk. 'You're the wife of a director of this company.'

Recklessly, not quite knowing where this is coming from, she gazes back. 'I know exactly who I am, Captain Leifsson.'

'And so do I.' Then: 'I believe I'm to see you both on the bridge? I'll do my best to make it sound interesting for you, although I'm sure your husband might be bored since he must have heard everything before. You yourself? Have you been on a ship's bridge before?'

The change is extraordinary. This is Captain Leifsson, master of his ship, relaxed but on top of his brief.

*

Kitty takes her time in going back to the suite, dawdling by the window of the jewellery shop in the mall to admire its centrepiece, a glorious opal pendant. She decides not to indulge in fantasies about broad-shouldered ships' officers but to concentrate on the disturbing elements of the conversation about the crew. She will never again take a cruise without considering the contrast between people like herself and them. On the surface, all is grace and ease, marble bathrooms and a fluffy towel sculpted into a different animal form every night. Below, there is fatigue and self-sacrifice, four bunks to a tiny room, a hook instead of a wardrobe, a shared shower room with a quarter of a shelf for your shampoo or shaving gear. She'd watched a documentary and, until her conversation with the captain, very little of what she'd seen and heard had penetrated. She was probably painting her toenails at the time.

She also decides, while admiring the dazzling jewel, the artistry of its creator, she will never again thoughtlessly flash a credit card, funded by her husband, to buy something glittery simply to hang around her neck. Because she wants it. Because he can afford it.

What had she become?

But she is confused. The captain spoke of clichés. This kind of thinking is cliché in its purest form, a tabloid headline, a video sidebar on Facebook: *Rich Bitch Sees the Light. Your Jaw Will Drop When You Watch This.*

When she lets herself into the suite she finds Saul lying on the bed in his pyjamas, sore leg propped up on a pillow, watching CNN. 'Dow's up,' he says, without taking his eyes off the screen.

'That's terrific, Saul,' she responds, without thinking, calling on her repertoire of standard replies. 'You selling or buying?'

'Not yet. It's a waiting game.' He switches the channel to Fox. 'So how'd it go with Cap'n Birdseye? Oh, by the way, you forgot your phone and there's been a call for you. I couldn't get to it, don't know how it got through. Probably because at that moment we were hugging the coast, going past Rome, or Corsica or somewhere, and your phone could piggy-back.' Still watching the TV screen, he indicates the phone on her side of the huge, double-mirrored bureau. She picks it up, and although there's no service it shows there's been a call. From Ruby. 'Can I use yours, Saul? It's Ruby. You have some kind of super-satellite, haven't you?'

'Marine. Paid enough for it. And it's still patchy – do you have to? Can't you wait until your own gets a signal?'

'Saul! It's *Ruby*!' She glares at him. 'Okay, okay, keep your hair on, you know how to use it? I don't know what it is on your phone but this one's an iPhone and it's the little green icon on the screen.' He eases his machine out from under his leg and tosses it to her side of the bed.

'Thanks.'

By mistake, she presses the Messages icon – which is also green – instead of the phone one and a string of names comes up in his inbox: Pip Pip Pip Pip all the way down the screen: 'My God, Saul, you've been working poor Pippa to the bone – how many calls a day have you been making to the poor woman, you sure have made her sweat – give her a break, eh?' She presses the correct icon which is at the bottom of Saul's screen and taps out Ruby's number.

Miracle of miracles, she gets through. 'Hello?' Ruby sounds cautious. 'Who's this?'

'It's Kitty, dumbchuck!' Then she remembers she's not on her own phone. 'Sorry, it's Kitty – you called me?'

'Oh!' Ruby audibly brightens. 'Listen, there's big news. They've found that rat Sherman. He was arrested at Miami airport when he got off a plane from Haiti, would you believe? There was a paragraph, one of those little boxes, on the front page of the *New York Times* this morning. I just saw it. Shall I read it out to you? The headline is "Former Model Agent Arrested". That's what grabbed me, naturally.'

She's excited, but Kitty can't yet sort out what she's feeling. 'Yeah. That'd be great, Ruby.'

'Here goes. "Sherman Read",' Ruby begins in a sing-song manner, '"fifty two, was apprehended last night by officers from the US Customs and Border Protection Agency as he came through Miami International Airport having arrived from Toussaint Louverture –" can't pronounce that, hon "– International Airport in Port-au-Prince, Haiti. Mr Read's wife of eighteen years, Lola "Lottie" Sudman, fifty, herself a former model, divorced Read in May 2006, six months after he fled the US, allegedly having embezzled the earnings of three top models for whom he was an agent at Solar Models, since gone out of business."

'Don'tcha love the "top models" bit, Kitty?' But without waiting for a response, she carries on: "'The FBI has never closed the case and, with the co-operation of other agencies, including Interpol, has been searching for Mr Read since that time. He is currently in custody and will appear before a judge later today in Miami-Dade federal court to face charges. Mr Read and his ex-wife have three children."

'That's it, Kitty, isn't it great?'

'Uh-oh,' Kitty says. 'You're breaking up, Ruby. We're at sea. Call you tomorrow.' She presses the off button. Saul's signal is still fine.

Why doesn't she feel as elated as Ruby obviously does? What the hell is happening to her?

'Ruby OK?' Saul asks, when she gives back his phone.

'She's fine. Just wanted a chat. I'm going out for a bit of fresh air, Saul. See you anon.'

Outside, despite the blast of frigid air on her face, she stays at the rail. Coming on top of Barry's confiding in her and her edgy discombobulating encounter with the captain, Ruby's news has tipped the balance in some way she can't yet define. All she knows is that it has triggered not just the feelings of that episode but something equally profound. She feels that her life, as she's known it, is spiralling away from her with the ship's wake, streaming incessantly until it subsides into the sea as the *Clara* glides onwards through the dark evening. The earlier storm is now but an inconsequential entry in her 'memory book', as that man had termed the book of condolence for poor Joshua.

Right now, try as she might, she can't catch firm ground.

18

Roxy Smith is disconsolate. It's early morning on day four of the voyage, a big day for her because she's to fulfil a lifelong dream by visiting the romantic island of Ischia, but with the trauma of the previous afternoon, the joy of anticipation has dissipated.

She will never forget the sight of Josh on the floor, his hair spread on his blood, like the wings of a wounded crow. She could still feel his weight as she and Charles had turned him over, but most vivid of all was the shock, recurring, of seeing his bloodied, near-lifeless face.

With him and Barry missing, it had been a sad dinner yesterday evening. Even Charles, who can usually be relied on to provide a laugh or two, had been down in the dumps.

And at the other side of the table, although they'd played no part in the events of that afternoon, even the two love birds had seemed to feel its effects. Roxy had noticed (it was kind of a relief) that, instead of holding on to each other when they were talking together, they were concentrating on their food as though it was their last meal ever.

But, tragic as it had been, Joshua's death was only one component of her upset this morning. The other is Roxy herself. Only day four of the trip, this unbelievable opportunity her mum has handed her, and already, shamefully, she's thinking of throwing in the towel because she's starting to believe she doesn't have what it takes to become a successful novelist. She now fears that *Heartbreak in the Cotswolds* had been merely a flash in the pan.

She's sitting on her *über*-terrific bed in her *über*-amazing suite, looking out at her *über*-fabulous balcony on the starboard side of the *Santa Clara*. She can see nothing through the windows, her own reflection, half lit by the table lamp on her bedside locker, obscuring all but a stretch of balcony rail. Beyond that sliver of silvery metal is a void, because it's just before six in the morning and it's still dark.

She had set the alarm on her mobile phone, planning to get out there to watch the ship dock in Naples prior to the trip to Ischia so she could give her mum and Ruth the full flavour of the day – and also, of course, to chronicle it for her novel.

The bloody novel . . .

There's no point in comforting herself with what other novelists have said in interviews about the 'very difficult second novel': by the time they're being interviewed, they've got through it, their books are on the shelves, thanks (writes the interviewer) to 'true grit' and 'application' or 'the inspirational advice' offered by publisher, editor, mother, English teacher of yore, even the late Maeve Binchy, who had famously ordered countless whining hackettes simply to get their arses back into the chair.

Maeve, by her own account, had started her own writing day at six in the morning, finished at noon and had been happily ensconced in the pub by half past, having lunch with her beloved Gordon, so that they had the rest of the day to themselves.

By contrast, here's Roxy. Yes, it's six in the morning and she's doing what? Staring into dark space. She's a shit writer. She'll never be able to pin down a viable idea. She's still stuck with trying to make choices. She's useless.

At one stage yesterday afternoon, following her conversation with the captain, she'd briefly considered a shipwreck or the *Clara* being overcome by pirates, but she had calmed down. She doubted now, having been on the Med for a few days, that, realistically, pirates would get too far with such a situation. It was all hopeless.

Temporarily juggling with shipwreck, she'd used some of the precious data allowance on her mobile to get an idea of how to frame the chaos on the bridge. She had googled 'photo, cruise liner, bridge' and had been shown a wide shot of what seemed to be an array of computer stations and screens. Sitting in front of them, widely spaced, were several men and a woman while in front of a series of massive panoramic windows stood two more men, one with binoculars to his eyes, the other with a coffee cup raised to his mouth. All calm, shiny and relaxed, no sign of a big mahogany wheel with spokes coming out of it. Not terribly dramatic, she'd thought, disappointed.

As for using Captain bloody Leifsson as a role model for her man, she'd initially had goose-bumps every time she'd glimpsed him – and she conceded that his speech during the dinner had been stylish – but in her view, he'd certainly displayed the need to lighten up. Right now he doesn't seem the type to take his eye off his joystick or whatever he uses to steer the ship.

Could she throw somebody overboard? She'd googled again – but found a very, *very* complex procedure to stop the ship, turn it, turn it the other way, warn everyone, launch lifeboats and more. 'MOB', it's called. Man Overboard. They train for it apparently. But by the time she'd authentically described all this in a novel, her poor victim would have been sleeping with the fishes.

And then, dammit, she'd found she'd used up all the data she'd been saving to send pictures of Ischia to her mum.

What had happened to her? With the first *Heartbreak*, she'd been able to start at the beginning with her heroine and anti-hero (a taciturn chap) encountering each other in the single shop of a tiny village nestled in the picturesque Cotswolds landscape. They'd hated each other on sight, but since he was stuck there doing a land survey on behalf of the council for the next six months and she was the local schoolteacher, they would inevitably run into each other frequently. That was the set-up and the rest had flowed, chapter after chapter. She didn't even have to revise. Well, not until her agent and her editor had seen the manuscript. She'd actually enjoyed the entire process.

And now? Floundering. Awash with ideas but they're all still tumbling about, causing each other to crash.

Roxy is not normally a quitter. She's a glass-half-full person in any circumstance, but now, she decides, she has only two choices: to dump everything and start all over again (maybe ask to be moved to a different table so she can be at close quarters with a new bunch of people) or reef through what she has already and tear out the dross. In a sense, though, both options amount to the same thing.

The captain could still be in the background as the 'enigmatic' foil to her strong, fiery heroine – in her notes, Roxy had been tinkering around with presenting this novel in the first person, centring it on herself as protagonist. It would make things a little easier, narrowing down the choices, because everything would have to be seen from a single perspective. She was nervous about it but if she continued with the bloody thing it was still an option.

What makes everything worse is that by blabbing about what she was doing, she had created expectations, especially with the Dunnes. She'd have been far better off if she'd kept her mouth shut.

To be harsh about it, the Dunnes had proven to be a washout.

Last evening, after dinner, she'd kept the appointment with them to distract herself, knowing what images would inhabit her imagination after she was alone in her bed. She'd met Mary and Gemma, with Gemma's husband Jimmy, along with Gemma's brother-in-law Larry, and his wife Dympna, who is one of Gemma's four aunties on the trip. Missing were two of the aunties and a husband, who had opted for an early dinner at a hamburger restaurant on board prior to a 'Broadway-style production' of *Cabaret*.

So expectations had been already high. They had insisted on including her in rounds of drinks: 'Keep your hands in your pockets, there, Roxy, we insist!' And with all of them leaning forward avidly to listen, she'd started her tape.

Immediately afterwards, although it was heading towards midnight, she had sat down at the desk in her stateroom to encapsulate Mary's story. Even while she was listening to it, however, her sense of doubt about how it could be incorporated into her novel was increasing.

In itself, Mary's was a moving story, but it had been done and done and done again, especially in Ireland, still enmeshed in such stories for real. She knew this would sound harsh and self-seeking on her part should she ever express the reason why she had lost interest; she was, in a real sense, ashamed of having done so.

Each individual story is harrowing – for the individual.

But since she'd moved to Ireland, she'd found that every talk programme on the Irish stations, especially those encouraging phone-ins, had frequently run Mary's story: pregnant girl is incarcerated against her will in an institution, baby snatched without much notice, maybe sold to America, decades-long searches as mother and baby, sometimes one, sometimes both, searched for each other; babies, in adulthood, frantic to find out who they are.

Roxy had seen the movie *Philomena,* had wept with other audience members, but in Mary's case, she'd been fired up to hear something different.

So? What was new?

After publication of her first *Heartbreak*, she had been invited to do a reading in her local Women's Institute, where her mum was a member. During the question-and-answer session afterwards, one woman in the front row, who'd been busy writing notes throughout, even noting Roxy's answers to questions about where she got her ideas, put her hand up. 'If you don't mind,' the woman said, 'I've heard it said many times that everyone has a book in them. Is that true?'

'Are you a writer yourself?' Roxy had asked.

'No, but like half of us here, I want to be,' she'd responded, raising a knowing titter throughout the room.

Roxy, a novice at this, had been slightly thrown: she didn't want to insult people by saying that authors had special skills but, seeing her hesitation, Tony Scott, her still-new agent, who'd been in the audience, had jumped in to cover for her. 'If I may, ladies, that's absolutely true. Everyone's life story is worth a book, but the kicker is that not everyone can write it! Certainly not as well as Roxy Smith up there!' The women had applauded, smiling and nudging each other. The questioner had joined in the applause and *Heartbreak*'s author, relieved, had been able to take the next question.

So, although not strictly analogous, her dilemma about Mary Dunne's story is similarly obvious. In her case, though, Roxy had made the running, conveying not just interest but excitement about its potential, and now the entire Dunne cavalcade, including Gemma and Mary, are expecting to see themselves immortalised. Before their meeting and despite the subdued atmosphere in the dining room the previous evening, each time she had glanced towards the Dunnes' table, one or other of them would catch her eye and give her a wide, conspiratorial smile or a thumbs-up. Gemma's husband, Jimmy, had made that a two-thumbs salute.

So she has to include Mary – or does she? Is she learning the hard way that this is what writers mean when they talk about having to be ruthless? The novel to be served above all else?

In the bar, expectations had been already high. They had insisted on including her in rounds of drinks: 'Keep your hands in your pockets, there, Roxy, we insist!'

As the tape unspooled quietly, Roxy had forced herself to think of nothing and no one but Mary while she, emboldened in the presence of her tribe, encouraging her all the way, spoke quietly, remembering.

She was sixteen, and pregnant by a local lad. He was eighteen, but the problem was that he was top drawer, son of the doctor in the midlands town where they both lived. The plan was that, after the Leaving Cert, he was to go on to the College of Surgeons in Dublin to do medicine and follow his da into the profession.

'Oh, he was gorgeous, Roxy.' Mary's eyes misted. 'Clongowes, a rugby player, and everyone said he'd even a chance of playing for Leinster.'

Roxy knew all about Leinster and Brian O'Driscoll. She had a picture of Mary's guy now but: 'What's Clongowes?'

They'd all looked at each other. 'Only one of the poshest

boarding schools in the country,' Gemma said. 'When you met a fella at a dance and he said he was from Clongowes – mind you, a lot of them said that but you could tell by the accent they might have passed the place on the bus. But if he was for real, you knew immediately he was set for life, doctor, lawyer, you name it – twig, Roxy?'

'I do.'

'He offered to marry me,' Mary took up her story again, 'but his parents kicked up a stink and there was this big meeting at home with my parents. Before I knew it I was on the boat with my father. They'd got a priest friend of theirs to organise for me to stay in a convent where I could have my baby and nobody would ever know. His parents paid for the whole thing. They even handed me an envelope at the end of that meeting with my ma and da. It was open and I could see two hundred-pound notes in it. "For maternity smocks," she said, the mother. "And pocket money," the father said, with this big, beefy smile.

'I threw it on the floor and my da lifted his hand to hit me, except he didn't – he wouldn't in front of anybody, especially posh people. My ma picked it all up and put it back in the envelope.

'They thought I was a prostitute.' Mid-transcription in her stateroom, Roxy had taken a break to consider her stance on the story. If she had been given it twenty years previously, she would probably have thought she'd hit the mother lode, no pun intended.

Mary had had her daughter, got to keep her, feed her, bathe her and care for her 'for three days, two nights, four and a half hours and six minutes' before she'd had to give her up for the adoption. Roxy found this particular detail, the precision of the four and a half hours and six minutes, very moving: she could barely imagine, even as a novelist, what those last few hours for Mary, with her baby, must have felt like.

'Well, thank you very much.' Roxy had heard enough. Throughout the original recital as she taped, she could see that Mary's relatives had been checking on her own expression to see how she was reacting to what they already knew.

Now, in her stateroom, as she gazes at the paused recorder, blinking its impatience to get going again, she envies their loyalty and togetherness. She and her mum are an item but it must be lovely to have a gang of supporters who would always be there for you.

The only realistic option, she believes now, is to make Mary's story the main event – and to use the romance between herself and the 'Clongowes lad' as a tragic romance with dreadful consequences. That could be authentic and would be a believable plot. But on a second hearing via her tape, as she'd hopped backwards and forwards, she realised something awful: she was no longer all that interested.

So what was new here? That sounded heartless and dreadful, but what was original? Even 'posh boy and simple girl' was clichéd. So of itself Clongowes doesn't cut it.

Desperately seeking ways not to let the Dunnes down, she wonders if she could use the tribe as a whole for background colour and minor incident, thereby lending a bit of depth and breadth to her novel: many readers would like to know what cruising's like, especially those who hadn't been – but she wasn't writing a travelogue.

All this brooding is doing her no good. She springs to her feet and almost runs to the shower, trying not to think about the admonitory notices pasted to the wall, begging that water, 'our planet's most precious resource', should be conserved, then spends at least ten minutes luxuriating in the stream of warm water running over her head, down her back and between her breasts to her toes. When she's towelled herself, dried her hair, got dressed and gathered up her bits and bobs for the day, it's almost a quarter to seven. To facilitate guests who, like her, are taking excursions, breakfast is available from seven.

On her way to the dining room, through glass doors leading outside, she sees Charles, muffled in a heavy coat, scarf and hat, on the deck. It's still dark, but he's standing, motionless, near a light. She goes out. 'Good morning, Charles. A penny for them.'

'Ah, Roxy!' He turns round. 'You're up early. Going to breakfast?'

She looks hard at him. Had he been crying? 'Are you all right, Charles?'

'Perfectly fine. I'll join you, if I may?'

'Of course.'

But as they walk along companionably, using up the minutes before seven, she sneaks another look at him and confirms her first impression: he had been weeping – his eyes are red-rimmed and puffy.

They manage to time it so that the doors are being thrown open just as they arrive. It's a comfort to Roxy to get into the blaze of light, the waiters, more relaxed than they are at dinner, attending to the various food stations, wearing white surgical gloves as they pile up croissants and pour chopped fruit into large bowls while chefs, in whites, slide hot sausages, bacon, fried and scrambled eggs, mushrooms, beans and hash browns into domed hot trays, or tumble bread into big baskets. Others fill the cereal containers and milk dispensers. It's at the same time industrial and domestic but very comforting, Roxy finds.

'Bowl of plenty' and 'cornucopia' pop into her mind. 'Are you hungry, Charles?'

'I can't say I am, m'dear. But you won't have to eat alone. I'll have some of this delicious-looking fruit salad to start with.'

'Well, I'm going to have a fry-up. It does keep you going, doesn't it? Can I bring you over anything, Charles? Even a couple of boiled eggs?'

'No, thank you, you're very good. I'm still ambulant, you know!'

'Right.'

When she gets to the table to deposit her plate of bacon, sausage, mushrooms, two fried eggs and two slices of toast, he's still toying with his bowl of fruit. He surveys what she's brought. '"And in this mountain shall the Lord of hosts make unto all people a feast of fat things . . ." I do love the King James Bible. I voiced one of the apostles, the Doubting Thomas character, in a recording of it once. I don't think it was a bestseller, Roxy, but it does exist somewhere, in the Bodleian Library perhaps, as a record of my own existence. A heap of vinyl LPs in an ageing box covered with dust, that's how I imagine it. It sums up my own life now, I suppose.' Then, obviously believing he's gone too far: 'But I'm sure you're too young to know what an LP was.'

'Not at all.' Roxy, who hasn't missed his allusion to being on the scrapheap, nevertheless plays along as she begins to eat. 'My mum has a pile of them – the original soundtrack of *My Fair Lady*? She still loves Julie Andrews so she has *The Sound of Music*, lots of stuff like *Fantasia*, *Gone with the Wind*, that kind of thing.'

'She sounds romantic, your mum. That must be where you get your talent for love and heartbreak.'

'Maybe, but my talent is a sore topic this morning, Charles.' She sighs.

'Oh?'

She changes the subject, indicating her food: 'Charles, all I heard from that Bible quotation was the word "fat". Yeah, I know, this is a heart attack on a plate, but it'll set me up for the day and I don't do it often.'

'You're young and healthy, my dear. Eat your fill and don't mind the conceits of a tired old man whose race is run.'

She looks at him, eyes wide, resting her knife and fork. 'You're scaring me, Charles. Am I going to have to cancel Ischia so I can watch you?'

'Oh dear. I'm sorry. Of course not. I'm just being dramatic as usual, old dotard that I am. Tell you what, if I may steal a slice of that wonderfully buttery toast, I'll show you that there's absolutely no cause for concern. We're all affected by yesterday's events.

'And, by the way, I do apologise for shouting at you! I surprised myself, actually – I didn't know I could produce that level of sound any more. Gives me heart.' He grins at her.

'No apologies necessary, old fella. But you did give me a fright.'

'Worked, didn't it?'

'I don't mean yesterday. Well, that too, but I mean now, this morning.'

'Oh, tosh! Please, my dear, don't give me another thought – you don't want to infect your art! I'd never forgive myself.'

'My art is another story, Charles.'

He gazes at her now, eyes shrewd. 'At the risk of repeating myself, "oh?"'

'We'll talk again, if you don't mind. Right now I have to eat all this.'

'Of course we'll talk. It'll be a pleasure, artist to artist!' He smiles, then takes a huge bite of toast, chewing ostentatiously. 'Gnashers still OK – that's a blessing!'

She chuckles and picks up her cutlery again. Abruptly she finds inspiration. 'Listen, Charles, I could really do with your advice about something, how to structure the novel, for instance. I'm a bit at sea.'

'Oh, very good. Very droll.' But he'd visibly brightened. 'I'd love to advise you, Roxy. I'm not a novelist, of course, but I've always thought that a good novel displays some elements of a good play structure.'

'I won't be back until at least four o'clock, probably.' Roxy slides a whole fried egg onto a slice of toast, cuts into it and spreads the yolk. 'So we can talk then?'

'That would be wonderful. I think I'll have some of that lovely granola over there. Excuse me for a moment, Roxy.'

As she watches him go towards the cereals, she's still worried. She's also beginning to wonder if, on top of all her other concerns, she and her stupid novel could be a jinx on this dining table.

19

Charles does not know what to do with himself this morning. With no class to prepare, or anything else useful on his agenda, he is unusually restless. Maybe his subconscious is still dealing with the aftermath of yesterday's events.

He'd go for a brisk walk, which normally helps with any kind of perturbation, but while from inside it had looked like a fine, calm day, out here on the port deck, there's a cutting onshore sea breeze rattling through the forest of cables and aerials overhead and cutting up the surface of the water at Naples port.

He could go for a shave and a haircut – availing himself of the staff discount – but he has already performed his ablutions this morning. The cinema doesn't open until after lunchtime when its fare is usually for children. He has no one for whom it would be appropriate to buy souvenirs, even if the shops on the mall were open. He doesn't swim, play bingo, bridge or chess, and while there is an art exhibition on display in the atrium (prior to an auction of the pieces tomorrow when the *Clara* is at sea), he'd caught a glimpse of it while passing through and the work, abstract and very modern, is not to his taste.

There's always the library. It can be pleasant there, quite peaceful, and with passengers encouraged to donate their own books when finished, there are usually a few, new to him, with which he can while away a few hours.

Now that he thinks about it, that's what he'll do. Kitty Abelson had told him last night at dinner about Barry having shown her Roxy's book. And he has to admit he'd been chuffed that the author had asked him for advice to help with her new book. He'll riffle through her first one to see what's what. Then he'll be in a better position to advise her. The library opens at ten. He looks at his watch: still twenty minutes to go. He'll take a few turns on deck and be there when it opens.

Roxy had come upon him at a bad moment earlier – she seemed somehow to have gleaned the impression that he was contemplating jumping into the sea. Far from it, he has no fondness for cold water . . .

Bloody clown – he's aware that the facile quip, for his own ears only, is customarily how he deals with a profound issue he doesn't want to face.

For he is deeply upset and not just about what had happened the previous day. It's that every mile the *Clara* travels towards her ultimate destination is one mile nearer the end of Charles's lifestyle, as he has known it, of his life, really, leaving him with nothing but memories and a cold hearth (will he be able to afford fuel for his fireplace?).

And the text he'd received from Jeremy, his agent, has put the tin lid on it. Like a snappy little Chihuahua, it had been waiting to bite him when he turned on his phone after waking up: *Sorry old boy, BBC passed on Book at B. Rotten shower, but worry not. Working on other avenues as of tomorrow. Hope acting course going well and you're enjoying sea air, have fun! Bring us back a parrot! Freezing here. Talk soon. Onwards and upwards! JB*

Jeremy's perkiness sometimes gets on his nerves.

He has tried to put the text out of his mind, to do the modern thing of living in the moment, but the ship has pretty much emptied again as the guests, including Roxy, scurried off on coach trips to Pompeii or ferries to Capri and the larger, less overtly touristy Ischia – where he knows from experience that in winter many of the shop owners put up shutters and leave to find winter jobs on the mainland.

For many, the main attraction of Capri is its beauty, but there's a certain cohort, in their vintage years like himself, who continue to gravitate towards it because for many years it was the home of the singing and acting star Gracie Fields, Our Gracie, as she was known in Britain.

He climbs up to the next deck, but on seeing there are a few idiots (to his mind) pounding around its jogging track, turns to go down again. Why do joggers always look so unhappy? Fancy Lycra gear in the cheeriest neon colours but faces as glum as basset hounds. Back on deck six, he wanders up and down, doubling back to stay clear of that winter wind.

At one point, he stops to lean on the rail and watch what's happening on the dock. Not much, is the answer, but it's impossible not to reckon with Vesuvius, glowering above the city as though losing patience with it, threatening that it's almost time to blow. With volcanologists agreeing that it could erupt at any time, Charles can never understand why so much housebuilding has been allowed on the flanks of the mountain, with whole villages straggling upwards, albeit very prettily and colourfully in the eyes of snap-happy tourists.

What's even worse, and not generally known by the casual visitor happily trundling along on sightseeing trips, is that under the serene-seeming Bay of Naples there exists, potentially, a far more dangerous entity. Campi Flegrei (Fields of Flame) is an underwater multi-cratered supervolcano, stretching some distance across the bay and so potentially powerful it could, if certain parts of it went up, affect the entire planet, including agriculture, atmosphere, even climate. Depending on the strength of the eruption it could even create a new mini Ice Age.

Currently still napping, but restive, its magma affects a commune very close by called Pozzuoli where, over the last ten years or so, the ground has been rising and subsiding because of intense pressure under the surface. Nature's warning?

Charles shivers. He's being dreary today. He casts a last glance at Vesuvius and its deadly hinterland, but as he turns away to go back into the illusory safety of the *Clara*'s interior, something on the dock below catches the corner of his eye and he pauses, moving back to the rail to check it out. It happens a second time and he sees that what had drawn his attention is the flare of a silver star on top of a Christmas tree, caused by the flash of a camera used by someone on board the *Clara*. She's the only cruise liner moored in the harbour today.

What he also notices, near the Christmas tree, is their table's Danish couple, Aksel and Elise, standing a little apart from one another, backs to the side of one of the buildings. He's intrigued by that little space, maybe three or four feet, because, like everyone else at their table, he's never observed them at other than cuddle-distance. Right now, though, maybe they've 'had words' because they're not even looking at one another while seeming to wait for something to happen.

Something does. A taxi drives onto the concourse in front of the terminal buildings. Aksel flags it down, and when it stops, he bends low at the driver's side to talk to someone, presumably the driver.

From his vantage point, Charles watches as the conversation stretches into minutes, as though there's a haggle about a fare. Eventually, the Dane beckons to his wife, the two of them get in and the taxi drives off. To Pompeii, Charles presumes, thinking that the behaviour of two people he'll never see again after the conclusion of this voyage is none of his business, and for all he knows, once inside their taxi they probably fell into each other's arms.

He had a policeman friend for years – dead now – who, in explaining the mindset on the beat, had said, 'You're just walking along, keeping your eyes open, and out of the blue you see that something or someone doesn't quite fit the general picture. You're not sure what it is – it could be posture, behaviour, position in a crowd, expression, an out-of-place sandwich board – but it's a hunch, a feeling. *What doesn't fit here?*

'It's like a mantra, Charles. We all learn to trust it and it becomes instinctive. Most times there's an innocent reason for what you've seen, or think you've seen, but sometimes there's not. It's like an extra sense, a sixth, and it comes with experience.'

And that was what had popped into Charles's mind while he watched the Danes – it hadn't been merely the gap between them: *something didn't fit.*

Irritably, he shakes this off. *Too much time on your hands, sonny boy . . .*

He leaves the deck and is waiting at the doors of the library when the man comes to open up. 'Hi, Charles! You're early today.'

'Why not? Poor *Clara*'s days are numbered, running out fast, eh? Have to make the most of what's left.'

'Yeah – who'd have believed it?'

'I find it a little unreal. How about you? Where will you go after we get to Rome?'

'I've got it all planned.' The young man throws open the door and places a doorstop in front of it. 'Me and my partner have bought a smallholding in Worcestershire, not far from Kidderminster, and we're going to raise alpacas for the wool. We're not going to make our fortune but we'll be self-sufficient. We'll grow our own veggies, have a few chickens. The place already has a little cottage – it's in bits but he's a draughtsman and a bit of a DIY nutter so we're going to fix it up. It also has a greenhouse with solar panels. There's a writing group in one of the villages not far from where we'll be living so I might even try my hand at writing books instead of reading and lending them. Can't wait!'

'Sounds wonderful. All the very best with it.' While Charles, a committed townie, would not have changed places with him, he truly envies his positivity and enthusiasm.

'Thanks.' The younger man smiles. 'Looking for anything in particular this morning?'

'Actually, yes. A novel called, I think, *Heartbreak in the Cotswolds*.'

'We have that. Not ours. Some passenger probably dropped it in.' He crosses to the shelves, plucks it out and hands it over. 'It's odd that you should ask for that particular book, just as my head is full of images of the Cotswolds where I'm going to be rather soon! Do you believe in coincidence, Charles?'

'I've lived a long time and nothing at all surprises me now. This was written by one of our guests.'

'Really? That explains why it's here. Sneaky but effective, eh?'

'Thanks. I'll settle in now, and I'll think of you when I'm back living in the Big Smoke.'

'Keep the book, Charles. No point in putting it back.' He gazes at his neatly catalogued collection. 'Don't know what's going to happen to all these anyway. They're hardly going to Malaysia with the *Clara*. I reckon they'll just be dumped, poor things. You do get fond of them, you know.'

'I'm sure you do.' *Another nail in the coffin of everything I held dear.* Then: 'Any chance of a piece of scrap paper? I need to make notes.'

'Take this. We certainly won't be using it.' From under his desk the librarian hands over a new book-loans ledger, then goes through the room, turning on lamps, while Charles settles into a chair and opens Roxy's novel.

An hour later, having read the first eighty pages, he knows that a Jane Austen or a Georgette Heyer she's not, but that Roxy (or her editor?) has a good idea on how to structure a book. That, for him, doesn't mean formal architecture: it means how to keep readers turning those pages. But, he thinks fondly, we don't need to see a cardigan as being both 'fluffy' *and* 'feathery', and the many coincidences stretch credulity – hero and heroine too often encounter each other randomly and in the most unlikely places, taking a tour of a heritage house, for instance, when one or other had felt an unusually strong urge to go there for reasons not understood – and, hey presto!, who's right there too? It's quite propitious, he thinks, that her next book is set on a ship, a limited arena where everyone encounters everyone else at least once or twice a day . . .

He had skipped to the last chapter and, on reading it, became convinced that, yes, Roxy herself had been the model for her heroine, whose romance had failed and whose passion for her hero, initially 'red-hot', had been thwarted: the writing on this theme felt authentic in the way a lot of the rest of the story didn't.

Closing the book, Charles has cheered up, feeling that his day now has a purpose. He had never fancied himself as an authority on literary matters, but he reads a lot – and eclectically, from his mother's Mills & Boon stash, all the way to Dostoevsky and Chekhov's short stories.

He says goodbye to the librarian, again wishes him luck in his new life and, humming 'If I Can Help Somebody', made famous by Mahalia Jackson, one of Mother's favourite singers (*you corny old buffoon, you, Charles Burtonshaw!*), leaves the library to go back to his stateroom.

His exercise with Roxy's book, trying to parse it objectively and mentally rehearsing how to talk to her about it, had reminded him of the work he used to do before going to the *Clara*'s ballroom each time he and his pupils embarked on their first acting class. It had felt good.

By lunchtime he's hungry. He hasn't seen his lovely Kitty or her less lovely husband all morning. And with Roxy in Ischia and the Danes, presumably, in Pompeii, if he went to the main dining room he may be on his own at that big table. He decides to eat at the Clipper Café, buzzier and far less formal. He takes his ledger with him to tidy up his notes while he's eating. In a way, he thinks, as he claims a table by the window of the huge, bright restaurant, this is the work of someone on a publisher's readers' panel.

Here was a thought – he, Charles Burtonshaw, could offer this service with virgin material: it has to be akin to the way directors ask for reactions to first readings of new plays and will take suggestions for improvements, even if the playwright is simmering at the other end of the table.

And if Roxy finds his thoughts and suggestions useful, he could apply for a position on one such panel. They probably don't pay very much, but it might help with his council tax. Even more importantly, perhaps, it would keep him busy.

Maybe, he thinks now, the librarian isn't the only man who can change career. This could be one of those lightbulb moments – funny how one small thing, like a negative text, can take you down, while one little dart of hope, realistic, of course, lifts you.

He has certainly become more emotional lately, but this is probably a symptom of no longer being forty or fifty, like having to wear vari-focal spectacles or seeing a concerned expression on the face of your doctor or dentist during a check-up. Despite his frequent self-abnegating quips about being old, he's far from old in his heart, he tells himself now. He's maturing, like good whiskey or wine. This might prove to be a good day, after all.

*

From a quarter to four or thereabouts, Charles is waiting for Roxy to return from her trip to Ischia. He's sitting in the atrium, near a bank of showy glass lifts, surrounded not just by the normal displays of plants and flowers but, hanging on every wall, the art for auction.

Near the reception desk, a space has been cleared, and two workmen are unrolling streams of fairy lights from large cardboard spools, testing them as they go, while two others, supervised by a third, are erecting a large Christmas tree. The place is filling with happy noise, lifts swooping up and down, guests chatting animatedly as, returning to the ship from their days out, they swap experiences and queue to hand in already written postcards.

He can see, on the mall leading off this central circulation point, the shutters are beginning to come off shop windows, and that between them, at a leisurely pace, stallholders, chatting to each other, are setting out displays of bargain jewellery, bric-à-brac, such as music boxes that play endless tinkling versions of 'O Sole Mio' and 'Santa Lucia', scarves, pashminas, baseball caps and watches. Lots of watches.

He spots Roxy, who has stuffed her blonde hair under a red woollen cap, with *Ischia Buon Natale* embroidered in yellow on the front. She hasn't seen him and is heading for the desk so he rises to intercept her. 'Hello there! How was Ischia – up to expectations?'

'Yes and no. Most of the shops were shut, but there were market stalls,' she touches her cap, 'and this huge Christmas tree lit up in the middle of a lovely square not far from the port. There were kids skating on an ice rink – I hadn't expected that – but what I really, *really*, loved was this incredible Christmas display in a wood, not far from everything. It's called Bosco something.'

'Bosco Incantato? I've seen pictures of it. The Enchanted Forest. Always meant to see it for myself some day, but,' he sighs 'not now to be . . .'

'You'd never know what might happen, Charles, so keep

your pecker up. And yeah, "Bosco Incantato"' she rolls the Italian around her mouth, 'that's the one. It's mainly for children, I suppose, but I loved it. It was very misty over on the island today and the place felt really mysterious, with the fairy lights lighting up all the trees and outlining big pink flamingos and reindeer and unicorns and huge big butterflies all over the place. And there were terrific forest and bird sound effects against music all around you. Probably because of the fog, you sort of felt your feet weren't on the ground, that you were floating. You were certainly off the planet and in another world.'

'Definitely a scene for the novel?'

'For sure. But I had imagined that island as sunny, like it was in *Avanti*.'

'Jack Lemmon and Juliet Mills? Lovely. You'll have to go back there in summertime so, Roxy?'

'Chance'd be a fine thing.' She smiles ruefully but then she notices that he's carrying her book. 'My God! You found it!'

'So it was you who dropped it in!'

She smiles cheekily at him. 'So sue me!'

'Shall we begin straight away, my dear? I've been thinking how to approach things for the novel –'

'Sure.'

*

The two of them are in the Starbucks coffee shop, each with a notebook, his open, its first page covered with dense writing, hers still closed, her novel between them on the table.

'So, what's your main problem, Roxy?' Charles opens the proceedings.

'Everything.' She throws up her hands. 'It's a bin chockful

of rubbish. It's going around in my head like a carousel, all colours and music and different people hopping on and off the horses or waving at me as they ride past me.'

'Do you know where you want to start? Where you want it to end?'

'That's the whole problem. I don't. And I know I've identified too many characters.'

'From people on board the *Santa Clara*?'

'Sure. Where else?'

'Tell me about them so far – just a summary of each one.' By the end of her recital, Charles is almost dizzy. 'You're right, my dear. You are in a mess. You're like a shepherd with your animals scattered all over a vast open plain. You're trying to gather them all in and keep them together without a dog to help you. So think of me as your dog, eh? And, by the way, did you ever think of starting your book in the middle?'

She hesitates. 'No. Do writers do that?'

'It sounds sensible to me. You have to start somewhere and the middle might be as good as anywhere else – it could take some pressure off. You can delve right into the action – then go back and show people how you got there, you'll have something to aim for – and that's half the book written!'

'It's Christmas Day on the *Santa Clara*, say,' he waves an arm around the coffee shop, festooned with poinsettias and red tat, 'everyone's happy but something major happens. Some accident, some incident, a fight? A man overboard? Don't wait to research the details, just write the action and the reaction from those at the Christmas table – don't worry about the scenery and setting. You can add them when you're revising. You'll probably find you'll be able to identify the people important to your story. You'll find some, a few, one or two, will interest you more than others.

'For now, forget all that research you've been doing. I'm guessing that when you sit down actually to write you'll remember the stuff that's important without ploughing through all those notes. And don't forget, you're not obligated to the people you've interviewed.

'As for the plot – based on what you've told me, you don't seem to have one so far, have you? It's just a lot of characters muddling along together.'

'I'm afraid so.'

'I've skimmed through this,' he indicates the first novel, 'and at heart, like all love stories of all time, the premise is simple. Have you ever heard of *Daphnis and Chloe*?'

'No.' She shakes her head.

'It's a romantic novel, generally agreed to have been written in Greece a couple of centuries after Christ. Apparently it was very popular in its time – and here's the plot. You'll probably recognise it or its equivalent used by countless writers down the centuries. Two abandoned children, a boy and a girl, are found, separately, by a shepherd and a goatherd. Each is adopted, one by the sheep man, the other by the goat man. As the children grow up, their foster parents put them to work, herding the animals.

'The inevitable happens, they fall in love, but events intervene. They are separated, and there are abductions, not least by pirates. Daphnis, the boy, falls into a pit, Chloe's kidnapped . . . It goes on in this vein, lots of incident, until, eventually, after much to-ing and fro-ing and an intervention by the great god Pan, they get together, marry and live happily ever after.

'Works every time. Simple, universal, full of action, but essentially it's boy meets girl, there are obstacles, they part, they can't do without each other, they overcome the obstacles, they get together. You've used it yourself already, and I'm guessing you'll probably use it again for this new one – although in the ending you chose for your first book, you wouldn't let them go happily ever after, would you? You gave them heartbreak.

'Would I be right in thinking you had to live up to your title?' Charles is enjoying this. She's frowning, concentrating. 'Not that I'm the Oracle, but as I'm talking, you're thinking, eh? So tell me again about your heroine. Leaving all your research aside, what's she like?'

'She's beautiful but a bit distant right now, maybe a bit cold, although she's not really. She's been wounded in the past. The man who secretly loves her knows that if he can get her to trust him he'll be able to peel away her reserve, like peeling an orange . . .'

Privately, Charles thinks this simile to be somewhat wanting, but smiles encouragingly. 'You see? You've already found the thread. You just have to follow it, like the author of *Daphnis and Chloe* did with his hero and heroine. Your problem has been, as I think you've recognised, that you've been drenched by obligation and too much research.'

He goes on in this vein – he's thought it through during the day – and he can tell she's now listening hard. 'It's the story first, my dear, and you already know that, but you've buried it under all those notes. Just get that story upfront!'

Abruptly, he realises he's been talking for at least a quarter of an hour. 'Am I being too hard on you, Roxy, moving too fast, being a bit of a pain in the bum? I hope you don't feel

I'm patronising you. After all, you're a published author. I'm the entertainer, the jester – I parrot other people's words. You create them, and that's a far higher calling, my dear! From down here, I bow!'

'Oh, Charles, you're wonderful. You've tunnelled right into the middle of the tangle. Starting in the middle is a great idea. I'll get going with what happened yesterday to Joshua, and once I have that down, I'll just think backwards and work forwards, like you say, to get to it, then away from it. I already feel that episode yesterday is going to be like a . . .' Charles can see she's fully engaged now '. . . like a lighthouse I have to get to!'

'Exactly. Bravo!'

'You're really great. Thank you so much – how can I ever repay you?'

'By inviting me to your launch party!'

'You'll have to come to Dublin – my publisher is in London and that'll be the main market, but even if they won't give me one in Dublin, I'm going to have a party anyway.'

'That's the ticket! It'll be a pleasure, my dear, and I look forward to it.' He stands up. 'Don't forget, I'll be around for another week, so if ever you want to talk again, please feel free.' He puts on his coat. 'I'm going to take a turn around the deck. It's almost dark, but it's very warm in here and I could do with a blast of fresh air. Care to join me?'

'I've had a whole day of fresh air although with all the mist it wasn't all that fresh! I have to get out of these jeans – what a great day! See you at the table, Charles?' Impulsively, she stands on tiptoe and kisses his cheek.

*

Charles finds the deck deserted. It's a crisp, clear evening, with a few stars beginning to show through the deep blue dusk, and his breath visible on the air. He tucks his hands under his arms, watching the lights blinking on and off on the pier's Christmas tree, the silver star now outlined with glowing colour, while behind and above it, the little streets and houses defy the louring volcano, defiantly strewing spangles over its lower slopes.

The dock below is still busy, but the pace has slackened and, in twos and threes, he can see people trickling back towards the *Clara* after their excursions ashore.

He takes a few deep breaths, appreciating the freshness, but it's too cold to linger and he's back inside five minutes after he went out.

He's returning to his cabin to indulge in a little nap before dinner, smiling and nodding greetings to others trudging past him towards their own suites when, just two doors away from his own, he spots the Danes among the next wave coming towards him from the lifts at the far end. Out of courtesy, he waits for them to reach him. 'How did you get on in Pompeii? It's quite an experience, isn't it?'

'Oh, it was wonderful.' Elise had clearly been deeply affected. 'Very, *very* moving. I cried when I saw that little baby – so innocent.'

'*And* the horse *and* the dog – you cried at those too!' Affectionately, Aksel puts an arm around her shoulders. 'Walking around with Elise, Charles,' he smiles, 'was like travelling with my own personal little fountain! We took a guide for ourselves,' he goes on. 'He was marvellous, wasn't he, Elise?'

'Amazing!' She nods.

'He knew the answer to every single question we asked,' he continues, 'so vividly describing for us how quickly everything had happened to all those poor people, how the lava flow came too fast for them to escape, burying them almost instantly with their houses, servants, animals, everything they had, so they were all caught in the attitudes we now see. We were expecting it to be interesting, weren't we, Elise?' Again she nods and smiles up at him. 'But it was a shock to find it so very emotional. I'm glad we went. It will probably prove to be the highlight of our honeymoon, a sad one, but I don't think we could ever forget it, could we?'

'Never.'

'Well, I'll leave you to it,' Charles says. 'I'm glad you had such a good time. See you both at dinner?'

'Yes.' Elise's eyes fill. 'It will be sad too, poor Joshua, but we must do our best.'

'We must.' Charles smiles again and stands aside to let them pass.

He's letting himself into his stateroom when something niggles at him. Something quite ridiculous, really, but it's demanding his attention . . .

Instead of going into his room, he backs out and, looking at his watch – it's just after half past five – removes the keycard, then lets the door close again.

Walking quickly, he goes back the way he'd come, taking one of the lifts to the floor housing the library, which he knows is due to close at six, although sometimes, if there are guests still inside, the librarian doesn't rush them to leave.

Lamps still on, the man is already tidying his desk and putting away his loan register. 'Gosh, Charles, I don't need that book back – it's not on our record.'

It's only then Charles realises he's still carrying Roxy's novel. 'It's not why I'm here. Sorry to bother you but do you still have those books about the ruins of Pompeii?'

'Sure – at least I believe we do, although I think a lot went out prior to today. Let me see . . .' He puts down the papers he's been holding and walks to a shelf. 'You're in luck, Charles, but this one doesn't have any pictures, if that's what you need, just drawings and illustrations of the digs.'

'Perfect. I'll just be five minutes – there's something I want to look up.'

'Fine. Take as long as you like. I'm in no hurry. I'm going to miss the old *Clara*.'

'Me too.' But Charles has already put aside *Heartbreak in the Cotswolds* and is opening the book, more of a treatise or a collection of essays than something for the casual tourist. He flips to the back to see if there is an index. Luckily there is. He identifies what he wants, finds fifteen mentions of it and, one by one, he goes through them. After six or so, he is satisfied.

'Thanks.' He closes the book and takes it up to the librarian's desk. 'Have a good evening.' Not forgetting to pick up Roxy's novel, he leaves the library.

It takes him twenty minutes to track down Frank Mitchell, who turns out to be backstage in the theatre. He's having a blistering argument with the wardrobe mistress responsible for the costumes in that evening's show, a dance revue based on the movie *Saturday Night Fever*. Respectfully, he waits in the shadows until they have resolved their differences and she moves back to the little room housing her glittering showpieces.

Turning to leave, Frank jumps. 'Charles! For God's sake, man, you frightened me.'

'Sorry, Frank, but there's something I want to say to you. It might be nothing, but it might be—'

'You're not making sense. Come out into the auditorium where at least we can see each other.' Still tetchy, he leads Charles across the stage and down a set of steps at its side, along a short corridor and through a door into the audience seating area. 'This'd better be good, chum. My heart's still banging. I thought you were a robber or something, going to bash my head in! You shouldn't creep around like that.'

'Sorry – but I thought it might be important. It mightn't be, and perhaps I'm going over the top or being senile but, well, something didn't fit.'

'You're talking bollocks, Chuck.'

Then Charles tells him.

*

It's coming up to half past seven and Charles is sitting on his balcony. He's been out here for some time, despite the chill, and is beginning to wonder if he's done the right thing.

Back in his stateroom following the chat with Frank, he had, as planned, got into bed for a nap. He hadn't slept, because as soon as he lay down his brain fired up, carrying a cargo of images, including those of the boy's face, beauty marred by blood and spittle. It chugged incessantly round and round, so eventually he'd given up, showered and, wrapping up warmly, had come out here to think.

It's plain sailing, *Clara*'s engines murmuring as they carry her across the water, flat and glistening under a crescent moon; he decides that introspection is getting him nowhere. What's done is done and it's nearly time for dinner. He goes back inside.

Ten minutes later, he's fully dressed and lacing up one of his shoes when there's a tap on the door.

It's Frank. 'May I come in for a second, Charles?' His friend rarely if ever calls him by his proper name, and Charles's stomach turns over with fear. Perhaps he's being charged with slander or making false accusations. He's no legal expert, but at home he sometimes takes the *Telegraph* and always reads the court cases and those little Corrections and Clarifications. 'Come in, come in.' He forces himself to sound normal.

The cruise director closes the door behind him. 'I want to update you, Charles, but I have to say "well done"! I contacted Jock immediately after our little chat and he organised a discreet search. They were in their cabin and there was a row, as one might expect, but in the end, the lads found what they were looking for. The woman broke down and, yes, they were dealing, insisting first that the coke was for personal consumption. My eye! There was enough to fuel a pretty good party at the very least.'

'Where are they?'

'We'd already left port, unfortunately, and as you know, we don't dock again for thirty-six hours, so unless we made them walk the plank, we couldn't disembark them, and you know Leifsson, punctual as a Swiss cuckoo.

'But for some reason, maybe it was all the tears from the woman, he went soft and decided not to put them in the brig. It's small, designed for only one person, although there have been times when we've stuffed in more than one. Anyway, even though they do have a balcony, we're pretty sure they won't jump so they're under the equivalent of house arrest, locked into their cabin. We'll feed them, naturally, but other than that they'll have no contact with anyone on board, and when we dock in Dubrovnik we'll put them off.

'Turns out, by the way, that although she's Danish he isn't, originally Bulgarian. They are married, that bit's true, and he adopted her name, as they do in Denmark. It's traditional and legal, apparently, according to the captain, and he should know.' He sticks out his hand. 'Put it there, Mr Maigret!'

As they shake, Charles, relieved that he hadn't gone overboard with his observations and accusations, falls back on his lifelong habit of treating a serious thing as a joke and a joke as a serious thing, like Seamus Shields in O'Casey's *Shadow of a Gunman* (in which he'd played Adolphus Grigson). 'All in a day's work, sir. But I feel a bit sorry for them now. What'll happen to them?'

'They'll be taken off to face the law. Unfortunately for them, we're at sea tomorrow so they'll have to cool their heels. Dubrovnik is next but to tell you the truth, Croatia isn't the worst they could face but one way or another they're probably going to see jail time. It's a first offence – certainly they say it is, but the cops will already have their details with Europol. Anyway, don't waste your time thinking about them, Chuck. You're not going soft just like Leifsson did, are you? They're greedy scumbags, the two of them.'

'Who knows about it?'

'Not many. Certainly not the main body of passengers. Although I know we won't succeed in keeping it tight, for now only your little lot, who were directly involved, are in the loop. The captain wants it that way until he decides what's best. He'll tell you himself, probably – there will be questions, of course, not this evening, because people miss dinner, go to other restaurants or just to bed, but someone will notice that those two are getting room service a lot over the next day and a half; some will smile knowingly about that story about them being honeymooners but it's inevitable that this time tomorrow, certainly by the time they're taken off, everyone on the ship will know.'

'They're not honeymooners?'

Frank shakes his head. 'They've been married for six years. By the way, Leifsson asks if you and the other three left at your table would like to dine with him privately this evening. I'll be there.' Sorrowfully, he wags a finger. 'Tsk-tsk, what are you doing to them all, Chuck? It's ten green bottles at that table of yours, eh?'

'Thanks, Frank. At one level, even when I was waiting for you down in the theatre, I was still wondering if I hadn't been watching too many episodes of *Inspector Morse*.'

'You weren't, thank the Lord. Cheery-bye for the present,' he says then, heading for the door. 'We'll sort out a smaller table in the MDR for your sad little entourage as of tomorrow – and, all joking aside, I do know all this must be terrible for you. Okay? See you later.'

Charles sits on the side of the bed to finish lacing his shoes, yawning. Who'd have thought that people involved in the highly dangerous pursuit of drug-peddling, even if those two were not big-time, would be silly enough to make the mistake they did during a routine, seemingly innocuous conversation about the glories and tragedies of Pompeii?

They might even have got away with it, too, if they hadn't invented the detail about the expertise of a guide they'd never met. It had all come down to lava.

From his many visits to the site, Charles already knew that in 79 AD, the unfortunate citizens of Pompeii and Herculaneum had not been overtaken by lava flows. Lava moves relatively slowly. Provided you stay at a reasonable distance, you can even walk beside it.

Every creature, human and animal, trying to outrun the wrath of Vesuvius that day had been caught almost instantly by a pyroclastic flow of hot gas and volcanic matter, which can travel at up to 450 miles per hour and reach 1000 degrees centigrade. The inhabitants of Pompeii and Herculaneum, with their homes and possessions, hadn't stood a chance: they'd been immediately buried by successive waves of volcanic ash and pumice.

Not lava.

Charles's second visit of the day to the library, just to make sure his memory wasn't failing him, had confirmed this.

20

Kitty is in the second bathroom of the Duchess Suite, the one she had appropriated as her own. It's early evening, still only day four of their trip – hard to believe with all that's happened that day.

In tandem with all this navel-gazing, however, she feels an enjoyable, if sneaky, tingle at the thought of an imminent meeting, two meetings with the captain, first, during a visit to the bridge, and also his kind offer of a private dinner with herself, Saul, Roxy and Charles. With Saul present, presumably dominating the conversation, it'll all go fine.

She's turning her head this way and that to assess her appearance and the minimal make-up she favours when her husband raps on the door. 'Kitty! Open up!'

When she obeys she sees that he is in a state of agitation. 'What is it?'

'We have to go back! We have to get off this ship.'

She stares at him. 'What's happened?' She fears the worst. 'Is it one of the children?'

'The children are fine, as far as I know. But we have to go back to the US immediately. Part of the scaffolding has collapsed at the site in Boise. I don't know the extent of injuries yet, but there are fears that two men have died. We have to go back.'

'That's terrible, Saul, really terrible. I'm sorry, I don't know what else to say. When did it happen?'

'Just after eleven this morning, local time there – they're hours behind so the shift was in full occupation.'

'Maybe it's not as bad as you think – do you have any idea how it happened?'

'Not yet. The safety people are already swarming over the site, cops too – we have to go back! It's our company that'll be sued even though it has to be the contractors who were at fault so we have to pack right now and this tub will be pulling away in less than an hour. We gotta get off!' He's overlapping sentences again, sure sign he's seriously stressed, she thinks, as he turns to rush towards the bedroom. His bad knee acts up, however, and he stops, wincing, rubbing it pointlessly.

She comes out of the bathroom. 'Sit down for a minute. Saul, I understand the urgency of this but it's not your fault.'

'We're wasting time!'

'Calm down a bit. Be logical.'

'Stop telling me to be calm! And start packing, unless you want your stuff to go to Malaysia!' Another indication of the degree of Saul's distress is how much it looks and feels like rage. She's used to it. 'Listen – *listen*, Saul—'

'Start packing, Kitty! That's an order!' He hobbles into the bedroom where, through the open doorway, she sees him wrench open the closet.

Watching him tear his clothes out and dump them randomly on the bed, Kitty's thoughts coalesce and harden, as clear as fresh ice. She goes into the bedroom, gazing at Saul's eviscerated closet, the messy heap of clothing and shoes on the bed. 'I accept you have to go back, Saul. I hope you can accept that I don't.'

'What do you mean?' He stops and, aghast, looks at her.

'You heard.' She clears a space on the ottoman at the end of the bed and sits. 'I don't have to go back to the US. I'm assuming you'll go direct to Boise, by whatever is the most direct route.'

'Of course.'

'After Dubrovnik, which I'm not that pushed about to be honest because if you remember, we were there before for a night on our way to somewhere else, I forget where. I'm meeting my sister in Venice on Friday. Remember? Why do you want me to go back to the US?'

'What? You never told me you were meeting your sister – don't be ridiculous! This is an emergency – you can see your sister any time.'

'Not in Venice.'

'What's with Venice all of a sudden?' He drags the bigger of his steel-framed wheelie bags from the floor of the closet, throws it open onto the bed and begins flinging clothes into it.

Calmly, she watches him. 'What's with Venice, Saul, is this. I did tell you. I told you I wanted us to give her and Paul an anniversary present of a weekend in Venice. You were to contact Philippa about it.'

'Okay, okay, I remember now, my bad! It slipped my mind.'

'Like everything else to do with my family.'

'Oh, here we go!'

'Yes, here we go, Saul. But you needn't worry about it because I organised it myself with a lovely young guy down at the reception desk, who deserves a very big tip. He spent at least two hours finding a decent hotel room for Geraldine and Paul in Venice and moved heaven and earth to get flights for them.'

'Great, they'll have a good time, but that doesn't mean you have to meet them. I need you with me, dammit! You're my wife, Kitty, or have you conveniently forgotten that?'

'Saul, you don't need me, except occasionally as arm candy at events you attend.'

He sputters and is about to launch, but she puts up a hand to stop him. 'Listen to me for once, Saul. I know only too well that I'm your wife. I know also that the voyage on this ship is business for you and wouldn't have been your choice, but we're here now and it would have been nice, just once, to feel we were on vacation together.

'Just take a look around you. You've turned that second bedroom in there into an office. The Asia markets are more interesting to you than—'

He cuts across her: 'I went with you to Nice, didn't I? And to that – that other place where my knee gave out. Now, if you don't mind, I have to get on with this.'

'Yes, you did come with me to those places. But your mobile phone was the centre of your life at Cinque Terre. Not those beautiful villages, not the sea, the cliffs, or even me. Listen, Saul, be honest. If Mount Etna is erupting when this ship sails around Sicily tonight, the rest of us will be up on deck marvelling at the fire-show, but you'll be watching the squawk box on CNBC, won't you?

'So please take this in. While you're in Boise up on a scaffold, I'll be in the Gritti Palace. I'm taking my sister Geraldine and her husband of fifteen years, Paul, to lunch there – thanks again to Wolfgang at Reception. Even he couldn't get me a table in the restaurant but he's reserved one for us in the lobby, which is lovely. I've seen photos of it online. He booked it for four, but naturally I'm going to have to change that. That place is five-star, maybe even six by some measures, and you would have felt at home there, Saul. But never mind, you'll probably get a great view of Boise from the top of your scaffold. The bosun's chair, right? You see, at least one of us does listen to the other.'

He stares at her, an absurd, misshapen bouquet of boxer shorts drooping from each hand. 'What's gotten into you, Kitty?'

'Maybe I've come to life. Maybe that poor boy's death has woken me up so I can admit that I've been half asleep for the past decade, slip-sliding through my precious one and only life – and, yes, before you say anything about *that* and you'd be right, you've been a terrific and very generous provider. You've lined my slide with chinchilla. And, in intention at least, I acknowledge you've been a supporter. But, Saul, I'm an unproductive leech – and even leeches serve a medical function. I don't know what I have to offer to the world any more since I've spent so long not being useful. Okay, all those charities, but a lot of what I do is self-aggrandising socialite stuff. Even a kid working in a McDonald's or Arby's can go home at night and feel he's being some kind of use to humanity. I've hinted this before, Saul, but you haven't heard me.'

'I – I never knew you felt this way.'

'I've mentioned it. I just haven't mentioned it in these terms – but now that I have, please take it that I'm not happy dossing around with people I'm supposed to respect just because they wear silk knickers and eat fully formed duck embryos marinated in raspberry jam or whatever. I don't respect myself any more and haven't for a long time.'

'Kitty, I . . .' He made a move as though to come towards her but again she holds up a hand.

'Wait! I'm not finished.' She couldn't have stopped herself now, even if she'd wanted to. Which she didn't. 'I respect my sister,' she went on. 'She lives a real life, unlike me. She's bringing up two lovely children who believe that going to Starbucks is the coolest, most exotic treat in the world. This' – she sweeps an arm around the suite – 'is lovely, of course it is. And we've met very interesting people, at least I have.'

'I did too.'

'You mean Barry? You saw him as another asset, Saul.'

'We were going to have dinner with the captain – it was going to be great, honey. I'm missing that. Don't you think this is hard for me?'

She stares at him with something approaching pity. She'd soften but she's too far down this road to stop now, although she does find her own unleashing a little frightening. Like that volcano outside, she's been keeping a lid on her feelings and thoughts for a long time but now that it's blown she has no way to put it back on or even to control the extent of the damage caused by the outflow. 'It's the status, isn't it, Saul?' she asks quietly. 'It's you starring again in your own birthday movie.'

He's still staring at her, those silly boxers still clutched in his hands. She gets up from the ottoman, goes over to where he's standing, removes them gently, folds them and puts them, all nice and tidy, into a compartment within the case. 'Saul, I . . .' She sits back down on the ottoman and, lowering her head, covers her eyes with both hands, suddenly fearful that what she'll say next could prove fatal. She's probably said too much already. 'Sorry, Saul,' she says, her voice barely audible, 'I know I'm repeating myself, but Geraldine and Paul are in Venice as our guests on the fifteenth anniversary of their wedding. At our invitation. It's as important to me as it is to them, and I intend to keep the appointment at the Gritti Palace.

'Again, please look at the way you live *your* precious life. Look around you at this suite, Saul.' She raises her head again. 'You've been out on that balcony, what, maybe twice? About five minutes at a time? It's nine hundred square feet – that's bigger than the whole house where my sister and I were brought up. I'm going to meet her.'

'Is it your time of the month, Kit?'

'That,' she gazes at him almost in wonderment, 'is the pits. It's low. You haven't really heard a word I've said, have you? I'll leave you to finish your packing.' She looks at her watch. 'You'll have thirty-five or forty minutes, by my reckoning, to get off. This captain seems to like punctuality. If I can help with anything, please feel free to contact me, but before six fifteen, please. Roxy and I are being collected at that time to go to the bridge. I'll convey your regrets and I'll explain what happened.

'Safe journey, Saul. I'll see you when I get back to the States – and good luck with what you have to do in Boise. I don't envy you that, it's rotten luck, but I'm sure you'll cope. You always do.'

She leaves, shepherding the sprung door so the sound it makes when it finally closes is only a click.

*

Saul, with a porter in tow, comes to Starbucks on the mall, limping, at the last minute. He is, strangely, on his best behaviour, possibly because Roxy and the paragon Wolfgang are present. 'You all packed, Saul?' She doesn't make a move to meet him.

'Yes.' He indicates the luggage trolley and the porter. Kitty, imagining the jumble inside the expensive set of metal, senses that treacherous softening, like a mother must feel when

her son goes to live with his mates in their first apartment/
dosshouse. She refuses to let this happen.

While Wolfgang and Roxy stand aside to respect their
privacy, he tells her that there are no direct flights, 'and we've
missed the best prospect, which is leaving Naples just half
an hour from now. I'd never make it even if there wasn't this
security situation at every airport on the planet. Philippa is
organising a charter jet. She really earns her stripes.'

'She sure does.' Kitty is stunned at how normal, even casual,
this conversation is. Had that been her in their stateroom less
than half an hour ago or some effigy come to life? 'How long
do you think it'll take?' she asks, as though it's routine that
her husband is going on a private jet from here to Boise, of all
places, leaving her alone in a majestic suite on a cruise liner.
And, she wonders, how will Portlandis feel about that since
he's the director, not she?

She'd like to think, in this strange new manifestation of
herself, that she cares not a fig what her husband, or any of
his companies, associates or partners, thinks of her not being
his loyal helpmeet at his side to comfort him in the light of
such a tragic accident, especially when he and the company he
partially owns are likely to face years of expensive litigation.
She does care, just not the way he wants, or the way she needs
to. 'Is there any further news?' she asks.

'Not really.' Saul glances across to where Roxy and Wolfgang
are standing. 'No good news anyway.'

'There have been deaths, then?'

'I'm afraid so.'

'I'm sorry to hear it, Saul.' She really is. 'I hope it won't affect
you too much personally. How long will it take you to get there,
d'you think?'

'Well, if we can leave before ten this evening, and right now Philippa thinks she's nailed it, we should be there around three a.m., maybe three thirty Boise time. There could be one stop for fuel.'

They might have been friends on Wall Street discussing a hostile takeover, she thinks, as she adds, 'All the best, Saul,' and pecks him on the cheek.

But her astonishing resolve caves a little when, with an expression she'd never before seen on his face, eyes stricken, he grabs her in a bear-hug and whispers, 'I love you, Kitty, please remember that, no matter what happens and—' into her neck. He doesn't finish the sentence.

She manages to hold on to her willpower with a kindly: 'Me too,' when he lets her go. She kisses him again, this time on the lips, albeit briefly, the commuter's wife seeing Daddy off at the station to go to his day's work in the city. 'See you soon. Take care.'

Saul nods at the porter, who has been waiting nearby, and they trundle off towards the elevators. Yielding to an impulse she did not quite fathom, not then, Kitty checks her watch. It's just after six fifteen. She joins Roxy and Wolfgang, and they head for the bridge. She is to remember the significance of that timing.

*

After their taut encounter in the captain's office of the day before, Kitty now has no idea how to handle this, especially with no Saul to play buffer.

As it turns out, she needn't have worried because the encounter with the master of the *Santa Clara* is brief: he welcomes her and Roxy with cordial courtesy, the ship casts off only minutes later, bang on the button of six thirty. And as they get under way, his role, she sees, is quietly but authoritatively to supervise everything going on around him. He introduces the staff captain, 'my second-in-command', who is at what Kitty knows is the helm. He also introduces them to the pilot from Naples port, and urges them to listen as he relays instructions to the engine room.

'God, it's very quiet,' Roxy whispers into Kitty's ear, 'isn't it?'

'Very professional I'd say,' Kitty murmurs back.

When the ship is safely headed in the right direction, Leifsson comes across to where she and Roxy are standing: 'I'm sorry, ladies, but once again, I'm afraid I have to be somewhere else. Please feel free to ask any questions you like.' His wave encompasses everyone on the bridge, the men and the woman attending banks of flickering screens, those at the helm, the sailor watching the horizon through binoculars. 'I'll see you both at dinner. I'm sorry your husband had to leave in such dreadful circumstances, Mrs Abelson. You'll miss him. We all will.' And with one of those little bows of his, he leaves.

*

Afterwards, the women had agreed they'd been highly impressed by their visit, not merely with the sense that not just anybody, but the right somebody, is in charge, but with the airiness, brightness and spaciousness of the bridge, the massive spread of window glass, the array of communications and technological equipment being monitored and operated. 'It's kind of like the *Starship Enterprise* only a lot bigger and nicer,' Roxy says, when they're having a drink together in one of the bars, 'but I wish we could have seen it in daylight. It must be spectacular. And what do you think of our friend the captain when he's on the job?'

'I haven't been thinking all that much about him.' Kitty is glad that the bar's lighting is dim. 'But, yes, he does seem efficient.'

'I wouldn't say he's the life and soul of a knees-up, eh?'

'Probably not. He seems rather serious, all right.' She's casting around for a way safely to change the subject but, to her relief, Roxy does it for her.

'If you don't mind, Kitty, why did Saul leave?'

Kitty tells her. Including the fact, knowing that it would tickle her interest, that her husband had had to charter a private jet since nothing commercial was available.

'And you didn't want to go with him? A private jet? Jeez!' Roxy's eyes are round, but Kitty is now sorry she introduced that element of Saul's departure. It feels as though she'd been boasting. She certainly didn't want to say she'd been in private jets more than a few times. 'I'm very happy here. I've never really explored Rome, Roxy, and anyway, I'm meeting my sister and her husband in Venice. It's their anniversary and it's been set up for ages.'

'Well, if you're stuck for someone to talk to, you know where to come to. Okay?'

'That's very nice of you. But you're so busy with your book.'

'Not that busy.' Roxy sighs. 'I had a chat with Charles earlier. He gave me loads of great tips. He says he's not a writer, but I'll bet he could produce a terrific autobiography. All those stories of his . . .'

'Why don't you suggest it to him?'

'I will. I'll do that.'

They're sitting in the ship's piano bar, where there's a low buzz of conversation just below the decibel level that would otherwise have overcome the work of the skilful young pianist who is segueing from one standard show tune to another. No one is paying him the slightest attention, even when he flourishes to a stop every so often and turns, as though to acknowledge applause, of which there is none. He doesn't seem to mind, however, launching immediately into another set.

'Poor guy,' Roxy is sympathetic, 'but if the two of us do clap it'll just show him that all the others aren't. Maybe on ships it's a tradition not to applaud. Are you looking forward to the dinner? Like, I can't believe we started out with eight at our table – look at us now. Just you, me and Charles, apparently.'

'You know about the Danish couple, then?'

'Who doesn't? I heard it from the two lads, Dilip and Angelo, in Housekeeping. They're lovely, but they say there's more to come. A drugs ring.'

'Now there's a plot for you, Roxy!'

'Yeah. I'll discuss it with my new mentor!' She grins. 'Although Charles thinks I'd be better off concentrating on what I'm good at. Like love stories. They're not as easy as you think, Kitty. You could probably write the plots on half a matchbox. It's stretching it out that's the problem. I read an interview with Edna O'Brien once, she's great, but she said something about the big set-pieces, the dramas and the major scenes, being the easy bits when you're writing. The hard bit is "getting them from lunch to dinner". I thought that was *really* clever. But, of course,' Roxy adds ruefully, 'she's so good she can always get them from lunch to dinner in some style! So, what are we expecting tonight?'

'I don't think it's going to be that big . . .' and Kitty tells Roxy how Charles had described the *Clara*'s 'dinner at the captain's table' when it's genuinely at his invitation and not a corporate event. She'd asked him in the context of Saul's birthday, upcoming on Christmas Eve.

The *Clara*, Charles had explained, is one of the very last liners afloat offering a private area for dining with the captain, rather than 'his' table being in either the centre, or somewhere else prominent in the main dining room. 'On the *Clara*,' Charles had said, 'it's in a large alcove off the MDR, but the diners in it can be seen only by a few of the other guests. You feel very privileged and exclusive in there. They do it beautifully – the table is dressed with fresh seasonal flowers, silver cutlery and crystal. I intend to make the most of it, if that's where we're invited to.'

'That must be where Saul's birthday was to be celebrated on Christmas Eve?' Kitty waits for the pang of regret. It doesn't come. Instead, there's a sting, brief enough, of guilt. 'It's his sixtieth, you know.'

'He told us himself, at least twice, to my recollection.' Charles had grinned but with affection. 'But I'd doubt if a big celebration like that, especially for a director of the company, would have been in a little place like the alcove. Those big occasions are usually in the centre of the room so everyone can participate. After the main course, all the waiters form a choir and give a pretty dreadful rendition of "Happy Birthday", while the pastry chef brings in one of his best cakes, with lit candles, and everyone joins in. The captain gets photographed with the guest of honour and his or her cake, but he doesn't stay for the full meal and makes his excuses to leave. Where we're concerned, though,' he adds thoughtfully, 'especially since there'll be no cake to be admired, he'll have to find another trigger. Don't worry, they do these things well. Honestly.'

'So with no birthday, no cake,' Roxy surmises, 'it's just us. Probably to help us get over the shock of what happened. But of course Saul could come back for his birthday in the private jet!'

'I doubt it!' Kitty smiles. 'But when he calls me I'll suggest it and I'll say it was your idea!

'Time's moving on, Roxy. I think I'll go brush my teeth and get ready. See you maybe outside the dining room? From what Charles said I guess we'll have to pass through the Main Dining Room to get into that alcove or whatever it is. I hate going into a crowd of people in a place like that alone.'

'I find that hard to believe. Someone like you, Kitty? With your looks and clothes and coming from modelling? You must be sociable, you have to be.'

'I was, a few years ago, but it wore off!' Kitty laughs. 'And you don't know me from the inside . . .'

'So I'll have to watch you a lot more carefully!' They get up from their seats to walk together to the elevators, Kitty marvelling at how lightly she seems to be taking Saul's departure.

*

The group at the captain's table numbers six, Charles, Roxy, Kitty, the captain, Frank Mitchell, and the staff captain, whose name, Kitty and Roxy learn, is Jock.

The four men are already there when the two women walk in. Charles, Kitty sees, had not exaggerated the care with which the table is presented. She has dined in many five- and six-star establishments, some with three Michelin stars, which, in presentation terms, pale in comparison. The lighting is cunning, playing on the silverware and faceted glasses, angled so it doesn't compete with the white candles around which the flowers have been arranged, low enough so diners don't have to strain their necks to see the person at the other side of the oval table. The sense is of luxe intimacy and perfect taste.

With only two women to four men, the seating has been arranged so that she and Roxy find themselves facing one another with a man on each side, she with Charles to her right, the captain to her left, Roxy between the others.

Charles, of course, is familiar with everyone, and as soon as the first round of wine has been poured, the conversation focuses on him. Accepting the spotlight, he jumps into top gear so that by the second glass the atmosphere, certainly among three of the men and Roxy, is relaxed and affable, even clubbable. Roxy is having a ball, flirting lightly with her companions on both sides, who obviously find her charming, and teasing Charles, who reacts in kind and with a ready wit. Kitty looks at him in admiration: he must have been attractive in his day and quite a dandy.

After ten minutes of enjoying the banter, she turns to the captain. 'Thank you for having us. Your staff go to a lot of trouble.'

'Practice makes perfect.' When this man smiles, which she now believes to be rarely, his entire face lights.

'It's wonderful,' she says. 'They're certainly enjoying themselves!'

'Are you, Mrs Abelson? It's such a pity that your husband had to leave us.'

'I thought we'd settled that,' she says boldly. The wine, strong and meaty, is going down a treat. 'I'm Kitty. Remember?'

'I remember.'

'What's your own name? I can't keep calling you "Captain".'

'Einar.'

'Einar,' she repeats. 'That's a nice name. I was afraid it would have about twenty syllables.'

'Two only.'

'Great. It's easy.'

Once again, conversation dies. But there is an outburst of laughter from the others and she raises her voice a little to be heard over it. 'Do you like hosting these evenings, Einar?'

'I'm not being facetious,' he responds, 'but their success or otherwise always depends on our guests.'

'Is tonight typical?'

'I don't think so.' He lowers his eyes. 'It's different every time.'

'How many do you usually have?'

'The table capacity is ten, so it could be six to four, six guests, four officers. Tonight is exceptional.' He's still not looking at her but his meaning, she suddenly realises, is clear.

Quickly she turns to her other side to tune in to Charles, who is holding the floor with one of his anecdotes, but she doesn't hear what he's saying. She is so conscious of the captain's presence, less than twelve inches away, that she seems to feel the heat from his body.

It's warm in the alcove, she tells herself, with all the lights and the flickering candles.

The main course is brought in and served. She feels lightheaded, almost giddy.

Seemingly oblivious to the tension at her side of the table, the other four continue with their revelry while waiters come and go, refreshing the glasses, whisking away empty plates. The captain hasn't said a word to her or, indeed, to anyone in the last ten minutes but her consciousness of his physical presence is increasing. She is now hyper-aware that he is deliberately ignoring her, but a wild fairy, whom she hasn't detected in herself since her teens (and later in her early twenties when she, Abegunde and Bertha had spent so many evenings gate-crashing parties to which they hadn't been invited) has now woken up and is tickling her tongue. She waits for a gap in the dialogue now taking place between Leifsson and Charles, then breaks into their conversation: 'Had you always wanted to be the master of a cruise ship, Captain?'

'Actually, no.' The essence of politeness, he smiles not directly at her but around the table, while signalling that their waiter should refresh their wine. 'My family's industry is widely dispersed. I have a great-uncle, still living, who spent his life on trawlers and I used to accompany him sometimes when I was a child – but that was before the fish stocks declined and he retired.

'Perhaps, however, those journeys had their effect. At college, I had decided to study aviation engineering, with a long-term view to becoming an airline pilot but, although I graduated, I found the lure of the sea to be strong. During college, I had signed on as deckhand on a passenger ferry for two successive summers and found I enjoyed it. The training started there, further study and training and stints on ferries and container ships – even on one occasion in an engine room – becoming involved in all aspects of ships and shipping, further exams, tests and interviews. It was a long road but here I am.'

It's quite a speech by comparison with what Kitty has heard so far from the captain's repertoire, and at the end, he looks challengingly at her, as though to say: *Enough, Mrs Abelson? What else would you like to know?* And then: 'I'm sure I've talked too much about myself for one evening.' Turning, across her, to Charles: 'We know a lot about Charles, but I'm sure there's more to learn.' And, the angles of his face relaxing, he grins. 'We've known you for a long time, haven't we, Charles?'

Charles gives a gracious little bow. 'And I you, Captain!'

She, she muses, is as much at fault as he is for the next silence. She can't think of anything at all to break it. A veteran of banquets and awards dinners, where she was usually seated with people she knew only slightly, Saul at the far side of the table, she should be able to come up with some conversational gambit. Something neutral.

'I'm meeting my sister on Friday in Venice. We're both very excited about it. Do you have brothers and sisters, Captain? Children?'

'No children, but I do have one sister.'

'Just like me.' Adding: 'Yes. Just one sister.'

'No brothers?' His tone is polite.

'No.' She shakes her head. 'And my parents are dead. Yours?'

'Mine died too. May I offer you some water?'

'Thank you.' She holds out her glass.

He fills it, then glances around the table. 'Ah, I see that everyone has finished.' Quickly he stands up and taps his glass. 'Ladies and gentlemen, if I may, but I shall be brief. I find I have to leave you. Please, be merry and happy and stay, please stay, for as long as you wish. I can guarantee that Chef Julian's tarte citron is the most heavenly you will ever taste. And, speaking of pleasure, it has been mine to host you this evening. Thank you so much for coming – and now a toast, if I may, to the *Santa Clara*. May she have safe passage to her next life, and may all who sail in her enjoy her as we have!'

'*Santa Clara!*' they all, including Kitty, intone, raising their glasses. And, with perfect decorum, he is gone.

When Kitty gazes after him, her eyes meet those of Charles, a faded blue, but shrewd and knowing.

21

Kitty, having set her little travel alarm, wakes very early on the morning they're due to dock in Venice.

The previous evening, the captain of the *Santa Clara* had made a ship-wide announcement on the Tannoy to his passengers: 'Ladies and gentlemen, this is Captain Leifsson, I hope you have enjoyed the wonderful city of Dubrovnik. Tomorrow morning we are to dock in Venice. It is a personal choice, of course, as it will still be dark initially, but I recommend that you rise early to go on deck to watch our arrival by sea into this city. It is an experience, I think, you will not forget. To get to our cruise terminal, we shall move slowly down the Grand Canal, past the famous St Mark's Square and all the landmarks you are familiar with from pictures, even if you haven't been to this beautiful city before. We shall be travelling very slowly as there are regulations concerning the ship's wash. I am sure you will appreciate that, not least because of concerns about rising sea levels, Venice is in a delicate state and we do not wish to add to her troubles. As I say, it is a personal choice as to whether or not you wish to witness this amazing arrival by sea. Personally, I do not tire of it. Tonight the weather is forecast for calm conditions all the way and into tomorrow morning, low temperature overnight five degrees, rising slowly from dawn. Tomorrow's high will be nine to ten degrees, and although at this time of year it is usually misty, we are not expecting any rain. In addition, ladies and gentlemen, because we know that our guests value their time in this lovely city, a reminder that to give optimum time ashore, we shall be departing later than usual tomorrow evening, casting off at eight thirty p.m. As a result we shall not arrive at our next port, Messina, until ten a.m. the following day, but you will have ample time to see the sights of the city, and even take a trip to the coastal resort of Taormina, just one hour away. All details are available in the daily bulletin left in your stateroom. But, I repeat, departure from Venice tomorrow evening at eight thirty. Please be back on board by eight o'clock at the latest. I wish you a good evening, a peaceful night and a wonderful visit to Venice. Thank you.'

Kitty had decided to skip dinner in the MDR – while she's happy with the companionship of her two remaining tablemates, Roxy and Charles, she was simply not hungry. Half a lifetime spent keeping her figure means she's learned not to use food for comfort or reward, or to eat purely by the clock. Food on the *Clara* is varied but rich, and the pastry chef's desserts are to die for, but although she doesn't mind putting on a couple of pounds, she doesn't want to waddle back to Manhattan.

But now, stretching her limbs in the comfort of her warm bed, she realises she's hungry.

She smiles as she thinks back to her sister's excited phone call yesterday afternoon. Geraldine and Paul had arrived in Venice at around lunchtime, had had lunch 'in the most gorgeous little pizza place, Kit, and it wasn't all that expensive, Dublin prices, and we sat outside right beside this little canal freezing our tails off. Thank God you warned us not to expect Riviera weather.'

'Did a gondolier float by, singing "Just One Cornetto"?'

'Hilarious – don't be daft. It was more a question of boxes of bananas going by, or tools, or bicycles, not a gondola in sight, but it was so exciting. We really could tell we were somewhere different. And, Kitty, the hotel is fantastic, everything you'd want, even a view of a canal, a bridge and a church from our bedroom window. Where would you get it? We'll get to the gondoliers tonight!'

'Whoa! Slow down. I can barely understand you. Glad things worked out.'

'Worked out?' Geraldine shrieked. 'That's the understatement of the century. We can't thank you enough, Kit. This is terrific. I can't wait to see you tomorrow in the Gritti Palace. Paul keeps calling it the Gravel Shed. I could kill him sometimes – it's that Monaghan humour, but I always worry he'll go too far some day and someone'll give him a dunt.'

'Ah, leave him alone. I like Paul.'

'I like him too.' Her sister's voice is tender. 'But, listen, he's cried off having lunch with us. I'm trying to get him to come and have a drink before we eat tomorrow but he says he's going to leave us alone to chat. He promised his ma he'd go to Padua – she's a lifelong fan of St Anthony so she wants him to light a candle for a special intention and, if possible, bring back a relic. There's some pal of hers has got cancer, poor woman. By the way, your last text said Saul won't be joining us either.'

'He had to go back to the States.'

'What happened?' Geraldine's tone had changed instantly. It always does, at the mention of Saul's name.

'There was an accident on one of the construction sites,' Kitty had replied evenly, 'but, look, it's probably good for you and me to be able to talk and bitch with no men around. It's been ages since we had a girly chat.'

'And you didn't go with him?'

'I wanted to meet my lovely sister. Anyway, I'm no help to him in these matters – I'd just be hanging around in some hotel room or other, waiting for him to come back.'

The silence at the other end of the line had spoken volumes. Then Geraldine, her voice a little forced, had said, 'Anyway, can't wait to see you, little sis, but this is probably costing me a fortune with roaming charges. See you tomorrow, one o'clock at the Palace. I'll be sure to wear my tiara!'

'On the other hand, smart-casual's more appropriate, I'd say. One doesn't wear one's diamonds before dinner.'

'Brill. See you.'

Must be some ancient golden curse hanging over her, Kitty had thought, as they broke the connection. They'd been eight for dinner, then six, then four, now three. She'd booked four for lunch ashore in Venice: now they are two. Is someone trying to send her a message?

But she resolved there and then to make sure Saul was *not* going to be the topic of conversation, as he has been so many, many times for Geraldine and herself. This trip is solely for her sister and Paul and their anniversary, no marriage counselling on the agenda. Even if Paul is not to be present, Kitty is determined that he and his wife, their lives, their children and their news, are to be front and centre.

Does she miss Saul? She glances across to where his head

had lain for the past few days. She's used to his absences when he's away on business, and had had no real hope that this trip would be a romantic get-together for the two of them, but except for mealtimes on the ship and those two excursions they'd taken, one aborted, he'd attended to business and had behaved more or less as though he were at home.

So, no, she doesn't miss Saul. What's to miss?

An hour later, having showered, then eaten a little block of Belgian chocolate from her mini-bar, she's on deck near the bow with hundreds of other passengers as the *Santa Clara*, moving ever more slowly, drifts along the water. There have been a few murmured conversations up to now, but the sound dies down and all eyes are fixed ahead as, through the mist, the city's lights, like a faint yellow globe hanging above the water, slowly appear.

Little by little, as the ship creeps closer, the globe flattens and spreads while the first wavering outlines of buildings, a tower, a steeple, become visible until, fully an hour after that first glimpse, Venice and its lights, still seeming to be a ghost city, spreads before their eyes in the pre-dawn light. Kitty, warned by the temperatures the captain quoted, is wearing her down-filled winter coat and hat, although the tip of her nose feels as though it's made of dripping, melting snow.

Still nobody near her moves as the crowd stands together to experience what their captain had so laconically summarised in urging them to get out of their warm beds this morning.

They enter the Grand Canal just as the first light of dawn seeps through the dispersing mist, illuminating detail: the crumbling stone of door and window frames, the dark hollows of boat docks under businesses and residences, the dark green algae of high-water marks while the silence of their arrival is interrupted by the whine and putt-putting of boats of all sizes, criss-crossing the canal in front and to both sides.

Conversation resumes as the people around Kitty remark on what they're seeing, although a few are now yielding to the dampness and cold, peeling off to go inside. Those remaining are rewarded by the sight of the first gondolas, flags drooping, bobbing at their mooring docks in the wash of busy *vaporetti* and other traffic in the choppy water, which is a filthy, creamy brown. Kitty waits to leave until after they get to St Mark's Square.

And here it is, unmistakable, the subject of a billion postcards. Streetlights are popping off, but under the roof of the colonnade along one side of the square, a profusion of fairy lights is already glowing, as are those on the enormous Christmas tree, between it and St Mark's Basilica, and while they're passing, the traceries on the upper storeys snap on too. All of these lights are white, giving an ethereal glow to the square in the haze. Strangely, she thinks, despite the Christmas decorations and redness in practically every corner of the ship, she had almost forgotten it's so close to Christmas – and Saul's birthday. Only thirty-six hours away now. She'll have to call him at midnight, his time, on Christmas Day, whatever it proves to be, Italy time. Dammit, one of her tasks today is to get an accurate time check for Boise – if, of course, he's still there. It's odd, she thinks, that he hasn't called her yet. It's not like him.

There is one difficulty – a big one. At the time she'll need to call him with birthday greetings, the *Clara* will be at sea, voyaging towards or around Sicily – hopefully close to land where there might be a signal. If there isn't, she can't and he'll just have to put up with it.

Despite the early hour, St Mark's Piazza is already busy. The brisk trajectories of locals, carrying briefcases, laptops or bulging shopping bags are in straight lines. Earlybird tourists, rendered obvious by baseball caps, backpacks and cheap waterproofs, wander randomly and are consulting maps or snapping – she can't wait to join them. She slips away from the crowd back to her stateroom and orders breakfast from room service.

It has to be routine for Captain Leifsson to urge his charges not to miss this magical experience, but now she wonders if he had been up there on the bridge, seeing it for the last time as the master of his ship. If so, had he been sad? *Enough!* She cuts off this line of thought. *Shut up! Don't do this – get a move on.*

She's still wearing her coat when the room-service waiter arrives, so she asks him to set up her breakfast on the balcony. She eats it while still slowly-slowly, the *Clara* moves through the increasingly busy water traffic, and the grandeur of the mist-wreathed city unrolls from the stern as if for her alone.

After docking, she's among the first to get off. She takes a water-taxi to St Mark's, getting there when it's still only a quarter to nine. Having equipped herself with a map from Reception, she now has more than four hours to herself before she's to be at the Gritti Palace.

*

It's amazing, she thinks, ninety minutes later, how small and compact the centre of the city is, yet how easy it is to lose your sense of direction, especially as many of the less showy bridges over the backwater complex of canals tend, to her unaccustomed eyes, to look the same. How many bridges has she crossed? Has she doubled back? Has she been on this one before? She doesn't recognise these buildings but this grey-green stretch of water seems the same as the last one . . .

She consults her map and decides to start again at St Mark's Square. She'd been leaving its glories until last but her feet, despite the padding of boots and the weight of the Murano piece she has found for Geraldine and Paul, have decreed they've had enough of cobbles and bridges for the moment. The cafés in St Mark's should be open by now, she thinks, and however 'tourist-trap' they are, it won't matter to her feet. Following her map, showing landmarks such as churches, pharmacies and hotels, she arrives back at St Mark's to sit gratefully on a chair outside one of the mega-cafés, many of its rows and rows of tightly packed tables already occupied. She orders a latte and a croissant from a waiter, who had clearly had a bad night and wants to be anywhere except at work, serving *stupidi turisti* – she doesn't know if that's accurate but it sounds good.

When he comes to take her empty cup, she orders a second, half because she needs one, half mischievously (further to wreck his day), and while she waits, she spreads out her map, on which the street layout is ringed with advertisements, and then unfolds the *Clara*'s itinerary. She needs to figure out approximately where the ship will be at the right time on Christmas morning, so she can make that midnight call to Saul. She becomes conscious that someone is standing beside her.

'*Buon giorno, signora!*' says a man, dressed in a pea jacket and jeans, a plaid scarf around his neck. For a moment or two she's confused, until she recognises him. 'May I join you?' Captain Leifsson asks, just as the surly waiter arrives with her fresh coffee, placing it in front of her. Hand on hip, eyebrows raised, he looks at Leifsson, who points at Kitty's cup. '*Sì, per favore*,' then, to Kitty, reiterating, 'May I?' indicating the second chair at the table.

Fleetingly, her body screaming, *'Yes, yes, yes!'* Kitty's brain recognises danger and manages to confine her response to a polite 'Yes, of course, please do.'

He sits, and they look at one another.

'You are checking our progress?' He nods towards his ship's itinerary.

'Actually,' *something to talk about,* 'you may be able to help me here because I'm trying to figure out where we'll be between four and six on the morning of Christmas Day.'

'Certainly. From four to six o'clock on Christmas Day, all going well, we shall be at sea on the last leg of our journey prior to docking at Civitavecchia for Rome the following morning.'

'And would you have any idea what the time difference is between Rome and Boise, Idaho, at midnight, Idaho time?'

'Just a moment.' He pulls out his mobile phone and clicks a few buttons while, around them, more and more people take tables. 'Eight hours,' he announces. 'Eight a.m. the following morning in Rome.'

'Thank you.'

There follows one of the rather excruciating pauses that seem to dog them.

'I take it that Mr Abelson is still in Boise?' he asks then. 'That was a serious setback for him and his company.'

'Yes, it was. I haven't heard, but I hope to be speaking to him this evening before the ship sails and before I lose network coverage.'

'How was Dubrovnik yesterday?' he asks, as the waiter comes with his coffee. 'Did you go to the old town? Walk the ramparts?'

'I didn't go ashore yesterday. I had some reading to catch up on. Roxy – you know Roxy?'

'Indeed I do.' *Of course he does – idiot!*

'She went ashore and, she said, spent ages looking for bullet holes.'

'Did she find any?' Leifsson's mouth twitches.

'No.' Kitty shakes her head. 'That, of course, doesn't mean there aren't any!'

'You're right. No, it doesn't. There must be a lot of bullet holes after what happened. When was that war?'

'Back in the nineties.'

'Was it that long ago?'

'It was.'

As their conversation dies away, the chatter around them seems very loud now to Kitty. 'Apparently,' she says now, feeling she has to raise her voice a little, 'she found a Christmas market in some church or monastery, St Clare's I think she said was the name. She brought back a candle for me and a bag of candied orange peel for Charles.'

'That was good of her.'

Another silence clangs awkwardly onto the table between them, although almost immediately (*thank God, Kitty thinks*) the campanile, which is quite close to where they're sitting, fills it, bells chiming eleven for what seems like many minutes.

When the reverberations have petered away, she again sips her coffee. 'You must know Venice very well, Captain?'

'Einar, please. I am off duty. But, yes, I do know Venice well. I never tire of it, as I may have said during my announcement last evening to our guests, and even after I am retired, I shall return frequently.'

'You're retiring?' She hopes she'd sounded surprised.

'Yes, this is my last voyage on the *Santa Clara*. I was very pleased to see Venice on the itinerary. To tell you the truth, sometimes I wonder about these Portlandis cruises. The itinerary decisions can sometimes seem rather arbitrary. I guess in this case, though, it may have a lot to do with off-season and which ports offer the cheapest fees! Will you be staying in Rome, Kitty?'

'You're very young to be retiring.' *What had he meant by that question – oh, God, this is crap.* 'Are you planning to stay in Rome yourself?'

'I will be fifty on January the thirtieth. Yes, I might be.'

'My goodness – I'd have thought you were much younger!' Had that been her chuckling? she thinks despairingly. It had sounded even more bogus than her dialogue. 'These cups are rather small, don't you think?' She takes another dainty mouthful.

'Yes, you would certainly need to have two for a proper hit of caffeine. Of course, that's how they make their money. The Italians are a clever people.'

Jesus. Please stop this! This is agony. 'It's amazing that we should meet here this morning.'

'Is it? St Mark's Square, one of the most famous tourist attractions in the world? And you are a tourist this morning, are you not? So is it that surprising?'

'Yes, but you—'

'I always come here. And this may be my last paid opportunity.' He lowers his head to stare at the ground as though analysing it. Then: 'Why not?' He raises his head and gazes directly at her. 'I came here, Kitty, knowing that sooner or later you would be here too. You were kind enough to let me know you were meeting your sister at the Gritti Palace. I was prepared to go there if I hadn't found you before that.'

'Were you?' Inside, her body is dancing.

'Yes.'

In front of my sister?

'In front of my sister?' The implications are clear.

'Yes. If this is not agreeable to you, I shall, of course, accept that and be on my way.'

And now, after, oh, maybe six hours or so – *calypso, calypso* – while his eyes stay locked on hers, she hears someone's voice, a woman's, maybe not hers, say: 'It is agreeable to me.'

Looking away from him she notices that she is gripping the edges of the table. Her fingers feel numb. Tentatively, very gently, he reaches out a hand, touching the back of one of hers, just for an instant. The contact fizzes, like a lightning strike. 'What are we going to do, Einar?' She still can't look at him.

'I don't know. Not yet. It is so easy to pilot a ship, to make life-and-death decisions on the turn of a coin, to be judge and jury, to seem invincible at all times and in all situations. To be the one in charge. This is hard. The hardest. But "I don't know" is the proper answer to your question. The only thing I did know up to now was that I had to be here. Like this. With you. I can't believe it that you think there might be—'

'Let's think only about this moment, Einar. Let's just have this day. I don't want to have to think ahead.'

'Kitty, please look at me.'

She does. She had noticed before that he has a tiny scar on his jawbone, a couple of inches from his ear. Rather than meet his eyes again she concentrates on it: a little crescent of white against his tanned skin.

'I have something for you,' he says quietly. 'I was going to give it to you, come what may, win, lose or draw for me.'

She's still studying his scar but can see him reach into an

inside pocket and take out a small cardboard box, a couple of inches square. Sees him put it on the table between them. Hears him take a deep breath.

'In a few days,' he begins, 'I will no longer be master of the *Santa Clara*, and protocols, officer to guests and so on, will no longer apply. I can walk around naked, hang from the communications mast—'

Her head jerks round, clearly as he'd intended.

He smiles at her, a little puckishly – she's beginning to differentiate his expressions. 'I have the pension cheque already,' he says. 'All I have to do is cash it, and I'm a free agent. There's nothing they can do to me then.' His chest rises as he takes another deep breath. 'I'm rolling all of my pension into one lump sum – Portlandis encourages this. Once you're gone, you're gone, and the company doesn't want to be involved in any way in your afterlife. I intend to invest it in a smallholding I already own, to build greenhouses, then live off it. I love horses very much. Do you know about Dutch Friesians, Kitty? They are the most beautiful animals on the planet. I want to cross-breed them with our own sturdy little Icelandic horses, beautiful in their own way, strong and very hardy. But if that doesn't work, all is not lost. I can join a trawler. My experience and skillset has to count . . .'

Abruptly, she realises what this is about. 'You're setting out your stall, Einar.'

'Am I? If that's how you see it, perhaps I am – but before you start thinking about that, let me add something else.' He pushes the cardboard box closer to her. 'I have to emphasise what I said already. It's win, lose or draw, Kitty, and the last thing I would want is you to feel I'm adding pressure to what I can already see, in the few days I have known you, is a pressure-filled life.'

She is now afraid to open her mouth in case whatever she says, the tone she uses, will shatter something fragile.

'It is my amulet,' he continues strongly. 'It has kept me safe during all the years I have been at sea. It had originally belonged to my late wife's grandfather, who had captained a whaler, and before he died, at a great age, may I add . . .' his eyes flicker sideways, with reminiscence, then come back to her '. . . he gave it to me, actually presented it ceremonially in front of relatives, on the day I got my master's ticket. I have worn it since, and it may be coincidence, but whatever about my passengers,' briefly, he looks forlorn, 'in all the time my ship was under my command, she has never had an accident.

'I am giving it to you because I want it to keep you safe now. And even if you decide I am living in fantasy and nonsense, if you decide to fly back this evening to your husband, I still want you to have it, to keep you safe in the air.'

Kitty, flummoxed and a little shaky, picks up the box. 'May I open it?'

'Of course.'

Inside, nestled in tissue, is a small, exquisitely carved figure of a whale, creamy-coloured, strung on a gold chain from a hook set into the animal's dorsal fin. 'It's a humpback, as I'm sure you can see,' he's watching her, 'and it's from a time when we were not as enlightened as we are now in their conservation. It's carved from a tooth, I'm told.'

'A whale tooth?'

'Yes, but the humpback is a baleen species. This is from a whale with teeth. I don't know from what species and never thought to ask.'

'It's too precious. Please, don't give it to me. I don't deserve it.' She pushes the box back across the table.

'I'm not a romantic man, and no-one could describe my offering you that little thing, which is probably of no intrinsic value, as a romantic gesture, but you're right, it has been my most precious possession, but you are wrong that you do not deserve it. I didn't deserve it – nobody deserves anything, really. I have worn it for more than half my life. That is why I want you to have it whether I win you or lose you – and it's strange that I should think in those terms, never having had you – but I have hope.

'So,' he adds, with the air of someone who has completed a difficult task and is pleased to have it off his desk, 'one way or another you must keep it.' He smiles again, a little wanly. 'I know this is going to sound utterly insane, but if I can't have you, I want to live the rest of my life with my DNA somewhere near yours. Even if it's stuck in the back of your sock drawer, our DNA will mingle!' He shrugs. 'There you are. I wish I could think of something more romantic, more poetic.'

'This is mad, Einar!'

'Utterly, utterly mad. Sudden love is mad. It steals in like a thief in darkness to carry off all rational thinking, leaving the victim searching in vain for his brain. That is what has happened to me since the first time I saw you as I escorted you from the boarding hall to the elevators. You were wearing jeans, one of those down jackets and a white sweater. At dinner that evening when I did my rounds I could barely look at you, you were wearing a white dress. At the cocktail event the following evening, it was a black dress with little sleeves that just covered your shoulders and the dress didn't touch your knees. I thought its colour was an omen of my doom because, of course, I never dared to dream that I could sit here like this with you. Shall I go on? Shall I tell you what you were wearing when I had the good fortune to rescue your beautiful ring?'

'Will I give you a tour of my wardrobe so you can't be surprised any more?'

He smiles faintly. 'I know I am being hyperbolic, it's a symptom of this madness, but I didn't ask for all this. I was going back to Iceland, quietly and happily to live my life and look after my horses and my land. You came on board my ship and everything changed. My instant attraction to you was a phenomenon I have never before experienced, and it was presented to me as a *fait accompli*. In a sense, to be prosaic about it, it was a chemical reaction.' He grins now: 'There! I told you I'm not romantic.'

Then he seems to realise he has perhaps revealed more than he had intended and: 'Oh, Mrs Abelson, madam, you have no idea how I have suffered!'

'That's what we'll call our new musical, shall we? *Oh, Mrs Abelson!* Has a nice ring to it, wouldn't you say?'

'Musicals are not my forte, Kitty,' but she thinks he's relieved, as she is, that the temperature has dropped a notch.

Or, her treacherous body prompts, *we're a few steps closer to being where we want to go*?

'I like movies,' he says now, apropos of nothing, 'especially old ones, *To Kill a Mockingbird*, *Twelve Angry Men*, *Casablanca*?'

'So at heart, despite what you say and under all that starch,' this from Kitty, fresh from the moors with Heathcliff and Cathy, 'you are a romantic!'

'My late wife wouldn't have agreed with you.'

'The mingling of DNA with old socks? Sounds pretty romantic to me. Tell me about your wife.'

By now, their coffee, not even half drunk, has developed a

cold, milky crust and they order two more from the waiter who as ever behaves as though this is an impertinence. Then, after it arrives, they barely touch it, lost together in the singular and heady chat of two people newly discovering each other while floating above an undercurrent of mutual desire neither has yet verbally acknowledged. Both then start and look around at the campanile, disbelieving, as it warns them it is now one o'clock – she's late for the Gritti Palace, he has to be back on board for a utilities meeting at two o'clock. It's lucky, she thinks, she has already bought her gift for Geraldine and Paul. They stand and push their chairs neatly under the table, both eyeing the cardboard box in the middle. He picks it up. 'May I fasten this around your neck, Kitty?'

She lowers her head and pulls down the collar of her coat. He takes the amulet out of its box and, instead of approaching her, goes behind her, draping the chain around her throat, fumbling a little with the tiny clasp. 'There!' he says and as he moves back in front of her, avoiding her eyes, he murmurs, 'sorry for being clumsy, I just wanted to touch your skin.'

She makes one last effort to stay clear of the abyss, for the moment . . .

'That was our Calvin Klein moment, of course!'

He frowns, puzzled.

'Eternity? It's a perfume. There's an ad for it where they try to represent the beach scene in *From Here to Eternity.*'

'Ah!' Comprehension dawns. 'Burt Lancaster!'

'Deborah Kerr.'

'Will you have an early dinner with me in Venice tonight, Kitty – or have you made arrangements with your sister?'

'Yes. I will. Five o'clock?'

'Five it is. I'll meet you outside the Gritti Palace and, don't worry, I'll be discreet. In the shadows. But you'll know me. I'll be the one wearing Calvin Klein Eternity.'

They turn to go their separate ways but, as they do, both simultaneously encounter the stares of the couple they'd met on the ship before Einar had 'interviewed' Kitty: the man who likes to dine at four, the woman who'd given her the once-up-and-down and had seemed to think she was the captain's wife. Their eyes, thinks Kitty, are out on stalks.

'I don't care.' Leifsson too, has seen them. 'Let them do their worst. I hope you're not upset?'

'No.' Kitty means it. This is all insane but it's the type of insanity that encourages people to climb Mount Everest.

'I'm sure to run into them again. I'll tell them we're married, but we've been keeping it quiet because you're on the FBI's Most Wanted list.' He sounds light-hearted, which, just twenty-four hours ago, she would not have expected of the *Santa Clara*'s captain.

*

Now she and Geraldine are seated at a low coffee table in the lobby of the Gritti Palace which lives up to Wolfgang's description: ultra-luxurious, all accoutrements glittering and gleaming.

Her sister is delighted to see her. 'Paul should be back before we leave – what time do you have to be on board?'

'About half five,' Kitty lies.

Her sister stares at her. 'What's happened to you?'

'What do you mean what's happened to me? Nothing's happened to me!'

'I'm your sister. I've known you longer than anyone else on the planet. Something's happened.'

'All right, I've lied to you. I've lied, too, about the time I have to be back on the ship. I'm meeting a man for an early dinner. But you and I will have plenty of time,' she rushes on. 'We've hours. I'm not meeting him until five.'

'So who is he? Where'd you meet? Does Saul know?'

'No . . .' Kitty hesitates. 'I've to ring Saul, at the latest, tomorrow morning. I'm not going to mention anything until I sort out my head.'

'When and where did all this happen, Kitty?' Geraldine is not smiling.

'I thought you'd be pleased.'

'I never thought I'd be advocating for Saul, but aren't you being a little unfair to him? Not telling him? I know people have affairs but—'

'I'm not having an affair.'

'What do you call this, then?'

'We haven't slept together.'

'Yet! I can *see* it, Kit.'

'Please, Ger, don't judge me. Anyway, you're the one who's always implying that I should leave Saul. "Money isn't everything" and all that. I've known Einar for only a few days, and this wasn't meant to happen.'

'That's what they all say, apparently! Who is he anyway?'

'I can't tell you.'

'Jeez, Kit, will you give over? I'm your sister. He's married, is that it?'

'No, it's not. He's a widower. But . . .' Kitty now discovers that the urge to talk about a new lover can be very strong '. . . if you truly promise not to tell *anyone*, even Paul, Ger?'

'So he's not married but there's a mystery here. Does he have money? Can he keep you in the style to which you've become accustomed? Or is it Rich Girl meets Penniless Homeless Man? "We're in love," he says. "At last!" she says. "This is the real thing."'

'I won't listen to this. That's bitchy!'

'Sorry, it is. I don't know why I'm fighting you about it. I guess I'm afraid you'll get hurt. I'll back off.'

'He's neither penniless nor homeless. He's from Iceland, he's just retired and he's going home to become self-sufficient on a little farm. And he loves horses. He wants to breed them.'

'This gets better and better. What's got into you?'

'You said you'd back off.'

'I meant it. I'm just being protective. After the life you've been leading, I can't see you in a dirndl skirt and wellies, mucking out stables. You have to see, Kitty, this sounds as though you're off your rocker.'

'That's what I *think* too. But I *feel* as though, for the first time in years, I'm happy. Aren't you always asking me if I'm happy? Well, I am.'

Geraldine sighs. 'Describe him to me, this Man of Iceland. How old is he?'

Kitty tells her.

'Well, at least you're coming down a decade.'

'Bitchy!'

'So he's retiring at fifty, from what? Being a blacksmith or something?'

'He's the captain of the *Santa Clara*.'

'Jesus! You're full of surprises, you are. But then you always were. So what time are you meeting him again?'

'Five.'

'We'd better get a move on. I'm certainly going to drink my lunch. Iceland? Land of the furry jumpers and volcanoes? We sure do have a lot to talk about – but I'm sorry I had a go at you. And I knew something had happened for you to look like this. "Radiant", I think they'd say in *Hello!* magazine. But, God almighty, Kitty! What are we going to do with you?' She waves at one of the waiters who, as though on casters, immediately glides across the carpet to take the order. After they've given it, Geraldine shakes her head. 'You're some tulip, d'you know that? Go easy on poor old Saul but, as you know so well, I've always thought he was married to work and money, and with the attraction of his money, he won't be single for very long. Deep down, I'd love to have your kind of body-glow again. Paul's great, I love him to bits, but after fifteen years? I envy you. Maybe that's why I was such a bitch. Sorry – forgive me? Give us a hug, you silly cow.'

*

That evening, after her dinner with Einar Leifsson, it's only when she lets herself into the suite that Kitty realises she's still carrying the Murano lantern she'd bought for Geraldine and Paul. She had brought it away from the Gritti Palace – at least Einar had, gallantly offering to carry it for her – but she'd been in such a tizzy she hadn't realised nobody should have been carrying it anywhere, except Geraldine and Paul back to their hotel.

The brief encounter between the captain, Geraldine and Paul had gone as well as could be expected in the circumstances. Paul had been his usual bluff bus-driver self. He was always hail-fellow-well-met, prepared to give anyone the benefit of the doubt until it could be proven otherwise.

Geraldine had been more circumspect, but when she was saying goodbye, arms around Kitty, she had hissed into her ear, 'Jackpot! Go for it!'

She and the captain, as she continued to think of him, had eaten at a bistro-style place off the beaten tourist track. They'd talked and talked, about their own lives, past and present, his with his wife: 'I loved her but was never in love with her,' he'd said sadly, 'and for her that was the tragedy. She complained that I was away so much. She was a good woman who wanted children and we did our utmost to have them, but when she and our first child died together, I made up my mind I would never invest in another close relationship.

'And then, Kitty, you walk onto my ship!' He'd twined his fingers with hers.

From the austere personality he presented on board, she'd thought, looking at him on the other side of their little metal table, with its red candle and paper napkins picturing Santa Claus, the change in him was miraculous. It was as though someone had removed a set of shutters to shed light all over him. Fearing it could not last, she nevertheless allowed herself to feel deliriously happy in his company, but just for today. He clearly saw a long-term relationship. She didn't dare hope – but there Hope was, whirling hula-hoops on her substantial hips, asking Kitty to join in the fun.

Despite his assurances that he didn't care who saw them come back to the ship together, she had insisted they should take separate water-taxis: 'Nobody else knows you have your cheque and all these new freedoms. If you won't protect your reputation, I'm protecting it for you! Until we get to Rome, you're still the master of the ship.'

'Right now I feel like the master of nothing. I feel nothing is tangible, that everything, whatever "everything" means in the context of what's happening, has turned to air and light and I can't grasp it . . .'

They're almost at the taxi stand but he pulls her into the shadows of a side alley away from the street lighting and puts his arms around her. She responds and they hold each other tightly. Neither moves to kiss. Kitty can't answer for him, but for her, it would have felt wrong, as if it might ruin something as evanescent as a dream.

*

Having stashed her sister's gift in her suite, Kitty's next task is the now customary one of removing the ornament from the centre of the bed. This evening's triumph of the towel-carving art is an elephant, with trunk, ears and even little tusks. She dumps the bed cushions on the floor, flings the pillows after them and peels off the bedcovers, exposing the sheets. Then, knowing she's being exceptionally silly (although who's to know?), like the child she once was, she throws herself backwards into the middle of the huge bed, spread-eagling her arms, pumping them in long, slow arcs, making snow angels with the Egyptian cotton.

Almost too elated to sleep, she manages to doze off in the company of CNN's anchors, as they drone on about Donald Trump's latest tweets.

The TV is still on when she wakes to a tapping on the door: 'Room service!'

'Wrong room. I didn't order anything,' she yells but, what with the TV and the thickness of the doors, the waiter hasn't heard her and knocks again.

'Room service, madam!'

'Shit!' She pulls on the first nightdress she can find, a full-length white cambric thing she believes makes her look like Betsy Ross, creator of the first flag with Stars and Stripes, because of its multiple buttons. She crosses to the door, pulling it open. 'I didn't order—'

'Good evening, madam,' says Einar Leifsson. 'Shall I bring this inside for you?'

Wordlessly, she opens the door to let him pass. On the tray are two ice-cream sundaes, complete with little umbrellas.

'I have to tell you, madam, that, unfortunately, when I was bringing the tray up here I think Mr Burtonshaw and I saw one another. However, I have an important question. Shall we have our ice cream before or after?'

'What?'

'There is, I believe, a freezer in this suite?'

'You've done this before.'

'Not at all, madam, but we must make our decision quickly or they will melt.'

Kitty is experiencing sensations all over her body that she has never felt to this degree before. She swallows. 'Thank you very much. They should be placed in the freezer. You will find it in the kitchen area beside the dishwasher.'

'Thank you, madam.'

'No, thank you, Einar. Do you have your receipt book with you?'

'Unfortunately not, madam. However, a gratuity is always welcome for extra service, although always voluntary, of course.'

'Let me get my wallet.' She fetches her handbag from where she'd dropped it beside the bed while he puts the sundae dishes into the freezer, then comes back to wait in the living area, hands behind his back. She opens the wallet as she goes back there, taking out a five-dollar bill.

He takes it and bows. 'Thank you very much, madam, you are very kind. May I wish you a good evening?' Then, discarding the money, he scoops her into his arms and carries her into the bedroom, depositing her on the bed. 'Hmm.' While she lies very still, every vein and artery rushing, he looks round at the wreckage she has wrought with the bed and its covers, the elephant towel, bottom-up on the floor, its little legs splayed and unravelling. 'Let's see now.' He sits beside her, stroking her hair, and slips his left arm under her shoulders, pulling her towards him to cradle her. 'What would you have said if I'd agreed with you that I had done this before? I haven't, by the way.'

'We'd have talked about it.' She closes her eyes and he kisses them, one after the other.

'Maybe debated a little?' His fingers, which have been playing with the pearl buttons on the nightgown, begin slowly to open them from the top down.

'And who'd have won?' Her body now seems to have a life of its own, straining to cast off ties as, methodically, he moves down the buttons.

'I would, of course.'

He's now on button five – she's been counting. There are fifteen altogether. 'May I ask,' she whispers, 'how come you're so good at opening little buttons?'

'Have you ever been a fisherwoman? Ever tied a fly, ever gently removed a hook from the mouth of a little fish to put him back into his home and let him live?' Button nine slides open.

Before he opens button ten, he takes his arm from under her and, using both hands, lowers the garment from her shoulders. Then, delicately, he pushes back the sides, exposes her breasts. 'There! Much better.' Gently, he kisses each shoulder, then her nipples, flicking each a few times with his tongue. Instinctively, she arches her back.

'No, I don't think we're ready yet.' Slowly, he opens buttons ten, eleven and twelve, exposing her belly and hips. 'Three more to go and we're done here.'

'I need to brush my teeth.'

'No, you don't.'

'What about a shower?'

'No.' He opens the last three buttons then parts the nightgown so she's lying, framed in cambric, exposed from head to toe. He inhales a long, slow breath – and, murmuring something incomprehensible to her, strokes her with both hands, from shoulder to ankle, then, sliding off the bed, leans over her to kiss the arches of her feet before quickly shedding his own clothes. He lies beside her, pressing his length against hers, turns her to him, wraps himself around her, kissing her mouth, whispering against it, 'We have to do this slowly because we must remember. Remember, Kitty . . .' He kisses her hard then, raising himself above her to look down at her face. He's so close she can see the flecks in his irises. 'I must insist that "Kitty" is no name for such beauty,' he says softly. 'My name for you is "Catherine". Remember, Catherine, remember . . .' His kisses become deeper and longer.

'Come what may?' she whispers into his mouth.

'Come what may.' Slowly he eases himself, full length, onto her, and body to body, they lie without moving for a few seconds, she, trembling a little, feeling the increasing speed of his heartbeat against her breasts. Then he raises her to him. 'Come what may, Kitty Golden, golden Catherine, Catherine Golden, Catherine . . .'

22

Twelve hours after she sailed out of Venice for the last time (unusually late because, as the captain had explained, he had wanted to give guests the longest possible time to explore that lovely city), the *Clara* had docked in the Sicilian port of Messina at ten a.m. the following day.

While standing at her bow Charles, blessedly because there is no wind, can shelter under his umbrella and look both into Sicily and into the toe of her mainland parent, Italy. The rain, light but incessant, had begun the previous evening at ten o'clock, just as he was taking his after-dinner constitutional around the decks. That dinner, his third-last ever on the *Clara*, had been a sad affair, with just himself and Roxy at the table.

They'd had another session about Roxy's novel, but as he was telling her about his working life, Roxy's journalistic background had kicked in, he thinks now, because she'd wondered if he would be interested in the two of them working together on his memoir. 'I live in Dublin, of course, but my mum's still in London. She's poorly and I think she'd like to have me home a bit more.'

Charles had been shocked at the notion that his humdrum career, as he'd always seen it, would be worth a book. But she'd set about trying to persuade him, telling him that it's well known in writing circles that while *everyone*'s life is worth a book, not everyone can write one. 'So how's about it, Charles? We work together. You help me with my novel, the way you have already, I work with you on a book about your career. Maybe you don't realise it, but at this table, until it all went pear-shaped, you were the entertainment. You tell wonderful stories about famous people. Wonderful stories, full stop. You're a born storyteller, Charles.'

'You really think so?' He didn't know how to take that. It was amazing that even one person believed he was worth a book.

'Yes, I do.' Ponytail bobbing, expression determined, Roxy couldn't have been more definite. 'We both win. As soon as I get home I'll contact my agent. We split the proceeds fifty-fifty – if there are any, of course. It's your life we're selling, but I'll be doing all the work. Judging by what I've heard already, it'll be a doddle. You can dictate your stories. I'll interview you about your views and background. That sound reasonable?'

'Heavens, Roxy, it's very good of you.'

'Not really. It's a business proposition. And I think each project will help the other. You're good at storytelling, I'm good at research. We complement one another. Have you anything major on for when you go back?'

'No.' Charles had been about to add the usual waffle about 'prospects, although nothing confirmed yet', but for once he didn't. 'No,' he repeated. 'I'm totally free.' In a way he found it liberating not to have to keep up a front.

'Done.' Roxy stuck out her hand and they shook to confirm the deal. Despite the rain, Charles had gone to bed in his stateroom on deck six happier than he had been for quite a while.

He wasn't stupid. He knew enough to accept that this could be a bucket of fog, but *someone* had faith in him – and he genuinely looked forward to having Roxy's bubbly company for however long it lasted.

In some respects, he thinks now, standing between Sicily and Italy in the bow of his lovely ship as the rain patters quietly on his umbrella, this last cruise has turned out to be the fulfilment of the old Chinese curse *May you live in interesting times*, with the humiliating collapse of his acting course and the horrifying fate of his sole pupil, but to balance things, there'd been his upgrade to the comfort of his lovely room, and now this, with Roxy. She's young enough to be the granddaughter he'll never have, and he cautions himself against getting too enthusiastic. Like dandelion clocks, cruise companionship tends to blow away on the cold winds of home.

Neither of them had seen Kitty all day yesterday. Roxy (who had, to her chagrin, slept late and missed the *Clara*'s spectacular early-morning entrance into Venice) had gleaned that the ex-model had never been to the city before. She had told him that Kitty had gone ashore early to be with her sister and the sister's husband.

Charles has a more fanciful take on this, but he keeps it to himself. Quite late the previous evening, after the *Clara* had set sail, he had seen the captain, incongruously carrying what looked like two dishes of ice cream into one of the lifts. Curious, he had watched the numbers climbing, and had seen them ascend all the way to deck eight. He wouldn't have been surprised had the ice cream reached a very interesting destination. Or if he'd just observed the hero of Roxy Smith's new novel; Mother's Mills & Boon had nothing on it, Charles had smiled gleefully to himself. He adores being ahead of the posse in the study of human behaviour, picking up what some are up to in the deep, while the rest paddle around in the shallows.

He gives himself a mental kick now. On the other hand, it might just be that the captain likes ice cream and in bringing two portions upstairs had been pre-empting the need to come down again to order a second. He is a good-sized man, probably eats a lot. (Being captain, though, he could have ordered a flunkey to fetch it for him?)

Absolutely none of his business, Charles had taken the next lift to deck six and his own lovely bed.

During this cruise he had been ashore only to Nice – not alas to Venice, where he had many times walked its streets and crossed its bridges, tut-tutted at the flotsam in the canals, marvelled at the churches and – admired his particular favourites – the beautiful handmade papers and pens in the city's numerous stationery shops.

Charles has always thought that cities have distinct personalities. Hamburg, where he once played with a touring group, has more bridges, canals and other watercourses than Venice, London and Amsterdam put together yet to him it is a stern and strict governess, corseted with steel, concrete and glass. If Edinburgh could talk, it would tell jokes as ancient as its huge store of listed buildings, while Venice is an old courtesan, combining mystery, intrigue and exquisite subtlety. It's not for nothing that its *Carnevale,* held in the run-up to Lenten austerity, is famous for elaborate masks. His memories of the city are warm and vivid, an archive of sensory delights he can draw on for as long as he has left to live.

Right now, eschewing the delights of Messina (for him, when compared with the sumptuousness of Venice, Rome, Lucca, Florence, Milan, Siena and Verona, Messina can't hold a candle) he is staying on board once again, determined to make the most of the last thirty-two hours he and his *Clara* can be together.

There is a reason why a man becomes attached to a ship, he thinks. She keeps him safe on dangerous seas – or rescues him when he's in trouble. Each vessel, like each city, also has a distinct personality (he's sure the captain would agree with this): the *Clara*'s is sturdy, calm, helpful, generous, reliable and welcoming – like a long-term wife (or partner, these days), sharp corners blunted, surfaces that had been angular and glittering, now worn and no longer posing danger. Overall the *Clara* is pillowy and comforting, and Charles fears that in two days' time, when he disembarks in Rome, he will feel he's abandoning her, sending a much-loved relative into a home, away from everything familiar.

On impulse, he pulls out his phone: yes, there is a signal, a good one. He dials Maggie's number.

She's recognised his and answers: 'Well, this is a surprise, Charles. What's up?'

'Nothing really, dear. I'm on the *Clara* for the last time – she's being sent to the scrapheap, I'm afraid. I'm just feeling a little sad about her so I thought I'd give you a call. Sorry, is it inconvenient? I know it's early for you.'

'Not at all. In fact, Leonie has just left for the day – she's doing her Christmas rounds. As I think I've told you, she has a large group of indigents she supports, gives them Christmas puddings and so forth. The kitchen looks like the local hunt's been through it. And the steam! She takes the puddings hot to them!'

'How is she? And how are Donna and Millie?'

Maggie and her partner have a pair of donor-sperm twins. 'Oh, big and bold. They're going to be eight next month. And how are you doing, Charles?'

'I'm fine.'

'Charles, how many years have we known each other? You're not fine, or you wouldn't be ringing me. Oh, no – you're not ill, are you?'

'No, Maggie, I'm not ill, I'm chipper.' He forces his voice into a higher register. 'I just thought I'd ring you to wish you a happy Christmas. I guess with the *Clara* going . . .'

'You're lonely. Look, why don't you come out here some time over the Christmas period? I'm sure the girls would love to meet you. They're on holiday until January the seventh and, after all, you are, I suppose, a sort of grandfather, well, a grandfather-figure. They don't have any granddads, like other children at school and on TV ads. They're nice. They have their moments, but we're trying to bring them up to be respectful to their elders.'

'And Leonie wouldn't mind?'

'Of course she wouldn't. My God, Charles, how long is it since we separated? And, by the way, I can't remember whether I said it at the time, but I genuinely appreciate that you didn't fight the divorce. You could have, I know that, but you paved my path and I'm grateful. So do come over. The trains are ghastly, but it's only an hour and twenty minutes, and Leonie does make nice cakes and puddings!'

'I will. I'll give you a call and we can make arrangements. Have a merry Christmas, Maggie.'

'You too, Charles. Merry Christmas.'

Charles's eyes glisten as he cuts the connection.

*

Kitty Golden is planning again to have breakfast in her room, rather than on the balcony today, because she's looking out at rails dripping under the grey, persistent rain of her Irish childhood.

The day before, in the Gritti Palace, when she'd managed, for a few minutes, to get Geraldine off the topic of Einar Leifsson and onto what was happening at home, they'd actually discussed rain and how it had changed. 'We're having monsoon rain at home now, Kitty. Sudden deluges, what we used to call cloudbursts when we were small. But they were rare then, weren't they? Remember sitting on the harbour beach in Rush, making little tents of our plastic macs and how it was actually fun to be getting pelted?'

'Sure I do.' Kitty had smiled. 'That *noise!*'

'But nowadays,' her sister had gone on, 'every bloody passing cloud seems to burst, coming down in stair rods, hopping off the roads and the roofs. It's kind of scary how fast this climate change is happening. It'll be okay for us, I suppose, we'll be dead. It's the kids and their kids I worry about. Do you notice it in the States?'

'Not in Manhattan – it's an island in every sense – but, yes, we are worrying, or some of us are, about what Trump is promising when he gets into the White House next month because to him climate change is a hoax. We're hoping, I guess, that this might be just campaign talk and that he'll get a few sensible people around him and listen to them.'

She leaves the gloomy prospect of her balcony, crosses the room and climbs back into bed. Although she knows that her sequential absences from the dining room will probably have intrigued her two remaining tablemates, she's not ready to don a mask to face them, acting as though nothing seismic has happened. She is also unwilling to relinquish the heavy imprint of the captain's warm body on hers.

She moves to lie in the space they'd both occupied and, like a teenager, luxuriates in her imagination's re-creation. 'I'm required by law to rest for ten hours out of every twenty-four,' he'd said after half an hour or so, while they had lain side by side, her hand in his. He had then hoisted himself on one elbow, softly to kiss her again. 'I could do this all night.'

'I could too. Do you have to go?'

'Yes. I'm on the bridge for arrival at Messina.' He'd looked at his watch. 'It's nearly midnight. I wish I could stay – but soon, Catherine? Soon?'

'There'll be a lot to work out.'

'Granted.'

'But not tonight. We have three more days.'

'Two and a half. And we have to be careful.'

'I understand.'

'And you have to telephone your husband to wish him a happy birthday.'

'I know that.'

'Am I putting too much pressure on you?'

'I can't believe this has happened. Is it a bubble, Einar? Will it burst soon?'

'Not if I have anything to do with it,' he'd said, grinning. 'Right now, I feel as though all the balls in the lottery have fallen into my basket. I would give them all to you. If you were with me, I would buy you a palace and a Rolls Royce – and a carriage pulled by four beautiful black Friesian horses, manes and tails flowing in the wind as they fly you to another world.'

'And you say you're not romantic?'

'When did I say that?' He'd touched the whale. 'That seems

to have been sometime in the last century. But in Iceland, Catherine, as I hope you'll discover, we tell stories to ourselves of gods and goddesses, good and bad fairies, monsters and demons in our epics and sagas. I grew up with them. Good night.' He'd kissed her again. 'I've broken every rule in the book today and tonight and I don't care – what have you done to me? I used to be the guy in charge!'

'You do know that this, like this' – he swept an arm over her and the bed – 'can't happen again on the ship? I must revert to type as the master of my vessel. So please do not be distressed if I do not register what we are – what I hope we are – in public. It's not much longer until we meet in Rome, and some of that, I hope, will be extremely nice.'

'A lot of it,' she'd said, 'all going well.'

'Yes. "All going well" it will be nice.' He'd kissed her belly, her breasts and then her lips. 'Are you going ashore in Messina tomorrow?'

'I don't want to leave this bed. Ever.'

'Shall I contact Housekeeping? This bed is a disgrace to the reputation of the *Santa Clara*!'

'Thanks but no thanks. I may go to sleep right now and sleep all the way to dinner.'

'I shall put out your "Do not disturb" sign as I leave, hopefully not scandalising any of your fellow guests in the process.' Having kissed her once more, he'd climbed off the bed to dress.

'I cannot wait for Rome, Catherine. My fear is that you will now have time to think, and that thinking will bring you back to your husband.'

'Do you really believe that all this, today, tonight, is a flash in the pan for me?' She pulled herself higher in the bed. 'I have never before strayed. Never once! And by the way, Einar, I wish your name was Bob or John – I'm going to have a lot of spelling to do!'

He showed her he'd understood the implication by coming to the bed again and kissing her where the little whale sat on its chain in the hollow between her clavicles. 'Good night, Catherine. Sleep well. Here's to Rome!' Quickly pulling on the rest of his clothes, he'd finally moved to the door and, taking the 'Do not disturb' sign with him, had left quietly.

Having gone over all of this again, Kitty changes her mind about having breakfast in her room. She gets up, makes a cursory attempt to tidy the bed – she doesn't want gossip, not yet – then has a long shower.

When she gets to the dining room, it's almost as full as it usually is at dinner, as waiting staff flit between tables with coffee jugs and sous chefs replenish the domed chafing dishes. Yet Charles cuts a lonely figure at the top of table thirty-two, otherwise empty. 'Good morning.' She sits beside him. 'I see we still haven't a smaller table. There are only three of us.'

'I've noticed,' he says, 'but all in due time. At my age you don't "sweat the details" as the movie characters would have it, you get used to routines and I automatically sat here. And, anyway, for some reason it seemed disrespectful to Josh and Barry. Waters closing over and so forth. And by the way,' he concentrates hard on slicing crusts off his toast, and cutting the remaining pieces into little triangles, 'only because you're so near and I can see the seams, your top is on inside out. Morning, Captain!' He looks up.

'Good morning, Charles, Mrs Abelson.' Leifsson, carrying an A4 manila envelope, stamped COMPANY MAIL, is not in chatty mood and avoids eye contact with them. He withdraws six smaller envelopes and, flicking through them, hands one to Charles and two to Kitty, one marked with her name, the other with Saul's. 'Could you also take Ms Smith's for her, please, Charles? And please give her my apologies for missing her. I also have one each for our two Danish friends although they are, of course, now redundant. I shall make sure they're delivered to the correct locations. I have already opened mine.'

'What are they, Captain?' Kitty asks, looking at her two letters. She is afraid to raise her eyes. 'Are they some kind of invitation?'

'They are from Mr Lee.' His voice is clipped, but a muscle in his jaw, she sees, when she risks an upward glance, is pulsing a little. 'Our Venice agent put them into our system with the rest of the company mail but I retrieved them only this morning. I shall let you open them in peace. Given the context, I felt I had to deliver them myself, rather than have them put into your rooms.' He acknowledges them with one of his 'captain's bows', as she has begun to think of them, and walks away, his back stiff.

Charles looks after him. 'It's really touching to observe how many ways you two can find to avoid looking at each other.'

'*Charles!*' Kitty, feeling herself go red from the chest up, is disconcerted.

'All I'll say, assuming nothing, I promise you, Kitty, is that you're lovely, body and soul. You need to know it and be celebrated for it.'

'Please don't say any more.'

'I won't. I'm saying it to you, not to anyone else.'

Kitty, needing to steer away from this, gazes at the two letters she continues to hold. 'I'm afraid to open this, Charles.'

'I'll open mine.' He does so, withdrawing a single typed sheet of thick, inlaid paper and starts to read. She watches his face but the expression remains impassive, and so, putting Saul's envelope aside, she opens hers.

Barcelona, December 2016

Dear Captain Leifsson, Charles, Kitty, Saul, Roxy, Elise and Aksel,

Please forgive me for being so familiar as to use only your first names, also for typing and printing this letter, but my time is short.

I feel impelled to write to you all since, apart from myself, you were the last people my darling Joshua knew in his young life. You were kind to him, and although he, as you may have noticed, was not one for social niceties, I know he would have wanted me to thank you.

He is to be cremated in this beautiful, secular city where the arts are part of everyday life. Somehow, with the aid of some very good friends in music, painting and architecture, we have managed to get him here, and we have obtained permission for him to rest in Sagrada Familia for an hour before we, my parents and I, his parents and his brother, carry him to the fire. I think this is to happen within the next few days.

For myself, I would be so grateful if you could remember him as the young man he was before evil destroyed his singular beauty. I need to know this and, in my opinion, our discourse at Table 32 was very civilised and kind, although Joshua did not partake all that much. But I would like you all to know that underneath all the braggadocio (I recognised it and I apologise on his behalf if he offended any of you) I also know better than most that Joshua's soul was pure.

I am so grateful to you all for your company and kindness to me during our too-brief stay with you all on the little Santa Clara and especially in the aftermath of the tragedy.

Thank you, Charles, for trying so hard to save him; thank you too, Roxy, for the part you played – and from the heart I apologise, on Josh's behalf, for the shock you suffered, it must have stressed you terribly; thank you, Kitty, for the kind way you broke the dreadful news; thank you,

Captain, for your professionalism in the immediate aftermath of Josh's collapse, but not just that, for your deep humanity and understanding of my grief.

Thank you, Saul, for your kind and flattering offer of a job with one of your companies in the USA. I had always wanted to try America but it was not to be.

So thank you, everyone, including you two, Aksel and Elise (how happy you were! Long life to you both!), for your politeness and concern for both of us.

After the cremation, I plan to go to Trieste, city of Joyce, where I hope to find rest.

Thank you again,

Barry John Lee

Both Kitty and Charles, almost as though they have rehearsed the moves, refold their letters in synch and replace them in the envelopes.

Kitty excuses herself. 'I must turn my T-shirt, Charles, thank you for letting me know,' and leaves the table to head for the Ladies outside the main doors of the dining room.

Once inside, not bothering to go into a cubicle, she takes off the T-shirt, turns it out and puts it back on. She is reeling. If Barry's intention in writing that round robin had been to ameliorate the effects of that dreadful afternoon on each of the recipients, it had had the opposite effect on her.

The letter, intensely sad in all respects, has brought her own sorrow careering back, as it must certainly have for Charles, who had been more centrally involved in Josh's situation than any of the rest of them.

For several minutes, she studies her reflection. Has the letter wiped out yesterday's magic?

No, it has not. What it has done, however, is to make

definite her next task: whoever first said life is short was right. Geraldine was right. Sooner rather than later she has to call her husband and explain she is leaving him for another man.

She has no doubt now about this: her interaction with Einar Leifsson has opened the door to a realisation that even if the two of them had never clapped eyes on each other, she has to save her self-respect. Even leaving carnality out of it, as the nuns who had educated her would have called sex, or even thinking about sex, she desperately needs joy in companionship. And not just any companionship: she feels that, out of all the men and women in all the world, this Icelander's company is what her spirit has craved for a long time.

She's going to leave her husband, even if Einar vanishes tomorrow, and she has to devise a form of words that will least hurt Saul. She has until eight o'clock tomorrow morning.

No, that's cowardly procrastination. To wish Saul a happy birthday, then give him the news that would hurt any man, especially one who had been through two divorces already? That's yellow.

The irony is, she thinks, that on this trip she had more than once remarked to herself that he had possibly mellowed a little; the work regime was just as punishing, but he did let her boss him around a little – in the matter of his knee for instance, and in not having a full-blown fit about her not going to Boise with him, apologising to her so profusely about the couple's table farce, even so surprisingly accompanying her to Cinque Terre. Could her desertion seem to him extra inexplicable and harsh?

It isn't being facetious, she tells herself, to bring The Donald and Melania into this equation, to ask herself, in the event Trump's wife decided to take their son and walk, which would cause the lesser wound to the president-elect? To let him think his wife is being horrible and selfish? Or to imply that another man is more attractive than he is? Of the two men, her husband is by far the more intelligent and educated but they share several personality characteristics, the main one being an ego as big as the sun but as brittle as a prawn cracker. Thinking about it, she decides that the least hurtful route is to leave Einar Leifsson out of the equation for the moment, although Saul could well ask about 'third parties'. She'll have to judge how to deal with that at the time. And she has always found that truth, although difficult and inconvenient, is usually the best option. So maybe, she decides now, the best option could be to come clean. Something along the lines of: *Saul, I'm desperately sorry but I think I'm in love with someone else* – and to wait for the fallout.

While they're in port and have a phone signal, she steels herself to make the call.

*

In the Main Dining Room, Roxy Smith sits in beside Charles, who is carefully spreading English marmalade on little triangles of toast. 'Howdy, pard!' she chirrups. 'No sign of Kitty, eh? D'you think she's sick? Should we check? Or should we tell someone we're worried?'

'She's in the Ladies. She'll be back in a jiffy.'

'Great. Listen, I'll be back in a jiffy too. I see Gemma over there with some of her family, and I need to make things right.'

'I thought we'd covered this. You have no obligation to them, Roxy, and, according to yourself, my dear, they don't actually fit into your story.'

'I know, I know – you're right,' she says. 'Of course you are.

I'll just go and say hello. Any further thoughts on what we agreed yesterday?'

'Plenty. The hell with the cost, Roxy, I'm going to stay in Rome for the couple of days. I'm fed up being as parsimonious as a field mouse. But as soon as I get back to London, I'm going to go through the mountain of cuttings I've kept – and Mother kept – over the years I've worked. I'll enjoy putting them in some kind of order and they'll be very helpful to our task. We're a most unlikely pairing, you do know that, Roxy?'

'The best kind, Charles. We like each other and we're not competitors. We can't be. We're in completely different genres, different generations. We'll broaden each other's horizons and can learn from each other. I'm delighted.'

'Will you have time for this, Roxy? Will you have to park the new novel?'

'Plenty of time. What we'll be doing is just journalism, a sort of assembly job and putting it into narrative form, and as I've found out, it'll be a doddle compared to novel-writing. I had no idea! Nobody tells you it's so hard! They think it's you just get this idea and the Muse sits at your elbow and off you go for a few hours every morning before you go out into your garden to pick strawberries for tea!'

'Any further on in your choice of heroine for the new one? Even a name?'

'Alice.'

'Wonderful. *Alice's Adventures in Wonderland*. You can't go wrong with an Alice.'

'She's still generic, an avatar, if you like – you know what an avatar is, Charles?'

'Funnily enough,' he smiles, 'I do. I'm old but not dead, a bit of a technophobe but I can still read! You know what? I think she's right in front of you but you can't see her yet.'

He swivels his eyes in the direction of the doors, and when Roxy turns to see what he's signalling, she sees Kitty Golden walking through, looking, Roxy thinks, like a million dollars although she's dressed only in a heavy cotton T-shirt she might have bought anywhere from Harrods to Primark, over navy trousers. The woman's style is effortless. She could cut a hole in a black bin bag, pop her head through, sling a belt around her waist and win a best-dressed competition at Ascot with just a beanie on her head. 'How are you, Kitty?' she says, when the other woman arrives. 'Great to see you. Charles and I have missed you. Had a good day yesterday?'

To her surprise, Kitty shoots a glance at Charles, so quick Roxy doesn't have time to interpret it. 'Had a lovely time in Venice.' Kitty slides into the chair beside her. 'I met my sister, as you probably know. In fact we were having such a good time I forgot to give her the anniversary present I'd bought for her and her husband. I only realised it when I got back to the ship.'

'What'd you buy her?'

'A piece of Murano glass. It's a lovely candle-lantern, cobalt blue, gorgeous. I'll show it to you, if you like.'

'And did you buy yourself that little dolphin around your neck?'

'This? No. I've had it for ages. It's a family heirloom – it's actually a humpback whale.'

'It's beautiful.' Roxy notices that, surprisingly, Kitty has coloured a little.

'I've seen that on you before, Kitty.' Delicately, Charles puts his last piece of toast into his mouth. He chews, swallows, then adds, 'Weren't you wearing it the day you came on board?'

'Imagine you remembering!' Kitty touches the little whale. 'I always think only women spot accessories and jewellery. So what's good here this morning? I'm famished!'

'Well, it goes great with that outfit, Kitty.' Roxy stands. 'I'm going over to the Dunnes for a sec, if you'll excuse me. Don't worry, Charles, I've taken what you said on board.' She hops up and goes across to table thirty-three.

'*Thank you,*' Kitty mouths to Charles.

'I recommend the kedgeree.' Fastidiously, using an index finger, Charles is gathering toast crumbs into a neat little pile in the centre of his plate. 'It's really good this morning. I fancy one of those Danish pastries. Shall I fetch you something while I'm up there?'

'I'll come with you. We might see something even nicer, but thanks again.' Together, they leave the table.

*

An hour later, it's ten o'clock in Messina, two a.m. in Boise, Idaho, and the rain is still falling on the *Santa Clara*. Kitty, who is back in her room, has her phone in her hand to ring Saul and get it over with – she's already feeling terribly sorry for him – when it pings. The number on the screen is his.

She panics and reacts by cutting it off – she's not ready yet – but within thirty seconds it pings again. 'Hello, Saul, I was just about to call you. Pressed the wrong button, sorry. Everything okay?'

'Sure, sure.'

'You still in Boise?'

'No, I'm back home, just arrived. I've a meeting later today with a bunch of lawyers. It's bad, Kit, but not as bad as we thought. Two dead, eleven injured. It could have been a lot worse. It's gonna be messy, though, six companies involved in the suits already filed. The relatives are going ape – not surprising. What's happening there? Still having a good time? When d'you think you'll be back in the States?'

As he continues, almost nervously, the stream of words rapid, his stress settles her a little. She waits until he draws breath, then: 'That's what I wanted to talk to you about, Saul.'

'What? I can't hear you, you're breaking up.'

'We need to talk, Saul.'

'That's better. I can hear you now. When you flying back? I was just thinking about this Rome thing. You should stay, sweetie. I know you want to see the city so stay and have a good time. You getting on okay with all those nice people? How's Barry doing? I was gonna hire him but with this Boise stuff I won't be hiring anyone any time soon, I guess.'

'Saul, will you listen to me for a minute? There's lots to tell you and, as a matter of fact, I have a letter for you from Barry.'

'You're breaking up again, sweetie. I'll call you back later today.'

'I'll be calling you for your birthday.'

'Oh, yeah, yeah, I nearly forgot. Gotta go, sweetie.'

'Saul, will I try the landline? Saul?'

But he had cut the connection.

She frowns. That was odd. He'd almost forgotten his birthday. Saul? Forgetting the most important day of his entire year? Every year? Things must be worse than he's letting on. *Dammit*, she thinks. How can she lay further grief on him? He doesn't deserve it. But she simply has to.

For the next half-hour she paces the suite, even braving the rain to go out on the balcony, not caring that she's getting wet. How is she going to handle this? She bats ideas to and fro in her mind, then realises there are no options. The timing is unfortunate but there's no benefit to be gained from delaying. In fact, doing so could make the break-up even more traumatic for her husband, who right now is carrying on with life as though things are normal between them. No, she thinks, the only thing to do is to face it. The Boise situation might even serve as a distraction for him. Saul, as she knows only too well, values work and business above all else.

Before she can change her mind again, she picks up the phone and taps out their home number.

By the fourth ring she is suffering more pangs of conscience. He must just have fallen asleep – what news to wake up to. She is just about to press the cut-off button when the call is answered.

'Hello?' says a woman, sounding sleepy.

Kitty instantly knows the voice. 'Philippa?'

'Yes? Who's this?'

'It's Kitty, Pippa. I'm really sorry, I must have hit the wrong number by mistake.'

The line goes dead.

23

I t's Christmas Eve on the *Santa Clara*, and all over the ship, her guests are primping for the evening's celebrations.

Just as on Embarkation Day, Charles is waiting for his old friend, Frank, to join him on the bar stool beside his own. He's reading through last night's bulletin enumerating today's events, thinking that the prose, normally chirpy, while excelling itself in its inclusiveness, has gone a little OTT.

> *Come One! Come All! This evening, on the Eve of Christmas and Hanukkah, two days after the Wiccan and Zoroastrian celebration of the winter solstice, two days before Kwanzaa, we celebrate together in our various and wonderful ways . . . So this evening, you should come to the Main Dining Room with empty stomachs and high expectations. As this will be the last ever such event on the good ship* Santa Clara, *our chefs have been planning and prepping all through her last week in Europe; our officers, crew and staff, from thirty-three different nations, have been rehearsing their farewell party pieces and under*

the baton of its trusty musical director, our showband, too, will be in fine form. Even Piano Man Marty has been persuaded to move his baby grand into the ballroom to add to the brouhaha as old friendships are sealed and (maybe!) new ones forged. There's still time because, as you will know, we're at sea tomorrow and alas! Monday morning and disembarking will come all too soon at Civitavecchia and transfers to the Eternal City of Roma where your four-star hotel, the magnificently modern and luxurious Hideaway Hotel Chilingua, awaits. But for tonight, expect to dance into the dawn of Christmas Day (no excuses – we have wheelchairs!) with the encouragement of our troupe of professional dancers, who have the virtually impossible task of training officers and crew not to step on toes, including their own! There may be surprises, there may be gifts, there may even be a special visitor at midnight. With his sack. So have a wonderful evening and God Bless Us Every One.

'Did you write this stuff?' Charles looks up from the bulletin as Frank arrives.

'Dickens wrote the last sentence for me.' Frank sighs. 'Everyone's a critic these days. What's wrong with it?'

'Zoroastrians? Wiccans?'

'You might be surprised. We don't ask our guests to fill in forms.'

'And we're getting gifts, are we? And who's the special midnight visitor?'

'Guess!'

'No! Charles acts as though shocked. 'Please. I have my pride!'

'You also have a lovely room, Chuck!'

'Dear God, "the bells! The bells"!' Quasimodo-like, Charles hunches over, then: 'Complete with sack?'

'And bell! Since you mention bells. You're wanted backstage in the costume room for a fitting of the fat suit.'

'No such thing as a free room, eh?'

'Oh, come off it, Charlie. You know you love it! A captive audience? Showering them with gifts?'

'What are they getting?'

'We're on the collection routes as we speak.'

'All the usual junk?'

'Surplus stock, if you don't mind.'

'Do I have a choice?'

'What do you think? Come on, think of it as your last appearance on the *Clara* – your final service to her. And you're sure to have an appreciative audience.'

'When you put it like that, dear heart!'

'"Dear heart" right back at you – I know we said we'd have a drink, but I just dropped along to tell you I can't. Duty calls. Tomorrow will be quiet but, just in case, you think you might be able to stretch to a trip to Miami?'

'"Fraid not, unless there's some kind of financial revolution and air travel comes free.'

'Well, it's not goodbye just yet anyhow. For me it's mostly paperwork tomorrow so I should be able to come and find you, but just in case . . .' Frank passes over a piece of paper on which he's scribbled his new address in Miami. 'I know you're allergic to technology, Chuck, but I've included my email address in case you have a change of heart. And you already have my UK phone number.

'I'm going to miss your ugly mug, you know – big old loony.'

He thumps Charles on the chest. 'We didn't see each other that often but you've grown on me, dammit! Oh, for God's sake, what am I on about, let's not get carried away. Anyhow, see you this evening, Fatman! Don't forget, tonight will be emotional for the crew. Some of them have no jobs to go to.'

'I'm well aware of that, God help them. I'll do my best, Frank.'

'Of course you will, you always do.' Frank lowers his head and walks away.

Charles coughs to clear his throat but looks back at the ship's bulletin he's still holding in his hand to read about what other delights are in store for them all this evening, although the print does seem to have gone a little fuzzy.

*

In her stateroom, Roxy Smith is getting ready to shine.

Her 'good' dress, from John Lewis, is a mid-length sheath of lime green linen with a plunge neckline. It's currently a little snug on her, unfortunately, but as she regards herself critically in the mirror on the back of her bathroom door, she is happy enough that she'll get away with it. Mercifully, it has three-quarter-length sleeves, concealing what she believes is pure pudge on her upper arms – although neither Ruth nor her mum, who is never behind the door in expressing an opinion on Roxy's weight issues – can see anything wrong with that area of her anatomy. 'You've been reading too many magazine articles, Rox,' Ruth had scoffed, when they'd Skyped each other before the cruise.

Roxy had pinched the flesh up there and held it as close as she could to the monitor's camera to demonstrate what was worrying her. 'It's definitely orange peel. How can you not see it, Ruth?'

'Well, I can't because it's not there. If that's orange peel I'm Taylor Swift. And I've just looked in the mirror and I ain't no Taylor.'

Roxy smiles at the recollection as she fastens on her 'bronze' neckpiece from Accessorize, inserts her long, gilt and garnet chandelier earrings, from the same outlet, fastens on the black plaited leather bracelet she'd bought from a street vendor in Dubrovnik, and gives her hair one last comb-through. Although she says so herself, she's used her straightener to good effect this evening: on both sides of her face, her hair hangs glossy and slick as a pair of silk curtains.

She climbs into her six-inch heels (in which she can walk only by bending her knees slightly but that's a small price to pay), loads up her clutch with lippy and her credit card, and she's all set.

*

In the Duchess Suite, Kitty is suffering from an overload of choices as she surveys her wardrobe. She's dithering about whether again to wear the cap-sleeved black dress she'd bought in Nice or would that be too obvious to Einar Leifsson?

She puts it on. The captain's little whale sits perfectly in the neckline – but then she remembers that, according to the day's bulletin, the evening has been billed as 'gala'. And if there's anything Kitty Golden can do well in life, it's gala. She pulls off the black dress and selects a full-length figure-hugging slither of ivory satin with matching satin cross-strap shoes on kitten heels. The rest of her outfit for the evening is easily chosen: a pair of pearl ear studs, a white-beaded evening bag and her angora shrug, also white.

She stares at her reflection, again thinking of what has

happened with Saul. She hasn't yet fully absorbed the complexity of it all, having consigned the tangle to a position at the back of her mind, where it seethes quietly across indignation, anger at her own stupidity, personal guilt and fury with both Saul and Pippa. Adding to the confusion of course is the sense that in her present situation vis-à-vis Einar Leifsson, she has no right whatsoever to be angry. How had she not seen this coming, she who had been so superior and critical of the wives and girlfriends of men like Saul, many of whom had openly disclosed their affairs at 'girly' lunches? And how had she not picked up any clues from Pippa – she who had somehow managed to play a straight bat in that farce about the table-for-two Kitty and her husband had played? The woman had let her, Kitty, make a fool of herself while *knowing* that Saul was already on the trail of a large table: she had bloody arranged it!

At the same time, what could the poor woman have done otherwise? Sneakily, Kitty admires her *sangfroid*, but she's now remembering the (very) slight hesitation in the woman's voice when she'd been asked, as a favour, to do the couples-table thing. But there'd been a Hansel trail of other clues that Kitty, blithely oblivious, had missed too: Saul's unusual mellowness; his uncharacteristic accompanying her to Cinque Terre, his allowing her to boss him around a little without demur, especially around his knee injury, his non-pursuance of sex with her – apart from the first night when he hadn't been able for it; she had put down his lack of interest in it in the days following to the fact that he could have felt humiliated about his failure in that department.

Then there was his teary 'I love you' farewell hug when he'd left for Boise, that was unusual too and now that she's thinking about it, it had to be due to guilt. Talk around the lunch tables of Manhattan is rife with tales of husbands arriving home with gifts, including extravagant armfuls of red roses 'for no reason, honey, just because I love you!' Sure sign of guilt, apparently . . . And now, apropos of that farewell she remembers that she had checked its timing. Had she been alert though? Had that been instinct?

He was turning off – or not answering – his mobile phone and then, he hadn't pushed all *that* hard – for Saul – to have her go home with him on the private plane.

And now that she is in analytic mode, she remembers their one and only phone contact after he'd left when he'd seemed keen to have her stay on in Rome. Of course he was. Wasn't he getting room service from his PA in his own home?

Biggest shout-out of all had been that incessant line of Pip Pipetty Pip labelling on his phone message inbox. Even Tim Cook couldn't have as many messages from one of his PAs.

So game, set and match to Saul. To think she'd been agonising about her phone call to him in order to refrain from inflicting too much psychic pain on the poor baby?

But Kitty doesn't really know with whom she's more angry – herself or the new power couple of Manhattan; herself probably because, again, she's hardly in a position to be lofty about adulterous affairs.

From her vanity, she puffs clouds of perfume into the air and walks through them. Then she feels ready to go down and face Christmas. It will be strange, without Saul's birthday to think about and yet, as she leaves the suite and walks towards the elevators, she asks herself if she can, despite all, so easily shrug off more than ten years of marriage.

She had taken those vows of fealty, love and honour in

all sincerity, if finding them a little frightening. At the time, however, she had labelled her misgivings as 'bride's natural pre-marriage nerves', but had Saul and Pippa even then been an item? Had Pippa been the real constant in Saul's life all along? The notion stung. But then, again, given present circumstances, let her without sin cast the first stone, et cetera.

Ironically, mention of 'sin' pulls her instantly back into events in her suite and the all-encompassing body-halo of physical desire. She presses the call button for the elevator and, as it clanks into motion far below, leans her forehead against the cool metal of its casing, closing her eyes. The elevator arrives, the doors open. With some difficulty Kitty retrieves her public face and steps inside.

*

At the *Clara*'s extraordinary dinner that evening, the staff show the results of their work and expertise. In honour of the occasion, it isn't waiter service but an enormous buffet, with waiters, chefs and ancillaries standing behind a speciality dish, or dishes, of their country of origin alongside a photo of themselves captioned with their name and nationality.

The idea is that you browse the serving tables, as the French display, for instance, coquilles Saint Jacques, escargot and tarte Tatin or, in honour of the *Clara*'s presence in Italian waters, under a set of proud, beaming Italians and a notice announcing *Feast of the Seven Fishes*, here's a spread of sea creatures in pasta, batter and simple olive oil, *baccala* (salted cod), calamari in linguini, and sardines. (This tradition chimes with Kitty's own childhood experience of the precursor to Christmas: no matter on what day of the week Christmas Day falls, in Ireland there were always long queues in and outside local fish-and-chip shops, a throwback to the fish-on-Fridays and fasting of Catholics. It was tradition, of course, but also designed to provide a ready-meal, easing the lot of women who, in the days before shrink-wrapped supermarket food, were up to their necks in steam, feathers and gizzards from very early morning, plucking and gutting the turkey and replenishing the bubbling water of the Christmas pudding for hours and hours and *hours.*)

In front of a contingent from the Philippines, including Dilip, with whom Kitty is familiar, she can have rice and coconut cheesecake.

The list goes on, including (uh-oh!) the Iceland table, showing a picture of Leifsson, captioned, *The Skipper*, beside a platter of *hangikjöt*, described as smoked lamb, ptarmigan ('wild bird') and skate ('a fish').

Iceland's show is a worry: if her relationship with Einar Leifsson – in this first phase of love, her stomach churns – is not to hit difficult flurries, she'll have to have a word with him about meat. Even fish, come to that. Don't they have an overwhelming desire to live too? Otherwise why the panic when a predator arrives on the scene?

She chooses gazpacho from Spain, a Thai vegetarian green curry, and two desserts, banoffee pie from England and basbousa from Egypt, made from semolina, butter, eggs and coconut, soaked in sugar syrup.

This evening, many of the ship's officers are dining with guests at the tables, and Kitty is enjoying the company of the staff captain, Jock. But the ship's captain chooses not to sit anywhere in particular but to roam, a handsome white moth alighting here and there at any table to which the occupants call him. He isn't seeming to eat at all, merely to sip from glasses of water poured by willing hands.

Kitty, while trying hard to refrain from watching him, can't resist stealing the odd schoolgirl glance in his direction. More than once, she attracts Charles's scrutiny.

There is a short hiatus after the main course, with the staff, smiling and giddy, each bearing the flag or emblem of his or her nation, filing in to take prearranged places throughout the room, at the rails of mezzanines and along all the staircases and steps. When they're settled, they fall silent, as does every diner in the room, at a signal from a man Kitty doesn't recognise. He gives them a note from a harmonica, they all hum it, as though they're a professional choir, and then, accompanied by two amplified guitars, launch into '*Mille Cherubini in Coro*', a traditional Christmas carol, popularised by Pavarotti, among others, but usually sung by children. To see all these nationalities combining in something close to harmony, even if enthusiasm does outrun pitch and timing, is, for someone like Kitty whose heart is open in any case, very moving and she feels her eyes fill. She keeps her head bent because if she doesn't, she may betray something she would rather, for the moment, keep as private as possible.

*

An hour after dinner, celebrations in the ballroom are in full swing when Charles and Kitty arrive, having had a couple of glasses at the champagne bar. The first thing she sees is a huge netful of balloons, slung under the ceiling, presumably for release at midnight. The second is Captain Einar Leifsson, who is concluding a speech from the little orchestra dais, wishing everyone a fun evening, thanking them for their patronage of his company and his ship and wishing them calm waters all day tomorrow.

He asks for three cheers for the *Santa Clara*. While everyone, including Charles, who has gone ahead of her into the depths of the crowd, roars, Kitty lingers at the door, feeling unexpectedly emotional. She sure is in a teary mood this evening, she thinks, and where the ship is concerned, she thinks she must have caught some kind of infection from Charles.

*

An hour later, the din in the ballroom is considerable. A lot of the officers, crew and administrative staff, especially the younger members, have been enlisted to mingle with the guests. Some are even dancing with them and with each other as the band, augmented by Piano Man Marty, rip through their repertoire, mainly show tunes. A few feet from the balloons the ballroom's glitter ball revolves in the spotlights trained on it, casting prismatic bands of colour around the walls and on the heads of the guests. Many of these, encouraged and led by the professional dancers, are now happily circling in concentric rings as the musicians and their lead singer belt out a version of 'Look at Me I'm Sandra Dee' from the musical *Grease.*

*

Right in the thick of everything, Roxy Smith is in brilliant form. Having partnered anyone she can find, including Dunne husbands and even Gemma, snatching them, willing or unwilling, onto the floor, she is now dancing with Charles, who, she has discovered, is light on his feet and is leading her as easily as if she were a butterfly. But when the song ends, over applause and general noise, he yells at her that he has to leave for a few minutes. 'Here!' He beckons to one of the staff who, having been on the floor with a woman twice his age, is just leaving it. 'Will you take over this lovely girl for me, please?'

And that is how Roxy Smith finds herself about to dance with Wolfgang Becker as the band again strikes up with a pulsing, persistent beat on the drum kit. To her surprise, Charles is ascending to a position at the front of the stage. The drumbeat, almost ominous, keeps its rhythm going as Charles takes up the microphone and then both he and the band, accepting a cue from the bandleader, launch into a thunderous version of 'Master of the House' from *Les Misérables*, Charles complete with prehensile, twirling fingers and villainous expressions. From this distance, Kitty thinks, he looks a little like Brucie – her Mum had always loved Bruce Forsyth – but that thought was fleeting because Wolfgang Becker, minus his jacket, takes her hand and leads her off. Half of those in attendance cram themselves into a tight pack at the front of the stage to watch Charles perform at close quarters. The other half, young, middle-aged and old (but mostly middle-aged), who have obviously seen the show, progress around the room, stomping and singing at the tops of their voices. Roxy and Wolfgang are swept into the parade; he knows every word of the lyrics and has clearly decided to throw dignity to the four winds, by swinging her arm in time with the rhythm, as a parent would a child. Roxy doesn't know the words, but she does recognise the catchy tune, so she and her new partner, he word-perfect, she la-la-la-ing enthusiastically, stomp and yell with the best of them around the perimeter of the room.

When the song finishes, Charles is cheered to the rafters. He bows, smiles and acknowledges it all, then comes off stage and makes his way through a door at the back as the band leader announces a little break.

'Come on, Roxy, let me buy you a farewell drink.' Wolfgang pilots her through the crowd and towards the open doors of the ballroom.

*

It's a quarter to midnight and Kitty has come out of the packed ballroom, has climbed the central stairs and walked out on deck for a breath of fresh air, so fresh it's frosty, the sudden blast catching at the back of her throat so she coughs a little.

Underfoot, the deck has been sprinkled with something – sand, salt, fine grit – to guard against falls. She pulls the angora shrug tightly around her shoulders and throat, and goes to the rail to watch the water streaming by as the *Clara* calmly forges ahead. Away to starboard she can see a row of tiny lights, sequins on the darkness, obviously a little town or village on the Italian mainland.

'I saw you leave – had enough?' As though teleported, Leifsson has appeared at the rail beside her.

'Were you beamed up? I didn't hear you. You gave me a fright, Einar!' But she smiles with gladness.

'I can't stay. Please come back down, Catherine. I'm no dancer, I'm afraid, but I'm fed up making small talk with *hausfraus* from the Ruhr as we push each other around the floor and I really, *really* want to get my hands on you. I promise I won't trip you up. You shouldn't have worn that dress, Catherine, it's torturing me! I need to stroke it. And I want to kiss you, I *have* to kiss you . . .

'Saul is having an affair. Has been, I think, for a very long time.' It's out before she can stop it.

From below, there sounds the peal of a handbell followed by a big cheer. Charles Burtonshaw-Claus has clearly arrived.

'Kitty,' the captain of the *Clara* allows his passion to show, 'I promise you – I *promise* that everything will happen the way it's meant to. Nothing is constant in this world except change. We can face anything now. You can face anything –' he touches the little whale at her throat before swiftly kissing her, hard, on the mouth, then: 'Follow me? I promise we'll talk later. I have to go and release balloons, would you believe – the things captains have to do! I was never taught that in training! Come? Please?'

And he's gone. Kitty follows. Slowly.

*

Further along the same rail, in the shadows, Roxy Smith and Wolfgang Becker, having been just about to kiss each other, gawp after them, then turn, giggling, to face each other again. 'Well, what do you know? Can you believe it?' asks Roxy, but then, throwing her arms around Wolfgang's sleek, lovely body: 'Where were we, Wolf?'

EPILOGUE

The Hotel Chilingua is not far from the centre of Rome. Kitty Golden, Roxy Smith and Charles Burtonshaw are sitting in the lobby at a tiny table on three uncomfortable metal chairs in the shape of spiders. The hotel is new and ultra-modern: its interior designer has obviously been given his head and the décor is dizzying – walls painted a deep purple with slashes of yellow and pink. The light fittings resemble even bigger spiders than the chairs. 'Daddy longlegs?' opines Roxy. There isn't a cushion in sight.

Kitty Golden's luggage is still in the boot of the taxi waiting outside for her. She had shared the car with the other two, initially driving directly from the *Santa Clara* to the Ristorante Sabatini, famous, overpriced but in the gorgeous neighbourhood of Trastevere. She had invited the other two to lunch, having the taxi come back for them and afterwards, she had accompanied them here, merely stopping off because she is moving to the Waldorf which isn't all that far away.

'This place is fine,' Roxy's assuring the other two, adding artlessly, 'It's probably because I'm the youngest but I don't mind all the colour. Cheery. I think it's quite nice, actually.' But then she turns to Charles: 'Sorry Charles but I'm afraid I won't be having dinner with you tonight – and you'd never know, with a bit of luck, I mightn't be having breakfast with you tomorrow morning either! Ah shit, I can't keep it to myself, I have a date at the Spanish Stairs.'

'Steps.' Charles automatically makes the correction. 'It's the Spanish Steps – and may we enquire if we know the other party for this date?'

Roxy giggles. 'You probably do!'

Charles and Kitty exchange an affectionate glance. 'He's a nice chap. Good at his job. Has he plans for the future?' This is Kitty.

'He's up for one in a travel agency – and guess where?'

'London?' the other two respond in unison.

'Well, not exactly, but you're close. If he gets the job, he's going to be an assistant manager with a really big crowd in Liverpool. And with the plan being for me to be in London more now because of Charles here – thank you Charles! It's only a train ride away, for God's sake, and I think there's a ferry from Dublin. Before you say anything, either of you, I'm *not* counting any chickens. Honest. But isn't it great?'

During the lunch earlier, Kitty had given each of the two a parting gift, the Breguet watch to Charles, the travel voucher to Roxy, explaining that both had been bought for Saul but that the moment had passed.

Both had been initially covered in confusion. 'It's too much, Kitty,' Roxy had said, on tearing open her envelope, paling when she saw the amount for which the voucher was worth. Then, very quickly bouncing back: 'If you're really, really sure, Kitty, I can take my mum to Australia – she's been told that dry heat is good for emphysema – *and* get to the States as well! And Israel to see my friend Ruth! Jeez, Kitty –' She had flung both arms around Kitty's neck, almost knocking the other woman off her chair. 'Maybe Wolfgang could book it for me – hey! Maybe he could come with me – ?' Then, hastily: 'It really is too much.'

'Take it and enjoy. I have different plans now. Too early to say, though.'

Charles was staring at the Tiffany Box. 'I can't open this. I can't take it –' he too had turned pale on being given the blue box – 'I can't. I've never in my life . . .'

'Oh, come on, don't be a coward,' Kitty had urged. Just say One Two Three and open it quickly, like ripping off a BandAid.'

Carefully, he'd undone all the fancy packaging and when he saw the watch, glistening in its cushioning, went paler still.

'It's to cover the loss of your own in such appalling circumstances, Charles,' Kitty had said gently, 'to replace the one your mother gave you. I'm telling you this next bit not to be boasting or anything but it's a very, *very* expensive watch and you might find it a burden to look after it, worrying about burglars or losing it, getting service and all that, which isn't cheap. If I were you, I'd take it to a fancy jeweller, swap it for something you like and is a bit less glitzy, then pocket the money, which will take you far. Even around the world on another ship of your choice.'

'I – I – I can't think what to say. Are you sure, Kitty?'

'I've never been more certain of anything in my life. Maybe the two of you could go on another cruise while you're working together! Joke, joke!' she had added quickly. 'But you have to admit that this one has been quite a blast, good and bad, but we've all come through, eh?'

'But you could get your money back.' Charles was still staring at the watch. 'You and the captain?'

They both knew about Einar and Kitty was no longer bothered about concealing anything in that regard. Charles had confessed he'd suspected right from the beginning, and Roxy had apparently seen something on Christmas Eve, but wouldn't say what it was.

'Saul won't miss it,' Kitty had insisted, 'he has other things on his mind – and anyway, he didn't know he was getting that watch – and he sure doesn't need it, Charles. He has gazillions of watches. Here, give me your wrist.' She had taken it from him to fasten it on. 'You deserve this, Charles. You've been the glue that's kept us all together, if that's not a lazy way to describe your presence at table thirty-two. And you're the kindest man I've ever met. We've all appreciated that. Certainly I have, and Roxy has too – she's said so.'

Charles was still in shock. In his left eye, a large tear had balanced itself precariously on the lower lid.

'Just think of it, Charles,' Kitty continued, 'we're all going on to better things. You're going to see your donor grandchildren and research your memoir, we could all be celebrating its publication this time next year – the same for you, Roxy, two books for you, and you could even have a new man in your life!'

'A new life for me too –' Her stomach had jumped at the thought and, knowing what awaited her in another part of Rome, she shivered. 'And all this has happened in what, nine days? That's amazing.'

'I suppose we could say we've all learned? All changed just a bit? You're the wordsmith, Roxy, how would you describe what's happened to us all?'

'Maybe –' Roxy thinks, then. 'We came for a cruise but discovered a voyage?'

'The only sadness has been what happened to poor Barry and Josh.' Kitty smiles: 'And there you were, Charles, right at the heart of it all.'

'Barry and Josh!' Roxy had raised her wine glass, so did Kitty, but as Charles raised his, that fat tear had spilled over to run down his cheek and he couldn't speak.

Kitty's taxi driver, getting impatient, is now tooting his horn outside the hotel. 'I must go.'

'You're sure you're going to be okay?' This is Charles.

'Are you all right? I mean, about, like everything?' This is Roxy.

They'd spoken simultaneously as they stood up.

'I will be,' she says, hugging each in turn. 'And good luck with everything, novels, memoirs, time-keeping, train journeys to Liverpool, world travel. Give my love to Wolfgang, he's a good one!' She smiles. They all hug. The other two watch as she hurries across the tiled floor, mustard and pink in zigzag pattern, towards the taxi. Before she gets in, she turns to wave. Both, still standing, wave back. Then Roxy sees Gemma and Mary Dunne come into the hotel, along with a tall, young woman, brunette, chic as only Italians can be: 'Hey, Charles,' she says, 'I won't be a minute', and she runs across the floor to intercept them . . .

*

An hour later, Kitty Golden and Captain Einar Leifsson are in bed in the Waldorf Astoria. As could only be expected, the room is well heated, comfortable and plush; the bed is big, the furnishings, drapes and linens are of high quality, the bathroom is marble, the TV has a flat screen. They have made good use of the bed and are now twined around one another, her head in the hollow between his shoulder and head, his cheek on her hair, each as reluctant as the other to break the physical contact. 'Are you contented with me, Catherine?' he asks softly.

'Need you ask? I am. I will be. There's a road to travel yet. I have to go back to the States. It's not going to be pleasant but it's something I have to face.'

'I'll go with you – '

'No,' she says resolutely. 'Thank you, but no. This is something I have to face by myself. And by the way, in four weeks time I have to go to Philadelphia with my pal, Ruby.'

'I will be there waiting for you when you come back to New York. I will be in the flophouse – or do you say fleahouse?'

'We say "Budget Motel"!' Kitty laughs.

'Then I shall be in the Budget Motel or in Times Square or Central Park.'

'It's obvious you haven't been to New York, Einar,' affectionately she smooths a strand of his hair, 'if you had been you'd know that they're not the best places to wait or loiter. But thank you for that. There's one thing we should talk about right now, however. Do you mind?'

'No, of course not.'

'In Venice, you laid out your stall in front of me. I have to do the same for you.' She takes a deep breath. 'I will want nothing from Saul. I do have some money. I may even have more coming in, my own, right after a court case I haven't mentioned so far because I may not get even a cent. It's from way back. From another life I had.'

'But there is a chance I'd come to you barefoot and in rags if you'd have me? So now,' she kisses him, 'with that deck cleared –'

He pulls away a little to stroke her cheek: 'I don't have my own words to talk of you, of us, not in English, not in any language. But I do have a quote that might tell you what I feel about you and what has happened between us so quickly. I have known it for a long time but I have never said it aloud because I had no reason to offer it. Now I have. It's from Victor Hugo. *Les Misérables . . .*'

'Victor Hugo?'

'The winter nights are long in my country. We read. We read books, we always have. We are big readers in Iceland.'

'So what's the quote? Could you say it in Icelandic and then translate? You're the first Icelander I've ever met!'

'I could. But I would have to kiss you three times. That's the fee.'

'I'll pay it.'

He takes her in his arms, cradling her, then, softly:

'Hvernig gerðist það að varir þeirra komu saman?'

He kisses her, lips gently brushing hers.

'Hvernig gerist það að fuglar syngja, að snjór bráðnar, að rósin þróist, að dögunin whitens á bak við áþreifanleg form trjáa á djúpandi hápunktinum á hæðinni?'

He kisses her more strongly.

'Koss, og allt var sagt.'

He kisses her mouth, hard, as he had on that gritty deck on Christmas Eve so she can't but kiss him back. 'That's a very tough language, Einar,' she says then when, with lips tingling, she pulls away. 'Even tougher than Irish for someone like me. What you said, what does it mean?'

He cradles her again, stroking her hair with his free hand, and recites, softly:

'How did it happen that their lips came together?

'How does it happen that birds sing, that snow melts, that the rose unfolds, that the dawn whitens behind the stark shapes of trees on the quivering summit of the hill?

'A kiss, and all was said.'

They both stay silent. Then: 'No fee for English? No kisses for me this time?' She pretends to be disappointed.

'I made that up!' He draws away a little and takes her face in both his hands. 'I've been thinking about this and that, Catherine. This, you and I, is all due to the *Santa Clara*. It's her legacy to me, her final gift. She has given you to me, you are the precious gift of my life.'

'So that's the "this"?' she whispers. 'And what's the "that"?'

'Shall I show you?' He grins, wickedly this time. 'Again?'

ACKNOWLEDGEMENTS

Patricia Byrne, nee Madigan, had a gift, beyond compare, for generosity of spirit and unshakeable loyalty to friends, of whom I was amongst the most fortunate. During our last meeting at her hospital bed, less than two days before she died, we both knew we were saying farewell without saying the words. Merely to cover one of the telling silences between us, I mentioned I had just delivered this novel. 'I can't wait to read it,' she said.

These were her last words to me. I loved her and still do and my gratitude to her for minding my spirit and spirits will go with me to my own grave.

Throughout my writing life, my husband, Kevin Healy, has supported me in every way possible and I thank him from the bottom of my heart.

I also thank my family members, my sons, Simon and Adrian (with Adrian's wife, Catherine and my step-granddaughter, Eve), my brother, Declan and his wife, Mary – and their extended families – including Mag and the redoubtable Larry and Pauline; my stepson and stepdaughter, Justin and

Zoe, along with Ciara and Claus, my cousins, Barbara, Philip, Stephen and Laura; all always show support (and show up!).

And then there is my wide and lovely circle of friends and neighbours, who have always featured not just in book 'Acknowledgements' but in the deepest recesses of my heart.

Also to be thanked again are my 'It Says in the Papers' colleagues in RTÉ's newsroom – Clodagh Walsh, Caroline Murphy, Fiona Kelly and John S. Doyle (and Valerie Cox, who has now moved on to a writing career of her own) – for accommodating all the roster swaps I've needed for all kinds of alarums and excursions ('confused activity and uproar' – Oxford Living Dictionaries).

Friends in the book world include the great Breda Purdue, Hachette Ireland's publisher; Ciara Considine, my editor there; and Hazel Orme, copy-editor in London, who ferrets out all the inconsistencies and timeline atrocities I commit. Ruth Shern is my cheery and indefatigable companion as we voyage to meet booksellers, including those in Eason, Dubray, Hodges Figgis, and the independent shops who have offered me such solid support over the years. And thanks to Susie Cronin, terrific publicist.

Thanks, too, to the rest of the gang in Hachette, Joanna, Ciara Doorley, Jim, Siobhan, Bernard, to the book's designer Claire McVeigh, to the all-important proofreader Aonghus Meaney. Getting a book out and onto a bookshelf is a team effort and don't I know it! Publishers of books don't get an easy ride these days but they are the world's most entrenched optimists and thank goodness for that.

Staying in the world of books, another Patricia, Scanlan, sometimes has to insert steel into my resolve when I quail before the task at hand and I thank her profusely.

I'm thankful to all the librarians around Ireland, North and South, who don't get enough limelight for their efforts in promoting not just a love of reading, but appreciation of the books' authors, welcoming us into their personal but increasingly complex and fascinating fiefdoms to promote not just the books themselves, but all their ancillaries, including live readings. Gratitude too to the organisers of reading, writing and books festivals who welcome us and our cargoes – and finally to editors, researchers and media professionals who help in the promulgation of books and reading and contribute so much to the continuation of a reading culture.

To all of you, I'm grateful for your help and courtesy to me, but also in ensuring that Ireland, like Iceland, continues to remain faithful to reading, even if book forms are mutating now and will continue to do so.

Deirdre Purcell. Mornington, 31 August 2017